THE OATH

THE OATH

Rankin Davis

Hodder & Stoughton

Copyright © 1999 by Keith W. Rankin and Anthony J. Davis

First published in Great Britain in 1999 by Hodder and
Stoughton
Published simultaneously in paperback by
Hodder and Stoughton
A division of Hodder Headline PLC

The right of Keith W. Rankin and Anthony J. Davis to be
identified as the Authors of the Work has been asserted by them
in accordance with the Copyright, Designs and Patents Act 1988.

10 9 8 7 6 5 4 3 2 1

All characters in this publication are fictitious
and any resemblance to real persons, living or dead,
is purely coincidental.

A CIP catalogue record for this title is available
from the British Library

ISBN 0 340 75064 2 Hardback
ISBN 0 340 69574 9 Paperback

Typeset by Palimpsest Book Production Limited,
Polmont, Stirlingshire

Printed and bound in Great Britain by
Clays Ltd, St Ives plc

Hodder and Stoughton
A division of Hodder Headline PLC
338 Euston Road
London NW1 3BH

This book is dedicated to the memory of Tsutsumi Sakamoto, the crusading Yokohama human rights lawyer who was abducted and murdered along with his wife, Satoko, and one-year-old son, Tatsuhiko, by the notorious Aum Supreme Truth cult in 1989.

OATH (noun; plural, oaths).

1. A solemn, formal declaration or promise to fulfill a pledge, often calling on God or a sacred object as witness.

2. An irreverent or blasphemous use of the name of God or something held sacred.

3. An imprecation; a curse.

'The true meaning of religion is thus, not simply morality, but morality touched by emotion.'

Matthew Arnold (1822–88), from
Literature and Dogma, 1873.

PROLOGUE

Mark Mason, Queen's Counsel, watched in quiet amusement as the floor manager skipped deftly through the endless lengths of unruly black cable. They were strewn across the studio floor like limp strands of spaghetti, occasionally interspersed with large black crosses made from electrician's tape to mark the camera positions. This of course was out of sight to the viewers at home but from his slightly elevated position on the experts' panel Mark could see the backstage glamour in all its glory.

The commercial break had signalled an open stage for the myriad of backroom personnel who unfurled noisily from the wings and went about their business in a flurry of activity. It wasn't the first time he'd seen the chaotic inside track of a television studio: in fact he was fast becoming almost blasé about his regular appearances as a legal pundit. Once or twice he had even dared to admit, secretly, that he quite enjoyed his status as 'leading human-rights lawyer', a catchphrase by which the media now universally described him.

The floor manager suddenly emerged from the darkness behind the autocue machine and declared very loudly that there were thirty seconds to transmission. The make-up girl standing right next to him couldn't resist one last dab of bronzing powder to the host's brow before snapping shut her fuchsia pink plastic vanity case. She trotted off studio left and Robert Blake, self-styled daytime television current-affairs supremo, turned automatically to camera one, setting his face in the way only he could do. His oversized jaw was hung low and his large eyes were set below a questioning frown all intended to lift the audience into believing he was someone to be reckoned with: in reality he was an intellectual lightweight.

Mark Mason watched him carefully, barely managing to stifle

1

a grin as his host opened a huge, pliable mouth. Big fleshy lips moistened ready to curl around the words floating on the scrolling autocue centre stage: he reminded Mason of an unusually grim-faced guppy he'd seen once in an aquarium at Regent's Park Zoo. The clapperman frantically revved the applause from the studio audience, saving Mason from the embarrassment of a full belly laugh on live television.

'Welcome back everyone,' Blake said, turning to camera two for a close-up as the clapping tailed off. 'For those of you who have just joined us today on *Getting Even*, the debate show where you control the questions, we are asking the fat-cat lawyers to justify themselves.'

The other panellists appeared suitably but unconvincingly bewildered that anyone would dream of adopting such a stance. Lawyers justifying themselves: whatever next? If only more would, thought Mason. He wondered if his fellow guests were harbouring any secret pleasure in the fact that their very presence here implied that they were that endangered breed of lawyer who lapped the golden cream from the legal saucer.

More applause was milked from the crowd but not from the one person watching Mark Mason. Who is that guy? Every time Mark looked up to the audience, the man was staring directly at him and no one else. Mark averted his eyes but concentrated his mind upon the expressionless face, which was so familiar. Where had they met? For he was sure by now that they had crossed paths, some time, somewhere.

Blake launched into his pitch quickly, manufacturing a tone of indigence.

'Everyone needs a lawyer some time in their life, but are they worth the money? We are joined today by four top lawyers from different fields of practice, who can no doubt eloquently explain the huge sums the system costs the taxpayer when it comes to facing commons select committees and judicial enquiries. But can they face, as they say in legal circles ladies and gentlemen, the man on the Clapham omnibus. Well, today before a live studio audience that ordinary onlooker is you and me.'

Blake rounded quickly on the rather timid-looking woman at the far end of the panel, stuck out his jaw and challenged her.

2

'Well, can you, Marianne Taylor? In your area of expertise, medical negligence, isn't it right that lawyers' fees in any one case are often considerably more than the annual salary of our National Health Service surgeons?'

Mark drifted off again, beginning to question what he was doing here in the first place. If only his wife Tamara hadn't drunkenly introduced him to her fellow dinner guests at that charity function as a 'celebrity barrister' when he had arrived unfashionably late, then he wouldn't be here at all. Blake and his showbiz wife had been at the same function and it hadn't taken long for Mark to find himself accepting the invitation to appear on this inane show in defiance of a suggestion that he was elitist. Not for the first time in his life he was regretting that he had never learned to say no.

The medical negligence expert was having a hard time of it, ploughing on politely through Blake's vitriolic soundbites, when Mark cast a quick glance to the audience.

He was still there. Staring.

Blake had swiftly opened the floor for questions and a number of hands shot up in the air. Mark breathed a sigh of relief to avoid the first one chosen, but was a little unnerved to notice that his watcher had raised his arm. Even while the expert to his left was dealing admirably with the tricky question of no-win no-fee litigation, the man sat, perfectly erect and silently insistent, with his arm still held aloft. Mark knew it was coming next.

'Yes, you, sir, in the third row: yellow shirt, blue tie. I see you're anxious to add a voice to the debate.'

'Thank you, Mr Blake,' replied the man a little too loudly, forcing the overhead boom microphone to retreat skyward. His accent was no-nonsense northern: hard vowels and clipped consonants. 'I'd like to ask Mr Mason there if he truly believes, as he has said publicly on many occasions, that everyone accused of a crime deserves the best representation possible.'

'Of course I do,' stumbled Mark uneasily as the camera centre stage rolled in a little closer.

'Well if that is the case, are we not in danger of developing a system of criminal justice in which the villains of this world are allowed to walk free simply on account of the fact that they have bigger chequebooks than the rest of us?' his inquisitor pushed.

'I think with respect, sir, that you are misconstruing my motivation to make such a statement in the first place.' Mark struggled not to sound courtroom pompous, but failed miserably. 'Let me make it clear: I firmly believe that, whatever the nature of the crime alleged and whatever the personal characteristics or indeed status of the accused, they are entitled to challenge the evidence against them. It is very simply the rule of law that exists in this country: the prosecution bring a case to court and the prosecution must therefore prove it. The fact that some lawyers are remunerated more generously than others is neither here nor there. I trust it is well known that my own chambers was established on a co-operative basis with at least fifty percent of our workload being dedicated to free representation. Money, I am afraid, does not motivate me: I am a great deal more concerned with righting wrongs.'

'That's highly laudable, Mr Mason,' interrupted Blake, 'but is this gentleman correct when he says that criminals are escaping justice because of an imbalance in the system? Are we as a society under-paying our police and our crown prosecuting authorities in comparison to these fat-cat lawyers who can command fees of a million pounds on a brief?'

'I can't possibly comment upon that because it isn't my responsibility to moralise about the priorities of society and how to manage the public purse, but I do know that in reality there doesn't appear to be a great deal of difference in the quality of advocates conducting cases in the courts: after all, most barristers accept cases from both prosecution and defence solicitors.'

'But not you, Mr Mason,' the man from the audience stated loudly to a few murmurs of encouragement around him. 'That's right, isn't it: you are only prepared to take on defence cases. Don't you think that all victims of crime deserve to have such highly principled and paid advocates as yourself presenting their case?'

'I'm not quite sure if that was meant to be a compliment.' Mark shuffled in his seat, attempting to appear modestly unaware of his reputation, but acutely aware that most of his colleagues back at chambers would be watching his performance and no doubt practising their jibes for later.

'Mr Mason, you don't remember us, do you?' said the man, gesturing to the people around him. Mark scanned the faces and again was hit with the vaguest of recollections, but it was no good: he had met so many people throughout his time at the bar. They could be anyone.

'I'm sorry, I don't,' he eventually confessed.

'Nearly two years ago you represented us all in connection with an allegation of criminal damage and harassment to a so-called church in East London.'

Suddenly it came flooding back to him: the Millennium Church affair, or so it was dubbed in chambers at the time. Jesus Christ, there had been some changes since then. He recalled that he had picked up the case from the free legal clinic run by his chambers. It had aroused his interest and he set about trying to dissuade the prosecution from continuing against a protesting group of parents who claimed their children had been abducted into a cult and not a church.

The church leaders had pressurised local police into action and sought protection under the recently introduced harassment law from the parents' constant compaign of abuse. The Crown Prosecution Service issued a summons against the group, but Mason countered by threatening a very expensive challenge in the European Court of Human Rights. He was asserting that the action represented no more than an official sanctioning of critic-silencing. He bartered with the Crown by adopting a stance that any action against the parents was an attempt at circumventing the unassailable right of free speech. The taxpayers might find it hard to believe their money was being spent on protecting an obscure group of radical churchgoers. He had won the argument. But what was this guy really doing here? More importantly what did he want?

Blake was just about to move on when Mason was provided with the answer. The man in the audience rose to his feet. 'I can't help but think, Mr Mason, that you are no better than the politicians when it comes down to principles: you change them as often as your shirt. I have had to sit here and listen to your empty suggestion that you are only interested in righting wrongs, yet you have consistently turned down my pleas for help . . .'

'I'm afraid our panellists can't possibly comment on individual cases,' interjected Blake, quickly trying to diffuse a potential problem for the station's libel lawyers. Mason was bewildered

5

and decidedly uncomfortable, but he desperately wanted to know what the hell was going on. He couldn't recall ever meeting the entire group before, let alone hearing of them since the case had concluded.

'I'm afraid I haven't the slightest idea what you're talking about, Mr . . .'

'Moody, Geoff Moody, and I think you do, Mr Mason: I have attended your free representation unit on several occasions, seeking advice in connection with a private prosecution against the Millennium Church for the abduction and rape of my daughter . . .'

'I think, sir, you have now had your say,' said Blake, battling against the tirade in his earpiece from the producer in the control room.

'. . . and I have been turned away, because you don't represent victims, do you, Mr Mason? You only defend the guilty these days. If you're so interested in righting wrongs, then why won't you help me; help my daughter.'

As the commercials came around again, for the second time that day Mason wished fervently that he had learned to say no.

CHAPTER ONE

They stood in the chapel at the centre of the Haven absorbing the images on the enormous monitor that served as an altar. The church had permitted them this glimpse at the outside world only as a lesson in their journey to salvation. Like a great pulsating wall of faith they watched the unfortunate souls on TV who could not be saved.

The Church had told them so.

The screen was slowly panning across the building site that was the Millennium dome in London. Promises of a golden future were oozing from the commentator's mouth. The viewpoint suddenly switched to Trafalgar Square when the neon spectacular exploded violently into life, flashing the legend:

'10,800 seconds to end of the century'.

The camera cut quickly to reveal the excited crowds buzzing in a sycophantic frenzy of goodwill to all mankind. They systematically joined together in a symbolic choreographed hugfest representing nations of the world uniting in expectancy of the glorious future.

But the congregation watching it all knew that the British government, like other administrations across the globe, had been cynically promoting that most fashionable of media concepts: 'a New World order'. An order where peace and harmony occupy the political platform now that conflict and disquiet have for two thousand years borne so little fruit. An order, also, which could conveniently excuse the mistakes of its predecessors.

The congregation knew because the Church had told them so.

There was no room for such recently acquired philosophy among the faithful of the Millennium Church. Their anticipation was rooted in two thousand years of biblical obscurity. Their hope was a different hope.

7

While revellers across the planet were noisily celebrating the New Year soaked in a heady mixture of champagne and expectation, these worshippers waited soberly, silently and reverently for the master to deliver his own vision of the millennium.

The screen blanked momentarily as the satellite link hustled to retain the transatlantic connections. A single, sweet treble note hummed from the surroundsound system and then they heard him speak. It was a voice of many colours, sometimes dark and thunderous with an undeviating sincerity as if it was driving a spike into its recipient's brain. At other times it could be soft and calming as if accompanied by the delicate tones of an orchestral harp, deftly slipping through willing ears and nestling deep into the cortex. Above everything, its charisma was obvious to all who were compelled to listen, taunting and pulling them in closer and closer.

'And I saw heaven opened,' the voice began, deliberately whispering, holding every syllable with meaningful satisfaction. 'And behold a white horse; and he that sat upon him was called faithful and true,' the pitch now rising into a strident confident march, 'and in righteousness he doth judge and make war. His eyes were as a flame of fire and on his head were many crowns; and he had a name written that no man knew but he himself.'

The silence pressed heavily on everyone's chest as they sat in unison awaiting his words.

'As you have seen tonight, the time is fast approaching, brethren, when it shall be revealed to us as the good book has foretold. The unclean ones cannot be saved, that is clear.' A murmur of agreement rippled through the assembly like a Mexican wave. 'Read with me now. Affirm our future.'

As one, the congregation began to recite a familiar passage from chapter seven of the Book of Revelations, adopted as their creed.

'And I saw another angel ascending from the east having the seal of the living God; and he cried with a loud voice to the four angels, to whom it was given to hurt the earth and the sea saying, Hurt not the earth neither the sea, nor the trees till we have sealed the servants of our God in their foreheads. And I heard the number of them, which were sealed: and there were sealed a hundred and forty-four thousand of all the tribes and the children of Israel.'

The congregation settled once more, each one of them appearing lost in their own hard-earned epiphany. Men, women and children, even those of tender years, carrying the same expression with dreamy eyes glazed by the ecstasy of their enlightenment, and fixed on some prized internal point.

The celebrant continued. 'In the months ahead as we approach our destiny, a great many will seek to lay temptation in your path. The unclean will strive to persuade you to turn your back on the journey.'

Suddenly, a shout of 'Never' pierced the atmosphere to be followed quickly by another, then another still, until the congregation was embroiled in a new mantra of affirmation.

'Never, Never, Never,' they cried while the master waited unseen. Inside, he felt touched by this spontaneous confirmation of faith. The only faith there was that mattered: their faith in him.

'I hear you, brethren, but believe me when I say this, that there will be those who pray with us today who shall stumble in the moment of truth just as others have done. You know I speak the truth,' he shouted. There was a long pause as everyone remembered. How could they forget?

'The fallen woman,' he went on, 'the one who lived among us, whom we all trusted as one of God's servants, seeks to frustrate us from the path. Rest assured that her name has been erased from the walls of the great new Temple. But still her lies go on. Many deceitful things will be said by the unclean to help you fall like her. The undeserving will seek to undermine your faith by repetition of these hurtful, wicked lies. Do not let this happen, no matter what is said in the poisonous propaganda of the media. I have no doubt that you may be called upon to offer great sacrifice in the fight ahead; sacrifice that is necessary if we are to march triumphantly into the new heaven and earth come the day of judgement.'

January 6th 2000

Mark Mason dived out of the taxi and hurried through to the security desk just inside the front doors of court. The queue was long, so he pulled rank with the first security guard frisking visitors. The old man was in no mood for an argument and allowed him to dump his bags and papers at the front of the line awaiting the X-ray machine's beady eye. Just as well his face was well known here, he thought, smiling conspiratorially at the pretty young girl in guard's uniform as she waved the metal detector cursorily over his body. She winked at him before he collected his robe bag from the conveyor belt, rushed across the foyer and through the double doors at the rear, which were marked 'barristers and solicitors only'.

He checked his watch: five minutes to ten, and he had promised to meet Greta Larson, the most junior tenant in his chambers, at the café round the corner at nine o'clock. Not good, he thought, being late: especially when he was asking for her assistance. What's more he liked Greta: he had been instrumental in getting her into chambers in the first place by winning over one or two colleagues who were a little sceptical about her attitude and motivation. The only problem he would concede was that she didn't suffer fools lightly and some found that difficult to deal with, but not him. Over the last two years he'd begun to use her not only as a sounding board for his legal problems but a sponge for his personal ones too. The fact that she was only twenty-five, a full nineteen years his junior, never prevented him from seeking her advice on developments in his war of matrimonial attrition. Perhaps he liked her just a little too much. Not only did she bring just a hint of politically incorrect glamour to their set, she possessed that directness and industry that meant she was duty-bound to succeed. One day, he knew, she would make a fine defence counsel and he wanted to help her get there. But today he was prosecuting. How could he forget?

It suddenly occurred to him also that he had meant to drop the papers for today's hearing at her place over the holidays, but what with the kids and Tamara, he just didn't have the time. Christ, she hadn't even seen the brief yet and he hadn't dared tell her which case it was before the holidays. As he approached the advocates' lounge he saw her hunched over the crossword in the far corner of the room. Before he got to her and without looking up, she said, mimicking his brogue, 'Nine o'clock, Greta, I promise.' She looked up, raising her eyebrows.

'Sorry Greta,' he mumbled, 'I got sort of tied up this morning.'

'Really,' she replied acidly. 'I say to myself, Mark Mason arriving at court before ten? No, he must be wrong, he never arrives before ten. No, no, he says, "Greta, I swear I'll be there at nine, by which time you'll have had ample time to grapple with the papers because I'll even drop them off for you over Christmas, maybe we could get a drink or something".'

'Yes, I know, I'm sorry about that too. I was sort of . . .'

'Don't tell me, Mark, you weren't sort of tied up for two weeks by any chance?'

'Yes, sort of, you know what I mean, what with Camellia's horse riding and Edwin's rugby practice and then we had Tamara's parents over for longer than she . . . er . . . I mean, we had planned.'

'Jesus, Mark, you can tell it's the first day of term. You need to get back to work quickly: too long spent at the homestead methinks. Did you swap Millie and Ted for new children by any chance?' she said, smiling knowingly and making him feel like an idiot for telling her at the Christmas party about his secret struggle with Tamara over the kids' names. He had drunkenly vowed a New Year's resolution to thrash the pretensions of his wife's existence out of his life forever.

'Very funny,' he hissed.

'Oh well, never mind: I guess oaths are there to be broken. Anyway, let's hope the next century is as lively as the last, or did you miss that as well on account of your domestic arrangements?'

'My word, sharp this morning aren't we!' he said, taking the armchair next to her. 'A happy Millennium to you as well.'

'Yeah, yeah, so what have we got then? Anything interesting? It had better be, to keep me away from that shoplifting in Wimbledon magistrates,' she said, sitting back, still clutching her crossword like a security blanket. Her embryonic practice rarely took her to the higher courts, so there was a lot of time spent doing puzzles on tubes to London's remotest trading posts as Mason called them. She snapped the broadsheet into the seasoned pro's preferred position, folded to a quarter page.

'A spot of PII in the case of Rose Moody versus the Millennium Church and the Right Reverend Perry Jon Rivers,' Mason replied as casually as he could.

'Very funny, Mark, you'll be vying for a role at this year's Benevolent Ball as a stand-up comedian next,' she replied, without looking up. 'What's this, do you reckon, before you tell me what we're really doing here?'

'Go on, then what's the clue?'

'Twenty across, five letters, nothing in, and I don't know if I'm pronouncing it correctly, but it just says H I J K L M N O,' she declared uneasily.

'Pass it over here while you read this,' Mark said as he pushed the brief over to her. He watched as she read the front sheet with its neatly typed titles, just as he had recounted to her a moment ago: it was indeed the case of Rose Moody.

'Oh no you don't. I just don't believe it, Mark, after the crap I went through,' she started, pushing the papers back towards him.

'I'm sorry, Greta, but you were the first person who came to my mind when I got myself into this. Come on, you know about these people: it'll help me carve an angle and I know I need it,' he pleaded, relying purely on charm but knowing it might take a little more than that to get her on board. The reason being that, when he had represented the protesting parents two years before, Greta had been in pupilage. As part of her involvement with the case, he had encouraged her to visit anonymously one of the Millennium Church's weekend introduction retreats, just to see whether there was any truth in the assertions of the parents. She had lasted fourteen hours at a country house in Somerset with so-called Church elders before leaving in the only taxi for miles around that would dare approach the place. She was unable to stomach one more fire and brimstone lecture, and what's more had run into one of her friends' parents while she was there, making the entire exercise a complete débâcle. Her experiences had, however, caused a good deal of merriment in chambers.

'I couldn't spend another minute in the same room as any of those freaks.'

'What about a courtroom this time, Greta? Look, this is different: let me tell you about it. Rose Moody is a fifteen-year-old child: a normal, happy, but by no means unusual teenager, she has her moments with her parents like they all do. One day she runs away from home and thirteen months later she ends up a wreck. And nobody apart from her father seems to care. How does that happen? How can people let it happen, Greta?

'She says she has been molested and raped all in the name of God. Still no one wants to listen, the police make some pretty basic enquiries and pass the file, then the prosecution give her allegations the once-over and decide not to pursue a case to court. Why? Now if for one moment she is telling the truth then I ask you, how can you not help? I mean, does it sound right to you that she should be denied access to justice? If it's a true bill then surely these people can't hide what they have done to this child. It's firstly subornation of her free will, then alienation from her own family and then the eventual desecration of her body all because God says it's OK to do that.'

He realised that his voice had been straining to keep below the general hubbub of the lounge, and when he focused on Greta he could see that she was smiling at him.

'Bastard,' she said softly, knowing that she couldn't refuse him.

'I prefer righter of wrongs, Miss Larson,' he replied with an affected courtroom pomp.

'I remember now: this is all because of that silly TV programme you did, isn't it?'

'Afraid so.'

'Is this the guy who washed the floor with your principles?'

'You got him. He wasn't lying when he said that he had been turned away from our clinic.'

'How come?'

'The pupil we had manning the desk was so far left up his own arse he told him we don't prosecute as a matter of policy, so the papers never came on to me until I met with him after the show. It's in a mess.'

'What's he like?'

'Geoff Moody? Oh I don't know, he's a little blunt but he's an honest man who loves his daughter very much and he needs our help: this is a private prosecution and he's spent just about everything he owns attempting to get the case off the ground.'

'What's the state of play now?'

'The church have retained a full line-up of heavyweights from Giles Callow's set in the Temple and they're the ones washing the floor with Moody's legal principles at the moment. Today they are seeking access to Rose's medical records.'

'I assume we say they are privileged.'

'Naturally, but they are of course third party documents in the hands of the relevant hospital trusts, or local authorities when it comes to case notes from social service involvement with the family. It means we have a voice but I doubt whether we can resist the application: their defence is that she is mentally unstable, that her story is pure invention, and furthermore that she has probably made ludicrous allegations in the past.'

'Is there anything in the records to compromise her credibility?' Greta asked, frowning as she leafed through the papers.

'I haven't seen them all myself, but from what I can gather from the Local Authority barrister she certainly was going through a rough patch before her disappearance from home. Geoff Moody seems reluctant to talk too much about the life she had with him, doesn't think it's remotely relevant. The fact is, he's fixed on one outcome only and that's guilty verdicts.' Mark checked his watch again: twenty past ten.

'Come on,' he said, 'grab a handful of papers: we'd better get to court.'

He led the way out of the lounge, nodding his greetings to a few familiar faces around the room. He held the door open for Greta and as she passed by him he said, 'Water.'

'What do you mean, water? Get your own bloody water. I'm not a pupil now, you know,' she exploded.

'No, I mean twenty across: the answer is water. H I J K L M N O. Don't you see? H to O, five letters, water. It's simple really. You would never have made a chemist, Greta.' He walked off in front of her with a wink as she looked on, still trying to work it out.

Geoff Moody grieved for a daughter who was not dead, but might as well have been. He sat in the public gallery of Court 5 at the Old Bailey, anxiously waiting for Mason, and picked at the frayed skin of his finger-ends. Those same fingers had worked a lifetime building a hardware shop, now sold at a cut price to pay for the private prosecution of the leader of the Millennium Church: PJ Rivers. In the last two years he had lost his daughter, then found what was left of her, seen his second marriage crumble under the

14

constant pressure of his quest for justice, and suffered two minor heart attacks.

Mason, long black hair peeping from under his greying wig, turned and gave Moody a slow nod as he entered the room. Moody ventured a raw smile that died before it touched his dry lips: there was nothing to smile about. Two slow, painful years to bring the case this far and he was still three months away from trial. Moody switched his focus to the defendant's lawyers and tried to tell himself that they were just doing their jobs, but his bitterness at those they represented tainted his usual even-handed approach. Giles Callow QC, an American attorney who had landed on the scene five years before, returned his look with a haughty sniff of a stubby nose and returned to his case papers. The transatlantic lawyer was as blunt as his mind was sharp. A love of the English law and British food had swollen his girth and his bank accounts to gross dimensions. Ginger hair sprouted from the sides of his frayed wig like red weeds and his face echoed the same florid colouration. He appeared destined for the ministrations of a cardiac arrest team, but Mason knew him to have the heart, longevity and appetite of an alligator.

Moody grimaced: he had put everything he owned into this citizen's prosecution, but it was not about him; it was about Rose. They had ruined her, tainted her and turned her against herself and her family, till all that was left was a husk of the loving fifteen-year-old, who had walked out of her home after an avoidable family squabble and had disappeared inside the Millennium Church. It had taken him eight months to track her down to a retreat in the Scottish Highlands, and a further six to finance and arrange for her enforced departure. The therapy might never end, but this case was another kind of healing. He was not a vengeful man, but he did not wish other parents to suffer as he had while their children were corrupted by PJ Rivers and his lunatic followers.

This hearing was called a public interest immunity application. Geoff had asked Mark Mason to explain what that meant, and as ever his reply sparkled with common sense and clarity.

'Well, basically, Rivers and his defence team want to see all of Rose's medical notes and all the records with the social workers, and we don't want them to, so we ask the judge to agree with our point of view, and they say he can't.'

Moody had grown accustomed to the law and its perverse anachronisms. He reached for his asthma inhaler and gulped a calming double lungful of air. Two years before he had owned and managed a thriving hardware business; now he had nothing. But he would see it through. The world needed to know what had happened. His only hope was the man below, wearing a wig.

Mason could feel the weight of Moody's expectation as he sat in the well of the court with Greta in the junior's row behind him. As he spread the papers on the bench before him, he was unnerved to uncover the small brass plaque that said 'Prosecuting Counsel'. The one and only time he'd sat in a similar position brought back memories that wouldn't shift from his mind until the day he died, and then perhaps some.

It had been in the summer of 1975 when, qualified only two months, he'd been prosecuting noting junior in a notorious case and proud of it. A young man by the name of John Wilkinson, in the prime of his life, had been savagely cut to pieces by a disgruntled homeless drifter in a drunken rage called Reggie Routledge. The evidence was compelling: a good eye-witness although it was dark, and Routledge was found with the murder weapon in his hand. The trial lasted four days and the defendant hadn't stood a chance with the combined weight of top prosecuting counsel and a judge who still couldn't understand why the death penalty had been abolished. Mason watched as they led him from the dock, his startled eyes wet with fear and helplessness.

He felt righteous at the time: they had convicted a dangerous murderer, said the press, and his parents were so proud of him. Their years of sacrifice to provide him with an education had proven worth it. The coupons his mother religiously saved to cut five pounds a week off the shopping bill. Those fishing trips his father had given up. The ritual of placing the money he'd saved into a post office savings account just so his son didn't have to work in the factory like he did. It had all seemed so right then.

The victory mess attended even by the trial judge was a marvellous affair in a private drinking club just off Greys Inn Road. He had been delighted to receive a compliment on his role from the famous silk leading the team. It was as good as a wink, said his dad. 'Not be long, son, before all the villains in England are quaking in their boots with you around.' He knew that his father would be down at the pub quietly brimming with pride and just waiting for anyone to ask how his son was doing now he was a barrister. He had left that night with a belly full of port, a big future beckoning and immediately proposed to Tamara Havering whose parents couldn't wait to get her off their hands, especially to someone who, they were assured by Tamara, was undoubtedly heading for the very respectable title of Treasury Counsel.

Two months later all the goal posts had moved.

It was the day before the wedding when the news first broke, changing the course of his whole life. During a routine search warrant for suspected stolen goods in a house in Greenford, North London, the police had discovered the remains of two bodies buried under the floorboards. A full-scale enquiry revealed a total of eight corpses scattered around the property and many items linking the owner of the house to a series of unsolved murders. One gold signet ring was found bearing the initials JW. Its discovery solved a small mystery hanging over the conviction of Reggie Routledge. The owner of the house eventually confessed to the murder of John Wilkinson, telling police officers that he had come across Routledge slumped on a bench close to the murder scene. It had been a simple job to leave the machete in his hand. By the time someone got round to checking on Routledge's progress they found that he had taken his own life four days into his life sentence for a murder that he did not commit. Mason swore two oaths on his wedding day: one to Tamara and another to himself that never again would he assist in the conviction of another human being. But today he was breaking one of them, and as Greta handed him a copy of the defence application he was seriously wishing he had the courage to break the other.

He shuffled through the brief, searching for his skeleton argument, which he had drafted some time ago, but without any real conviction. He had realised after that first meeting with Geoff Moody that any defence counsel would go straight for the girl's previous history. He had taught Greta the self-same thing, and could hear himself saying to her, 'In any defence where you have to deal with the uncorroborated evidence of a complainant in a sex case, begin by assuming she's a liar, then start trying to prove she's pathological.' He glanced across to Giles Callow who was chatting happily with his instructing solicitor and looking every bit as though he were totally confident. Probably being paid two thousand pounds for this hearing which won't last more than two minutes, thought Mason, then it would be off for a good lunch.

A sharp rap on the black oak door behind the judge's bench heralded Mr Justice Withnail's arrival.

'Court stand.'

Moody shuffled to his feet along with the others as the judge stalked on to the bench. Previously, Mark Mason had put his evaluation of Withnail in his own crisp way:

'Mind like a steel trap and an attitude like a wounded bear. Hates private prosecutions; says it undermines the state.'

He would be the trial judge in less than three months' time. Tall and robust with ruddy cheeks, trimmed by black Victorian sideburns, his bleak smile was winter to Geoff Moody's hopes. Mason shared the same view. It was a bad draw from the pool of senior judges. In his more paranoid moments, he believed that the appointment was a deliberate attempt to sabotage the case. Withnail was still annoyed by a Court of Appeal decision some months earlier in which he had been heavily criticised for his constant interruptions in the trial. Mason had argued the appeal, and consequently expected no favours in this hearing.

'Mr Callow,' Withnail bellowed, addressing the only one of the three QCs briefed by Rivers, the absent defendant to appear that day. 'Why, exactly, do you wish to see all of these records on the child Rose Moody?'

Callow, employed for his excellence in all matters of procedure, nodded thoughtfully.

'These allegations against Mr Rivers, the leader of a recognised church . . .'

'Cult,' Mark Mason whispered. Callow ignored him.

'. . . are based solely on the evidence of one girl, a minor, who has severe behavioural and psychological problems. We submit there is no independent evidence to support her claims. The jury's assessment of her credibility as a witness is therefore of paramount importance. We know from the case papers that she has been

18

the subject of investigation by social services and the medical profession. The defendant maintains that he should be allowed to read the results of those investigations. If he is not allowed to do so it will prejudice his defence.'

Withnail pondered, but Mason knew it to be mere show. It was Rose's word against Rivers'. He was the leader of a powerful church and she was a damaged nobody from nowhere. In his heart he knew that was why he had taken the case. He also knew how destructive the information would be. Mason climbed to his feet.

'She is a minor, my Lord. While every defendant has rights . . .'

'Yes, and normally it is you who is demanding them,' Withnail said, through lightly clenched teeth.

'Those rights have to be balanced against the rights of the child, which, as statute lays down, are "paramount".'

'True, true: but paramount does not mean absolute. This is a balancing exercise,' the judge continued, having already decided which side of the equation he preferred.

'No, my Lord,' Mason interrupted sharply, 'it is a fishing exercise: they don't know what they are looking for.'

'But,' Withnail said, one hand in the air, to kill further argument, 'unlike the defence, I have read the documents they seek disclosure of, and I can well see why they want to view them.'

'But my learned friend wants to dangle his hook in the waters of evidence and see what he can catch, and that is not, and cannot ever be, a reason to agree with my learned friend's application.'

'But I know what they will catch, Mr Mason,' the judge continued, enjoying his new-found status as the defendant's friend. 'You seek to persuade the jury of a man's guilt on allegations of a savage nature. All this on the word of a girl suffering at best temporary emotional instability, and at worst permanent mental ill-health. And yet you submit that the defence is not entitled to examine her records, merely to allow the jury to take your word that she is sane.'

'She's not mad,' Geoff Moody shouted, angered by the flippancy of his Rosie's judicial dismissal. The room held its breath. Mark Mason sighed. Callow grinned. Geoff Moody felt the colour rising up to his face. Withnail pointed a finger towards him.

'Mr Moody, I take it. You have a barrister to represent your

19

daughter's case; you have no right of audience in this matter and I can have you removed at any moment.'

'But . . .' Moody began.

'Silence,' Withnail thundered as Mark Mason turned and raised one finger to his lips, his dark brown eyes shining with empathy. 'I will not tolerate any further outbursts. Mr Mason, you will control your client's father, or I will. Do I make myself clear?'

The barrister nodded, only too aware that any prospect they had to defeat the application now lay in a shallow grave.

'Now, to conclude this matter formally, it is my view that the defence can see all the documents they seek: to refuse access would be to anticipate a miscarriage of justice.'

'Certificate of appeal?' Mason pressed, hoping that this time-saving device would save a mountain of legal legwork and what little money Moody still had left.

'No, Mr Mason. How can I make an order then immediately state that it is wrong?'

'Because it *is* wrong, my Lord.'

'Do not attempt to make me appear foolish: the Court of Appeal has stated that judges are far too forgiving of counsel's behaviour.'

Mason raised an eyebrow.

'I hope your lordship didn't take that as a personal criticism.'

The clever, stinging remark struck home.

'We will meet at the trial, Mr Mason.' He narrowed his eyes. 'I shall look forward to it, have no doubts.' He nodded to Callow, who returned his gesture, then rose to his feet and swept swiftly from the bench. Geoff Moody stared down at his hands: his outburst had cost them dearly.

Mark and Greta made their way out of the courtroom to meet with Moody in the corridor outside. Callow was beaming widely, no doubt looking forward to an easy trial for serious money now that Withnail had firmly nailed his colours to the mast. Mason looked at him and now truly understood why the expression 'fat-cats' had found favour with the press: Callow had cream spread all over his whiskers.

Moody was waiting for them.

'Don't feel too bad, Geoff,' Mark Mason said softly. 'We were never really in with a chance. I would have argued the same points.'

'It was just the things he said about Rose . . .'

'I know, but we've discussed this before: they are going to say far worse things than that at trial, particularly now.'

Geoff shuddered at the prospect, but they had to proceed; there was no turning back now.

'I'll keep my temper under check.'

'It's not *your* temperament I'm concerned about,' Mason whispered, and Geoff understood his concern: the outcome of the case all came down to Rose's evidence and she was as fragile as a flower and damaged beyond repair.

'Am I doing this for myself or for Rosie?'

'You are doing it because it's right,' Mason replied, 'and the right choice is often the hard choice.'

'You're not even being paid, Mr Mason.'

'No, but I'm trying to right a wrong.'

Mason shook his hand and left; Geoff followed forlornly behind. He was just a little man with a little life, not some dashing hero of the people. His blazer was worn at the cuff, his trousers creased and his striped Marks & Spencer tie was stained with a trace of egg after his lonely breakfast at the boarding house in Paddington. Geoff Moody had never been a religious man, though he loved the Christmas celebrations and Rose's choir's carol service, but in the battlefield, atheists became converts when the bullets flew. He closed his eyes and prayed for a miracle.

CHAPTER TWO

W hite. White and speed. An aching vacuum of cold air, and hot breath robbed from his straining body by the freeze. A wall of startling blue ice banked high, his body 90 degrees to it being held only by centrifugal force and sheer velocity. His skis fought to find purchase on a brittle, unforgiving surface. His knees were bent almost sideways, one into the other, ski poles rammed under sweating armpits.

The wall began to dip away, but it wasn't over yet. Joss dropped his centre of gravity to accommodate the change in local geography and began to feel the slide. He had expected this and used the sideways momentum to exert his balance until, when he reached the foot of the bank, he sprang to the opposite side and was flung like a human missile from a sub-zero slingshot.

'Hold it, Joss,' he muttered and almost lost it at the bank's lip. His outside ski flirted with disaster briefly but a tiny sway of his hips pulled him away from severe injury. As he hurtled across the top of the bank, Joss saw the frowning mountain peaks of the Austrian Alps jut into the impossibly azure sky.

'Not today,' he shouted. 'Not any day.' This was better than the snow he was used to; same colour, different kind of dependency.

Joss Lane, twenty-four but feeling sixty five, felt a hand gently shake his arm, then jerked awake, wild-eyed and lost in the 747's interior. He focused on the concerned face of the Air-Swiss stewardess,

'Sir, are you all right?'

Joss nodded, then glanced sideways at his fellow travellers on the adjacent seats, who had swayed away from him toward the aisle, 'Sorry, just mind-skiing' he explained, though their set faces offered no understanding; he couldn't blame them, even those who

23

knew him found difficulty with the concept. Joss Lane watched the stewardess move away suspiciously as the flight continued on its path to London, Heathrow. He exhaled slowly and watched the soft pillows of the clouds drift underneath the wing, like great banks of brain-jangling cocaine and wondered how many cumuli he had snorted before re-hab and how many dark slag heaps of smack he had injected before the cure with Kristina Klammer at the Complott Clinic in the Alps.

'Cure!' He almost laughed out loud, then remembered the growing fear of his aisle mates and coughed his ironic humour away. For the past eighteen months, Dr Klammer had been his addiction counsellor, guru, friend, and harshest critic. In his mind he could see her now; chestnut curls softening the pinched concentration of a cerebral face. A slim figure with a needle-sharp mind which was more bed of nails than pin cushion.

Eighteen long months in an antiseptic prison, a year and a half of gut wrenching ache and unrequited need until he was pronounced 'well enough to leave'. Dr Klammer had accepted her patient as a filthy, dreadlocked wraith and seen him leave whip cord fit with close cropped hair; clean, inside and out. His wasted musculature had been firmed by endless hikes, climbs and Telemark ski-ing. At a shade under six feet the addict's stoop had been replaced with a straight narrow back, but the kinks in his brain still remained.

The thought of an armful of best made him go weak momentarily, until he bit his lip and remembered his pitiful state; a vast bear-pit of sweat, shit and self-loathing. No friends, just dealers. He recalled his favourite T-shirt, bought from a hawkers' market in Burma, which sported a picture of an alien smoking a joint and, underneath, the legend, 'Take me to your Dealer'. Joss had found it hilarious at the time: hip and trendy, a gobful of spit in the eye of his father, Callum Lane, and the rest of the pathetic straights who traded precious freedom for a mortgage, second car and a week with the kids at Center Parc. It took him some time, many stomach cramps and unheeded cravings later, to learn that he had been that alien: a sad, wasted creature from another world, lost in an unfamiliar landscape of chemical need. Now, at least for the moment, he had a focus, of sorts.

The anxiety of returning to his past life threw his mind into

24

tumble-weed confusion. At times like this Klammer had forced him into a routine, to bring a sense of calm and definitive focus. He reached into his pocket and produced three small, well-worn, playing tiles from the Oriental game 'Go'. They were parched bone and smoothed by use, but each represented a different aspect of his life. He breathed deeply and placed the first tile down gently on the plastic tray attached to the back of the seat in front. It had on it the ideogram signifying love. Joss focused and thought of Greta Larson. He reached down again, inside his world travelled ruck-sack underneath the seat in front, and removed Greta's letter. It was the first link he had experienced with his past since the Amsterdam Court had given him the option of accepting treatment or going to prison; it hadn't taken long to make his choice, though he regularly regretted it at the Clinic. The writing on the envelope was unmistakably his girlfriend's, he corrected himself, ex-girlfriend's. Joss had not touched her nor had sight of her since the inquest into his mother's death. He shuddered, then placed the second 'Go' tile down quickly; this represented the past. Joss concentrated on inner peace whilst he fixed her kind face in his clouded mind's eye. Jennie Lane. Mum: Dead for two years and, despite his Doctor's arguments to the contrary, it was all his fault.

Joss heard the squeak of the drinks trolley approach and acknowledged the vapid smile of the make-up caked server, asking in her sing-song voice if there was anything he wanted. He ordered two whiskys and a lager chaser to calm himself before re-reading Greta's letter. Greta had been his 'Wonderwall; when Noel Gallagher had crafted the song, Joss knew that he had someone special like Greta in mind. They had first met at the L.S.E. Joss was in his final year reading Economics, she in her second year of a law degree and destined for life at the criminal bar. However, it was not in the lecture room but in the field of dangerous sports where they had met, sharing a mutual love of danger, excitement and athletic sex. But it was more than that; at least to him. He raised his Chivas Regal to the memory of the other members of In Extremis, the extreme sports club, and his friends Ben, Barney and Tom, themselves ghosts from the life of a different other, but they were unrepresented by the tiles.

Now, he removed Greta's letter from its envelope and laid it flat on the plastic tray next to his lager can.

Dear Joss, it seems trite to ask you how you are, but at the risk of appearing cloying I hope you are well, really well, in mind and body. The newspaper pictures from outside the Amsterdam drug court were not of your best side, though neither were your recent exploits.

Joss grimaced, typical Greta Larson, a bitter-coated sugar pill,

I would not write to you unless there was pressing need. When you disappeared after the inquest I accepted that you needed space and time to gather yourself to face the past and the future, but needs must. Things have moved on.

Joss nodded and took a sip of the fiery whisky. She had always been single-minded and he was proud that she had not been diverted from her ways.

I am involved in a case that you need to know about. It is a rape case, involving a religious cult called the Millennium Church. Joss, your father is a member of the sect. I know he is, I can give you all the details later, but believe me, they are pure mind control evil and Callum is caught up with them. As yet there is no evidence that he is involved with the abuse, but this is a very ugly can of worms. We need to meet.

There followed details of her home and work telephone numbers, and Joss had already left a message on her answer-phone and another with her clerk at chambers.

You have lost your mother; I could not forgive myself if you lost your father as well. He is in very deep. Please contact me, Joss.

She had signed her name and Joss had been dismayed that the message was signed merely 'with best wishes' and not 'love', though in reality he could have little complaint.

26

Joss stuffed the missive back in its paper home and sat back. The two tiles sat next to each other before him: love and the past. Two women he had loved more than life itself; both lost to him by dint of his selfish cravings. He needed to see Greta; he had to. When his re-hab had been at its grimmest, her image had been a talisman against despair. But before he could go in search of her, he had to drop in on Niall Robertson. Uncle Niall, the family solicitor and his father's trusted business partner. If anyone knew what was really going on, it was the dapper Irish lawyer. Joss felt his face crack into a smile as he pictured the busy little solicitor, darting about like a flustered mole, his distinctive tight grey curls and thick, steel-framed glasses bobbing furtively. He always seemed to be talking, never stopping to take breath. 'Lot to say, kid, not a lot of time to say it' was one of his catchphrases. When he did give people a chance to speak, however, you knew he was listening really hard, as if he really wanted to understand you. Niall was part of the family and Joss knew his father trusted him completely. At the thought of his father, Joss stared hard at the ideograms on the tiny pieces of bones; love and the past, but where did Callum Lane sit between the two? He had been a distant figure throughout Joss's childhood, almost cold to the touch. Joss felt more warmth toward his Uncle Niall, who had always been there: weddings, funerals, christenings and family conferences; same old conspiratorial smile with a wink for his favourite nephew. It had been Uncle Niall who accompanied them on holidays abroad as a youngster. In fact, Joss thought that it was probably Niall who first encouraged him in his pursuit of dangerous sports. One of his earliest recollections was a trip to Rosas in southern Spain at the foot of the Pyrenees, when he had begged and grovelled for permission to try parascending from the back of a speedboat in the Mediterranean. His mother and father had flatly refused him, but Niall eventually managed to persuade them to relent. In the same way, he had managed to persuade the speedboat owner that Joss was old enough to be dragged a hundred metres into the sky. He was a very persuasive man, Niall Robertson. Perhaps that's why he became a lawyer, although with a mouth like his, it was difficult to imagine him becoming anything else.

Joss knew that Callum and Niall had studied at university in

Dublin together; he had seen the old black and white photographs often enough. Strange thing was that he could never be quite sure that the tales he heard from Niall about their youthful antics were true when he considered his father in his favourite chair studying his favourite pink newspaper in his favourite grey suit. While Niall had always retained that mischievous sparkle in his deep green eyes, Joss's father's had simply dulled over the years, until they died completely after the day it happened. Niall would give him some answers, he was sure, and after all it was the only place to start looking.

As the in-flight announcement informed the passengers that in ten minutes they would be landing, Joss produced the lonely third of the 'Go' trio and carefully placed it down. This represented the future and was as unreadable as his father's face. It was intended to force him to ponder the answers from the past as a guide to the future. Joss already had one answer and by now Dr Klammer would know he had forced the lock to her filing cabinet to discover the secret that had been troubling him throughout his stay at the Complott Clinic. For months he had asked the question; 'who is paying my bills, and why?' and for months Kristina Klammer had met his enquiring gaze with her own flat expression, but no answer. His illicit search of the filing cabinet had finally revealed the answer, which dove-tailed with the contents of Greta's letter; the Millennium Church had forked out over a quarter of a million pounds on his treatment. Him. Joss Lane. A raving junkie; he had to know why. The three bone counters held the secret, he was sure of that, he had to read their meaning, but for the present the future was still clouded and obscure.

And he was not the only one with questions to ask. Klammer had had her own questions for him, all attempting to resolve his guilt over his mother's watery death, but she had one specific enquiry that dogged him for a year and a half. She sang it to him, whispered it to him as he lay prone with exhaustion,

> '*Joss and Jill went up the hill*
> *To fetch a pail of water.*
> *Joss fell down and broke his crown.*
> *His Mum came tumbling after.*'

He had explained to the point of repetitious exhaustion that this was his mother's favourite lullaby which she sang to him when he was a child. Kristina, however, was always dissatisfied with his reply and pressed,

'Yes, but what does it mean to *you*?'

Joss still could not provide that answer nor could he fathom why she continued to press him so diligently on a minor, dimly recalled point from his past. Like a student who had failed to revise for a major examination, he had too many questions and insufficient answers.

He swallowed the last of his drinks and readied himself for action. He replaced the tiles in his pocket, then Joss Lane, motherless son, ex-junkie and once dangerous sports fanatic, fastened his seat belt and descended into the dark clouds lurching ominously over his country's capital city.

CHAPTER THREE

March 1st 2000

Mark Mason ran troubled fingers through his dark hair as he made one further note on the case of 'PJ Rivers'. It was the eve of the trial and Mason was worried. He'd conducted several very serious cases in the two years he had been a QC, but none quite as desperate as this.

He swigged back the dregs of his coffee in the cramped room of his Pump Court chambers. The walls were crammed with crumbling law reports, the floor with spilled briefs, as messy as his mind was clear. It was his very own chaos filing system.

Outside, in the tiny waiting room, Charmers, Moody's solicitor, sat and waited, but as yet there was no sign of Rose and her father. Mason sighed: there had been four abortive attempts to take her through her evidence already, when for one reason or another Rose did not attend the scheduled appointments. Yes, things looked desperate: without Rose, the Millennium Church and Rivers would win and the Moodys would be ruined. Mason could not allow himself to consider what effect it would have on the trembling girl.

They were playing for the very highest of stakes, and the defendants would do everything in their power to defeat the case; they had already done much. This was the first action against the Church that had ever gone to trial: all the others, both civil and criminal, had been defeated by a mixture of fear and clever technical points of law. Rivers and his associates had the money and had briefed the best.

The defendants had three QCs in their attack. Callow, who had been acting against Mason at the disclosure hearing, had been brought in at the personal insistence of Rivers. He was still a regular visitor to the United States and held dual rights of audience at the Californian bar. He saw himself as a legal innovator and would no doubt be drafting grounds of appeal before the first day of the trial was through. Rory Fannon was a highly respected Old Bailey crime silk, whose silken voice and reasonable demeanour was judged to be a tactical must in front of a jury. The defence would use him at the end of the case to sway the jury in their favour; if they got that far. Finally, and worst of all, the savagely brilliant Thynne QC. Nobody ever called him by his first name; Mason doubted if anyone even knew what it was. Even the bar-list of practitioners failed to disclose it. His cross-examinations were looked upon as textbook studies in sly innuendo and bombastic destruction. Each cross was as individual as the case itself, but he had not lost a legal action in years. Some said that was because he only picked winners, but Mason had seen the crafty performer in action and knew that his cross-examination skills were the super-structured foundation of his success. He feared for Rose. Thynne had had months to prepare himself for the onslaught; he took no prisoners and either executed witnesses in public or forced them to self-destruct in the box. How could Mason possibly prepare Rose for a public savaging if she refused to attend his chambers for a briefing?

Greta was sitting behind him at the small desk positioned under the window. He stretched back in his chair and tapped her on the shoulder.

'You finished noting that yet?' he asked, referring to the lever arch file, which contained the evidence gathered by the original official investigation into Rose's allegations.

'Everything but the final report from the office of the procurator fiscal: I didn't see much point; you only need remember one line from it.'

'What's that?'

'Insufficient evidence. It's stamped in big red letters on the front.'

'What do you make of it?'

'They are going to crucify us with it and the jury can come along for the ride.'

'I know what you mean. If the offences she alleges had all taken place in England or Scotland things may well have been a lot different. At that time, when Geoff Moody marched into the police station in Edinburgh clutching Rose, nobody could be sure where some of the events she was alleging had taken place. She was certain that she had been abducted in England and all the evidence pointed that way from her father, who gave the account of her going missing that night. But where she was taken to after that was a mystery. All they knew was that her father claimed he had rescued her from the church's retreat called the Haven on the Isle of Skye: her recollection of the early days was so poor at that stage. It's gradually coming back to her now with the help of therapy, according to Geoff, but how reliable is that when you take into account that the defence will allege that it amounts to no more than forced recovered memory syndrome?'

'And look where that stands in terms of legal credibility these days,' Greta mused. 'There's a lot of case law against us.'

'Precisely,' answered Mark, recalling the recently discredited line of authorities involving twenty-year-old allegations of sexual abuse thrown out of court because of the inherent risks of convicting on evidence acquired by similar techniques of memory retrieval. The current fashion for defence counsel was to call experts who could convincingly throw doubt upon that entire field of forensic psychiatry. He decided to leave that issue well alone for the time being and moved on, trying to clarify the peaks and troughs of his case.

'Go through the sequence of events with me following the arrest of Rivers at the Haven,' he invited Greta; she began,

'When he was first questioned by the police he was held under the Criminal Justice Scotland Act. He was detained and questioned for six hours, which was the maximum permitted under that statute. He made candid and categorical denials to all of the central allegations put to him.'

Mark nodded. 'And that was all without the benefit of a solicitor: the defence will say that is further evidence of his innocence. He wasn't running scared or refusing to co-operate: in fact, he invited the police to check his personal documents through his office, giving them times and dates of his movements around the world.'

Greta rubbed her head. 'Reading through the interviews it strikes me that the police just weren't interested: this guy was an American citizen and they have him in a dirty cell declaring his innocence. I expect they couldn't wait to get him out of there before the Embassy got on board.'

'Hence the decision not to get any medical evidence from Rose or the defendant at that time.'

'That's right. Similarly, no consideration was given to expending resources on the collection of forensic samples from any of the inhabitants of the Haven. They had written her off at this stage, I reckon.'

'So, OK, we have a very weak report going to the office of the Procurator Fiscal. He is the local head of the independent Scots prosecution service working to the central body, the Crown Office. Do we know if the Crown Agent himself ever reviewed the file?'

'There is no indication that he saw it personally but there are file notes to indicate that someone at the office reviewed it. He came to the same conclusion as everyone else: there was insufficient evidence to mount the prosecution. They had potential jurisdictional problems and effectively passed the buck. Geoff Moody was told that he ought perhaps to contact the English police when he returned home but the moment had gone.'

Mason wandered over to Greta's desk and looked out to the street below. The familiar old guy who lit up the ornamental gas lamps around the square was going about his business and Mark reflected that he wouldn't mind swapping places with him right now. The case seemed utterly hopeless, but he had to nail his own colours to the mast before the night was through.

'Right', he continued, 'let's think the main issues through, where do we have to score with the jury? Starting with the kidnap and unlawful imprisonment, what have we got?

'We open up with Geoff giving the background and circumstances of the night Rose left home. We have the police report of a missing person that he made. We have some statements from young kids who saw her talking to a couple of strangers at the amusement arcade, but no evidence of any struggle.

'We have to prove that she was abducted against her will. It comes down to Rose on that and she is pretty sketchy: one minute she is sure that she asked to leave their company after a while but they wouldn't let her and the next minute she isn't. This is a fundamental point for us and she has to come up to proof: if we lose the jury at the outset then there's no way they are going to take on board the more subtle arguments about mental assault during the time of her unlawful imprisonment. We need to get them on our side quickly and use the malice they should feel towards the defendant at that stage to convince them that her free will had been suborned,' Mark concluded grandly.

'Sounds easy in principle, but are you sure we can rely on the jury coming into court with a natural antipathy towards the defendant?'

'I've never defended a case where they didn't,' he replied smartly. 'Are all the statements in order from the psychologists and nutritional experts?'

'As far as I can see, but in terms of pound-for-pound expertise the defence have out-bought us.'

'Never mind about that now: we haven't cross-examined them yet. OK, that leaves us with the central issue concerning the sexual abuse including, most importantly, the rape by Rivers. We have the indictment drafted to cover the date of her disappearance to the date of her rescue.'

'Yes, but she can't pin the date down.'

'So what. We say that the date is not a material averment: it's the fact that it happened at all.'

'Maybe so, but it has become the issue because the defence are prepared to provide evidence of Rivers' whereabouts on any particular date she cares to name. They say we would be hard pushed to find any dates during the indictment spread that will coincide with his visits to the Haven. He travels all over the world and they have flight plans of his private jet, minuted meetings, press coverage from all over: everything. Sounds to me like they are confident she's making it up: otherwise, why would they risk it?'

'It may seem like that to you but it smacks to me of manufactured evidence. Anyway, what about our medical evidence: is the doctor warned and ready for trial?'

'Yes, but I don't think it takes us much further,' Greta replied shaking her head slowly.

'How come? We have physical evidence that she has been penetrated. It's a prerequisite.'

'But so is the fact that the victim doesn't consent.'

'She was under sixteen, Greta: in law she couldn't consent.'

'But her sixteenth birthday fell when she was inside the church,' she reminded him. 'What about the allegation that she was subjected against her will to routine group sex?'

'What about it?' he asked.

'There is a possible winner for the defence here, in that any evidence of penetration is entirely irrelevant. They are saying, in effect: so what, it proves she has had sex but it doesn't prove she had sex with Rivers. In fact, the more sex we establish she has had the better as far as they are concerned.'

'Why?'

'Because after her birthday they could say any sex, which may be proved to the jury's satisfaction that she engaged in, could have been consensual. She hasn't been able to provide any coherent evidence of identification of the persons involved so nobody has been interviewed. If they had, they may have raised the issue of consent at the time.'

'It doesn't matter. I'm holding Rivers vicariously liable for the acts of his apostles. Consent isn't an issue because she had no free will to consult,' Mason said slowly, feeling quite pleased with the soundbite but unhappy that when all was stripped away this case depended entirely on the evidence of one frightened, fractured girl who at present was nowhere to be seen.

He checked his watch: it was 7pm and still she had failed to show. In fifteen and a half hours he would tell the jury all, outlining the horrific allegations against the Church and Rivers; it would be disastrous if Rose failed to prosecute her own case.

The chamber's junior assistant pushed the door open and smiled brightly.

'Mr Moody's just come in with a lady.'

Mason smiled a sigh of relief.

'Thanks, Sandra, bring them in.'

A second later, Charmers, unusually flustered, led the way into his room, followed by an anxious Geoff Moody and a woman, who was a complete stranger.

'Where's Rose?' Mason asked.

Charmers rolled his eyes. Geoff Moody shrugged and turned to him.

'This is Susan Morris, who's been helping with Rose.'

She held out a slim hand. He shook it, and felt her skin to be surprisingly coarse for a woman, as was her grip. Mason found himself meeting a knowing, watchful gaze. An elegant black trouser suit, nipped around a trim waist, reinforced the look that said 'I'm serious'.

'But I'm not doing a very good job; isn't that what you're thinking?' she said, a half-smile revealing astonishingly white teeth. Mason shook his head, then stopped. His entire belief in the law stemmed from an adherence to complete honesty, at least from his side: he wouldn't change that habit now to save her feelings.

'I know how important you are to Rose,' he began. 'Geoff has kept me informed of her progress, but she still isn't here, is she?'

'Obviously,' the woman replied without a hint of sarcasm, 'but I guarantee that she will be at court tomorrow.'

'I don't wish to appear rude, Miss Morris, but could you please remind me of your qualifications.'

'I'm a qualified therapist, specialising in addiction work.'

'So not a professor of psychiatry?'

'I know her,' the woman countered, ignoring the implication.

'And you will be a witness on our behalf. The defence team have half a dozen experts lined up with qualifications longer than a boa constrictor and twice as deadly. Does that not frighten you?' Mason was concerned that Susan Morris too would become one of Thynne's courtroom victims.

'I can look after myself,' she said sweetly. 'It's Rose I'm concerned about.'

'As are we all,' Mason said, shaking his head. 'What makes you think she'll go through with it? I mean, she's hardly hammering at the door of the court.'

'She's ready, that's all, but she's only strong enough to go through with it once.'

'I've spent some time with her today,' Geoff Moody added. 'There's a change all right; she seems more like my old Rosie. Why, she even laughed the other day.' He forced a smile; Mason could feel nothing but sympathy for the tattered remains of the Moody family.

'We have no choice,' Charmers the solicitor said. 'We have come too far even to consider abandoning the case, but Rose must attend.' He turned to the counsellor. 'Miss Morris, we know you to be well meaning, but I cannot stress enough the importance of Rose's personal appearance in the witness box in pursuit of her allegations; she must tell them her tale in her own words.'

'She will tell them the truth,' she replied icily, her eyes boring into him.

'Of course she will,' Mason soothed, 'that was what Mr Charmers meant.' But the solicitor was clearly angered by her outburst. 'We are all under a lot of pressure; none more so than Rose,' Mason continued. 'But the trial has to get off the ground, then one way or the other it will end.'

'Not for Rose,' Geoff Moody muttered wistfully. The woman reached out and touched his arm. Mason felt helpless.

Soon, too soon, the girl would be exposed to public humiliation, her wounds torn open and exposed to the cold stare of the Millennium Church and PJ Rivers. Theirs was a religion without mercy. They would not forgive her betrayal.

Later, when the others had departed and Mason was packing up his case papers for the next day, he heard a thump against the chambers room window. Moving towards it, he could see that a small sparrow had flown into the glass and fallen to the outside sill. He opened it and reached down. It was warm, so warm; yet so dead. Mark Mason QC shuddered. He was too practical to believe in omens, but he shuddered none the less.

CHAPTER FOUR

The following morning, Mark and Greta walked the short distance to the Royal Courts of Justice from chambers. Fine drizzle hung in the air, misting over Mark's face and sticking to his suit in small globules. The smell of wet wool drifted into his nostrils, reminding him of the fell walking he had loved so much in his native peak district. It was, however, a different kind of mountain he had to climb today.

After last night's abortive conference without Rose there was simply no way of telling whether she would attend court. Her father's involvement hung like the sword of Damocles over the entire case. His unrelenting quest for justice was something to be admired, but at what cost, Mark reflected, thinking of the pressure Geoff Moody must be exerting upon his own daughter. If she had cracked and refused to appear, then he knew the defence would strenuously resist any attempt to have the case taken out of the list at this stage of the proceedings. He could foresee they would claim that any failure to attend by Rose was merely a reflection of the fact that it was her father who was the prime mover behind the case.

As they rounded the corner from Fetter Lane and joined the Strand, they could see the crowds gathered outside the front entrance to the courts. He counted at least five television cameras and unconsciously began brushing the front of his pinstripe. Greta smiled as she noticed him.

'Don't worry, you look fine,' she said.

'What?' he replied distractedly.

'I said you look fine,' she said, motioning to the cameras ahead.

'I don't feel it,' he said forlornly. 'In a way I hope she doesn't turn up.'

'You don't mean that,' she stated.

'I do, Greta. I'm afraid they'll make mincemeat out of her. What happens if she never recovers from it? Whose responsibility is it at the end of the day? I should have been firmer with Moody; persuaded him not to go on.'

'You can't do any more than follow your instructions, Mark: at least, that's what you always taught me.'

'Did I? How remiss of me.' He winked at her playfully, but could feel the real bite of hopelessness deep in the pit of his stomach.

Just as they approached the edges of the crowds, Mark could hear an American newscaster talking directly into camera with the magnificent backdrop of the stone archway to the courts behind him. He bounded immediately towards Mason.

'Mr Mason, Mr Mason, sir.' His shrill West Coast accent drilled the air like a siren attracting a number of other reporters to the spot. 'Mr Mason, Dale Winters, CBS, reporting on the Moody case. You may know that there is a great deal of interest in the United States: the Reverend Rivers has claimed to be a victim of a wholly unfair legal system. Our own legal experts are highlighting this case as an example of the inherent weaknesses in the United Kingdom's antiquated system. What do you say?'

'No comment.' Mason waved him aside.

'We have heard that the complainant is unlikely to turn up today: will that be the end of this litigation against the Millennium Church?' The reporter thrust the large round microphone under Mason's jaw.

'I am afraid you have been misinformed. The complainant is on her way to court as we speak. Now, if you'll excuse me, I'm sure you will appreciate that we are busy,' Mason replied confidently.

'Will the jury be sworn today?' the reporter pushed as a spray of microphones from the other journalists blocked Mason's exit.

'Of course the jury will be sworn today: I expect to begin opening the case against Mr Rivers before lunchtime.'

'Aren't the defence seeking to cross-examine the jurors to eliminate any possibility of prejudice?'

'They can try,' smiled Mason, 'but they won't get anywhere. This is not the United States of America, may I remind you. One of the finest principles, in my humble opinion, for which this unfair system, as the defendant puts it, earns most respect the world over is the calm expedition of jury selection.'

'The Reverend Rivers is well known for his controversial vision of the future, Mr Mason: he maintains that there can be no fair trial of these allegations unless the court is prepared to show caution before admitting jurors who may have opposing religious beliefs. What do you say to that?'

'What you fail to recognise is that it is essential we know nothing of those twelve people. We must not care what their opinions are, or where and whether they are educated or what their hobbies may be and especially that we allow their innermost thoughts to remain a matter for them. The more anonymous the better, to reach an impartial and incontestable verdict born out of those very secret deliberations. The defendant can only be promised justice if there is no connection between him and the twelve faces that try him. Now, if you will excuse me, ladies and gentlemen,' Mason said, forcefully leaving the crowd in no doubt as to his intention.

A pathway through appeared out of nowhere. Mason strode through the gap, and Greta followed, smiling to herself. Mason may have doubts about the case but he certainly wasn't going to share them with anyone else except her.

They were ushered quickly through security and walked down the stone staircase leading to the robing rooms. As they reached the bottom, Greta was forced to turn left into the door marked female advocates, and Mason reflected momentarily on the accusation that this indeed was an antiquated system. The porter stood to attention and gave Mason his usual cheery grin.

'Big 'un today, sir. Here, let me carry that case for you,' he said, reaching for Mason's hefty black leather pilot's case.

'It certainly is, Charlie. The opposition in yet?' he enquired.

'In the lounge, sir,' the old man replied over his shoulder as he led the way around the corner to the rows of wooden lockers with their sparkling brass nameplates uniformly gleaming. Mason spotted the team huddled over papers in the far corner of the room.

He expected an onslaught from his opponents, but not as early as it came. As he brushed down his silk gown by the side of the locker he felt a movement behind him. Without turning, he whispered,

'No carving of this one, gentlemen.'

'Carving' was the legal slang for settling a case out of court, without a jury's decision. Mason plucked his wig out from the black and gold tin that bore his name and had done so since he had saved up to buy it from a Chancery Lane wigmakers eighteen long years before.

'Are you so sure that is wise?' Mason recognised the lilting voice: Rory Fannon. They had sent their friendliest emissary across to exert subtle pressure. His face said it all. Rounded by good will and marked with a ruby glow, he could have been the human embodiment of the blarney stone. He was fair of hair and humour and rarely failed to see the ludicrous irony of a job that paid him so well to do what he did best; talk. His robes were relaxingly shabby, his wing collar far from pristine and his wig well-nicotined by the cigarellos he often shared with clients many years away from the parole board. Mason liked him. They had co-defended a few times and always gelled well, but today they would eat from different tables. Mason gave him a curt nod.

'You wouldn't be talking to me if you were completely confident.'

Fannon smiled, 'Hate to see you make a bad career move, Mark, that's all.'

'That's touching.' He glanced across to a corner where Callow and Thynne, the other QCs, muttered darkly between themselves. Three silent junior counsel, there to assist the three leaders, gathered bundles of documents.

'Quite a team,' Mason murmured, as he swept back his hair and placed the ancient wig on his head. 'I can understand why they got involved, Rory, but not you.'

'Needs must, young Mark, needs must. Tax bills and school fees have a way of dulling the conscience.'

'And expanding the wallet,' Mason chided. Fannon shrugged.

'This is going to be bloody, Mark: no good will come of it.'

'You'll get paid,' Mason snapped, annoyed by Fannon's repetition of the obvious.

'There must be room for manoeuvre before we kick this off.'

Mason spun around. 'Callow is running the show, we both know it. What message does he send?' Fannon appeared rebuked and shamed by Mason's accurate assessment of the defence team structure.

'The Millennium Church and Rivers do not wish the girl to be further scarred by the trial.'

'A little late in the day for that, wouldn't you say?'

Fannon shook his head. 'We are not yet through the courtroom door.'

'All your clients are afraid of is adverse publicity. If Rivers goes down, he goes down for ten years at least.'

Mason's verbal bravado was not matched by his demeanour and Fannon could sense it.

'You will never win this one, Mark. She is too damaged. Thynne will screw her up for good. Do her a favour: advise her to offer no evidence.'

Mason nodded thoughtfully. This wasn't a compromise; it was a legal lynching.

'What about costs?'

Fannon grimaced. 'Stumbling block there, Mark.'

'Let me guess. Geoff Moody agrees to pay all your costs until he is destitute and therefore taken out of the ring? What are your costs? Half, three-quarters of a million?'

'Substantially more, Mason,' Thynne said from behind his shoulder. His voice dripped like sour honey. 'Tell me, has Miss Moody graced us with an attendance today? I gather it has been rather difficult to take instructions from her.' His blubbery lips pursed together like two mating slugs.

'Yes of course she's here,' Mason replied, forcing a confident tone into his voice. 'Ready, willing and . . .'

'Mentally disabled,' Thynne concluded. 'On your own head be it. Frankly I feel sorry for the girl: that father of hers has pushed her into this. Still, I am looking forward to a chat with him.'

'I'm sure you'll be rewarded with much increased understanding,' Mason replied breezily. He was always happy to trade slights with Thynne.

'How very droll, Mason,' he snarled. 'What impresses me most after all these years is this sudden interest in prosecuting: a role reversal, wouldn't you say?'

'Oh you know how it is,' Mason chided. 'After this I may start taking on a lot more: nothing to it really.'

'Surely not – the great defender turns inquisitor – whatever next?' Thynne smiled smugly. 'You do realise, Mason, that there really is a great deal more to it than the shoddy performance you've put in so far at the pre-trial hearings. Then again, I don't suppose it's entirely your fault: of course, you never had the proper pupilage under old Findlay for a prosecution practice.'

'You could say that, but then again I watched my old master whip your backside often enough when you prosecuted him. Does that qualify me?' Mason asked, raising an eyebrow to underline the insult.

'I dare say that he enjoyed one or two victories, but they were rare,' Thynne smarted. 'How is the old devil anyway?'

'As right as rain, but you didn't come over here to talk about Tom Findlay, Thynne, so let's get on with it, shall we,' Mason said, adjusting the starched wing collar on to the brass stud in the neck of his shirt.

'By all means, dear boy, but before we do, it would be as well to remember the words of Judge Avory. Prosecuting counsel ought not . . .' Thynne was interrupted from behind by the deep transatlantic drawl that belonged to Giles Callow.

'. . . To struggle for the verdict against the prisoner, but they ought to bear themselves rather in the character of ministers of justice, assisting in the administration of justice. An admirable concept, which no doubt you have well in, mind, Mark.' Callow eyeballed him briefly before moving off at a funereal pace, a bulky folder wedged under his arm.

As the others followed Callow out of the room, Mason carefully tied his legal bands and adjusted his ageing wig precisely on his head. He glanced at his reflection in the mirror and wished for once that it was a crash helmet.

44

CHAPTER FIVE

Mason headed up the stairs and met Greta who was leaning over the balustrade looking down on the chequered black and white tiled floor below in the main body of the magnificent building.

'Ready?' she asked quietly.

'As I'll ever be, Greta. Come on, let's do it. Have you seen Rose arrive yet?'

'No, Charmers is down there just inside the security barrier but I haven't seen Geoff or Rose: sorry, Mark.'

'She'll be here, she has to be. Besides, I anticipate the legal arguments will take up most of the morning so there's time yet. We need to get some authorities from the library: Callow is bound to have some obscure points to make before we kick off.'

They walked wearily along the long stone-flagged corridor, which encircles the Royal Court on the first floor, and turned right at the end heading for the main library. Once there, they spent half an hour retrieving case reports from the shelves in the ancient room. Mason believed that a series of applications would be made by Callow dealing with the admissibility of certain parts of the evidence. The trial judge would then rule upon each individual application at this preliminary stage to ensure that the continuity of the proceedings wasn't interrupted too often when the trial was under way. They piled the books on to one of the trolleys provided and walked briskly to Court number ten.

The public gallery and press box were packed to capacity and a sign on the door forbade any further admittance. Mason chose at first not to look over at the defendant, who was chatting easily with his legal team. But the man's reputation and Mason's knowledge of the evil he had wrought upon Rose Moody demanded that he look into the face of the beast. Mark had seen many photographs of the Reverend Rivers. The black and white of press shots gave his face a blurred quality like a photo-me-booth picture smudged by an excited thumb. The reality was very different. The sepia tones were now fleshed with the strident high colour of the healthy in body and soul. His oval face appeared strangely kind and well meaning, almost like a Doctor with good news to impart. There were lines around his deep forehead and cheeks but they suggested an appearance of deep concern rather than worry or debauchery. He was of average build, height and breadth but carried the dignity of his place in the world with knowing ease. The dark blue suit he wore almost sang with decency, whilst a black tie with a rakish red slash promised a twinkle in the character. He was impressive, Mason had to admit it. This was no raving, bible-belt monster with a penchant for young girls, but a saintly man wrongly castigated by a disturbed young woman. Mark saw Rivers look towards him and smile. Rivers's eyes fixed him like a rare moth on a collector's board. He felt pinned by the sheer power of the stare. He forced himself to look away. Mason looked over to the panel of potential jurors who had been brought into court by the jury bailiffs. They sat in a specially dedicated section of the court facing the judge's bench, but out of view to the public. He studied each of the twelve faces in turn, thinking about the question that had been raised by the American journalist outside the court.

A panel of jurors is chosen by taking their names and addresses from the electoral register entirely by chance, almost with a pin. When the summoning officer sends out the brown envelopes stamped with the crest of Her Majesty's Lord Chancellor, he has no idea whether any of them might fall within a specific category: they could be convicts or clergymen. He must rely upon their honesty when they arrive at court and claim exemption from service. Should a potential juror fail to reveal grounds for his or her automatic disqualification then there is no way of discovering that disqualification and there would remain one liar on the jury. This, Mason thought is the best system in the world.

When the potential jurors were assembled, the clerk of the court shuffled the cards upon which their names appeared and called out the first twelve to appear. Callow was well known to be a fierce advocate of the American system of selection and a highly vocal critic of the restrictions imposed in England on challenges to jurors. In the United States the courts had become so ultra-cautious of admitting any juror who may have an opinion of any sort that they allow weeks to be spent on cross-examining prospective jurors with a view to weeding out those who think. Mason believed that this calamitous system had evolved through the efforts of over-zealous and sometimes unscrupulous lawyers who imagine their job is to ensure that their client is tried by an approved committee instead of twelve men good and true.

Suddenly there was a sharp rap on the door leading from the judge's dais to his chambers behind.

'Court Stand,' shouted the usher as Justice Withnail bounded on to the bench and sat down quickly with a curt nod in the direction of the advocates.

The clerk rhymed off the traditional starting point for all court proceedings. 'All persons having any business before Her Majesty the Queen's justices draw near and give your attendance.'

'Are we ready to empanel the jury, Mr Mason?' Withnail enquired in an unusually polite tone.

'Yes, My Lord, the prosecution is ready for trial, although I trust your lordship is aware that my learned friends seek your Lordship's ruling on several preliminary matters, one of which I anticipate involves the swearing of jurors,' replied Mason positively.

Withnail was probably surprised that the case was still proceeding, given his comments at the pre-trial review in January, and although Rose still hadn't arrived Mason decided that any judicial wrath coming his way could happily be delayed until Callow had received his first. He was sure that his opponents would try to challenge some of the jurors, and that was bound to incur outrage from the bench.

'Is this right Mr Thynne?' snapped the Judge.

'My Lord, my learned friend Mr Callow will deal with the preliminary issues,' Thynne replied, sitting down hastily.

'Will he now, well we shall see about that,' Withnail snarled as he nodded to the clerk of the court to begin empanelling the jury.

Mason had calculated correctly that whilst Withnail was an angry and unpleasant judge to those who appeared before him, more than anything he was a traditionalist. He held as a sacrosanct rule that his function was to assist and protect the jury at all costs. Any legal meandering at their expense by the defence, Mason felt sure, could only improve his own chances of swaying the judge in his own favour.

It has long since been the law that the defence did not have the right to a peremptory challenge of any potential juror, but there still remained a limited right to challenge if they could prove good reason for excluding those who were possibly unfavourable. The clerk read out twelve names in succession and eventually there were eight men and four women sitting nervously in the jury box in the well of the court. Callow rose slowly to his feet as the first juror, a middle-aged man in a blazer and grey slacks was about to take the oath.

'Challenge,' shouted Callow.

'On what basis, Mr Callow, do you seek to challenge this man?' asked Withnail, throwing his pen into the crease in the middle of his red judicial notebook.

'Upon grounds of general prejudice, my Lord,' Callow replied calmly. It was obvious to Mason that Callow had expected some animosity from the judge and wasn't about to rise to the bait.

'The burden of proof is on you, Mr Callow, and you must provide *prima facie* evidence of your grounds before I will allow you to go any further.'

'I respectfully apply to your Lordship for leave to cross-examine this potential juror on the *voir dere* to determine the precise basis of my challenge. It is the defence contention that no fair trial of this defendant can take place unless each juror is prepared to disclose his or her particular religious persuasion to discount any possibility of prejudice against our client.'

'Denied, Mr Callow. It has long been the practice of these courts, as you well know, to refuse any such attempt at circumventing the natural process. I do not consider that you have laid any firm foundation for your submission in relation to this or any other juror. Lord Parker as long ago as 1964 declared that in these circumstances it is no good saying simply that this man or this woman appears antagonistic, therefore he should not try my case.

Similarly, despite the practice that has become commonplace in your native shores, it is no good in this court simply saying he or she may harbour a secret religious prejudice.'

'I am fully aware of the authority to which your Lordship refers: however, may I be allowed to submit that this case represents an exceptional set of circumstances wherein a departure from the normal practice is merited. In the notorious case of the Krays in 1969 defence counsel was permitted to cross-examine jurors upon whether they had read certain newspaper articles discreditable to the accused. In the present case, many such scurrilous articles have appeared in the press, which cast aspersions upon our client's religious beliefs and ceremonies of worship. I can now produce before the court many of those pieces.' Callow motioned to a disinterested Rory Fannon who handed a large folder crammed with the offending articles. It was passed to the judge who didn't even bother to look past the first one.

'Mr Mason what do you have to say?' he asked.

'My Lord, it is a matter for the court, but with respect to my learned friend's argument I find it difficult to see how they can show that any of the jurors have read and digested these articles, let alone been prejudiced by them. The Krays case was wholly exceptional historically, but this case is not. Furthermore, I would be surprised if the defence can point to any information peculiar to any individual juror that may strengthen their case for exclusion.' Mason gambled on the fact that Withnail was against the defence and any admission made by them tending to suggest that they had already vetted the panel secretly would be met by cries of invasion of privacy.

He glanced over to the defence and noticed a slight shake of the head by Rivers to Callow, clearly indicating that he shouldn't pursue this one any further.

'I entirely agree, Mr Mason,' said Withnail. 'Now, can we please get on with the case without further pointless argument.'

Mason was on firm ground, but only for the moment. He quickly scribbled a note and passed it to Greta behind him. It read simply, 'Rose?'

Two of the jury members chose to affirm and not take the oath on the Bible: a fact that wasn't lost on any of the lawyers watching the procedure. None of them asked to be excused and Withnail warned them that if they did do so he may well not allow the request in any event. He then went on to tell them of the heavy responsibility that lay ahead and that they must bear it alone, for they could discuss the case with no one.

'The chief danger is when you go home from this court: on no account must you allow members of your own family or friends to proffer their views to you. You may discuss the case among your number as the trial proceeds, but only if you are all present and can each hear what is being said.' Withnail delivered all this with the avuncular charm of a great-grandfather and it appeared to Mason that the jurors were visibly grateful for his clear explanation.

As Mason watched the jury listening to the judge it was only possible to guess at who they might be. The front row consisted of one middle-aged woman who appeared professional, smart, attentive and wearing expensive clothing and discreet jewellery. Another was probably a housewife in her thirties, careworn but cheerful looking. Two of the men next to her were stout white-haired types well into their sixties and the next two were barely twenty years old, one wearing three earrings and the other a bright green button-down shirt. As the case progressed, Mason knew they would gel together in these unnatural circumstances immediately ennobled by the trust that was being placed in them.

As soon as the judge had completed his introductory remarks, the jury was sent out of court to its retiring room in order that Callow could complete his legal arguments. He began immediately by proposing that the judge should prevent the trial going any further upon grounds that the cardinal principle of fairness which underpinned the criminal justice system had already been compromised by the delay in the proceedings being brought. Again, Mason felt relatively comfortable with this abuse of process argument, figuring that Withnail was going to allow this trial to be heard publicly come hell or high water despite the fact that he had shown initial hostility at the pre-trial hearings. It was a well-known fact that Withnail had ambitions for higher office, and one way of succeeding to the lofty position of Lord Chief Justice was the successful and speedy expedition of high-profile cases such as this.

He listened carefully to the arguments concerning publicity, delay and lack of opportunity given to the defendant to provide details of alibi with great care. His concluding remarks were, however, designed cleverly to ensure that no one was left in any doubt about where he believed he was destined.

'I have well in mind the powers of my brother judges in the court of appeal and beyond: if I have erred in any of these rulings I am convinced they will not hesitate to correct my shortcomings.'

And with that he invited the jury back into court, and Mark Mason to his feet.

The court fell silent, save for the ticking of the courtroom clock, and Mason began by introducing the barristers involved in the matter. Then it was time to introduce the players.

'You will see and hear from Rose Ann Moody.'

The judge had refused his earlier request for Rose to give evidence over a video link, and even denied her a screen so that she would not have to face the man she accused. Mason then turned to introduce Rivers, the defendant, who nodded openly to the jury: no smile, but the concerned expression of a man of God, defamed before his deity.

'Ladies and gentlemen,' Mason continued, 'this case is about freedom; the right to a life free from abuse: mental, physical and spiritual. Rose Moody's right. We all know about the Millennium Church; or do we? With the arrival of the year 2000 its rise in popularity has been rapid. We are not here to question its beliefs but its methods. Religious freedom is vital to a multi-cultural society such as ours. It could be put no better than the words of Mr Justice Latey, and I quote:

'"In an open society, such as ours, people can believe what they want to and band together and promulgate their beliefs. If people believe that the earth is flat, there is nothing to stop them believing so, saying so and joining together to persuade others."'

Withnail grimaced. He had been planning to use that portion of Latey's judgment himself, to sum up the case to the court. Mason continued.

'Fine, elegant, liberal words, but it goes further.' He leaned forward for emphasis. 'They have to pursue these rights within the framework of the criminal and the civil law, and it is the case for Rose that this is precisely what the Millennium Church

51

failed to do. They did not fail by negligence, but by design and purpose.'

Mason paused and scanned the jury: they were listening, waiting for him to list the catalogues of horror inflicted on Rose, like a drop-dead punchline, the build-up enhanced the effect.

'We all think we know about the Church of the Millennium, but by the end of this case you will know the whole dark, shocking truth, and the cancer at the very heart of that truth is PJ Rivers.'

Mason heard muttering from Callow, but the wily Thynne hushed him to silence, not wishing to alienate the jury at an early stage. They were three and he was one; the English loved an underdog and despised a bully.

'But what do we know about Rose? We know she is seventeen years old and that she has a loving father. But you will hear how, between leaving the family home, after a minor argument, aged fifteen and being rescued by her father from the clutches of the Church, she suffered horrors and indignities that will chill you as they are given in evidence. What happened to Rose Moody at the hands of the Church and PJ Rivers in particular? It was no less than murder of the soul and the slaughter of a child's innocence. You will see a pathetic specimen before you.'

He didn't want to describe Rose so but, if they had any hope of winning this case, their argument would have to be partially based on pointing out the savage physical changes her experience had brought.

'Once she used to laugh with friends; all the laughter has now gone. She was a keen sportswoman; now she rarely leaves the confines of her father's rented accommodation. She had boyfriends – tragically it was a boyfriend who caused the row that led her to storm out of the family home, that day she was swept into depravity by the Church; now she flinches even with accidental male contact. What happened to the vivacious, popular, pretty young woman who disappeared that day? What awfulness did she suffer at the vile hands of Rivers and his followers?'

Mason steeled his voice, dropped it to a deep whisper and began.

'It was worse, much worse, than she ever could have imagined . . .'

CHAPTER SIX

J oss emerged from the tube at Temple station and gazed along
the embankment. He took in the cityscape as his mind harshly
compared the snow-capped beauty that had been his home in
the Alps with the monumental cage that now surrounded him.

The sun was behind him low and heavy in the sky, bouncing
orange shrapnel off the river toward the city. The gleaming glass
tower blocks beyond Blackfriars Bridge contrasted sharply against
the eerie Fabergé dome of St Paul's, and so, so many cars were
crawling along the road towards Westminster.

He turned up the steps to his left and headed past Inner Temple
gardens intending to cut across Fleet Street. The exceptionally mild
London winter and early spring had forced the flower bulbs through
into pockets of furious colour, providing him with some faith that
nature hadn't been forgotten entirely in the city. Soon he reached
Bell Yard on the eastern side of the Royal Courts of Justice and
headed for Serle Street.

As he walked through Lincoln's Inn he must have smiled to
himself a hundred times as he caught glimpses of the inhabitants
going about their business. A posse of students from nearby
King's College passed by him. He stopped for a moment. It
was the irony of the proliferation of sports clothes, more than
anything, that astonished him. Virtually every colour in the psyche-
delic spectrum was represented in abundance. Strange: when he'd
been a teenager walking the same streets dressed head to toe in
green and yellow mountain chic he had turned heads, but now
it seemed everyone was dressed the same despite the absence of
wilderness.

It wasn't long before he stood outside the cream-stuccoed frontage of number 8, Lincoln's Inn Fields with its discreet oval brass

plaque declaring the simple legend: Robertson, Bartlett and Hurst Solicitors.

It all seemed so restrained in the quiet of the square, yet he knew on the other side of the elegant walls Niall Robertson would be busying about, disturbing the air space like a mini tornado. He stood on the doorstep for just a second then pressed the small shiny intercom button.

'Good morning, Robertson, Bartlett and Hurst,' said the faceless machine.

'Right, er, good morning to you. I'm here to see Niall Robertson.' Joss said nervously.

'Do you have an appointment, sir?' the voice enquired suspiciously.

'No, should I?'

'Most certainly. Mr Robertson is a very busy man.'

'That figures.'

'I'm sorry?'

'No matter, but it's kind of urgent,' he pleaded in his youngest voice.

'Please state the nature of your business.'

'My name is Joss Lane.'

'I'm sorry, sir. Did you say Joss Lane?'

'That's right: Jocelyn Lane. I'm Mr Robertson's nephew, sort of.'

'Just a moment, sir.'

A gentle hiss indicated that the intercom was still open as Joss listened to the receptionist's heels clicking rhythmically into some unknown distance.

The brief silence that followed was punctuated suddenly by the sound of a chair screeching across a wooden floor, and the almost comforting but still barely comprehendable County Donegal rap of the man himself broke the airwaves.

'Joss, is that you? I thought you were dead.'

'Last time I checked everything was functioning, Uncle Niall.' Joss smiled to himself.

'Why didn't you answer my letters?'

'What letters?'

'The ones I sent you, genius.'

Joss suddenly realised this conversation was still being conducted with him talking to a brass box,

'Uncle Niall, it's kind of inconvenient out here,' he hinted.

'What do you mean?'

'I mean, do I get to see you, then, or do I have to make an appointment?'

'Oh for God's sake, of course you don't have to make an appointment.'

'Well.'

'Well what?'

'Are you going to let me in?'

'Oh, sorry, I sort of lost meself there for a moment. Come on up. For sure, there's a lot to do . . .'

'. . . And not a lot of time to do it,' Joss finished for him.

The door buzzed angrily and Joss pushed it open, emerging into a circular hall. Deep plush lilac wall-to-wall Axminster covered with a Chinese rug of striking purple wisteria and yellow roses dominated the floorspace. The plastered panels that swept his eyes up the staircase were painted in deep tones of regal blue against oyster-shade marble walls. The place stank of money.

He walked into the reception area and gingerly dumped his backpack at the foot of a mahogany coat-stand. A grey-haired woman with the thinnest, darkest lips stared vaguely in his direction while still managing to hold an interest with one eye on the latest edition of *Country Life*. Joss smiled self-consciously in her direction as another door behind the empty desk opened and Niall Robertson's jam-jar spectacles loomed into view. He was exactly as Joss recalled and he bounded across the room at a frenetic pace. Joss offered his hand, which was immediately swept aside only to be replaced with a tight hug from the little Irishman.

Joss felt the pressure in the small of his back as Niall led him to a corridor off to the left. Soon they were in an office dressed in traditional Irish tartan wallpaper: green and yellow squares with a black crosshatch. Brass everywhere. Hunting prints adorned the wall and a rather sad-looking stuffed fox stood rigid before an intricate fire-surround.

'Dig the wildlife.'

'What?'

'The fox.'

'Yeah, caught it myself.'

'You're kidding.'

'Would I?'

'Yes.'

'OK, OK. So I bought it in Shepherd's Bush. Impresses the punters.'

Joss smiled and walked over to the perfectly proportioned bay window with fifteen millimetre glazing bars and 200-year-old glass gently curving either side. The square looked magnificent below. Manicured flowerbeds brimmed with golden daffodils and waves of deep purple grape hyacinths. The ancient oak trees, still leafless but bursting with muscle, that peppered the perimeter were magnificent because of their sheer dignity. He turned to Niall who had appeared at his side.

'What's happened to Dad, Niall?'

'Long story.'

'It's never stopped you before, Niall,' Joss quipped while noticing that Niall had shifted away from him and was now gazing into the fireplace with an anxious expression. 'What's the matter?' he asked.

'You'd better sit down, Joss.'

'What is it, Niall?'

'Sit, please,' he implored.

Joss walked the short distance to the two green leather benches perched upon brass rails at either side of the fire and designed for those intimate winter conferences. He sat down, never taking his eyes off Niall Robertson.

'This OK for you or would you prefer the couch?' said Joss, spreading his arms wide.

'I see you have managed to regain your cockiness, Joss,' remarked Niall while seating himself opposite. 'You know, I half-expected never to see you again, young man. You look well.'

'Better than the last time you saw me, that's for sure. How did you do it?'

'It wasn't just down to me, Joss, your father called in a lot of favours to dig you out of that mess.'

'I don't remember much about it.'

'I do, and believe me you weren't a pretty sight.'

'Don't remind me.' Joss looked away briefly; he didn't want to hear, this.

'Guess you're right there.'

'What's going on, Niall, just tell me.'

'Your old man . . .' Niall hesitated, avoiding Joss's eyes.

'Spit it out,' Joss pushed.

'Well . . .' Niall paused again, searching for the words. 'I suppose you could say that he's a changed man.'

'How come?'

'I guess he must have decided shortly after your mother died to sort of pursue a different kind of lifestyle.'

'What do you mean?' Joss uncrossed his legs and moved closer.

'He hung up his calculator and checked out of the mainstream.'

'Niall, look: I know you've seen me grow up and all that, OK? So why is it that you're choking on me now? I've stopped growing: believe me, it's a biological fact, it's called adulthood.' Joss sighed in frustration. 'What has happened to my father?'

'He found God.'

'Rubbish.'

'Not rubbish, Joss: reality.'

'Ridiculous, he's a numbers man, a scientist: he's never had room for anything that couldn't be seen or counted. I mean, one of the only things we ever did together when I was a kid, was watch the moon launches. He said there were so many planets to explore that one God couldn't be responsible for them all. I remember him telling me he was an atheist, for God's sake.' Joss rose to his feet.

'Unintentional, I hope,' Niall remarked.

'What?'

'You just said "an atheist, for God's sake",' Niall snorted sardonically while measuring the new Joss Lane before him. 'I suppose you were bound to turn up sometime; you always do.' He shook his head slowly, a lingering frown etched across his forehead.

'Why hasn't he contacted me while I've been at the clinic?'

'I guess he must have thought you'd just blow away again if you ever came out of your hidey hole, and the odds weren't looking promising, I can tell you.'

'So I got better. Will you get off my back with that guilt thing?' Joss snapped. 'You don't have to remind me that I let people down. I know that, I want to make amends. I've had a long time to think about things.'

'That's an understatement, Joss. Just when are you going to learn?' Niall reacted sharply. 'You know, he gave up on you before the débâcle in Amsterdam: he wouldn't listen to anyone. But I knew you'd be back after the inquest. And back you came all right, Joss, almost in a body bag with handcuffs on. What's he supposed to think, Joss? Have you ever considered that you might have lost a mother but he lost a wife and then, just when he didn't need it, his son turns his back on him before becoming a freaking junkie. I can tell you, by that time he seemed to have lost all sense of purpose, and energy, and who could blame him?'

'So that's when he found God, was it?' Joss bit back. 'What's the deal then? Don't tell me, he goes to mass on Sunday and calls himself a Christian now, does he? I expect he will be banking on receiving eternal salvation in return. Don't make me laugh, Niall, he probably sees it like a contract.'

'Afraid not, Joss: he joined a group of people who call themselves the Millennium Church.'

'That figures,' said Joss quietly, remembering the papers in the filing cabinet back at the clinic and Greta's letter, but decided to keep the information to himself for the moment. Niall seemed too keyed up. The welcome had been shortlived; there had to be a reason for his agitation.

'What did you say?' Niall asked sharply.

'No matter, go on.'

'They hold some very strong beliefs, these people, and your father thought it important that he should commit himself to them.'

'What do you mean, "commit himself to them", exactly?' Joss asked cautiously.

'He diverted all his assets to them including the family home and his business interests: liquidated everything and joined their community.'

'Jesus Christ.'

'There's worse.'

'Go on.'

'There were heavy, heavy losses to his clients.'

'They weren't clients, they were charities,' Joss snapped. 'You worked together.'

'I only advised him, son, I didn't press the buttons. Money has disappeared; a lot of it, but his limited liability status saw them off.'

'What about the Fraud Squad?' Joss asked.

Niall shrugged. 'Mis-management, neglect, bad investments; he was negligent not criminal.'

'My father would never have acted like that.'

'Joss, son, he isn't the same man as he was.'

'Where can I contact him?'

'I don't know exactly where he is at present; I haven't spoken to him in a long time.'

'You must have some idea, Niall.'

'It's very sensitive at the moment.' Niall shifted his gaze momentarily.

'Come again?'

Niall moved over to the desk and picked up a copy of the newspaper lying on the top of some hefty-looking case files and threw it to Joss.

'I guess you'll find out soon enough.'

The bold headline read, 'Rivers Private Prosecution Opens'. Joss quickly read through the article, which recounted the opening speech by the prosecuting barrister, Mark Mason QC. Niall watched him in silence as he reached the end, closing the paper carefully and handing it back; this had to be the case which Greta mentioned in her letter.

'I want to see my father, Niall, as soon as possible,' Joss said flatly, his expressionless face disguising his confusion.

'I can't guarantee that I'll be able to locate him.'

'And I can't believe you have allowed him to get mixed up with this bunch of whackos, Niall, he must have been out of his mind.'

'Not according to his sworn affidavit at the time.'

'They made him sign something?'

'Yes, I saw it myself.'

'I have to speak to him.'

'Just leave it, Joss; he must be happy where he is. His commitment to the Church is unequivocal.'

'I just want to see him for myself. I mean, for crying out loud,
he is my father. Besides, if the end of the world is coming and he
knows something about it, don't you think he might want to pass on
that sort of information to his son and heir?' Joss said, flippantly.

'Glad you reminded me.'

'More good news? What? Have you become a Moonie?'

The businesslike lawyer ignored the comment. 'Your dear mother
died Intestate.'

This was news to Joss, it was his mother's joke that he would
be dis-inherited from her own independent wealth if he didn't stop
playing such dangerous games with his life.

'Of course there was a will, I've seen it.'

'Well, it couldn't be found, son. I'm sorry. Your father acted as
Administrator and beneficiary; the lot's gone.'

'I couldn't give a shit about the cash; I need to see Callum.'

'You have no idea what you're dealing with, Joss. This is no
Mickey Mouse cult thing, you do realise that? This organisation
has three million devotees across the globe all preparing for
Armageddon. You're talking about some very serious people:
Adventists with a passion.'

'You don't believe in all that crap, do you?'

'Who knows what to believe in these days, Joss.'

'I know enough to tell you that Callum Lane could never in a
million years join an outfit like that.'

'Wake up, Joss. Look, I've got a contact number in one of the
old files. Let me make the call and chase him down. Where are you
staying, by the way?'

'I'm not yet.'

'OK, the least I can do is put you up for a few days. Come
down to the farm; Jennifer will be delighted to see you,' insisted
Niall.

'No thanks. No offence, Niall, but I want to crash in town
somewhere; get my head round this thing. Besides, I need to
check out a few people.'

'Greta, I suppose?'

'Maybe.' Joss looked away. 'I don't even know if she's still around,' he lied, but had no idea why he should be so anxious to keep his cards close to his chest

'Come off it, Joss.'

'OK, so she's on my atonement list.'

'Pretty near the top, I'd say.'

'When I was in the clinic I imagined it would be so easy just to walk right up to her, but now I don't know any more.'

'I'm not going to disagree with you, Joss: you've got to expect she will be more than a touch mad at you.'

'Do you know what happened to her?'

'A little.' Niall looked shifty for a second

'Married?' Joss asked cautiously.

'I don't think so: more of a career girl type, I hear.'

'She always was,' said Joss with a smile, forced through by relief. 'What did she do after the inquest?'

'Last I heard of her was when I got a request for a character reference from a set of Chambers in the Temple at the end of last year. She was up for a pupillage.'

That fitted with Greta's message.

'That's the sort of irony I can do without, Niall: I hope I won't need a brief.'

'Greta is working on the Millennium Church case. She's junior for the Prosecution.'

Joss glanced down at the newspaper article.

'She'll be at court today then,' he said, suddenly feeling cold at the prospect of maybe seeing her again, but at the same time driven by a compulsion to be next to her, to touch her, hold her, just to *be* with her.

'My advice would be to keep away. The girl will have enough on her plate.'

'I have to see her,' Joss exclaimed. 'I'm going down there now, maybe I can find out something about my father if I do. Meanwhile, will you try to locate him and tell him I'm back?'

'I'll try my best, Joss. Look here, take this with you.' Niall reached into the inside pocket of his jacket and retrieved his wallet. He took out a platinum cash card and handed it to Joss. 'The number is treble two six. You can draw what you need until we get this thing sorted out.'

'I don't know what to say.'

'Don't say anything.' Niall retreated behind the desk and began scribbling on a sheet of letter-headed notepaper. 'OK, seeing as we don't have any client visiting at the moment why don't you use the firm's hospitality suite at the Ritz. I'll get my secretary to arrange it. That do for you?'

'Niall, I can't thank you enough.'

'No you can't, now get moving. I'll be in touch later.'

Joss left, still not knowing why he hadn't shared what he knew with his father's best friend, still wondering why Niall had seemed so nervous; no it wasn't that, he wasn't nervous, he was scared. It would have to be something serious to frighten the little legal street fighter; Joss needed to know what that something was and how this fitted together; that was, if it fitted together at all. He fingered the three tiles in his pocket and wondered if the one marked 'future' was beginning to show its secrets.

CHAPTER SEVEN

Mark and Greta sat in the lawyers' canteen sharing her home-made Caesar salad amid the smell of over-boiled vegetables. He nudged his food around the plate distractedly and Greta knew not to lead; only to listen if he needed it. He was secretly preparing himself for the first real test that would begin when the jury could start putting faces to the names he had told them about. He looked around the familiar room: it was just like his old school in Derbyshire with its dark oak panelling giving the entire space a gloomy air. Large stained-glass windows at the far end let in coloured sparks of fractured daylight, but the skies beyond were blackening. He flicked his fork disconsolately on to the tabletop and stretched his neck skywards, grinding away the pressure. He knew it had been a good opening speech. The jury was with him already and he couldn't help reflecting upon how much an advantage it was, being allowed to draw an image that they could relate to. The difficulty was: now that he had given them the silhouette it was up to his witnesses to fill in the detail, but with fifteen minutes to go before the court reassembled they still hadn't shown.

'Where the hell are they?' he whispered to Greta.

'They'll be here, don't worry,' she answered, trying desperately to keep a lid on Mark's temper.

'They'd better be: the last thing I want is a wasted costs order against me personally. It was my decision to go ahead this morning. I should have asked for more time.'

'You did the right thing, Mark. If you have to ask for more time, then so what? Withnail won't do anything now that Callow has got up his nose. I think he's on our side.'

'Don't bet on it for one moment, Greta.'

Just then Charmers loomed into view at the door with a flustered look about him. He rushed over to Mark and Greta.

'You're not going to believe this, but they had an accident in the taxi on the way to court,' he said breathlessly.

'What! Are they all right?' exclaimed Mason.

'A bit shaken up. Rose is worse than her father, but he's due to testify first and we won't get through his evidence by close of play, will we, so at least she can recover overnight. I've sent her away again with Susan Morris.'

'This is all I need. What happened?'

'A guy ran into them at some traffic lights, hit the taxi pretty hard, according to Geoff, and they both got a bit of a shock. The cabby reckoned it was his right of way but the bloke was having none of it, the police were called and the cabby wouldn't let Rose and Geoff go until they had given a statement. The other guy made off before the police arrived. It was a stolen vehicle.'

'Did they catch him?'

'No way.'

'Sounds a bit suspect to me.'

'Exactly what Geoff thinks. But surely you don't really believe the Church would pull a stunt like that?'

'Anything is possible, but there's nothing that we can do about it now. We've got five minutes. OK, is he ready?'

'What do you think? Just light the touchpaper.'

'That's what I'm afraid of.'

Withnail was renowned as a stickler for punctuality and, sure enough, five minutes later Geoff Moody was standing to attention in the witness box. A film of sweat was forming on his brow as he sought to suppress the needling pain developing in his shoulders as a result of the car crash. Mason wasted no time and opened up by alerting the judge and, more importantly, the jury to the incident. Withnail started to look suspicious, but under pressure from the jury's sympathetic faces asked politely whether Moody wished to delay giving evidence until the following morning. Mason hoped that Moody would play it up some more, but true to type he said that he wanted to get on with things.

'Mr Moody, you are the natural father of Rose, the complainant in this case, is that correct?'

'Yes, sir,' Moody replied, eyes straight ahead in the direction of the jury just as Mark had taught him. 'She is the single most important thing in my life.'

Mark began by taking Moody steadily through his evidence about Rose's background. He spoke of an unremarkable but happy childhood in the North Riding and painted a picture of family stability. Although her real mother had died of cancer when she was only seven it hadn't affected her for long, as Rose had grown used to the fact after the prolonged illness, which her mother had insisted was spent at home rather than burden a hospital. Geoff it seemed had always been the one who had cared for Rose as well as his wife, although he had later remarried with Rose's blessing.

Mason was slow and methodical in his examination. The Church's legal team watched stony eyed and unsympathetic as the jury were drawn further in to the intimate lives of this unfortunate family. Withnail's eyes bored into Moody as he spoke and only occasionally did he jot down notes. They moved on through the years when Geoff had begun to build up his hardware business. He told them all of the happiest years when, side by side, he and twelve-year-old Rose ran the shop together – when she wasn't doing her schoolwork, he added for good measure.

'I would like you to tell the ladies and gentlemen of the jury a little about Rose the teenager, if you will.' Mason was moving on to the difficult times and hoped that Moody would keep to his proof.

'She was just like any other young kid, really. We had our ups and downs: anyone who's been a parent will know what I mean.'

'Well, for those of us who haven't had that experience, what do you mean, exactly?' said Mason, not wanting to alienate any of the younger jury members.

'I mean when she got to thirteen and fourteen she was wanting to be out all hours with her friends and that.'

'And you disapproved?'

'Of course I did: her step-mum did too, her place was at home with me, she had responsibilities. We had a home and a business to run,' said Moody sharply and Mason knew that the remark hadn't gone down well with the youngsters. Overbearing parent syndrome crossed his mind. He pressed on quickly hoping to repair the damage.

'Is it true to say that the business was in difficulties at the time?'

'Bank was putting us under a lot of pressure, I was working long hours, and I admit a lot of the time I just couldn't cope with her so she was pretty much left to her own devices for a short while.'

'What do you mean by that?'

'I wasn't getting in from work until late almost every evening and when I did she would have that boyfriend of hers around: right bloody clip he was, as well. Bad influence on her, I said.'

'Is that what led to arguments between you?'

'I suppose so, but we always got through. Thing is, I always told her, the only thing you really have is family. Although my second wife was rarely at home at the time.'

'It is not in dispute that around this time Rose became involved with a group of people who belonged to the congregation of the Millennium Church, but can you remember precisely when it was that you became aware of that fact?'

'She didn't become involved, sir, she was snatched.'

'Objection, my Lord,' Callow interjected. 'This witness can give no direct evidence of any alleged abduction.'

'Yes I agree, Mr Callow,' said Withnail, turning to Moody. 'Do you see the point, Mr Moody? I acknowledge that you have strong views about these matters, but please try to remember that this is a court of law and we are trying to determine the facts of these allegations. It would be far easier if you bore in mind that you are here to assist in that process. Listen carefully to the questions that your learned counsel puts to you and try to avoid, if you will, impressing your own choice language on to the jury. Do you understand?'

'Yes, my Lord,' replied Moody sullenly.

'Good. Now, you were being asked if you could recall the date that Rose became involved with the Church?'

'The first I heard of it was the 15th of May 1998, three days after she disappeared from home.'

'And how did that come about?'

'We argued again about Greg, her boyfriend: she stormed out of the house and didn't come home that night. By two in the morning I was out of my mind with worry so I drove around the seafront and contacted all her friends' parents, but she was nowhere to be seen. The police started a search, there were appeals on the local TV and radio but still nothing. I couldn't eat or sleep: it was just terrible. I wouldn't wish it on my worst enemy, that feeling of hopelessness.'

'How did she eventually contact you?'

'I received a telephone call from her saying that she was staying with friends in the London area. She cried and said she was sorry and that she didn't want to be with these people but no one would take her back home and she didn't have any money.'

'What did you do?'

'I begged her to meet me, but she didn't seem all there; kept saying I wasn't to make a fuss. I could tell those freaks had given her some drugs or something.'

'My Lord,' pleaded Callow. 'This witness has already been warned about innuendo and opinion.'

'Yes, I agree. I won't warn you again, Mr Moody,' Withnail said solemnly.

'All right, but she didn't sound herself, that's all I can say,' Moody replied.

'When did you hear from her again?'

'She contacted me the next day and I told her the police were looking for her and it was only a matter of time.'

'The police, of course, didn't find her.'

'No: they couldn't do anything about it as she was declassified on their priority list. Declassified: I ask you, a fifteen-year-old girl,' Moody said, exasperated.

'What did you do next?'

'I began to find out more about the group she was with and met some other people who had similar problems. I started to track her down.'

'My Lord,' interrupted Callow, 'this witness is now talking about a group of people known as Cult Awareness, the very title being prejudicial to our client. Notwithstanding that, the jury ought to be made firmly aware that not one valid legal claim has been made against our client or his organisation at the inception of this group of hysterical scaremongers.'

'Have you quite finished, Mr Callow?' said Withnail sharply.

'Speeches generally come at the end of the trial. Carry on, Mr Mason.'

Mason continued.

'But track her down you did, to the Isle of Skye: to a retreat known as the Haven.'

'That's right, sir. The Cult Awareness group had evidence she was there; they were right.'

'Did the Church admit that fact?' Mason prodded.

'Not at first, no: they lied about it until they realised that I wasn't going away. I threatened them with the police, lawyers, all kinds of things, until they eventually admitted that Rose was staying there.'

'Were you allowed inside?' Mason asked.

'Never. They had things to hide.'

'Objection, my Lord,' Thynne QC bellowed, without bothering to rise to his feet. 'Moody was never allowed inside, therefore his evidence is prejudicial conjecture.'

'I agree,' Withnail murmured. 'Ignore that comment, members of the jury. The witness may only tell you that which he has seen or heard, not what he suspected. Control your witness, Mr Mason.'

Geoff Moody felt his face flush. He knew the bastards had all kinds of stuff to hide: why else would they keep the world out?

'But did you meet with your daughter?' Mason continued, hands flat against the bench in front of him.

'Outside the perimeter fence, but it wasn't her, wasn't my Rose.'

'Please explain, Mr Moody.'

'Well, it was like they'd taken something away, sucked the life out of her: she was a husk of herself.' Moody seemed to attempt to shake away the memory.

'Were you left alone at any time with Rose?'

'Never. They insisted, or the meeting would never take place. There was a small guard's hut beside the fence; we went in there with the others. She had a prepared speech already made, about how she was happy there, happier than she'd ever been. Told me not to worry, that she was with God, and he was all loving, that Rivers was her saviour: rubbish,' Moody spat.

'Like a robot in a film, she was: all flat-voiced. Never once looked at me. Not my Rose at all. It was over in about three minutes. I tried to reason with her, even took her by the arms and begged her to come home, but they just rushed her away.'

Mason risked a glance towards the jury. Their faces were masked in sadness for this decent man and his turmoil.

'What, if anything, did you decide to do?'

Moody stuck out his chin.

'I had to rescue her, Mr Mason. What father wouldn't?'

The jury seemed to be in agreement, but Mark Mason knew that when Thynne rose to cross-examine, the picture that would emerge would be very different.

Geoff Moody glanced around the court. He had just outlined how, with the aid of three paid helpers, he had rescued Rose from the Haven and escaped on a boat to the mainland. Mason deftly wound up Moody's testimony, dealing with his lodging a complaint in Scotland and Rose's return home.

Mark Mason had laid the groundwork for Rose's eventual testimony by allowing her father to tell his side of the story in his own words. Now, Moody nervously toyed with a pen as Thynne climbed wearily to his feet. The QC adjusted his half-glasses on his nose and nodded to the jury before beginning.

'There was violence when you kidnapped your own daughter from her chosen life, was there not?'

Mark Mason rushed to his feet.

'It was a rescue, not a kidnapping, my Lord. I object to the use of inflammatory language.'

Withnail clasped his ermine-cuffed hands together.

'Whether it was one thing or the other is surely what the jury are here to decide; the rest is semantics. Carry on, answer the question, Mr Moody.'

Moody swallowed hard; what he had done was only the necessary.

'It had to be done: they wouldn't let her go voluntarily.'

'Yes, of course,' Thynne commented dryly. 'Three men beaten unconscious and Rose screaming for you to leave her alone – that *was* what she shouted?'

'They had her brainwashed. I was told how it would be.'

'You carried baseball bats and knives, correct?'

Moody nodded.

'You must answer,' Withnail drawled.

'Yes, for self-protection,' Moody accepted.

'Taken into a retreat of God?'

'Into the pit of hell,' Moody snapped.

'I have warned you before about your temper, Mr Moody,' Withnail frowned. The jury appeared puzzled by the remark: when? their faces asked. But Thynne just smiled. Mason tapped his fingers; this was textbook stuff.

'But you did not hesitate to use the weapons?'

'Not to save Rose, no.'

'You wanted her back? Needed her back? Desired her?' Thynne's voice was oily and insinuating.

'I wanted her home.'

'We all know what for, don't we, Mr Moody?'

The witness seemed perplexed, but Mark Mason knew exactly where this was going and he was powerless to stop it. Thynne produced a document with a flourish and handed it to the robed usher.

'Take a moment to read this sworn statement,' he whispered. Moody did so, his face falling from pink, to grey to white as his trembling finger followed the document's content.

'I . . . it's all lies, it's false, I never . . .'

'Now,' Thynne said, his face grave, 'you can attest that the document is signed by your daughter and dated three weeks before her kidnapping at your hands?'

'Yes, but . . .'

'You have been sexually abusing your own daughter since she was thirteen, haven't you, Mr Moody, and that is why she ran away and didn't want to return?'

Moody's mouth opened at first. He had no words. Then he shouted.

'That evil bastard must have made her sign this.' He began to move towards Rivers, who sat gravely in the dock. An usher barred his way. Moody was about to push him away, then he thought better of it.

'Clear the court,' Withnail snarled. 'This case is adjourned until sanity has been restored.'

Mark Mason slammed his hand down hard on the bench. He had chosen and chosen badly. He had known of the statement's existence and its content, but had relied on Moody's stunned innocence to show up the inaccuracy of the sordid, incestuous allegations. Instead, Moody's failure to comment had made him look guilty as charged. The jury's own hardened faces confirmed this assumption. The prosecution had suffered a body blow. Mason prayed it would not be fatal.

CHAPTER EIGHT

The walk from Niall Robertson's offices in Lincoln's Inn Fields to the Royal Courts of Justice, on the Strand, took no more than ten minutes and during it Joss was thoughtful. Callum Lane must have experienced some kind of breakdown. It was the only rational explanation. He smiled to himself grimly. Callum. His Dad. But the distance between them was the result of a lifelong embargo on affection, and that was probably why he referred to him by his Christian name. There had been no backslapping drinking sessions down the pub when he was too young to drink legally. No trips to see the struggling local football team with a thermos of weak Oxo and stale pork pies; just a frosty greeting and yet more work to be done, Callum's work, financial work, now shattered into a million monetary shards. He was all Joss had left and as yet he could not be sure whether even that small link with the past was retrievable. Joss found it impossible to believe that Callum – pragmatic, God-denying Callum – could have fallen for the empty promises of a phony religious organisation like the Millennium Church. It was like being told that Madonna was a man, or that Keanu Reeves could act; beyond belief. He had to see it for himself.

Joss approached the stern black railings that formed the perimeter around the Gothic Royal Courts of Justice. Just outside the vast, cast-iron doors of the courts, where successful litigants normally preened before the waiting press, a large crowd was gathered. They held sad, badly-crafted, home-made banners aloft and chanted, 'Where are our children? Where are our children?' in a weary monotone. Some banners repeated the question, red on white, while others obliquely mentioned the 'Missing 32'. They linked arms and swayed to the hypnotic chant. It was a strange mixture of people, as if the contents of any early morning tube had been decanted onto the court steps. Young and old, some well dressed, some in shabby hand-me-downs, Asian, black and white, they were united in their cause. They were in the process of being filmed, photographed and interviewed by a legion of media representatives, but their main focus was on the grand entrance to the Courts of Justice. They clearly believed that justice would be the one thing denied them.

Joss shook his head. They were ordinary people, not the politicised fanatics who sometimes gathered for publicity purposes. They seemed to emanate sadness; the air lingered with loss.

He approached a photographer in a leather jacket, in the process of speed-loading more film, and asked what it was all about. The snapper looked at him quizzically. His stare seemed to say, 'Where have you been?' Joss waited patiently. The photographer shrugged before replying.

'They've all got kids or relatives who they say disappeared into the Millennium Church: say they haven't seen them again. Load of runaways; on the game, if you ask me.'

Joss nodded, then spoke: 'Don't look like a pack of nutters though, do they?' The photographer for once viewed the crowd with his own eyes rather than through the profit-making lens.

'Suppose not,' he admitted, then unashamedly raised his camera once more.

'Not my problem,' he muttered, moving down on to one knee, to snap a picture of a young boy, bent into his mother's waist, barely holding back the tears. Joss wondered if it would become his own problem.

He checked his watch: 4.30 p.m. The court would be rising soon. He waited nervously. The last time he had seen Greta – Joss bit his lip, it was so painful to remember. Had that really been him? Standing there in the witness box at the inquest with a one-way ticket in his pocket and his mother in a grave. He hadn't spoken to anyone after he'd given his evidence; he'd just picked up his backpack and walked. He didn't look back because he knew he had to go. Not one single glance at Ben, Tom or Barney sitting in the front row of the gallery; even Greta and his own father had had no idea that he wasn't coming back. It was the only way he could deal with things back then. The question was: what would he do now that he *was* back? What would *she* do, despite her invitation back into part of her life?

Can you just walk back into people's lives?

Can you, Joss?

After all that's happened.

Really?

Within minutes, lawyers with thick briefcases began to emerge, followed by a phalanx of bulky, black-suited minders hiding a figure within their muscular midst.

The chanting grew to a new volume, the bleak repetitive question filling the air. '*Where are our children? Where are our children?*'

The press surged forward, but the protest group held its polite line. They were not anarchists, just concerned parents and families desperately needing the answer to a simple question. Joss was moved at the sight of their innocent, stoic passion and knew that if his mother had been alive she, too, would have applauded their peaceful, heartfelt protest. Joss moved with the press stampede, sliding between cameras and microphones, trying to get closer, to see the focus of their controlled anger, but within seconds an escape trail had been forged and the unseen figure had been smuggled into a waiting car and whisked away.

Joss looked around for inspiration whilst the media addressed their film crews, or hastily phoned in copy to hungry editors. Then, suddenly, he saw her: Greta. He stopped, frozen by the moment. Greta. The last time he had seen her she had glared at him across a crowded courtroom, whilst the coroner reluctantly returned a verdict of accidental death on his mother.

The two years that had passed had hardened her features slightly around the eyes, as if trust had been replaced with the need for proof. He was used to her striding into athletic danger wearing jeans and fleeced jackets; now she strode away from the scene in high heels and a well-cut, sombre suit.

Was he hallucinating? Joss savagely pinched his own flesh, but the tingle he felt was real enough.

He knew that toss of her head too well to be mistaken. She had been his living goal during his prolonged stay in the rehabilitation clinic and now she was here, only twenty yards away.

Breathing rapidly he walked quickly towards her as she stood by the roadside in the Strand, one arm raised to halt a black cab, her fine profile fixed on her task. She glanced sideways at him, then away, then slowly turned back, blinking, as if warding off her own fear that he was a phantom. She began to smile, but it perished quickly. She dropped her arm. He whispered, 'Greta', and her arm whistled through the air and stopped a centimetre from his cheek.

'I swore to myself I wouldn't do that,' she sighed miserably.

Joss shuffled.

'You didn't; great control. Anyway I deserve it.'

Her eyes lanced through him. 'No, you deserve much worse, but now isn't the time for any of this.'

Joss smiled inwardly, what she had just said might mean there would be a later for them.

'You got my letter?'

Joss nodded and tapped his breast pocket; Greta shook her head dismayed.

'You still have no idea just how fucking serious this is, Lane. For once let's play grown ups.'

Joss felt his cheeks glow hot, like a boy asking a woman for a date and being shamed by her indifference and ridicule.

'Can we go somewhere to talk? I left various messages,' he whispered, glancing away.

'Not now. There's too much work to be done with the trial. I have to meet Mark for a working dinner.'

'Mark?' Joss whispered, feeling a burning lance of hopelessness slice through his empty stomach.

Greta tutted, then softened. 'Look, he's the QC who's leading me in the trial. I wrote to you because I thought you should know that your father is involved with the church. They are bile, Joss, pure smiling bile; I felt I owed it to you.' She began looking for another cab.

'You don't owe me anything', he muttered miserably. This wasn't how it was meant to be. She was supposed to scream a little, maybe give him a couple of slaps, give vent to a pile of accurate expletives then some tears; instead she was business-like and almost indifferent. Joss reined in his childish self-pity.

'I need to find my father, Greta. Can you help me?'

'I'll do what I can'. Her voice sounded strangely harsh.

A cab stopped and sounded its horn. Greta waved it away.

'I came here to ask Rivers about my dad.'

Greta smiled bleakly. 'Same old Joss; brave as a commando, naïve as a child. Look, I shouldn't talk about the case with you but these people are bad news, Joss. Callum is with them, his name keeps cropping up in connection with this trial; he could be in more serious trouble than the business collapse. I can't talk now, there are other things I have to do. Besides I'm just not ready to see you: I don't know if I ever will be.' She shook her head, fighting to remain in control. 'Where are you staying?'

'Niall's putting me up at the firm's place in the Ritz.'

Greta raised her arm once more.

'Hit me, will you?' he asked, a playful smile on his face.

'That would only make you feel better,' she replied, reaching forward and gently stroking his cheek. 'You look thin, Joss.'

He reached out his hand to cover hers, but it was slapped away.

'You need to know what you are dealing with. I've gathered together a mountain of clippings and articles on the Church. I'll send them round to you later at the hotel.'

'Thanks, Greta.' He was about to place his hand on her arm, but she flinched instinctively.

'Don't thank me till you know more about Rivers and the Church.' She nodded towards the banner-waving vigilantes. 'Ask them, poor bastards: they know the truth.'

This time, when a cab stopped she swooped inside and slammed the door. He bent down to wave a farewell, but Greta stared fixedly ahead. Joss nodded. There were a lot of apologies he still had to make; perhaps too many for one lifetime, but that didn't mean he shouldn't try.

CHAPTER NINE

J oss headed along the Strand. The pavement was jammed with the same noisy protestors shouting angrily across the enforced divide at the object of their hatred. He glanced beyond the line of police officers and looked over the Church supporters whose orderly presence offered an almost benign contrast. The sheer normality and composure of the faces which stared back at him was strangely disquieting as he struggled to hear himself think against the abuse being thrown in their direction.

Aren't these people meant to be freaks, Joss?

Isn't your father one of these people?

He shook the thoughts away and made for the bus stands outside Charing Cross station. The streets were packed solid with theatre crowds teeming out of the matinee performances of the West End musicals. The soft drizzle floated incessantly out of the darkening sky, clouding his vision as he padded disconsolately along the Strand. He reached a pedestrian crossing and paused for a moment trying to get an angle. He adjusted the hood on his puffer jacket, pulling it tight around his face, as the rain became heavier. The euphoria of his return to the real world had been short lived.

What if he really does believe in all this Millennium stuff?

What are you going to do then, Joss?

No plan. No parents. No home.

No Greta?

He tried to snap his mind into gear as he walked along, dodging the pedestrian traffic by skipping into the kerb while keeping one eye on the countless courier bikes speeding dangerously close to the pavement. He conjured Greta in his mind and could see each line and contour of her face, as if it had never been away. Notwithstanding the shock, her eyes had been less forgiving than

79

he could ever remember; but then again what exactly could he have expected after his walkout two years ago?

She wasn't going to understand, that much was clear; but worse, it felt as if she wasn't even going to try. He kicked himself once more and was now beginning to appreciate where Niall was coming from with this guilt thing. He'd hurt a lot of people, he knew that, but all he wanted was the chance to explain, let them know what it was like for him; then they'd realise.

His self-pity didn't last, however, and before long he'd rationalised the situation; in fact, by the time he'd reached the bus stand he had stupidly convinced himself that he didn't care any more. He never gave a second thought to the maroon people-carrier that crept along the road and stopped twenty yards behind him.

The number 43 bus to Piccadilly and St James Park was already packed solid with students and tourists, loudly and excitedly competing for airtime. Suddenly Joss longed for the simple cocoon he had left behind in Austria.

As he was beginning to doubt the quality of Kristina Klammer's signature on his clean bill of health, his hand made for the St Christopher medal around his neck. Elsa, his nurse, all bosom and rude cheer, had given it to him when he left the clinic.

The conversations around him were being conducted in a polyglot of French and German melting together in a cacophony of incomprehension.

'Talking Italian,' muttered the old man sitting across the aisle from Joss.

'Yeah, right,' replied Joss, not wishing to be pedantic. Not wishing to talk at all. He sat quietly looking out of the window, taking in the damp, grey London pavements. The woman sitting next to him was absorbed in the limp pages of the latest *Big Issue*, hungrily circling potential bedsits with a thick marker pen. Joss focused on the raindrops biting at the black umbrellas outside for what seemed like an eternity.

Then another group, Japanese this time, excitedly squeezed its way along the aisle, water dripping from the profusion of colourful Gore-Tex rainwear. A large haversack balanced precariously on one young back brushed against Joss's face, depositing a fresh layer of rain on his skin. The carrier was clearly unaware of the problem as he trudged along the bus leaving several passengers to dodge the trailing straps and flaps of the wayward bag.

As Joss was wiping his face with a scrap of tissue retrieved from his pocket, he saw her watching him. This was the second time their eyes had clashed. While standing at the bus stop he'd noticed her stately walk and fluid movements despite the long brown wax coat she wore buttoned tightly against the weather.

She was at least six feet tall with wisps of impossibly blonde but clearly natural hair peeking out from underneath a curiously incongruous green denim hat with a stylised yellow daisy in the centre. Joss checked again from behind the and ragged tissue. He was right, she couldn't take her regal blue eyes off him. He shifted his position slightly and pretended to be distracted momentarily by fishing for something in his pocket. Still, like the Mona Lisa, her eyes followed his every move.

Joss felt tightness slowly developing in the pit of his stomach. It was like the dull queasy anticipation before the first drop on a roller coaster. He couldn't quite get a handle on it but when he suddenly looked up at her, meeting her eyes once more, it was almost as if there was a re-awakening somewhere inside him. All traces of his long-awaited reunion with Greta had momentarily deserted him. Things were stirring within him that hadn't moved for so long he'd forgotten the natural high they brought.

The bus was just approaching Dover Street opposite the entrance to the Ritz, and Joss was beginning to panic. Should he stay on the bus unnecessarily in an attempt to further this embryonic romance or should he just forget it? He was more used to taking the latter course. In a swift movement he propelled himself up out of the seat, slinging his bag over his left shoulder, made for the doors and the rain.

Should you stay, Joss?

Or should you go?

He was just about to disembark when one final impulse drove him to check over his shoulder. He turned too quickly, momentarily forgetting about his own rucksack, and immediately bumped into something. He heard a little gasp and saw a flash of green falling to the floor. He bent down to retrieve the hat and quickly stood up. He opened his mouth to speak but, two inches away from his face, there she stood, with a challenging but rather shy little grin pulling at the sides of her full lips. All it did was to make her look even more beautiful.

'I'm so sorry,' Joss blurted as he handed back the daisy cap.

'It doesn't matter.' She had a Scandinavian lilt in a voice that was nearly as deep as his own. In the brief silence that followed the grin became a smile revealing perfectly matched teeth shining white against the ever so slightly tanned skin. She eventually nodded over his shoulder but he just stood there still vacantly lost in her smile.

'Excuse me, I think the bus is waiting,' she prompted, nodding again.

'Shi . . . er, yes . . . I mean . . . sorry . . . of course, the bus . . . yes.' He bundled along the aisle, apologising to all and sundry as she followed. The students collected on the running board giggled as he eventually managed to get off, not before becoming entangled with a coat hanger carelessly protruding from the wastepaper ducket. The top pocket on his sack ripped open causing a cascade of socks and shredders to fall on to the wet pavement below.

The rain was beating even harder as he frantically tried to restore his dignity, wondering what on earth to say next as she handed him his favourite Bart Simpson boxers.

'At least they're clean,' he offered.

'I'm delighted to hear it,' she replied, reaching for a stray cotton handkerchief. 'Do you often lose control on public transport?'

'Now that's unfair.'

'You think so?'

'Why yes, it's not every day I bump into beautiful sirens on the number 44,' he said, in the full knowledge that it sounded cheesy but banking on her European naivety to be flattered.

'43,' she said simply, without altering her expression.

'What?'

'The bus: it's a number 43.'

'Oh, right.'

'But thank you for the compliment anyway. I'm sorry to have placed you in any embarrassment.'

'Not at all. Now it would be embarrassing if I asked you to have a drink with me and you said no.' Joss pushed on now, not caring. Greta had her Mark and her career. Her Miss Jean Brodie act almost ruled out any future; or was he just rationalising in order to justify his desire for the stranger?

'Of course I shall,' she said.

'I didn't think so.'

'Excuse me?'

'I'm sorry, but did you just say yes?'

'That's right.'

'What! I don't believe it. You said yes to having a drink with a strange man you meet on a bus. My grandmother warned me about women like you.'

'And my grandfather warned me about men like you.'

'What did he say?' Joss smiled as he thrust the backpack over his shoulder.

'He said always make sure you choose a man with clean under-wear.'

'Touché,' Joss laughed. 'He sounds like a good bloke.'

'He was. He died of dysentery in a Filipino brothel.'

Joss broke into freefall laughter. 'I'm Joss,' he said, offering his hand. 'It's always a pleasure to meet a fellow cookie. I could do with cheering up: you don't know what sort of day I've had.'

'I think I can guess,' she replied, taking his hand and holding it gently. Joss could feel the stirrings again as she smiled at him from under the rim of her soaking hat. 'Monica,' she said soothingly.

'Honestly, Monica, don't try: it will freak you.'

'OK. Where are we going?'

'How long have you got?'

'All the time in the world. I'm travelling but staying with friends in Earl's Court at the minute.'

Joss jerked her hand, signalling them to cross to the other side via a gap in the traffic.

'OK, that's great, let's go to my hotel.'

'You move quickly, Joss.'

'I didn't mean it like that,' his face reddened.

'Nor did I,' she replied coyly, 'I meant across the road.'

'Oh sorry,' he said, blushing even further. They moved under the green canopied frontage of the Ritz mall, passing the front entrance to the casino.

'You apologise too much. I'm only teasing you. Where is your hotel anyway?'

'Right here.'

'Where?'

'Here,' he replied with a theatrical sweep of his hand gesturing toward the opulent archway leading into the elegant foyer of the Ritz.

'I don't think so,' she said flatly.

'Honest injun,' he said with his hand on his heart.

She looked at him dubiously then shrugged her shoulders in resignation. 'In for a pfennig in for a pound.'

The green-liveried concierge dutifully held the door open with that look of disdain reserved only for those whom he considered didn't deserve the privileges to which they were born. Joss gave him a bare-faced wink as they walked through to the reception desk. True to his word, Uncle Niall had sorted the room for him and, after registering, they made their way to the bar.

The Kir Royales tasted wonderful and Monica was even more attractive than he had first thought. They sat in the window seat overlooking the crowds below, talking travel and swapping stories.

Like all Scandinavians, she was tactile and it was only after the first hour or so that Joss began to relax at the constant fondling of his knees and thighs when she went to emphasise a point. He also realised that each contact was longer and more searching than the last. Her nails nipped at the hard muscle on his arms and lingered over his forearms and hands.

After a couple of hours, a perfectly manicured bellboy with a plastic expression disturbed them when he informed Joss that there was a telephone call for him at reception. Joss excused himself and followed the boy through to the marbled area where he was directed to a velvet-lined booth towards the left of the lifts.

'Hello, Joss Lane speaking.'

'Hi Joss, it's Niall. Look, I've been making a few calls: I think we can get this thing moving.'

'Great, let's get it on.'

'Hold on, tell me first: how did you get on at the court?'

'I saw Greta.'

'And?'

'And nothing.'

'Come off it, Joss, you're talking to family here.'

'We didn't get much of a chance, she was kind of busy. Besides, I get the impression we turned different corners too long ago to find the way back,' he said, with a forced nonchalance.

'I'm sorry to hear that, Joss. I know she meant a lot to you but, like I said, you've got a lot of making up to do. Now listen: good news. I think I'm waiting for a call back: maybe late tonight but more likely tomorrow morning first thing. I can't guarantee you'll get to see him, but Callum will be told that you're back.'

'From what I've heard down at the court, these people don't give guarantees, Niall, they take them. And anything else they can get their hands on: insurance policies, bank accounts, children, mothers, fathers, homes, you name it. There's a lot of very angry people out there willing to testify to that.'

'I can only pass on the information I've received, Joss, don't shoot the messenger, lad.'

'Yeah, OK, I'm sorry, Niall; I'm just wound up.'

'It's OK: sit tight until I contact you.'

'Thanks, Uncle Niall, for everything.'

'Don't thank me till it's over, Joss. How's the accommodation?'

'Barely adequate,' he laughed.

'Ungrateful little tyke. Look, relax, have a night on the town and I'll speak to you tomorrow, God willing.'

'It's not *his* willingness I'm interested in at the moment.'

'What's that you say?'

'It doesn't matter, Uncle Niall. I'll see you tomorrow.' Joss returned the receiver to its cradle, and for the first time since he'd landed back in England he felt the warm glow of hope.

As he walked across the foyer another warm hope settled inside him, but it disappeared just as quickly when he saw that Monica wasn't sitting where he'd left her. He slumped into the empty chair and stared forlornly at the trace of her peach lipstick on the rim of the crystal champagne flute. It was then that he noticed the single word written in the same lipstick on the table mat underneath his own glass.

It read simply 'bathtime!'.

His hopes bounded back when he realised that Monica wasn't the only thing missing from the scene. His room key had also gone.

She had cleverly left the door open with a wedge of tissue in the latch. As he walked in he could hear the gentle echoes of bathwater splashing softly from the far side of the room. He extracted the tissue from the door and placed the 'do not disturb' sign carefully over the handle.

She smiled at him as he pushed the bathroom door open and stood in front of her. Her firm pear-shaped breasts stood proud of the bubbles, nipples erect with the flush of need. She was perfect in every way: the undulating curve of her tight stomach and swell of her long thighs were accentuated by the refraction of the water.

He soon felt the rush of blood to his groin as he reached down through the water and stroked her lower leg. She laid back her head on the towelled rest and closed her eyes in response opening her thighs slightly as he pressed gently against her softest place. His fingers explored the hot cavern within and she moaned.

'I want you, Joss,' she whispered as she caressed her neck with those long slim fingers. He bent down to kiss her. Her lips accepted his and he could taste the remnants of her flavoured lipstick, making him want to eat every inch of her.

His eyes never left her face while he undressed, without any hint of the clumsiness he had displayed earlier, and soon he was kneeling between her legs ready to put paid to twenty long months of celibacy.

The first thrust took him higher than he'd ever been as she wriggled beneath him, encouraging every inch of him into her body. Soon his rhythm was causing the floor to take the brunt of tides of water but neither of them cared.

Five minutes later and the first knock on the door went ignored as they writhed around the bathroom floor.

Open doors, Joss, don't close them.

She begged him to disregard the second knock but he couldn't and he clumsily disengaged himself from her tight hold, grabbing a thick white towelling robe from the wardrobe on the way.

'OK, OK,' he shouted as he reached the door just as a third knock began making the frame vibrate. 'What's the rush?'

He opened the door to be confronted with the rain-speckled back

86

of a Burberry trenchcoat bending over. He saw the files in the briefcase before he saw her.

'I brought these,' said Greta, gesturing to the case.

Greta.

Christ.

What you gonna do now, Joss?

'Er Greta, hi, I sort of didn't expect to see you so soon,' he said hastily, closing the inner door behind him.

'Clearly,' she replied acidly, glancing down to where his insistent erection strained against the luxuriant bath-towel. A cool frown scoured across her forehead. 'You seemed desperate, so I went back to chambers for my research file.' She hesitated, her face colouring profusely, then something snapped.

'You tore my fucking world apart and then you come waltzing in like some whirling dervish, telling me you're sorry. It's just a little bit too late for that, don't you think?' Her eyes locked on to his in that way only utter honesty allows.

'Why are you here, then?' he chanced quickly, but wished he hadn't.

'Niall phoned me, told me how pathetic you were: he was absolutely right.'

Monica moaned loudly from the space behind him and whispered, 'Come and fuck me, Joss.'

'You bastard,' Greta spat, handing him the files. 'You'd better take these if you want to get Callum back, although I doubt very much whether he'll be any better off with a snake like you back in his life.'

She turned away from him just as Monica appeared at the door.

'Greta, wait, I can explain.'

No you can't, Joss.

No you can't.

And Joss Lane knew that a constant brilliant light in his life had been extinguished for ever.

CHAPTER TEN

Mark was waiting in the bar area of Chester's diner as Greta walked into the restaurant thirty minutes late. He could tell by her face that something wasn't right. She flung her trenchcoat on to the outstretched arm of the waiter and slumped in the seat beside him.

'You OK?' he said quietly.

'Of course I'm OK. Just sick of the weather outside: I couldn't get a taxi for ages; got bloody soaked.' She smiled but didn't look him in the eye. She looked flushed and brushed herself down unnecessarily.

'Are you sure, Greta? If you're not feeling well, I understand. It's been a lot of work for you, and don't think I'm not grateful.'

'Get off my case, Mark: since when have I been frightened of the work?' she snapped, glaring at him.

'Slow down and tell me what's wrong, Greta, please.' He could see her eyes were wet and reddened.

'That's just typical of men: "If the work's too much, honey",' she mimicked sarcastically, clearly in no mood to simmer down. 'The graft isn't the problem, Mark, it's the fact that I have to deal with your fucking mood swings all day that gets me. It's not easy propping you up, you know.'

'Hey, I'm sorry, OK? Let's settle down here. I know it's a poison chalice case. I shouldn't have asked you in the first place to get involved: I didn't realise it would get to you so much,' he said, genuinely worried. She had never reacted this way before. Something really had got to her.

'Just leave it, Mark, OK?' she replied, realising her outburst had been overheard by the couple sitting opposite them at the bar who judiciously hid behind the oversized menu card they were sharing.

'No, I mean it: I must have been a bit difficult over the last few days. You're absolutely right; I promise tomorrow will be a day of calm.' He held up his hands and smiled at her.

'No, I'm sorry, it's not your fault at all; it's something else. Just forget I said anything and get me a drink.'

He summoned the wine waiter and ordered a bottle of white, then turned back to her. 'Man trouble, I bet,' he pushed on bravely, knowing that in all the time she'd listened to his own problems he hadn't once dared to quiz her about her own private life. She had never offered and so he hadn't asked.

'Mind your own business,' she said, but he could tell she didn't really mean it.

'But you are my business,' he challenged with an innocent look, just waiting for her either to take the bait or walk out.

'Man trouble,' she laughed in resignation. 'More boy trouble really, but what makes you think for one moment that I'd want to share the secrets of my lovelife with you?'

'Oh, I don't know: I've shared mine often enough with you. Problem shared is a problem halved, that sort of thing.'

'Yes, but your half is totally dysfunctional.' She laughed.

'Try me. Honestly, I used to be good at this sort of thing before I got married.'

'It's a more of a saga than a short story.'

'I'm an expert on sagas. You're not the only one who's read Jilly Cooper, you know.'

'Some other time, perhaps,' she said, reaching for the menu.

'Whatever,' he said sadly.

'Don't be like that, Mark.'

'Like what?'

'All that puppy dog eyes stuff: it doesn't suit you.'

'Never failed before.'

'Well it has this time. Anyway, it's over now for good.'

'Where have I heard that before?' he mused, ostentatiously adopting the thinker's pose.

'I thought we really had something,' she relented, 'but I suppose I was wrong to hang on to the past.'

'Doesn't everyone – think they have something, I mean?'

'I guess so, but at least they both realise it at the same time during the relationship. This guy never grew up at the same rate I did.'

'Who is he, Peter Pan?'

'It doesn't matter; just another guy,' she laughed, feeling a little better but still not wanting to let Mark know the full history about her and Joss.

'Sounds like he's more than that, Greta. You've never mentioned anyone before: I thought you were, you know . . .'

'Like a nun, lesbian, what?'

'No, I mean you're not the sort who would ever have problems with guys: I can't imagine anyone would be stupid enough to mess you around.'

'Thanks, Mark, but it doesn't work like that. Worst thing is I thought this guy could help us. I was the stupid one: I should never have written to him.'

'What do you mean, this guy could help us?'

'I don't know, you probably think I'm talking rubbish.'

'No, go on, please.'

'It was something Rose Moody said in her proof of evidence: it's probably nothing.'

'What is it, Greta?'

'Rose said that she used to clean the administration offices at the Haven. One of her jobs was to spend hours with a tiny brush getting dust out of the keyboards on the computers. She said there were lots of them, and that takes serious money.'

'So what?' Mark asked as the waiter returned with the wine.

'It got me thinking about the financial operation of the Millennium Church. This is a big organisation we're talking about, and by the sound of it they have a lot of IT hardware to look after it. So I started digging around the published accounts about a month ago, figuring that at least we may be able to attack River's credibility if there were any scams going on with the tax man.'

'And you found nothing, right?'

'Pretty much so, but this is a global charity, Mark, they have money all over the place. It would take years to unravel the set-up, especially with a guy called Callum Lane running the show.'

'Who?'

'Callum Lane: he was the guy I met when I went to that crazy induction weekend. He was the one I told you about, remember? The father of one of my friends,' she prompted him.

'Yes, I remember, what about him?'

'This guy is a genius when it comes to numbers, believe me.

Strange thing is when I saw him he was totally burned out. His wife died in an accident and after that he lost himself completely in the Church. He was full of Rivers's vision for the future and couldn't care less about the outside world, or so he told me. I found it kind of hard to believe, but as you know I didn't hang around long enough to join the party. Anyway, now I keep seeing his name all over the accounts, and I thought maybe we could get some information to help.'

'How come?'

'Through his son.'

'Is he the guy causing you the problem?'

'It's not a problem any more,' she said firmly. 'Anyway, let's just forget it now. Like I say, it's all over and he can't help us; I was dumb for thinking that he could.'

'Whatever you say.' Mason knew she wasn't to be pushed any further. He suddenly felt a huge swell of indignation that anyone could hurt her so much. It was the sort of feeling he knew that he couldn't tell his wife about. He glanced at Greta out of the corner of his eye: she was pretending to study the menu but in reality she was miles away in places he could only guess about.

'Shall we order?' he said gently.

Twenty minutes later she was toying with her poached salmon and telling him the results of her searches of the social services records relating to the Moody family.

'There's a pile of confidential case assessments about two weeks before she left home. It seems that her school referred her to the social services after prolonged truancies.'

'Wasn't Geoff made aware of the situation?'

'Like he said in evidence, he wasn't at home too much during that period. Letters inviting him to appointments were sent to the house and must have been intercepted by Rose, but it was only a matter of time before things caught up with her.'

'Hence she ran away,' he concluded, letting out a long sigh.

'It's what the defence will say.'

Greta was right: damn Geoff Moody. Why hadn't he explained all this before? At least he could have laid the groundwork in examination-in-chief, but as things stood he was bound now to get another pasting in the box when court resumed in the morning.

CHAPTER ELEVEN

His eyes felt welded shut. Thick sleep bound his upper lids to his lower. Joss rubbed the gritty slough away and narrowed his vision to the other side of the bed. When he had come back from chasing Greta through the hotel, Monica had gone. It had been wild and wonderful, unfettered and meaningless in a meaningful kind of way. Junkies barely bothered with sex. The smack was their passionate significant other and would tolerate no casual dalliance with lesser pastimes. It felt good to have terminated their long-time affair. The world might have lost some of its magnificent chemical-induced colour but those dimmer hues that remained were rendered more acceptable by their honesty.

How could you do that, Joss?
To Greta of all people.
Go on, explain yourself.

The voice crackled in his head like a distant radio signal. He could distinctly make out the clipped tones of Dr Klammer.

'You never question your own actions, Joss. You must learn to listen to a rational, inner voice. When you leave here that voice will guide you through the stormy seas ahead.'

He turned over and buried his head deep in the pillow. Looking up, he saw that the files she'd given him were lying on the dressing table. He suddenly realised that whatever they might be; they were a way back to Greta.

He yawned away his sated tiredness and pushed back the feather duvet. He reached for the top file without disturbing the remaining stack and headed for the marble-faced bathroom. He turned the bath taps full on and sat on the vanity stool trying to avert his eyes from the heap of sodden towels in the corner: the only remaining trace of

Monica the Valkyrie. He opened the file entitled 'Radical Religious Communities' and began to read.

The document was a detailed study of cultism through the ages and recognised three common denominators; isolation, control and domination. Joss had followed the news, like every other young person, through the horror of Jamestown, the poisonous Aum cult of Japan, to the deranged and murderous David Korresh, but he had never begun to consider the logistics of complete control over the will of others. It took intelligence and real willpower. Such cult leaders' twisted beliefs, so laughable when standing aside and snickering at the gullibility of others, were food and drink to their followers; so vital that they would kill and die for them. This, then, was something of the measure of what Callum had fallen into.

Another file contained heartrending newspaper clippings featuring bereft parents pleading for their·children to come home, or at the very least to contact them. Their photographs, now yellowing, in grained black and white were sad-eyed testimony to their continuing loss. Joss felt their insistent pull. These people, too many different lives, had been shattered by cultism of one category or another. As the chronology approached the present it was the Millennium Church that featured predominately. He watched the count of the missing rise to the present '32' as the bereaved banded together to form a pressure group with no real head of steam.

At the epicentre of their collective disgust stood the enigmatic PJ Rivers: Perry John, the baptist's son. Within a bare fifteen years he had built an empire of belief across the world. Movie stars, musicians and hard-nosed businessmen had flocked to his banner of Armageddon, and with them their own admirers until the coffers were full and the pews packed with the faithful. Those who had interviewed Rivers all remarked on the calm, mesmeric manner of the leader of the Church. One renowned Fleet Street hack, the ever-inebriated Bill Botcheby, had even sworn off the drink and was now a champion of the cult's aims.

Two hours later and Joss was reaching for the last file when he spotted the note underneath. He picked it up.

'Thanks Joss it was terrific fun. I hope you don't feel cheap but some of my friends said that you needed comfort. Arrangements

have been made to take you to your father. A car will be waiting at twelve o'clock outside the hotel.'

It was signed Monica.

That was a low blow. The bitch clearly knew who he was and, what's more, she now knew a great deal more than he would have let on under normal circumstances. His face hardened into a scowl when he realised that he had compromised his future with Greta for no more than a honey trap.

A honey trap, Joss?

Why?

Then it dawned on him that someone must have had him under observation: how else could Monica have so conveniently bumped into him like that?

What now, Joss?

And who was watching him?

He glanced quickly at his watch: it was five minutes to the hour. He reached for the telephone and asked the reception desk to contact Niall Robertson. Frantically, he spent the next two minutes slinging his kit back into the flight bag and was just about to leave when the telephone rang. Nobody at the office knew where Niall was this morning, so Joss left a message saying that he would try again later. He replaced the receiver and not for the first time began feeling very much alone.

CHAPTER TWELVE

Mason sat in court waiting for Withnail to come on to the bench. Greta was sitting behind him looking a lot brighter than she had done last night when they had parted company, but still he knew her mind was elsewhere. Over coffee in the robing room she hadn't said very much and didn't seem at all interested in the crossword, her traditional kick-off to the day. Mason looked across at the jury who were avoiding eye contact with anyone but their own number.

When Thynne had accused Geoff Moody of sexual abuse and produced Rose's account of it, the playing field had changed. Moody had, of course, always maintained that Rose gave this account under duress from the Church when its leaders realised that she wanted to leave. She would later tell the court the same thing, but the seed had been sown: it was a possibility that the jury would be invited to consider. Thynne had introduced it as a darker motive for this ludicrous tale invented solely to gain compensation.

The clock struck 10.30am and Withnail strode on to the bench. The morning press had been full of the case and he had obviously enjoyed the picture presented to the public of a commanding and compassionate judge who wanted only that the truth should come out. The *Telegraph* had done his cause no harm, in posting the accolade that he was emerging from the case as a judge of the people, and certainly his lady wife was pleased that his normal scowl had disappeared. Mason thought that Mr Justice Withnail was thoroughly revelling in the attention. He nodded a greeting to the jury and apologised for the abrupt close to proceedings the previous day. Addressing himself to the barristers, he reminded them to proceed with caution, given the highly volatile nature of the allegations and counter-assertions. He enquired whether the complainant and her father had recovered from their shock, and even invited Mason to take as much time as he liked before calling Rose to the stand. Mason hurried to assure the court that Rose and Geoff were fine and that he was ready to continue.

'So be it: let Mr Moody be recalled.'

Moody walked into court with his head bowed, nervously biting his lower lip. He climbed into the witness box and immediately reached for the glass of water in front of him. Thynne waited a few moments longer than necessary before reminding Moody that he was still under oath.

'Now, Mr Moody, we were dealing with the question of your relationship with your daughter, were we not?' he smiled thinly.

'If you say so,' replied Moody sullenly.

'Perhaps you could explain why on earth your daughter would sign such a document as this.'

'Like I said yesterday, she was under pressure from that lot to find some way of preventing her return to my lawful custody: she was only fifteen years old, for goodness' sake.'

'Pressure, you say.'

'I do.'

'Duress, even?' Thynne posed, baiting him further.

'Your words not mine, but I should think that covers it.'

'The sort of duress, perhaps, she had suffered at home?'

'I've told you before, she has never suffered at my hands.'

'Are you quite sure about that, Mr Moody?'

'Of course I am.'

'Wasn't it you who yesterday was for saying that when Rose was merely thirteen she had, how did you put it, responsibilities?' He let the word linger as if he'd just tasted something nasty.

'I meant that she had schoolwork to do and there was just the two of us left after her mother died. We had to look after each other, that's all.'

'But wouldn't you agree, looking at things another way, she may have been quite resentful of your hold over her.'

'I don't think so,' Moody snapped.

'But why not, Mr Moody? Here we have a thirteen-year-old girl who wants to be out discovering things for herself – nothing sinister in that – yet she is lumbered with the housework, the cleaning, the cooking, helping out with your paint business . . .'

'Hardware business,' he corrected unnecessarily. He was losing the jury and Mason knew it: they were in uncharted territory and Thynne was planting all the insinuations Mason had predicted. He was questing subtly and cleverly, allowing the jury to infer rather than know for sure.

'Yes, of course, hardware business: I'm so sorry. And Rose helped, you say. Helped in what way?'

'Well, she worked in the shop at weekends and school holidays: she seemed to enjoy it.'

'Are you sure about that also, Mr Moody?'

'Yes I am.'

'Or wasn't it the case that you were obsessed with this child, and indeed you still are.'

'I love her. I'm not obsessed with her in the way you seem to be implying.'

'I suggest she was no more than a replacement for her mother, as far as you were concerned: I gather the similarity is quite remarkable.' Thynne was at him again, allowing the jury to leap ahead in their own minds.

'What you are suggesting is sick.'

'It is what I'm suggesting, Mr Moody, but I do so upon this sworn statement by your daughter: shall we examine it in more detail?'

'If we must, but it's all rubbish.'

'Of course, you say my clients manufactured all of this and threatened the poor girl if she would not sign it.'

'I believe my daughter.'

'I see, so when she says that your violent jealous rages when she brought a boyfriend home were too much to cope with, she was being truthful, was she?'

'Like I say, everything in that statement is rubbish, but you're twisting things.'

'That you started to explore her sexually around this time,' Thynne pushed on.

'Rubbish.'

'But is it, Mr Moody? Is it not right that at around this time she was truanting from school and the social services were anxious that she should be placed upon the Child Protection Register?'

'It didn't happen that way.'

'Well, what way did it happen, Mr Moody: you tell us.'

'I was neglecting her, I admit; she just wanted attention.'

'And what did she do?'

'She contacted some stupid child-line and made up a story: the police never brought any charges; it was totally false.'

'But, Mr Moody, you have on the one hand told us that you believe your daughter and that this court should do the same. On the other you are telling us that she is capable of manipulation and deceit. Which is it to be?'

It was a clever cross-examination, leaving Moody trapped under the weight of his own evidence. Mason could only hope that Thynne would alienate the jury if he made Moody out to be an idiot.

Thynne, however, was far too astute for such errors of judgement and pace in a situation like this. Moody began backtracking and became more argumentative as the accusations went on. Thynne was breaking him down relentlessly. The jury had two alternatives: firstly, they could speculate as to the situation, based on Rose's own account, or, secondly, they had the portrait of a lying young girl. Thynne had built up a picture of a forlorn, abject thirteen-year-old, a misused, confused manipulative girl going through puberty without a mother and a saddled with a father too busy to care; or worse, one who abused her. The defence didn't care which version the jury chose as long as it brought the right verdict.

Eventually Thynne left Moody in the witness box quietly ambushed and seemingly destroyed.

Mason stood up to re-examine and try to repair some of the damage. He took Moody through his years of trying to bring Rose up without a female figure in the house and emphasised strongly the fact that no proceedings were ever initiated against him as a result of Rose's complaint or the social services' investigation. When Moody was released from the witness box he took one long look at the Reverend Rivers, who sat staring straight ahead with not a hint of concern in his saintly face.

'You bastard,' Moody shouted, moving for the glass in front of him. The water only just missed Mason as it flew through the air, but pathetically it splashed against the dock and dribbled pointlessly down the wood panelling. The jury could hear the commotion in the corridor outside as Geoff Moody was arrested for contempt of court.

CHAPTER THIRTEEN

At twelve o'clock, Joss emerged from the elevator and walked the short distance into the reception of the hotel. He quickly checked out at the main desk and looked around the luxuriously decorated public area, searching for his contact.

At the far end, next to the revolving doors, there was a large group of yashmak-clad women busily hounding the bellboys, who were struggling with a dazzling array of jewel-encrusted chests and expensive designer luggage. A few businessmen were hovering around the entrance to the restaurant and just to the left of them stood a slightly built young man wearing a sombre grey pinstripe suit and black tie. He was sporting a completely bald head and clutched his chauffeur's cap tightly in his lap. Joss caught his eye almost immediately and walked over.

'Are you waiting for Joss Lane, by any chance?' he asked politely while noticing the small silver lapel brooch the youth wore in the shape of a cross with the letters MC inscribed underneath.

'That's correct, sir. The car is waiting. May I assist with your case, sir?' the young man replied.

'That's OK, I can manage. Where are we going?'

'My instructions are to transport you to the airport, sir. I'm afraid I am not aware of your ultimate destination. Someone will meet you at the terminal,' he replied flatly.

Joss followed the man outside and into the midnight-blue Daimler Sovereign, which was double-parked in the street. He climbed into the rear and sank into the cream leather seats wondering just how much of his former inheritance was being spent on keeping this monster fed with fuel.

The journey to Heathrow took less than thirty minutes, during

101

which time his attempts at conversation with his driver were met with a stone-wall consistency.

True to his word, when the driver deposited him at the front entrance to Terminal One another similarly dressed young man guided him to the private flier's lounge at the eastern end of the building. Once there, he only had fifteen minutes to wait before being ushered through to an airport people carrier, and a short ride later he was standing in front of the sleek white Douglas Rapier jet. A smart uniformed stewardess deposited him in the middle seat and told him that his destination was Broadford on the Isle of Skye.

It was clear to Joss that there was to be no great revelation from the crew during the flight so he settled back and reached into his flight bag for the last of Greta's files. Fifty minutes later, and he was left contemplating her chilling conclusion concerning the rise in popularity of the Millennium Church and its many imitators.

As the cold war recedes into history, we leave behind a strange stability from the balance of terror that once existed. It was a time of mutually assured destruction when communist and capitalist super-powers divided the world into two well-controlled camps. Terrorism was, by and large, state sponsored and politically motivated. Now, in the new millennium, we face another kind of threat, one of unrestrained killers and renegade states armed with the deadliest substances on earth.

The word is out. A college education, some basic lab equipment, recipes downloaded from the Internet – for the first time, ordinary people can create extraordinary weapons. Technology and training have simply become too widespread, too decentralised to stop a coming era of do-it-yourself machines for mass murder. We are reaching a new stage in terror in which the most fanatic and unstable among us can acquire the most powerful weapons.

In late 1995, the US Senate permanent sub-committee on investigations took a long hard look at the listed millennial activists around the globe. The results were astonishing, even to those already deeply immersed in hard-hitting probes into organised crime and terrorism.

The Aum cult, responsible for the Tokyo subway sarin gas attacks, is merely one example of what may be the most dominant, emerging threat to our national security. Senator Sam Nunn, heading the investigations, concluded in the closed committee hearings which followed the study, that the growth of these cults was a warning to us all. Nunn is one of the leading defence experts in Congress: what better authority do we need to at least begin contemplating stricter supervision and control of the spread of Radical religious communities?

These groups are capable of great harm in the service of a perceived higher calling. They are responsible only to God and the scripture; they feel absolved from the laws and values that govern the rest of us. In that sense, the Millennium Church, like the Aum cult, belongs in the company of Islamic fundamentalists, other apocalyptic Christian sects and messianic Jews. Their violence transcends this world and becomes a sacramental rite, a divine duty. Such beliefs justify the act of mass murder as we have witnessed many times.

In the year 2000, the proliferation of apocalyptic sects has become extraordinary. The aptly named Millennial Prophecy report claims to track 1,100 such sects in the United States alone. The 1993 mass murders of the Branch Davidians in Waco, Texas, and, a year later, the Solar temple suicides in France, Quebec and Switzerland are but two extreme examples of the phenomenon. These groups are not limited to the west. In 1995, a police officer named Vissarion drew Russian media attention by building a community of intellectuals in Siberia and declaring himself Christ. In China that same year, authorities arrested fifteen members of a doomsday cult called Bei Li Wang. In Thailand, police raided the headquarters of the Sri-ariyia cult, whose guru claims to be the master of heaven in the 'millennium kingdom'.

More worrying still are the Islamic fundamentalists who bring to bear their own form of apocalyptic judgement. These believers in Jihad have proven time and time again their willingness to kill and die for Allah. The fanatics who struck at New York's World Trade centre in 1993 clearly meant to commit mass murder and, as it transpired, that attack was meant only as the first in an internationally co-ordinated campaign of terror said to include bombings, assassinations, and the destruction of the United Nations.

103

Militia movements in the United States bring a similarly evan-gelical and heavily armed response to the world. Dozens of these grass-roots armies have arisen, such as the Militia of Montana, and the Hillsborough Troop of Dragoons in New Hampshire. They are disturbing on account of their white supremacist and anti-Semite survivalist philosophy. Many members of the so-called Millennium Church are disaffected militia who share a deep-rooted Christian fundamentalist view of the world, combined with the kind of intense paranoia that infected the Aum cult and Branch Davidians so deeply.

The Millennium Church was founded in about 1827 as one of several Christian religious sects that hold an implicit belief in the return or second coming of Jesus Christ. This belief is based upon various utterances in the New Testament, particularly in the Book of Revelations, and some of the writings of the later Old Testament prophets, including Daniel. They share views with Christadelphians and the four-square Gospel Alliance. Essentially, theirs is a philosophy of millenarianism, the notion that Christ will return to the earth to rule over humanity for one thousand years. Various dates have been predicted for when this period will begin but thus far, naturally, none has proved correct.

The Church represents the youngest of a trio of Christian sects. It claims not only to have certain knowledge that judgement day is close at hand, but also to have privileged information about when it will happen. They believe that Armageddon will qualify them to rule a new universe with Christ, while the remainder of less fortunate humanity disappears into oblivion. Originating in Pittsburgh, USA, the Church bases its views on the central belief that a precise number of the chosen flock, 144,000 members, known as the 'anointed', will travel the expressway to heaven, while the remaining five million members will populate an earthly paradise. The members subscribe to the ancient pulpit rhetoric of Arius: the holy trinity does not exist, but rather the term 'one God' means what it says. They also believe that Christ is merely the mortal image of the Supreme Being.

They have relied consistently on predictions of the imminent date of judgement day as the most persuasive tool with which to recruit new members. Followers take a literal interpretation of the Bible

104

and have thus assumed that all the important moments of salvation or catastrophe will be presaged by a time of great tribulations. They have variously predicted Armageddon in 1914, 1925 and, most recently, in 1975.

The church's incumbent leader, the Reverend Perry John Rivers, has prophesied that the end of the world will occur in the late autumn of 2000.

Joss breathed in deeply, then exhaled. His mind was crashing with the earth-quaking extent of the cult's beliefs.

This is Callum.

This is what he believes.

Can you save him?

Does he want to be saved?

The seatbelt light flashed on with an accompanying chime: he would soon find out.

CHAPTER FOURTEEN

Rose walked into a silent courtroom. She wore a simple black and white striped dress, which accentuated the pallor of her face. A symmetrical, short black bob framed her cheekbones; her elfin appearance made her seem even younger than her seventeen years.

Mason watched as she crossed the floor in full view of the jury. They followed her every move as she took the oath, gripping the Bible tightly. The court usher told her to read the words on the card, and for the first time the court heard her speak.

'I swear by Almighty God to tell the truth, the whole truth and nothing but the truth.'

It was barely audible and some members of the jury were already straining with the acoustics. Reverend Rivers appeared deep in his own prayers, eyes closed, refusing to acknowledge that Rose was standing only a matter of yards away, ready to destroy his reputation.

Mason stood and told her to keep her eyes on the jury, and her voice as loud as possible. He looked at her, wanting her to succeed, for when all was said and done, he believed the girl. What she had to say was of such ineradicable sadness that he wished she could be spared this ordeal of revelation and abasement.

Mason began by asking her about her relationship with Geoff Moody in an effort to deal head on with the defence's assertions which had caused so much difficulty during Geoff's testimony. He had to turn it around so that the jury saw just how close these two were.

'After your mother died, is it right that your father was solely responsible for bringing you up, Rose, even though he had re-married?'

'He did everything for me. My stepmother didn't take much interest,' she answered meekly. 'I couldn't have wished for a better father. I still couldn't,' she added without prompting. Despite everyone's reservations about the state of her health, she seemed to be quite strong at the moment and Mason wanted to push on quickly while she was looking comfortable. It was as if at long last the day had come to shift the burden she had carried for so long.

'It has been suggested in this court that he is a possessive and jealous man as far as you are concerned.'

'That's not fair: he has only ever had my best interests at heart. I was just a kid and didn't know any better,' she said, but her answer sounded a little too rehearsed.

'You're referring to the time that you reported him to Childline?'

'Yes.'

'Were your allegations true?'

'No, none of it was true: I just wanted attention,' she said, but once more Mason was worried that to the jury it sounded as if her father had written the script for her.

'But this time you are here to tell the truth?'

'Yes I am. That was then and this is now,' she said forcefully.

Mason didn't want to revisit the contested sworn statement produced by Thynne to Geoff Moody: he would deal with that later when the jury had taken on board the ideas that he was about to ventilate after Rose's introduction to the Church.

'What happened, Rose, the night that you left home?'

'I had brought my boyfriend, Greg, home from school. Dad wasn't back from work, my step-mum was out drinking again, so we played some records and had something to eat. I hadn't made anything for Dad's supper so when he came back we had a fight. He told Greg to leave the house and I was to be grounded, but I sneaked out instead.'

'You didn't tell him you were going?'

'No, I was really upset at the time. I wish I had just done as he said and never gone out.'

'Where did you go?'

'I went down to the arcade on the seafront to see if I could see any of my friends.'

'And did you?'

'No, there was no one there: it was late.'

'So what did you do?'

'I asked some men and a lady for some change to ring Greg.'

'And,' Mason pushed, begging her to give a credible explanation of the kidnap, which she had only recently begun recalling although the details were still sketchy. He had no idea whether the defence were going to call witnesses to the abduction, because Rose had never been able to identify anyone.

'They were, or at least they seemed, nice at first: talked to me and asked if I needed help. I guess I looked a little upset still.'

'Go on, Rose, please,' invited Mason gently, cajoling her into recalling the facts.

'I tried to ring Greg but his mother said he was in bed: that's when I asked if they could give me a lift home.'

'And did they?'

'They took me to a van, and I can remember them giving me a drink. Some time later we had passed the turn-off to my house and I started to worry. I asked them to take me home straight away but they said they needed to go somewhere first. I must have fallen asleep, because the next thing I knew they told me I was at a house somewhere in London.'

'Didn't you protest?'

'I did at first, but I kept feeling strange: I can't explain it. It was like I belonged there, almost, it all seemed so right. They were so nice to me one minute, then horrible to me the next.'

'Didn't you contact your father?'

'They said they would do it for me. I was scared to go back at that stage because of the trouble I had caused.'

'Did you have any means of getting yourself home?'

'No.'

'When did you contact your father?'

'On the third day, I think.'

'Did you say you wanted to come home then?'

'Yes, but I was petrified when my dad told me the police were looking for me.'

'What happened after that?'

'They suggested that I should get out of the way for a while.'

'Did you agree?'

'I didn't know what I was doing then; my head was in bits. I was all over the place.'

Thynne never took a note of her testimony, preferring to shake his head or mutter to one of his colleagues as the tale unfolded. Rose watched him, aware of the danger he presented and the impact his treatment of her father had caused. Mason then turned to her time at the Haven.

'We know that you ended up in Scotland at a retreat belonging to the defendant. What was your first experience of this place?'

'I was examined.' She dropped her gaze as she answered.

'Please give us more information,' Mason said gently.

'Down there.' She nodded shamefully towards her lower body. 'They put me on a table in the medical block and put their fingers inside me.'

'Why? How did they explain that?'

'They said that God wanted to see if I was good; whether I was still intact.'

'A virgin, you mean,' Mason probed.

'Yes,' she whispered.

'I do not mean to be intrusive, Miss Moody, but were you?'

Her eyes blazed, then died down to low, beaten embers.

'I was, then!' She stared at Rivers who blessed her with the sign of the cross. Mason noted the jury had seen the exchange, but he decided against raising an objection. He still didn't know what they made of Rivers.

'Were these people medical staff?'

'They said so.'

'Why did you allow them to do that to you?'

She shrugged.

'They were so persuasive, so kind; *then*.'

'And,' Mason continued, 'did that attitude change?'

'Yes. Oh God, yes.'

Mason nodded understandingly.

'Tell us, Rose, in your own words, what kind of treatment you received.'

The girl gulped in some stale court air to steady herself, and began.

'They don't want you to think for yourself. They exhaust you with lessons, exercise, anything to tire you out so you don't know which way up is any more.'

'Please explain to the ladies and gentlemen of the jury how that was achieved.'

Mason was pleased with her account so far. She had shown the right degree of hurt and indignation when outlining the repressive nature of the cult, but the mind- and body-sapping techniques the leaders employed still needed to be firmly established in the minds of the jury.

Her father had been allowed back into court on the firm promise that he would remain silent throughout, but the jury watched him with suspicion.

Mason began, 'Rose, you had been in the clutches of the cult—'

'Emotive, my Lord,' Thynne declared. Withnail nodded his agreement.

'With the members of the sect,' Mason continued, 'for two weeks. In all that time had you had any food or drink?'

'Not what you would describe as either.' Her voice was fuller, more confident, despite the best efforts of the defence barristers, who conferred noisily to put her off her stroke. 'They give you thin food, like grain and watery soup; it makes you feel light-headed, like you're dreaming and not really there. And stuff with lots of sugar in it; that gets you high and buzzing.'

This was the very evidence Mason wanted. He would later call on a chemist and a physiologist as expert witnesses to describe the effects these meagre portions would have on a young girl of Rose's age and weight.

'And how did it affect you?'

'I thought everything they told me was true. I was too tired to argue, even if I disagreed with what they said.'

'Did you meet Mr Rivers around that time?'

Her eyes began to blur.

'Would you like a minute to compose yourself?' Mason asked. She shook her head and looked to her father, who smiled grim encouragement.

'Yes, when he raped me,' she whispered, tears coursing down

her face. 'When he took me in the mansion, telling me this was God's will, and I was his servant.'

Mason paused. Whilst the jury had heard the allegation referred to in his opening address, this was their first opportunity to witness at first hand the victim's utter misery in remembering the awful incident. They looked from Rose to P J Rivers, who remained deep in prayer, too wily and well prepared to utter a single denial.

'Did he take your virginity, Miss Moody?'

'Again and again and again, until it didn't matter,' she said, her voice as flat as a new road.

'I'm afraid we have to go over the details, Rose, so that everyone understands exactly how this occurred. Are you all right to continue?'

'Yes I am.'

'How long had you been at the Haven before this occurred?'

'I can't be sure.'

'Please try.' He had to get a least a vague date.

'It seemed like a few months after I got there, but I honestly have no idea: I was spaced out.'

'Did the Reverend Rivers come to stay at the Haven often?'

'As far as I knew, it was the first time he had visited since I had arrived. There was a big buzz around the Haven: everyone was excited.'

'Were you?'

'I suppose so. You couldn't do anything at the Haven without hearing his voice over the loudspeakers or seeing his picture or reading his words, so to have him stand there in person to pray with us was wonderful.'

'What happened after his arrival that day?'

'There was a big meeting which lasted for hours: we prayed and listened to him speak.'

'What was it like?'

'It was like he had hypnotised everyone.'

'Captivated?'

'I'm sure the jury knows what she means, Mr Mason: stop leading,' interjected Withnail.

'I apologise, my Lord. Rose, what happened after the meeting?'

'Later on that night I was woken in my dormitory by one of the

112

elders and the hut leader. I was told to go to the big house where I would be met. They said the Reverend had chosen me personally: I was to go to him for special instruction.'

'Just pause there a moment, Rose,' said Mason, wanting the clinical description given by the girl's mentors to sit in the jury's mind before she moved on to describe exactly what was meant by 'special instruction'. 'Did you go there willingly?'

'I did, sir: it was a privilege, they said.' She answered without emotion.

'What happened when you got to the house?'

'I was taken into a room where there were already three other people: one was the Reverend and the others were girls my age. One of them started undressing me and I didn't know what to do; I was frozen to the spot.' Her timid voice began trailing away, yet managed to fill every corner of the court. 'The other girl started touching me between my legs and all over my body. I screamed to be let go but no one could hear me.

'The Reverend had a veil in his hand and he placed it over my head. The material was wrapped around my head until I couldn't see properly. I couldn't breathe.' She started to sob and cleared her throat, reaching for her neck with her hand as she recalled the feelings of panic.

'Take your time, Rose,' said Mason softly, holding the moment.

'My wrists were strapped behind my back and then he raped me.'

'Did he penetrate you with his penis, Rose?'

'Yes.'

'And did you consent to that happening?'

'No. I was screaming and screaming until I passed out. I woke up when some of the elders took me into another room: it was full of men I had seen around the Haven from time to time.'

'What happened in there, Rose?'

'It was horrible. I was thrown down on the floor while two of them held me down and the others raped me in turn.'

'So this was your initiation to the Millennium Church?' Mark knew it was a comment and not a question. He didn't have to wait long for Callow to get to his feet.

'My Lord, it is only right that the jury know that this matter was fully investigated at the time by the police and procurator fiscal in Scotland, and not one charge was preferred against my client.'

Withnail was more than a little annoyed with the silk: they would have their own case to present in due course.

'It rather seems as though they now have the point, Mr Callow. Please desist from interrupting the witness's evidence again.'

As Mason feared, Rose had been thrown off her stride by the mention of the fruitless police investigation.

'They didn't believe me, either,' she stuttered, and began to sob.

'No one does,' Thynne whispered towards the jury with a sad shake of his head.

Mason bit back his own disappointment and asked for a further adjournment.

CHAPTER FIFTEEN

The stark beauty of the Scottish landscape had unfurled before his wondering eyes; its snow-blessed peaks catapulting his mind back to the Austrian Alps and Kristina. The strip hugged the ocean tightly where the jet halted smoothly by a waiting Range Rover Discovery. A man leaned back against its driver's door, arms folded, face set.

Joss took his leave of the crew and walked calmly down the five steps to the smooth tarmac. A chill Highland breeze whipped through him as he approached the one-man reception committee, who smiled thinly at Joss's arrival. He looked like a man unused to showing his teeth in friendly welcome. About forty-five years of age, small and stocky to the point of squareness, he exuded a cloud of palpable control. A black suit, white shirt and sombre tie were in stark contrast to Joss's own thick Arran sweater and faded jeans. His complexion was pale as if he favoured the indoor to the out, the dark to the light. His eyes were a watchful shade of hazel. Joss knew the look. He'd seen it in the eyes of solo climbers who took the biggest risks and amassed the largest reputations. He held out a powerful hand. Joss grasped it firmly.

'Harrison Trainer.' The voice was deep, the accent American. 'Who the hell are you, and what are you doing on the Reverend's jet?' The words were hardly ones of welcome and Joss had the impression he was being sized up.

'Where's my father?'

'Tell me who he is and I may be able to help you.' Trainer was bristling with violent energy.

'Callum Lane,' Joss replied, never taking his eyes off the compact American. A moment passed whilst he appeared to assess the information.

'Thought you were dead; Joss isn't it?'

'Or his holy ghost. Where's my father?'

Trainer smiled, attempting warmth but achieving menace. 'Let's get you out of this wind,' he replied evasively.

'When can I see him?'

'After I have seen him myself,' he snapped, clearly angry that Joss's appearance was not of his own arranging. 'Then,' he added as an afterthought, 'when the time is right.'

'And when will that be?'

Trainer grasped Joss's hand-grip and threw it inside the Discovery.

'That's not for me to say,' he eventually replied, gunning the diesel engine into life. Joss clicked his seat belt into place and folded his arms.

'I need some answers,' he said bluntly.

'Don't we all, Joss, don't we all. For now, it's sufficient for you to know that I will drive you to the Haven: there, you will receive further instruction.'

'The Haven?' Joss asked innocently, though the Millennium Church's retreat had featured prominently in Greta's research files.

'A sanctuary from the outside world.'

'McWaco!'

Trainer turned his face towards Joss, eyes deadpan, mouth thin like a scar.

'You have a lot of pain,' he whispered and made it sound like a threat.

Joss swallowed hard.

Trainer manoeuvred the vehicle from the landing strip and began the journey to the Haven, the beating heart of the Millennium Church.

The vehicle scaled the steep crests of the jutting isle with contemptuous ease. Heather and rusting bracken softened the dour leaps and sharp falls of the lush green landscape. What roads they took were rough, unwelcoming tracks of ridged and rutted rock.

They travelled in silence. It was clear to Joss that Trainer did not care for him. That was fine. This wasn't a glee club. He wasn't looking to swap friendship rings; he was looking for answers.

They swept around a promontory where the road dipped away down into a great green valley. At its centre a towering hunting lodge dominated a large compound, which contained several newly built single-storey outbuildings. They were all surrounded by a tall perimeter wall that sprouted broken glass shards embedded in the concrete.

'To keep the guests in?' Joss asked.

Trainer laughed.

'To keep the others out. Anyone is free to leave at any time.'

'Including my father?'

'Of course.'

'Glad to hear it.'

Trainer steered the vehicle towards a security gate some half a mile from the huge manor house. Joss could see that there were people everywhere. These people were active; hyperactive. The land was a teaming mass of involved activity. There were men, women and children running, jumping, cycling. Some were practising callisthenics, others Tai Chi and yoga. Hundreds of fit and active specimens of humanity dressed in tracksuits and shorts, singlets and jogging pants.

'A Haven but not a rest home,' Joss commented, as they were waved through by the armed guard. 'Why the firearms?' he asked.

'Reverend Rivers has been troubled by a stalker for some years; it's all perfectly legal.'

'Sure,' Joss replied acidly. 'It couldn't be to stop people from jumping the wire.'

Trainer aimed the Discovery toward an outbuilding to the far left of the great house.

'I hope we can be friends,' he commented.

'Are you a friend of my father's?'

'Of course.'

Joss doubted that very much. Callum Lane was a man renowned for his ability to read behind the bogus smile and beyond the nodding heads of sycophantic flunkies. But that was the old Callum; before his wife's death.

'Has he changed?'

'Only for the better,' Trainer replied. It sounded like a well-rehearsed response.

'How long has he been here?' he pressed.

'Long enough.'

Joss was becoming irritated by Trainer's continuing evasion.

'Do you ever give straight answers?'

'All the time.'

It was pointless to pursue his enquiries. Whatever answers he sought would not be provided by his driver. The vehicle drew to a halt outside the long thin outbuilding. A group of people sat on the grass outside in front of a blackboard. An energetic man with a goatee beard was using a pointer to emphasise his delivery. He paused momentarily to nod to Trainer who returned his silent greeting.

'Orientation,' Trainer explained, as he climbed down from the Discovery's interior.

'Looks like disorientation to me,' Joss replied.

'We don't know we are lost until we are found,' Trainer remarked coldly.

'Golden words of Perry J Rivers?'

'Common sense.'

'Gobbledegook,' Joss responded. 'Trite, esoteric nonsense.'

Nice work, Joss!

'You will learn.' Trainer smiled as he spoke as if he could see into the future and enjoyed its secret status.

At that moment, a stunning girl in a grey jogging suit bounced up to Joss, reached forward and hugged him in a smothering embrace.

'You are Joss,' she gushed. 'I recognise you. Oh, it's just so wonderful that you are here at long last.'

She released him from her arms. Joss was at a loss.

'Well . . . thanks, I mean . . .' he stammered.

'I'm sorry,' she blurted, 'about hugging you like that.'

She appeared almost on the verge of tears; he placed a comforting hand on her shoulder.

'Hug me any time you want,' he said with his best winning smile. The girl's face was transported to delight.

'I knew you would be just perfect.' She turned to Trainer. 'I did, didn't I, Coach Harrison?'

'Seems everyone else but me knew you were going to drop by,' Trainer drawled angrily then nodded his head. 'He's perfect, all right,' Trainer agreed without enthusiasm.

'I'm Fiona,' she said and hugged Joss again. A cute button nose peaked perkily beneath waltzing blue eyes with dark lashes that swept over her jutting cheekbones.

She was perfect, too perfect, and from anything more than a yard away could have been Greta's identical twin.

'What now?' Joss asked, slightly alarmed by the coincidence.

'Orientation,' Trainer barked, moving swiftly away.

'I'm already perfectly oriented in time and space, thanks.'

Trainer halted immediately.

'Those are the rules. Play by them or leave. There are no exceptions. That's if you still wish to see your father.'

'He wants to see you,' Fiona added. 'I spoke to him this morning. Oh, Joss, it will be wonderful.'

Whilst he didn't trust Trainer for a nanosecond the girl's childish sincerity appeared incapable of duplicity. Joss raised one eyebrow.

'Orientation, Coach Harrison?' he asked.

'Orientation,' Fiona and Trainer replied simultaneously: what that word encompassed Joss would soon discover.

In the security of his office, Trainer furiously established the sequence of events. A radio telephone conversation with the Rapier jet's pilot proved that Callum Lane had ordered the collection of his son from a swanky London hotel by one of the members, and thereafter his rapid transportation to the Haven. It was a breach of security, and any breach of his security was serious. Trainer considered communicating the information to the Reverend, then reconsidered: it would reflect badly on him and PJ had more than enough to deal with at present, the snivelling little bitch, Rose Moody, had seen to that. With the court case and the massive organisation of the forthcoming Hyde Park rally, Rivers did not need to be distracted.

He still felt uncomfortable. Trainer prided himself on his sixth sense for trouble. He had caused enough himself in the past, and Joss Lane had trouble tattooed all over his arrogant forehead. He had never fully trusted Callum Lane, even though the Reverend had given the financier a stain-free bill of health. Lane senior was blessed with a rare and cunning intelligence, on the face of it, a true convert, and this action might be construed as the concern of a loving father, but Trainer remained unconvinced. He would monitor the situation carefully. Meanwhile, Lane junior would undergo 'orientation'.

He smiled grimly, then opened up his computer link to the Police Criminal Records data bank.

'Now, Joss Lane,' he muttered, 'let's find out if you're a bad one or a sad one.'

CHAPTER SIXTEEN

Fiona led him by the hand to a dormitory containing twelve beds. It was stark and clean and reminded Joss of public school. The plain walls were bare and denied any personal identity to the occupants. Glancing upwards, he could not fail to see one large single picture fixed to the ceiling; the very Reverend Rivers, eight feet by six, in monochrome with a benign smile gracing his features. It would be the last vision the occupants would be granted at night and the first to greet them in the dawn. It was more 'Big Uncle' than 'Big Brother', but was clear evidence that this was a 'cult of the personality.'

Fiona continued to chatter mindlessly about how 'wonderful' everything was and how 'terrific' things would be now that he was here. Joss glared suspiciously at the bed that had been allocated to him.

'Hard mattresses are very good for spinal development,' she lectured. 'Coach Rivers says that any back complaint can be cured after a few days here.'

'What is this "Coach" stuff?' Joss enquired, throwing his bag on to the bed and noticing that it barely dented the concrete structure. Fiona smiled, appearing slightly embarrassed.

'You will get used to it.'

'Will I?'

'I know it seems silly at first, but what it really means is that we are all on the same team in this place. He says we are his Spiritual athletes and he is our—'

'Coach,' Joss concluded. 'I get the picture: he has the big game plan in the sky and you are here to bring home the silverware.'

Fiona looked crest-fallen. 'Are you always so cynical?'

'Sorry, it's all a bit . . .' He shrugged, fighting his natural urge to speak his mind.

'Different?'

'Different, it certainly is.'

Fiona reached underneath the bed and removed a holdall. She unzipped it and began to remove a set of sports clothing.

'You will find that these fit perfectly. Your father chose them himself.' She smiled and nodded toward him and the clothes.

'What?' he asked.

'Get changed.'

'I'll see you outside,' Joss replied.

'We have no secrets here, Joss, no hang-ups. Our bodies are the vehicles of our souls. They must be serviced and cared for, polished and buffed until they gleam in the sun.'

Joss pulled his sweater over his head.

'The wise words of Chief Mechanic Rivers or Grease Monkey Trainer?'

'There goes that cynicism again.'

She watched unabashed as he stripped down to his underwear.

'You have a fine body,' she remarked approvingly.

'There's a few miles on the clock, but it's a great little runner: one careless owner.'

Fiona laughed appreciatively. 'You are funny, but you are beginning to get the general idea.'

He donned a pair of dark blue sweat pants, sky blue running singlet and some intricate shoes with garish patterns.

'You said my dad chose these?'

'Personally.'

'His tastes have changed.'

'This place cannot fail to change you.'

Joss didn't doubt it for a moment.

'What now?'

She reached for his own travel grip bag.

'We'll put this somewhere safe.'

Joss grabbed it from her.

'It's safe with me.'

'We are not allowed things of our own.'

She tried to wrench it from his grip, her face rigid with determination.

'No. Look, Fiona, I do not want to let you take it and I am not going to allow you to do so.'

'Then I have failed and I deserve to be punished.' Her eyes were accepting, not frightened.

'What the hell are you talking about?'

'Please, Joss.'

'Let me think about this for a moment. I'll see you outside.'

'I'm not supposed to leave you alone.'

'That's the deal.'

Reluctantly, she moved miserably away from his view. Joss was spooked. This place, these people were weird; what the hell was Callum doing with them? He must have lost the intricate plot to be floating around in hug-heaven with the loonie-moonies.

Quickly, he unzipped his luggage and removed his passport and wallet then glanced around for a safe hiding place. There was a communal bathroom at the far end of the dormitory. Joss glanced up and noticed that the ceiling was constructed of individual polystyrene tiles. He climbed up on to a white porcelain sink, and pushed at one of them until it lifted. He slipped his passport, his credit cards, his lucky 'Go' tiles, Greta's files inside, replaced the cover and dropped nimbly down. It seemed highly likely that the suspicious Trainer would search his luggage once it was surrendered, and having searched would double-check to see if he had secreted any objects in his bed. It was a far from perfect solution, but the best that could be achieved in the circumstances. He walked from the dormitory and handed the bag to Fiona.

'Joss, this is a kindness I will not forget.'

'What now?'

'The medical block.'

She began to walk away; Joss followed warily behind. She greeted scores of happy beaming people as they walked, each time stopping to introduce him. On every occasion he was mortified to be hugged unselfconsciously by them; it was overwhelming but then again, he figured, it was meant to be.

The medical block was situated behind the imposing manor house and had the same unremarkable structure as the rest of the

123

outbuildings. At reception he was greeted by a nurse with a ruddy complexion dressed in a clinical white tracksuit.

'Welcome, Joss,' she began, and he was delighted to note the absence of an embrace: perhaps the 'hug-fest' was over.

'We will begin on the treadmill. You will be wired up so that we can test your lung capacity and heart rate.'

He grunted.

'Standard procedure. We have your medical records and they need to be brought up to date.'

She was not to be argued with and within five minutes he was pounding the rubber surface of the escalated running track, with wires trailing and a lung monitor fixed to his mouth; Fiona beamed a huge smile as his legs stamped their way through two kilometres.

'And rest,' the nurse ordered. Joss didn't need the command. 'That is excellent,' she continued, reading the print-out.

'You used to be a heavy smoker.'

'Some,' he replied. Fiona tutted.

'Self-pollution,' she commented sadly.

'Your lung capacity will return eventually,' the nurse said disapprovingly, and despite his best efforts Joss felt guilty.

The rest of the afternoon was spent in a tornado of frenzied activity. Next he was led to the swimming pool where he was encouraged to swim laps down lanes with others. The monotony became a rhythm, then mindless repetition. He swam and thought. The pulse of his activity became a slow beat as he breathed every four strokes. It matched the time signature of the lullaby his therapist had been so fixated on. He sang it in his head.

'Joss and Jill went up the hill' – breathe,

'To fetch a pail of water.' – breathe,

'Joss fell down and broke his crown,' – kick turn, breathe,

'His Mum came tumbling after!' – arm over, head turn, swim.

Joss would sing along tunelessly to the nursery rhyme in his chubby innocence, never realising the quiet desperation of the words. As they finished the duet his Mother had always hugged her 'Jossie' and whispered, 'But they both ended up safe and sound in a secret place where no one could find them?' However Joss had grown up to discover that happy endings only happened in songs and poems and stories, real life was more like the Brothers Grimm.

Joss felt his pace fall as his heart sank, just as she had done that terrible day. He reached the end of the pool and his own endurance and had to be hauled out by a delighted Fiona, proud that he had swam so far.

Afterwards he was taken to the Foundation refectory where a meagre portion of salad and tofu was placed proudly before him; he was too hungry to refuse and wolfed it down furiously.

Next he was asked to cycle around a walled and banked track; by now he was near exhaustion. By 8pm he was one of the walking dead. His eyes could barely focus, his legs wobbled at the knees, he fell asleep in front of his bowl of thin broth. He didn't know how long he had dozed off for but he was woken by a gentle shake.

'What? What?' He felt his mouth, where a thin trail of saliva had snailed down to his chin. He focused as best he could: a thinly smiling Trainer whispered, 'Still oriented in time and space?'

Joss, despite his very best efforts, replied, 'No, Coach Harrison.'

He was helped to his feet and half-carried back to the dormitory by Trainer, who undressed him carefully, noting the pale and ancient track marks on his arms.

'We will have you chasing a very different kind of dragon,' he murmured. Joss heard the words and lodged them in the shattered recesses of his brain.

'I want to see my father,' he said, his tongue feeling thick and alien in his mouth.

'It won't be long now, Joss,' Trainer replied, patting him hard on the head. Not long at all, Trainer thought, we will see how smart your arse is then; junkie drop-out.

Callow, Thynne and Rory Fannon sat in the drawing room of the magnificent suite that Rivers and his entourage had taken for the trial's duration. They had been provided with tea and coffee, but Fannon's request for something to 'keep out the cold' was met with the provision of a tartan blanket by a well-meaning acolyte. Thynne grinned at the trans-atlantic misunderstanding but Callow was merely irritated by the intrusion into his busy schedule. They had waited thirty minutes whilst the Reverend was in prayer.

Fannon sipped his Earl Grey. 'Think we're going to be invited to join the club?' he muttered.

The door to Rivers's private quarters opened abruptly and Rivers himself strode in. The presidential candidate image of the courtroom had been traded for a white silk shirt and peasant hemp trousers. 'Gentlemen,' he said warmly, 'I thank you for your kind patience, but the Lord's work cannot be rushed by earthly matters.'

Fannon whispered, 'Christ,' and Rivers's eyes flashed in his direction.

'Precisely, Brother Fannon.' His voice was warm, belying the hostility of his gaze, 'I presume you wish to discuss the day's proceedings,' Callow interjected abruptly.

Rivers nodded thoughtfully and took the remaining seat around the Queen Anne table, 'Indeed I do, indeed I do,' he nodded to himself, then stared into each man's face in turn until they dropped their own gaze. Thynne lasted the longest.

'I listened today, gentlemen; I judged like Solomon, and that poor deluded creature was found wanting before God.'

'Wait until she is cross-examined, then you'll . . .'

An upraised hand silenced Callow. 'Forgive me,' Rivers said, 'But please wait until I have finished my thoughts in words before you give me your considered reply.'

Callow's face flushed, Fannon shook his head; the man had a powerful presence, all right, They had already held a number of conferences with their client, but during those earlier meetings he had been meek, happy to await the benefit of their advice.

'As I was stating, before your well-meaning interjection, the girl was found wanting. The devil himself has her ear as he has had her tattered body; poor wretch. She will not be saved come the great day and I, as the gatekeeper to salvation, regret that she is lost.'

The three senior barristers sat in silence, awaiting the real point of this homily. Rivers clasped his hands together, closed his eyes and rocked for a moment, back and forth, back and forth. Just as Rory Fannon was looking to the others and beginning to shrug, the Reverend's aquamarine eyes flashed open.

'But lost she is. Gentlemen, we must not be afraid to meet the devil's emissaries with his own weapons. She is the dark one's mouthpiece and as usual, the dark one has chosen well. You men are the finest lawyers in your country, you are my friends, you know the truth in your hearts, yet those that seek to judge me are strangers.'

Rory Fannon looked towards Thynne who was nodding sagely. Callow looked blank, seeming almost mesmerised by the performance.

'But the girl appeared convincing,' Rivers pressed. 'Why, if the Lord and myself did not know the truth, we might even be swayed by her filth.'

Thynne waited for a pause, 'Reverend?'

He was graced with a pious nod.

'I think I speak for all of us; your friends and believers; you have entrusted us with the advancement of your mission and we undertake that heavy burden with seriousness and purpose'.

'You have already been well rewarded for this,' Rivers pressed. 'In earthly ways of course, but please come to your point.'

Thynne attempted to smile, but even he was slightly put out by the oblique reference to the huge briefs' fees they had commanded.

'We are experts at reading a jury,' he went on. Rivers nodded his encouragement. 'And in estimating the effect of a witness upon them.'

'I am delighted to have your expertise re-affirmed, my friend; please continue, your words find favour with me,' Rivers said gently.

Thynne nodded, then spoke once more, 'The girl will be destroyed in court when we have a chance to question her fully. We will not shirk from using everything in our arsenal to see that her evidence is discredited.'

Rivers closed his eyes in deep contemplation for long seconds, then opened them slowly and fixed each man with a beatific smile.

'I believe you will, my brothers. I truly believe you will. All heaven may well rejoice when a sinner is saved but the legions of the damned scream in despair when one of their own is unmasked.'

Rivers stood abruptly and like iron filings they rose to his magnet. 'I must go to my room now to pray for the lost soul of Rose Moody. Good night.'

The three gathered their belongings in silence and walked toward the door. As Callow opened it, Rivers spoke, once more.

'I am the Vicar of the Lord, the gatekeeper to the doors of salvation, and the baptist of the found.' He paused dramatically. 'But I also pay the piper and I choose the tune; make sure it is played loud and clear, loud and clear.'

Callow allowed the others out into the corridor and toward the lifts. Thynne seemed stunned, Callow mesmerised by the show and Rory Fannon whistled under his breath. He whispered, but only to himself, 'You are also the most dangerous and powerful lunatic I've ever seen.'

CHAPTER SEVENTEEN

'A BODY IS FOR LIFE; A SOUL IS FOR ETERNITY.'
'What the hell is that?' Joss murmured from his bed. He looked up to Rivers's picture, which seemed to be speaking to him, then concluded that there must be hidden speakers in the ceiling that continued to pump out the decibels.

'AWAKE AND STRIVE AND YOU TOO MAY BE FOUND WORTHY.'
It was still dark outside but the dormitory's strip-lighting rose gently from dim to bright. Joss watched in total fascination as the others sprang from their beds and began to perform stretching exercises in their underwear. Joss pulled the thin cover over his head and rolled over. It was pulled back by the man he had seen lecturing so enthusiastically on his arrival.

'Come on, Joss,' he said determinedly. He sounded Swedish, or Danish perhaps; Joss had always had difficulty telling the two apart when they spoke their perfect English.

'I am Lars, the hut leader. You were too tired to meet last night. The day is young.'

'The day is still a sperm,' he replied sleepily. 'Give me a shout when it reaches puberty: then we can discuss which school to send it to.'

'Up we get,' Lars commanded peeling back the sheet, plucking Joss from his rest and setting him on his feet. Joss almost buckled. The previous day's exertions had his muscles tied in reef knots.

'Stretching will relax the muscles,' Lars said. 'It will get the precious heart pumping.'

Overhead, there was a change of audio personnel and a mellifluous female voice began to count as all the room's inhabitants dropped to their stomachs and began fifty press-ups. Lars eyed him warily; Joss shrugged and dropped to the floor. The first twenty were painful, then his blood pumped and surged, fuelling energy through straining limbs. Annoyingly, Lars was right: he did feel better when the fiftieth exertion subsided.

'Breakfast,' Lars barked. The others dressed hurriedly, conversation absent, faces set in stone; Joss could only shake his head.

Fiona was waiting for him at the simple wooden breakfast table in the refectory. She glowed with rude good health.

'Joss.' She went to hug him; he backed away and sat down.

'It's a little early for me. Mother always said "no hugging before 6 am".'

'Grumpy,' she chided playfully. 'We'll soon have you trilling like a lark: you will wonder why you ever wasted your mornings.'

'Can't wait. What's for breakfast?'

She led him to a table, straining under the weight of freshly squeezed orange juice and grain. The bowls were tiny, almost doll-like.

'This is crazy,' Joss said. 'The calories you people expend is huge. You need carbohydrates; energy food.' He pointed down to his bowl. 'With this stuff and the sugar in the juice, all you'll get is light-headed.'

Joss knew these lessons well from his days with In Extremis: diet was as important as skill and courage when you were hanging by your fingertips to a ledge two inches thick with a two-hundred-foot fall below.

'It makes us more spiritual.'

'It makes you more gullible,' he replied, filling his bowl to the brim. 'Look at this; skimmed milk. Jesus, it's no more than white water.'

He walked back to the table; Fiona sat next to him.

'You are not at your best in the morning,' she cooed and Joss was reminded of the sing-song voice of a Sunday-school teacher.

'How long have you been here?' he asked, spooning the mixture in.

'We have a busy day ahead,' Fiona answered.

'Two days, two months, two years?'

'A full schedule. If you thought you were tired last night, why, you will be sleeping like . . .'

'A happy-clapping camper.'

130

'A baby.'

'How long? Where do you come from? Where are your parents? How old are you? What are your dreams?'

This last question caught her attention.

'To be worthy, to be chosen.' She turned to face him. 'You can be worthy, you can be chosen; you can take the Oath.'

'The what?'

Fiona's eyes darted around the room, but she seemed relieved that nobody appeared to be listening.

'I shouldn't have said anything.'

'Tell me about this Oath.'

'What Oath? I have no idea what you are talking about.'

Abruptly she clambered to her feet.

'You know I have tried very hard to make you like me, I really, really have.' She jabbed a finger, almost in his eye, he flinched. 'But you have to make things difficult, don't you?'

Lars approached the table apparently from nowhere.

'Problem?' He eyed Joss coldly, then smiled at the girl, but the smile did little to unfreeze his features. Joss shrugged and drank his juice.

'He hates me, Lars,' Fiona spat.

'Then we will have to find him another "friend" for the duration of his stay,' Lars said and Joss knew it was a threat.

'I don't need any friends, and as for staying here, I am leaving as soon as I see my father; now where the fuck is Callum?'

Joss felt a muscular hand clamp onto his shoulder. He attempted to move his head but a voice, Trainer's, warned, 'Still!' Joss was powerless, the grip merciless.

'You cannot be allowed to upset the running of this place, Lane. You are here under sufferance because your father wishes it. You are free to leave at any time, but you will not be allowed to see him until you have finished orientation. Are we clear? Do we understand each other?'

Joss nodded. Fiona looked smugly delighted by the occurrence; Lars challenging. He felt the grip loosen slightly.

'You have not been a good son to your father,' Trainer continued, his voice sounding more reasonable now. 'It is not yet too late to put that right.' Joss could see that Trainer's cold aggression of the previous day had been exchanged for open loathing and his reference

131

to Joss's failures as a son was evidence that he now had a grip on Joss's coloured history. He nodded. This was not the moment but he would have his day with Trainer, it was inevitable.

'You'd love to rip my head off, wouldn't you, Joss?'

He was startled by Trainer's apparent prescience.

'But you would try and you would fail. Many have.'

Fiona appeared upset by his words. Trainer pretended to change tack.

'But that is not the way things are here. We are all on the same team.' He let go of Joss's shoulder. 'Now, I came to give you some good news, and look at us!'

'A good breakfast would be welcome,' Joss snarled. 'What good news? Two weeks in the Hebrides in winter living off the land? A Channel swim? I mean, how much good news can a man take without bursting into song?'

Trainer tutted. 'If you make it through the programme today you get to see your father tonight for supper.'

Joss was about to bite back, but this was about him and his father: once he saw Callum, things could be sorted out.

'Deal,' he agreed.

'We don't make deals, only promises,' Trainer replied.

'That is when you are not too busy swearing the oath.' Joss stared directly at Fiona as he spoke. Trainer and Lars followed his gaze. He was darkly pleased to see the colour drain from her face. Trainer nodded once. She was about to speak then he raised his hand to quieten her. Head bowed, she left the refectory.

'You complete orientation; you see your father,' Trainer said thoughtfully.

'Whatever you say, Coach,' but this time the response was deliberate, not the exhausted reaction of the night before, and Trainer knew it.

'Lars will put you through your paces.'

'A pleasure,' Lars replied, smiling thinly.

Joss pushed his bowl away and climbed to his feet.

'Lead the way, ice-man.'

Joss followed behind. Their game had become all too clear, exhaust the body and freeze the mind. But there must be something more; there had to be a point to all this. He could only hope that Callum could provide the answer.

CHAPTER EIGHTEEN

Joss had expected day two of orientation to begin with some trite PJ Rivers-inspired lecture on the body as temple to the soul, but a gruelling five-mile cross-country run with the easy-breathing Lars came first.

Whilst fighting for breath he attempted to get some perspective on this weird place. The inhabitants appeared happy enough in a vacant kind of way; the quarters clean and well kept, the organisation smooth and seamless. They had money, the sumptuous lodge and grounds were clear evidence of that, yet there was a totalitarian numbness about the whole enterprise that caused him disquiet.

On several occasions he felt desperate enough to consider stopping for a rest but he refused to give his grim-faced companion that satisfaction. He struggled up hills and ran disjointedly down slopes, through clear spring streams, scrabbling across the dark grey shale until eventually they completed their circuit. Lars nodded to him as he dry-heaved his stomach and, hands on knees, gulped in clear fresh air.

'Not bad,' Lars commented. 'In a couple of weeks you will be treating that as a gentle warm-up.'

Joss's heart rate began its slow descent. 'No, Lars, my old mate. In a couple of weeks I'll be flat on my back with a hot novel, cool breeze, warm woman and a cold drink.'

Lars appeared darkly amused and almost smugly unconvinced.

'As you like; follow me.'

'Delighted,' Joss replied. 'What now? A quick triathlon before a revitalising mug of lemon tea?'

'No, ECG and CAT scan.'

'My heart and brain are fine.'

'We all have them, every day without fail: even your father.'

Joss shrugged. 'My dad really does need his head examining. Still, if that's the form let's get it done.' If it was a necessary qualification to see Callum then he had no choice in the matter.

Lars led Joss across the courtyard, past the lodge and into a modern, breezeblock, flat-roofed building, which had been white-washed. The large red cross emblazoned next to the front door telegraphed its purpose.

'You mean people actually get sick around here? You surprise me, Lars,' said Joss as they entered the reception area.

'Not very often,' replied Lars, 'but we strive for self-sufficiency, in mind and body: you'll find that we have many skilled and highly committed doctors at the Haven.'

Joss was guided into a sparsely furnished anteroom just off the main waiting area, which was crowded with devotees chattering happily among themselves. He sat down next to a woman, in her mid-fifties he guessed. She had long, wispy grey hair and a deep chestnut weathered face born through years of exposure to the sun. She looked over to him and smiled, her eyes were the colour of frosty blue marble and looked as if they had seen a thousand lifetimes. Next to her sat a shortish man a little older than Joss with broad shoulders, who was absorbed in a book.

'Hello,' Joss said to the woman. 'What's the waiting time like?'

'Not long, young man. You're new, I believe,' she replied.

'Just visiting. Got here yesterday. What about you?'

'Oh, I've been here quite some time. Welcome to our community.'

'Thank you, but I don't plan on staying too long.' Joss glanced around. Lars had left the room and the other guy was still staring at his book intently. 'I'm really not into this cult thing, but hey, one man's poison?' he ventured politely.

'This isn't a cult,' she stated flatly.

'No? What is it then?'

'Exactly what it claims to be: a church, what else?'

'I guess you haven't seen the newspapers then.'

'I have no need, young man: what can newspapers possibly tell me that I should wish to know?'

'The truth, maybe.'

'What is the truth?'

'You tell me,' Joss chanced but wished he hadn't.

'Truth is not a feeling, it is not an idea; the truth is found in the Bible.'

'What's that supposed to mean?'

'It means those who are not chosen, who are not here, the ones who read the contaminated press reports: they have a false understanding of God the father.'

'And the Reverend Rivers has true understanding, I suppose.'

'He most certainly has, as you will discover soon enough.'

'What does everyone do around here?'

'Everyone has a role to play preparing for the glorious day.'

Just at that moment a harsh-looking woman wearing a lab coat appeared from the examination room at the far end of the room and called out the name Thurman. The man with the book rose to his feet and followed her without a word, casting a quick glance at Joss on his way out.

Half an hour later the examinations had been completed. Joss stood, his arms folded over his chest and awaited further instruction.

'To the pool,' Lars ordered.

Once more he lost himself in the mindless repetition of the swim until he collapsed on the side of the pool, legs as untrustworthy as an hour-old colt's. After drying off he was led to a small lecture room with an overhead projector on its tiny table. There was one chair and Lars sat smugly in it.

'Movie time?'

'Instruction,' Lars barked. 'Discipline is directionless without philosophy.'

'I wondered when we would get to the great brainwash. Do you think I'm tired enough now?' Joss asked, leaning his exhausted body against the wall.

'Stand up straight,' he was ordered. Joss raised his eyes to the ceiling, but told himself that playing the game by their rules was the only way he would get to see his father.

'Our founder, Reverend Rivers, made this film in all honesty and humility. Few would possess the singularity of vision to be so forthright.'

Lars depressed a switch and the screen before then flickered into life. Joss watched as an overtly overweight PJ Rivers in a tight business suit sweated uncomfortably under harsh lighting whilst signing a contract of some description. A soft voice with a trailing 's' began to speak. The tone commanded attention and respect.

'Recognise the fat man? Neither do I. Yet he is me, or was me in 1971. Note the sweat, the greying pallor, deep bags and drink-reddened eyes. Me; a sad, weak stranger in a tight suit. The last time I was seen in public before my heart attack. I was pronounced clinically dead but I was brought back to life.'

The presentation moved on to show Rivers wired up to a ventilator clearly gravely ill.

'There was no tunnel of light, no outstretched arms from loved ones who had passed over, just death; stark and cold and forever.' The screen faded to black, then through the darkness the tiniest speck of light began to form.

Gradually the speck grew larger and was accompanied by the whistling chimes of faraway tubular bells. Eventually it formed into the recognisable shape of the universe taken from deep space. The swirling elegance of the cluster moved hypnotically across the screen as Rivers's voiceover continued.

'While I drifted through this cosmic hinterland the good Lord came to me, Brethren: he came with a message. He said unto me that I must return to this earth and become the rock upon which this great institution of ours is founded. I seek no elevated status, Brethren, but accept humbly my role as carpet upon which you can walk to your destiny. I seek only to be of service come the great day when all who have chosen the right path will be saved.

'The turn of the century is upon us: the age of Pisces has come to an end and the age of Aquarius has begun, the new dawn when only the anointed ones will emerge victorious after judgement day. I ask each one of you to prepare for the times ahead, summoning all the passion shown by Jesus Christ our Lord in his first coming. There can be no room for the unclean, for upon his return only the righteous among you will find their place secured in the great temple that is the New World.

'Cast aside all that you have learned before and submit your-self to the new teachings of the Lord, which have been handed down to me.'

The screen then filled with light and the man who now appeared had left his intensive care unit behind and jogged briskly through a leafy park.

'I was spared for a reason. I was given a mandate from the good Lord to save humanity from itself and its worst excesses and weaknesses.'

The jogger was then transformed into a younger, leaner, fitter version who rowed a single scull boat up to the camera, climbed nimbly out and turned toward its lens.

'All you need is the right path; the Millennium Church *is* that path.'

He began to walk away, then reached a hand behind him.

'Come, walk with me.'

From off camera a young girl ran and took his hand, followed by others, who formed a human chain walking resolutely toward a low autumn sun. A deeply reverential voice spoke over the moving tableau.

'The Reverend Rivers is with you; go in peace.' Then the screen faded to black and Lars switched the light back on.

'Very slick,' Joss whispered, genuinely impressed.

'It is the truth; you saw the evidence,' Lars whispered, endlessly awed by the film's contents.

'How long have you been here, Lars?'

'Five years,' he replied dreamily, defences weakened momen-tarily by the cautionary movie short.

'What was your problem?' Joss pushed.

'Killed a man in a fight over money. My family did not want to know; the Church did.'

I bet they did, thought Joss with an involuntary shudder.

'Any chance of some popcorn and a hot dog?'

Lars granted him a stare of undiminished contempt.

'You are beyond his help,' he spat.

'I never said I needed help.'

'That is not your decision. Come with me. The gentle exercise has not yet curbed your acid tongue.'

Joss was led through the throng of busy disciples to the gym where he was forced through another hour of rigorous circuit training. Eventually he was allowed to enter the refectory to consume a bowl of wheatgerm cereal and more over-sweetened juice at an isolated table. He noticed Fiona scowling at him as she ate bread and drank water. Clearly his remark about the 'Oath' had found a sensitive target and she was suffering accordingly. Whatever the oath was, it was only for the faithful to know. Joss mused over the footage he had seen earlier. The film had a shuddering strength to it. Joss could now begin to understand how mesmeric Rivers could be. In person, he imagined, the impression would be magnified accordingly. The Reverend claimed to have experienced an epiphany – a moment of complete spiritual truth, when all the trappings of mundanity had been washed away by a tide of faith – or was it merely the ravings of an oxygen-starved brain? Whatever the explanation, the Church followers appeared genuinely convinced by him. Joss wondered whether the jury were sharing the same enlightenment at PJ Rivers's trial.

CHAPTER NINETEEN

R ose had asked to be seated on the resumption of her evidence and, reluctantly, Withnail had concurred. The press box was still brimfull and, whilst a court order prevented those journalists present from naming Rose, nothing could stop them outlining the allegations against the defendants. They scribbled their shorthand notes of when, where and how Rivers and others had continually abused the girl, as Rose, her voice now a monotone, detailed the occurrences.

After some little time, Mason noticed that the jury's attention was wandering. It never ceased to amaze him how quickly human beings could become de-sensitised to the unthinkable.

'Were these acts ever filmed?' Mason asked, and immediately the jury's attention was refreshed.

'Never with Rivers,' Rose replied. No, Mason thought, he's far too clever to have himself caught on video tape.

'But with others, yes, lots of times.'

'Where?' Mason asked.

'Different places. He had a camera crew – "God's film-makers" he called them – they knew what they were doing, made all kinds of films about the Church, but I think they enjoyed this best.'

'I have no doubt about that, Miss Moody, and were you filmed having intercourse with men?'

'Not just men, sir,' Rose replied, before her chin began to quiver. Mason glanced around to where Geoff Moody sat with his miserable head in his hands.

'I think it is time we adjourned for lunch,' the judge declared and walked heavily from the bench. Greta ran across to Rose and hugged her tightly.

'You were brilliant,' she whispered.

'It's not over yet,' Mason warned her, never more aware of the truth of his words.

It was 2pm and time for an hour's reading in the simple trestle-tabled library. Lars had provided Joss with a clutch of information on the Millennium Church with the words, 'Only those willing to look will be granted true vision.'

Joss nodded thoughtfully, and replied, 'I always keep my eyes open.'

'You wear the blinkers of the old world: look inside yourself for the new order of the soul.'

Let it ride, his chastening voice suggested. *Learn, think, then respond.*

Joss smiled as warmly as he could and Lars, though obviously unconvinced, left him to his religious education.

Several followers were deep in concentration, hunched over religious books. Occasionally they nodded their heads in agreement with the words they read, their faces glowing with the joy of enlightenment. Once more, Joss was impressed by the mind-grip this place held over its inhabitants. He looked down to his own studies: he'd had no idea that Rivers was such a prolific writer of books and pamphlets, which each reinforced the simple yet powerful message of the film: the end is in sight. But that was only the start: the documents codified into a quasi-religion built on self-sacrifice, blind obedience and personal poverty. That would explain his father's gift to the Church. Joss was no amateur theologian, but it was clear that the Church had redefined Christian doctrine and now operated on pure guilt with mindless subservience.

Joss was aching and tired. His arms and legs had never felt so drained of energy. His back was stiff and his shoulders cramped by the demands of the overpowering regime. Lars returned and led him to a sauna that smelled strongly of eucalyptus where, totally naked, he sat, too tired to feel uncomfortable amongst the other chattering devotees. Yet, strangely, he felt at peace with them, as if their shared punishing experience formed an unusual, unspoken bond. It was not long before he fell into a warm, deep sleep.

CHAPTER TWENTY

Mason dragged Rose through the rest of her evidence dealing with her recovery and current condition, aware that she was becoming ever more anxious. The time was fast approaching when she would have to face the defence lawyers. He had hoped to close the examination-in-chief just before 4.30 pm – just right to give her a rest overnight – but it was now just after three.

Thynne QC appeared slyly confident as, at the judge's gruff invitation, he clambered to his expensively shod feet. Rose had her chin tucked down into her neck and, despite Mason's calming attempts at encouragement, was trembling. Mason tried to catch her eye for one last nod toward courage but she seemed fascinated by the rail of the witness box. The jury were still; all twelve pairs of eyes locked on to the girl. The press box waited, pens poised for the onslaught to begin, the public gallery crammed once more.

Thynne slowly turned the pages of the lever arch file on the lecturn before him.

'I said "yes", Mr Thynne,' the judge remarked, his head already propped on the palm of his hand, but Mason knew that Thynne was just exerting more pressure and would ignore the rebuke. He raised one hand to silence the judge and leant forward to read his notes again, looking every bit as if he were enjoying the moment.

'Miss Moody,' he began. 'When you first met representatives of the Millennium Church in your home town were you frightened of them?'

'No,' she whispered.

'Please speak up, your evidence is being recorded,' Thynne admonished, his voice calm and reasonable.

'No.'

'That's better. They showed you great kindness, did they not? Listening to your problems and drying your tears?'

'Yes, *they* were all right,' she replied unsteadily.

'And it was an argument with your father that sadly, I believe, led to the upset and distressed condition in which you were found?'

Mason watched the jury's eyes flicker behind him to where Geoff Moody sat, then back to his daughter.

'Yes, but it wasn't really anything,' she muttered, 'now that I look back.'

'It was enough to make you decide to leave home at the time, was it not?'

'They told me we just needed some space, some time apart to understand each other better.'

Thynne nodded in understanding. 'But they were complete strangers. You must have been desperate to place yourself in their hands.'

Mason admired the build-up; the line of questioning all stemmed from the abuse statement she had sworn against her father.

'They seemed to understand me,' Rose answered.

'In a way your father did not?'

'No, well yes; it felt like it at the time.'

'Let us be quite clear about this: you went along of your own free will?'

'They were very clever,' Rose snapped, her head lifted up for the first time.

'Or to put it another way, they were very caring,' Thynne said smoothly, 'wouldn't you agree?'

Rose looked down once more, shaking her head. Thynne seized the advantage.

'Come along, now. Is it not the case that they cared for you: otherwise you would never have gone along with them. You were not abducted, were you?'

'No, not what you would call kidnapped. It was cleverer than that . . .' She grappled to find the words.

'You were not drugged or struck, tied up or threatened in any way?' Thynne pressed harder.

Rose dropped her head into her hands and cried out, 'No, it wasn't like that.'

'In direct contrast to how your father kidnapped you from the Haven?' Thynne drove on mercilessly.

'He had to,' she blurted. 'They had me, they wouldn't let me go.'

'But very, very different, you will agree?' His voice was calm once more.

'I suppose so,' muttered the beleaguered voice of Rose Moody, her shoulders quivering.

'And at the time he abducted you . . .'

'Rescued, my Lord,' Mason tried to interject, but was waved down by Withnail.

'Thank you, my Lord.' Thynne opened the document before him. 'You fought him off, even clawed his face with your fingernails, didn't you? Screaming "leave me alone, you filthy pervert",' he said, referring to a statement he now held in his hand. 'Now what made you do that?'

'They convinced me that he had been abusing me,' she shouted, her eyes wide and staring.

'Did what?' Thynne asked, feigning shock. 'Some complete strangers told you your father had been committing incest with you and you simply went along with it?'

Rose shook her head.

'I know it sounds stupid, but they had me believing everything they said.'

'No, Miss Moody, you told them what he had done to you, they took you away to safety, believing your distress was genuine,' Thynne suggested. He turned to Withnail. 'My Lord, live evidence will be called in due course to substantiate this matter.' The judge nodded.

Thynne returned eagerly to his task.

'You even asked them to examine you as you feared he might have infected you with herpes.'

Mason heard a noise from behind him and turned quickly. He locked eyes with Rose's father and shook his head sternly. Moody was blue with rage.

'My dad,' Rose said, her chin shaking, 'my dad has never touched me or hurt me in his life.'

'So you say.' Thynne snapped his fingers and a document was instantaneously produced from his junior counsel.

143

'Yet another statement that you signed before your abduction affirms otherwise. Please refresh your memory.' Thynne handed the paper to an usher, who placed it before Rose. She refused to look at it.

'Identify the document,' the judge snapped. Rose took it in her shaking hand.

'I know what it says,' she whispered. 'But it's not true, they made me sign it.'

'In it you detail exactly when and how the abuse began, do you not?' Thynne continued. 'The bathtime incidents, his climbing into bed with you, and worse; indecency, gross indecency, oral sex, leading on to intercourse.'

'Please,' she muttered. 'Please, it wasn't true, he never . . .' She turned to where Moody sat in quiet desperation. 'Dad, I'm sorry, I didn't know what I was doing.'

'This is distressing for us all, Miss Moody, particularly for Mr Rivers,' Thynne said. Mason did not have to turn around to envisage the defendant appearing piously concerned for the girl, who was now sobbing freely. But Thynne went on regardless.

'The allegations you have made are most serious, though I have no doubt you appreciate that. Now, the statement you claim the Church forced you to sign is very detailed. It deals with your home life, friends and boyfriends, school and recreation; only you could know all those details, Miss Moody.'

'They asked me, all the time, about things like that, I was so tired.'

'So you did not merely sign the statement; you also helped to prepare it?' Thynne asked triumphantly and waited for an answer. Mason was powerless. The line of cross-examination was ruthless but within the rules. Rose started to weep hysterically.

'I want to go home. Let me go home,' she shouted.

'We all want to go home, including Mr Rivers,' Thynne replied acidly. 'His name and Church have been sullied relentlessly in the public eye, because of you and these lying allegations.'

'They are not lies,' Rose screamed.

'Which?' Thynne asked. 'Which are not lies? Those allegations in your statement or those in your evidence? They cannot both be right, or have you lost the ability to tell the difference any longer?'

'My Lord,' Mason said, climbing to his feet, 'This is monstrous. A witness should not have to suffer this indignity at my learned friend's hands.'

Withnail appeared unmoved.

'Someone has abused this child, it is inhuman to allow this onslaught to continue.'

'Yet the allegations are grave indeed, Mr Mason. Reverend Rivers is a man of the cloth and therefore in a position of trust. I must allow the defence every latitude to put their case.'

'Every latitude?' Mason snapped.

'Within reason, of course. I shall adjourn this case until the witness has pulled herself together, but I do not have all day.'

With a curt nod to the jury he walked slowly from the bench. Mark Mason felt a hand on his shoulder.

'That was bad, that was,' Geoff Moody said. 'You took your time stopping it.'

He turned around quickly. 'The defence are entitled to cross-examine the witness: it's ugly but it is the law.'

'Then the law is a bastard,' Moody spat as he walked toward his daughter under the suspicious eyes of the jury.

CHAPTER TWENTY-ONE

H arrison Trainer still had his eyes closed in deep meditation as Joss woke in the hot dreamy atmosphere of the sauna. It was deserted now save for the squat frame of Trainer, his legs folded beneath him like human origami. Suddenly Trainer's face exploded into life and Joss noted that behind those hard eyes lay a barely hidden self-satisfied smile.

'I suppose you think that I'm just going to roll over and take all this shit,' Joss said while urging himself into a more comfortable position against the slatted wooden benches.

'Quite the contrary,' replied Trainer. 'I anticipated that you would be a troublesome element in our community: let's just say that I have a sixth sense about these things.'

'Is that right? I guess I didn't impress Monica then,' Joss spat.

Trainer's brow furrowed in his attempt to understand Joss's reference.

Joss nodded; whoever it was who had set up the honey-trap with the pliant Monica, it was not with the knowledge of his steaming companion.

'Has your God granted you second sight?' he asked, moving the focus away from the mysterious girl.

'You know so little,' Trainer replied in a world-weary whisper.

'And I suppose you know so much, is that it?'

'Something like that.'

'You're a freak, Trainer, you and all your people: cooped up in this godforsaken hole, pretending to care but contributing nothing.'

'Rather like yourself then, or so I gather,' Trainer snarled cynically. A superior sort of smile broke across his features as he looked directly at Joss. It was the sort of smile where the recipient is only afforded the briefest glimpse of sharp little teeth.

147

'Spare me the compliments, why don't you. I know where I've been but now I'm back,' Joss snapped, 'and I learnt along the way that whackos like you should carry a government health warning. This whole set-up is one big cancer cell: once it's got you there's no escape.'

'I'm afraid you'll find that's a fairly unusual attitude around here, Joss, or hadn't you noticed? These people are here because they want to be here, not because it's some kind of circus for the disaffected. We are simply here to help people develop themselves.'

'Into what?'

'Into a state of worthiness.' Trainer rose from his seat and carefully poured water over the simmering white coals in the corner of the sauna. Great clouds of steam temporarily erased him from view.

'For what?' Joss pushed through the mist, trying to harangue Trainer into a sweat for, no matter the heat, just like a desert lizard his skin was biscuit dry.

'For the future.'

'What about the present?'

'The present is but a product of the past.'

'Stop talking riddles, Trainer.'

'If you knew what the enlightened know, then all things would make sense.'

'I like things the way they are, the way they were, and I don't want to be enlightened by you or anyone else. I just want to get my father out of this place and back to reality where at least he can get on with his life.'

'Maybe your father doesn't want to go anywhere. Have you thought about that? What kind of life can you provide for him out there anyway? Your track record hardly smacks of stability, now, does it?' Trainer lingered over the word smack in a thinly disguised reference to Joss's recent past. 'No, I think you'll find that your father is devoted just like the rest of us to the Reverend Rivers.'

'I'll believe it when I see it,' Joss shot back defensively, but for the first time he was beginning to feel the awakening of doubt. 'What about you, Trainer?'

'What about me?'

'What exactly do you do around here?'

'I look after things.'

'You're so forthcoming. That's unusual for a Yank,' Joss snorted. 'Seriously, I mean, you're an educated man, I can tell that, so how come you fell for all this rubbish about enlightenment? Where's your own family?'

'Back in the US,' he replied.

'Whereabouts? It's a big place.'

'East Coast, where I started out, the grandson of Jewish immigrants from eastern Europe.'

'Don't tell me, in the rag trade,' Joss quipped. 'Spoiled rich kid finds God.'

'No, I had a lower-middle-class upbringing in the burbs on Long Island. Sure, I did well at school: we all did well at school in my neighbourhood; we were made to do well. Strange thing is, even way back then I always felt it wasn't enough.'

'What you mean? Education?'

'Formal education, yes. When I went on to Rochester I kind of got interested in alternative thinking, history of ideas, mysticism, that sort of thing.'

'I get the picture: we used to call your sort the meaningful ones,' Joss laughed.

'I was seeking something else,' Trainer went on, ignoring the slight. 'I graduated with honours in comparative literature and came to Europe on a travel scholarship seeking answers. All I got was lonely: you know the feeling, Joss.' Trainer's eyes bored into him and Joss could feel himself drifting back to his own soulless moments.

'I know the feeling,' he replied uneasily.

'I came to a point in my life when everything seemed to be poised at the verge of total failure, but then I started studying Beckett, which had a deep influence over me. I was directionless and consumed with the idea of an apocalyptic future, so how I ended up at Berkeley in the late sixties will always be a mystery to me. Anyway, a bit like you, I was studying for a masters and somehow slipped into the drug culture. It changed my whole outlook to a sort of confused but radical Utopian philosophy.'

'I had some highs like that but I never actually really trusted them. It must have been good shit you were on,' Joss giggled, feeling so tired he didn't care that he was strangely relaxing for the first time in Trainer's company.

'All the communes at that time had good shit – I should know, I lived on plenty – but they were all disappointments to me. I could never find people to relate to.'

'Did you go to Vietnam?' Joss enquired, figuring Trainer must have been in his late teens around then.

'No, I skipped the draft and went to mine jade with a friend of a friend in Mendocino County. I was hanging with all kinds of losers and the business lasted only two months anyway. I couldn't get a handle on my life, I was the unemployed black sheep. I even changed my name to avoid the authorities and started drifting. Most of the time I was looking for people to buy land with and start a community but I could never find the right people.'

'Let me guess: that was, until you met Rivers.'

'In the spring of 1972. He opened my eyes.'

'Sounds as if someone needed to.'

'You may mock, but I found the very synthesis I was looking for personified in PJ Rivers. At once he was a spiritual teacher and a down-to-earth human being. To me he represents the Nietzchean "Overman": he builds that bridge of transition between the human animal and the human being. He is sacrificing himself for the cause of human overcoming on a myriad of levels.'

'Superman, overman, spaceman, postman: it's all the same to me.'

'But you should experience him for yourself before you judge him, just as your father has done: he is a psychic technician, a person with an extraordinary imaginative mind power who uses it for good.'

'For whose good, though?' Joss challenged.

'The anointed ones, Joss: one hundred and forty-four thousand of them only will survive the day of judgement; the good book has told us.'

'And I suppose everyone here has already got their tickets booked,' Joss interjected bitterly.

'As we speak, arrangements are in hand for a day of devotion.'

Joss tutted. 'What, like old men with sandwich boards in Oxford Street on a Saturday afternoon?'

Trainer's gaze seemed to pierce far beyond the environs of the sauna.

'Just for once expand that imagination of yours without narcotics, Joss. Open your third eye and see them flow from every continent in the world: almost one hundred and fifty thousand of the most devout all homing in on Hyde Park to worship, all of them hand-picked for their pious belief by the Reverend.'

'Sounds like a bitch to organise,' Joss commented drily.

'Nothing is beyond the power of the Lord, so no one is guaranteed a place in the New World. All that we can hope to do is to serve, to be, to grow and to learn the riddle of our own insignificance. We have been chosen to help build a future in the shadow of the apocalypse. You and the rest are simply in denial.'

'Wrong.' Joss slammed his hand down on the bench beside him angrily, but he was already drifting into sleep again. 'I don't want to hear any more of this. You only think you have been chosen; you have no proof that your way is the right way,' he slurred.

'We have our faith and that is worth more than anything. You see now I look back on the past as if to another world, a dead and dying world. I could have achieved success in that world but I was unable to fit in, and look where it left me: just like you, a disillusioned junkie. There was no help and support from the world that created me, that's why I am eternally grateful to the man who saved me.'

'I want to see my father, do you hear me, Trainer? I want to see . . .' Joss trailed off and didn't hear Trainer promising faithfully that he would. Soon.

CHAPTER TWENTY-TWO

Geoff had sat slumped outside the court unwilling to talk to Mark Mason, Charmers or Greta. Mason knew the reaction well. A thousand grieving families had run the 'if only' guilt trip on him before, but they didn't mean it; it was just a symptom of their desperation and impotence in the face of the system.

Whilst Mason had been sitting in the robing room, flicking through a newspaper, Rory Fannon had approached for a brief word of commiseration, but Mason had waved him away with the broadsheet; there was no going back now.

In court, Rose appeared drained. Thynne had sucked out what little life she had. Blue veins stood starkly from her neck against the pallor of her skin. The jury appeared sympathetic to the undoubted truth that she had been abused, but they now had two potential sex offenders to choose from. One had the protection of the burden and standard of proof lying with the prosecution, the other the fetid smell of no smoke without a flame. It was ironic to Mason. For so long, in so many cases, he had battered the jury with those two legal rules and now he was frustrated by the very fairness he had advocated.

The court was ordered to stand, and Withnail made his appearance. After he had sat, and folded his hands inside the ermine-fringed wrists, he nodded for Thynne to continue.

'My Lord, my learned friend Mr Fannon will continue the cross-examination of the witness,' Thynne began. Withnail raised an eyebrow. 'He will cover fresh ground with Miss Moody; there will be no repetition of previous questions.'

'Unusual,' Withnail commented.

'But not unheard of,' Thynne concluded.

The judge turned, obviously puzzled by the turn of events,

toward Mason. 'What do the prosecution say about this?' Mason hesitated. Clearly the defence team had considered that Thynne's harsh treatment of Rose might alienate the jury if it went too far, and they were seeking to conduct a more sympathetic line of questioning of her. If he objected then he would be subjecting Rose to more vitriol; if he didn't, Fannon's lilting voice would melt any anger the jury felt toward the defence approach. He was damned if he didn't and damned if he did. He sighed.

'Only if this is the last time the hired staff is changed mid-witness,' he stipulated.

His contemptuous description of the high-powered advocates raised a nervous titter from the jury members, a wry smile from Fannon and a cold smirk from Thynne.

'That seems only right and proper to me, Mr Thynne,' Withnail pronounced.

It was Thynne's turn to hesitate, but he was renowned for his mental agility. He quickly pulled himself together and answered, 'My Lord, we are all here to ensure only the right and proper treatment of both the defendant and this poor abused young woman.'

'Neat,' thought Mason, appreciating that Thynne was already laying the foundation for Fannon's empathetic cross-examination. Withnail nodded for the new questioner to begin.

'Now Rose,' Fannon began, in a voice deep as the sea but soft as cotton-blossom. 'May I call you Rose?' She nodded, Fannon smiled. 'Thank you for that. Now, Rose, we all know you have been through a lot, more than any man of strong disposition, let alone a young girl, should ever have to suffer.'

Rose seemed to relax her shoulders a little, and began to raise her head toward him.

'And it's cost you dear, hasn't it?' Rose looked perplexed. 'Let me be a little clearer, Rose, and I don't want to embarrass you in any way, but you've not been yourself have you?' he whispered, dripping sympathy with every syllable.

'I suppose not,' she replied.

'You have tried to harm yourself on many occasions, haven't you?'

She began to nod, then remembered the presence of the court tape.

'Yes, when things got too much,' she stammered.

'On at least seven occasions, you've taken tablets, and cut your wrists, haven't you Rose?'

Mason could see fat, silvery tears dripping down the girl's gaunt face. Some members of the jury dropped their heads in their embarrassment for her.

'You poor child,' Fannon continued. 'Could you just pull back your sleeve for us, Rose?'

Obedient as a beaten dog, she dumbly did as she was asked. The white vertical scarring ran like pale rail tracks across her arm; the jury seemed to shake its collective head.

'Thank you, Rose, you're being very brave. Can you help me with this?' Fannon asked, dropping his voice to a whisper. She nodded once more, grateful for his unexpected kindness.

'None of those injuries happened when you were with the Church, did they?'

'No,' she answered flatly.

'And none of your attempts at overdose occurred during that time, did they?' She repeated her denial.

'They took place when you were back with your father?'

'Yes.'

Fannon, wily and seasoned, left that matter there: the accusation remained suspended, unsaid, between the jury and Geoff Moody.

'Things were not easy on your return home, were they, Rose? You and your father argued constantly?'

'Sometimes,' she conceded.

'Didn't you want to hurt him?'

'Sometimes.'

'You stole some things from him, didn't you, Rose? A cashpoint card and over a thousand pounds?'

'I was mixed up,' she replied defensively.

'You were angry, Rose, you wanted to strike out at him. Why?'

'It was his fault, it never would have happened if . . .'

'But it did happen, didn't it, Rose? And then you turned your anger on the people who had helped you.'

'Of course,' she replied, 'but I had every reason to.'

Fannon paused. 'But you chose your father first. You have never met Mr Rivers in your life, have you?'

155

The girl shook her head, as if she had not heard the question correctly.

'But you told the people in the church that you loved him, didn't you?'

'My Lord, with respect,' Mason objected, 'that is two questions, not one: which would my learned friend like the witness to answer first?'

The judge nodded.

'Well have you and did you?' he snapped. It had given Rose time to think as Mason had intended.

'I met him when he raped me, then after that when he did it again and again, and yes,' she paused and dropped her voice to a whisper, 'I did tell the others I loved him.'

'Unrequited love for a stranger you had never met?'

'No, no, no,' she chattered, 'they make you love him: it's how they do it; how they get away with it . . .'

'But Rose,' Fannon continued, 'poor Rose, you are a sick girl, one who can't distinguish the difference between fantasy and reality.'

Fannon shook his head sadly, almost appearing to blink back a tear, turned slightly toward the jury, nodded to them and resumed his seat with miserable dignity.

Mason exhaled. He had chosen wrongly and should have insisted that Thynne continue the cross-examination. He performed a perfunctory re-examination of Rose's evidence to stress the fact that she still insisted that she was telling the truth, but he had little doubt, when he resumed his own seat, that they were not even halfway through the fight and yet were way behind on points.

CHAPTER TWENTY-THREE

Joss woke with a start and tried to focus on the ceiling. He was back in his room and was lying fully dressed on the bed, but how he'd got there was another mystery to him. The intoxicating aroma of the sauna lingered in his hair and his head was still buzzing. It took him a few moments to realise that Trainer was sitting beside him watching quietly.

'It's time, Joss.'

'You mean you aren't going to give me any more crap? I don't believe you,' Joss replied while raising himself to his elbows.

'Like I said, it's time.' Trainer rose from the chair silently and gestured for Joss to follow him.

'But I'm not brainwashed yet,' he muttered. Trainer stopped and turned, then placed a pointing finger over Joss's chest.

'It's your soul we want to change, not your will.'

'Has my dad's soul been given Royal approval, then?' he asked, and for once Rivers's glib acolyte seemed unsure of his answer. He doesn't trust Callum, Joss thought, and wondered if the suspicion was reciprocal.

As they walked along a corridor linking the accommodation blocks to the lodge, Joss began to lose all those well-rehearsed lines he had vowed to say to his father. One by one, all notions that he'd harboured during the seemingly endless months of rehab that this moment would be a redefining event in his new life seemed to desert him. He felt oddly detached and very much alone. What would he find in place of the father he used to know? Joss had been submerged in the spiritual machine for a few scant days, yet he could feel its insistent undertow. Callum had walked hand in hand with them for months and Joss feared for him. He couldn't afford to lose anyone else from his life.

157

Suddenly he was standing in the hall of the lodge with its magnificent balustrade and flickering candlelight. Trainer turned abruptly and opened a heavy door to his right. Joss followed him into the room beyond, and by the leaded window noticed a figure slightly obscured by the wings of the red leather armchair in which he sat. Joss moved quietly towards him as Trainer pulled the door closed behind him and left them alone.

It looked like his father but it wasn't; not the dour, stentorian patriarch who had shaken his head silently at Joss's sporting excesses. It was his face all right, that was if you were to wipe a decade of brow-furrowing high finance from his features. It was his body, if you were to flatten his stomach and erase the vestigial stoop from his broad shoulders. But these things were physical; it was something more and less that troubled his son.

'Jossie,' he whispered. 'Jossie.' Then he rose and embraced Joss tightly.

Joss was bewildered. His father had not used that name since he was a small boy, but he felt one of his father's hands press something into the back pocket of his jeans.

'It's good to see you, Dad,' Joss stammered; the closest contact they had ever managed in the past was a manly handshake at Christmas.

'You have changed,' his father said, pulling back to view his son carefully.

'You too,' Joss answered, looking deep into Callum's eyes. They were the same colour he remembered, timber wolf grey, but lacked the fierce spark of incisiveness that had marked Callum out as a 'player' in the financial world. Callum now held Joss by the shoulders.

'You look more like her than ever,' Callum said sadly.

Joss nodded dumbly. This emotional honesty was too swift, too early, their familiar, family protocols uncomfortably replaced by unfettered truth.

'How are things with you, Dad?' He continued to stare. 'You look, well, younger, have they been feeding you ground rhino horn for breakfast?'

Callum moved slightly away and appeared troubled. His eyes flicked from side to side in warning; they were being watched. Joss frowned; what was this bullshit? He shrugged, unclear as to whether his father was being paranoid or petrified for good reason.

'This is no time for flippancy,' Callum whispered, and for a moment his old dad was back, then suddenly his face fixed into a forced game-show host smile. 'What kind of a host am I?' he grinned, offering Joss a drink. Joss took it and sipped carefully; grape juice.

'Unfermented wine nouveau,' Joss said cheerfully. 'You've changed your tastes: Chateau Neuf du Pape used to be your favourite.'

Callum smiled.

'A lot has changed.'

'I can see that,' Joss answered, and not for the better, he thought. His father indicated with a gentle sweep of his hand that they should sit at the simply-laid table, adorned with a fresh bunch of wild heather as its centrepiece. Before them a cold vegetable terrine with fresh chives offered some small respite from the inadequacy of Joss's previous diet. He took up his knife and fork.

'Why wouldn't they let me see you until now?' he asked.

'It's the same for everyone.'

'Maybe so, but what's the logic behind "orientation"?'

Callum chewed thoughtfully.

'In my old life, if I head-hunted an executive from another firm, he would be sent on a correction course to wipe away the habits formed at his old employers; it's a similar idea.'

'Brainwashing?'

'Brain-management,' Callum replied. 'Not quite so sinister; just a way of establishing new brain patterns.'

'Sounds like fascism to me,' Joss remarked, attempting to connect with the flash of his old father he had seen earlier.

'I can tell you must be off that filth now, but look at the methods used to cure you. Your brain told your body that you needed the drugs until your brain was changed; I hardly believe that you would call re-hab fascism.'

'There were times.'

'Denial,' his father stated.

'That's the second time I've heard that expression in as many

159

hours,' Joss said, thinking back to his conversation with Trainer. His father continued, between mouthfuls of food.

'You have met Harrison, I gather?'

'Once met . . .'

'A remarkable man.'

'You don't call him Coach then?'

'We go back a very long way.'

'Did you know I was at the clinic? Did you know where I was all that time?' Joss asked innocently. His father's eyes widened.

'I don't know what you're talking about, Joss,' Callum said flatly, his concentration now focused on the Spartan table-top.

Joss breathed out slowly.

Great question, Joss!

Next one might just give him a thrombosis.

Evidently, the clinic was not a topic Callum wanted to explore; he seemed genuinely hostile to the mention of it. But Joss still wanted some answers.

'You never phoned, never wrote? In all that time?'

Callum shook his head.

'I didn't know where you were. Besides, listen to you, Joss, you sound like your mother and I did when you went away to university.'

'But you never answered my letters.' Joss was becoming angry. 'I needed you!'

'And now I am here, and we can be together again. The past is negative power; the future is ours, but only if we can believe in the same vision.'

Joss threw down his fork.

'That is mumbo-jumbo psycho-drivel shite.'

His father looked genuinely distressed by the outburst. He placed his hands against his temples so that his eyes were shielded from all but Joss; they were wide once more in warning.

'Was I really ever so cheap and banal that you dare not take my word now?' He nodded sadly. 'I suppose I was; I am still coming to terms with that.'

'Let's go away, Dad,' Joss said, his voice brimming with enthusiasm. 'Just you and me. We never did when I was young. You were either too busy, or I didn't want to. A Greek island perhaps? We can get to know each other again.'

What he really meant was: for the first time.

'I rarely leave this place; it's my home now. I'll tell you what, Joss. I have to travel to the mainland tomorrow on Church business. When I return we will talk again.'

'But you are not saying no?' Joss pressed. His father appeared confused; but just then the outside door opened and Trainer entered.

'Sorry about this, Callum: something important has come up.' He failed to acknowledge Joss's presence. 'You are needed in the business room now!'

Callum almost jumped to attention.

'Can't this wait?' Joss pleaded, aware that Trainer's entrance had interrupted at a crucial moment.

Trainer indicated towards the door.

'You know the way back,' he said coldly. Joss put out his hand to his father who looked at it vacantly then shook it without enthusiasm: what happened to the barnstorming hug of half an hour ago? thought Joss. Callum did not glance at him as he left, but Joss patted the back of his pocket where the slim piece of paper his father had secreted remained. Obviously, his dad was terrified and was in real fear of Trainer. Joss felt protective towards him; it would seem that the son had become the father and the father the son. He vowed to himself that when they met again things would be very different.

Trainer ordered Callum Lane to the chapel for additional spiritual guidance. He had not liked what he had seen on the video screen in the security office. The meeting between the Lanes contained a sub-text that he had yet to fathom. There was nothing Lane senior had said that he could pinpoint as subversive, yet he was sure there had been a hidden conversation within the spoken one. Lane junior had appeared genuinely aggrieved by the injustices of the past, but was then placated far too easily.

Trainer re-ran the covertly recorded transmission of the meeting frame by frame. Then, he isolated each part of the conversation and attempted to analyse the points of conflict. By the end of his first full, concentrated dissection of the video he was more convinced than ever that something was wrong, but as yet he could only watch and wait for something more tangible to emerge. The clues would have to be teased out. The Reverend would not move against Callum Lane unless there was hard evidence to back it up.

Once more, Trainer considered putting through a call to his leader, but decided instead to hold the fort without superior orders. Lane senior was leaving for the mainland in the morning, and with him would be two of Trainer's men; he had yet to decide whether Joss Lane would form the last part of the quartet. Father and son needed more rope: perhaps that would give them the opportunity to garrotte themselves. Trainer hoped so. Callum had been twitchy ever since he learned of the internal audit commanded by Rivers.

As he watched the still of the bear hug between father and son, something caught his eye. Trainer was about to use the zoom facility on the video equipment, when a telephone call interrupted him. It was one of his more trusted 'sleeper' members, who worked in the media. After the phone call, all thoughts of further investigation of the video footage were lost: they had a traitor in their midst at the Haven and there could be but one penalty for treason.

Joss had followed the men back out into the hall and decided to take a walk in an effort to clear the murkiness that had crept into his head. He emerged into the courtyard to find that night had fallen swiftly over the compound. A three-quarter moon stared wanly down through the chill breeze that was cut with the salt of the sea, but the light it provided was insufficient to read his father's secret note. He was about to head down to the cliffs where the security lights would provide sufficient illumination, when he noticed that there was light streaming from the main community centre at the far end. He was tired by his exertions but his feelings were running adrenaline high: whatever was in the note was vitally important to Callum.

You have to, Joss.

Don't you?

A light frost crunched under his feet as he tramped toward the seat of light. In the distance he could see the sentry box also illuminated and obviously manned twenty-four hours a day. A swell of noise rose from the community centre as he approached. Joss didn't want to make any kind of grand entrance and waited until a further roar leapt from the crowd before gently pushing open the door and sliding inside.

There must have been at least three hundred people inside; their backs turned toward him as he hugged the relative shadow of the back wall. On the dais a young man was tied into a rowing machine. He was sweating profusely as he sculled furiously away, but there was something strange: he was smoking a cigarette as he did so. The curls of smoke pumped from his lungs around his head and toward Lars who held a packet of Benson and Hedges and a lighter. When one cigarette was smoked down to the butt, it was immediately replaced with one more by the triumphant Lars.

'Another and another. He has brought this poison here, adulterating the health of our children,' he shouted: the young man's face was green. 'He must learn that it is not his individual choice that matters but the will of the Church.'

Joss felt ill himself, but knew it was not his place to intervene.

'The body is sacred,' Lars continued. 'He was caught with these tools of self-destruction,' he said, raising the depleted packet high. 'His body must renounce them.'

Joss wanted to do something, but what? He was one, they were a fanatical three hundred. If he showed himself now, showed what he thought of all this, how could he help his father? Sick at heart, he watched the nauseating spectacle conclude when the rower vomited then passed out.

Joss decided to leave before the populace turned in for the night, the evening's entertainment over. He glanced to his left and, skulking in the shadows, he saw a dark-haired, stocky-looking man, whose expression mirrored the look of revulsion on Joss's own face. Just then, he realised it was the one called Thurman, whom he'd seen earlier in the medical block. Ignoring him, Joss made for the toilets and locked himself inside a cubicle. He removed the piece of paper from his pocket, flattened it out and began to read.

My dear Joss.

If you are reading this now it means that we got away with

its transference, but how long we have is another matter. I am helpless here and have prayed for the day when you would come. Help me, Joss. They have twisted my mind until things are clouded most of the time. It is only moments like this when I can think clearly. You must come to the mainland with me; you must get me away from them. We must go to Paris: your Dr Kristina Klammer is there for a symposium. She helped you so she can help me. Please, please help me to escape this misery, this awful sham. The things they have done, that I have seen! Destroy this message or we will both die.

Your father, Callum Lane.

Joss did as his father asked and watched the scraps of paper whip around the swirl of the toilet's flush then disappear.

He left the centre with only one thing on his mind. He was leaving tomorrow with his father and neither one of them was coming back.

CHAPTER TWENTY-FOUR

Mark Mason rubbed his tired eyes wearily. His chambers were deserted. Even the legal night owls had struck out for the wheezing tube trains that would wend them home to clock-watching partners and sleeping children. Charmers's notes of Rose's evidence were spread out before him; but they were only words. Mason had been taught by savage experience that juries assessed cases more on impression than the witnesses' words themselves.

He sipped some tepid Java, and lit his one cigar of the day. He ran his finger down the page and read on, but even the diligent solicitor could not bring Rose's living misery to life. The histronics of the day had both helped and hindered their cause. Mason would argue that her emotional scars were reliable evidence that she was telling the truth; the defence, on the other hand, would say that this damaged young woman was a dangerous fantasist who had convinced herself that she was telling the truth. Mason had to admit the fact that both propositions were equally valid to the jury.

If only he had some independent evidence, just something to support her account. Mason dived deep into the recesses of his mind for the shining window of corroboration, but came up both empty-handed and empty-headed. For months they had searched for others who had suffered at the cult's hands, but the only ones they could find were either unwilling or unable to support Rose's case. Many were too frightened to attend court, others were in such an unstable state that they would be completely unreliable.

Mason switched off the brass reading lamp on his desk-top and picked up his papers. They needed someone or something to give them a break, before it was too late, or had they passed that moment already? He did not dare to answer his own question.

*　　　*　　　*

It was 3.00am when he sensed one of them, his guess was Trainer, stop by his bed and watch him for several seconds. Joss fluttered his eyes across his eyelids in a fake approximation of REMs; whoever it was seemed satisfied and the footsteps retreated into the distance.

Joss breathed deeply as the snores and night sounds began to whisper through the long thin room. He had his outdoor clothing under the thin sheet, his shoes next to his bed. Slowly he began his night move. Lars slept at the head of the dorm, next to the door. Joss peeled back his cover and was for once grateful that the iron mattress was incapable of betraying him with a creak. His feet were snug and silent in thick socks as he reached down for his footwear.

Silently, one step at a time, he padded up to the exit. Lars seemed to be breathing deeply enough. He reached for the door handle and pushed it down. It squeaked, only slightly, yet to Joss it sounded like a fanfare of trumpets. Lars flopped over like a fish, then returned to his deep sleep once more.

With care, Joss shut the door from the outside, skipped lightly to a dark corner and fastened his shoes tightly. He skirted the silent, darkened outbuildings carefully and noticed that lights still burned in the lodge: he had heard that the elders conducted seminars throughout the night. But it wasn't the lodge he was interested in. Ahead lay the target of his intentions.

The medical block was lit by a single night light in the reception area. Joss scouted his way to the rear of the premises. By now the light breeze had deepened its voice to a sonorous boom. Joss was relieved he could make some noise, which would be masked by the roaring wind. He spotted a slightly open window on the second floor and was suspicious as to why it had not been closed when the weather worsened, but he didn't have time to contemplate further and scanned the area instead.

Joss stared hard at the wall, which was constructed from Highland stone. It had stone guttering inlaid flush with the surface. No footholds. He looked for a way up. Between the individual slabs were tiny crevices where the salt had begun to erode the binding cement. It had been some time since he had climbed but he remembered the words of his friend Ben, founder member of In

Extremis and climber *par excellence*: 'If you can work a thumbnail into the top of your flesh then it's all yours.'

He tried. There wasn't quite enough and Ben's rule of thumb was less than he had hoped, but as it was he had no option. Slowly, gingerly, Joss began his ascent. It was all about finger strength. Ben could hang by one finger for what seemed like all too dangerous minutes whilst he scanned a sheer rock face for his next move. Joss was way out of training and his fingers ached as he climbed, whilst the gathering air buffeted him from all sides. It was only twenty feet, but it took him half an hour.

Eventually, he pushed the target window open, sneaked a look into the darkened room and dropped to his pain-wracked feet. He spent a minute massaging them and stemming the flow of blood from several broken fingernails; he now realised why Ben regularly treated himself to a manicure.

He had not been in this part of the building before and the dark totally disoriented him for a while.

Eventually he emerged from the room into a corridor and edged his way forward. Rounding a corner, he suddenly bumped into a trolley. Quickly, he grabbed it to stop it tumbling away and down the staircase to his left. He breathed out silently, looked up and saw a sign marked MEDICAL SUPPLIES: it pointed past the stairway and to his left. Just then he heard someone padding up the stairs, and froze, pushing his back against the wall.

A man appeared, crouching low, obviously as anxious to avoid detection as Joss himself. Joss moved quickly, clamping a hand over the man's mouth and felt him freeze with fear.

'It's OK, I'm a friendly,' he whispered directly into his captive's ear. The man stiffened once more. 'If I wasn't I would have given you away by now.' The man seemed to relax at the proposition's logic. 'I'm going to move my hand away, and you are going to exhale slowly and quietly.'

The man did as he was told. They looked at each other in the half-light and both wondered what to do next. Joss spotted a room marked 'laundry' and pointed toward it. The man nodded his agreement and followed. Once inside, Joss pulled the door to, but did not close it fully. He turned: his companion was sweating heavily. They spoke in edgy whispers.

167

'I saw you earlier in the gym,' Joss began.

'Jim Thurman.' He was American, Joss guessed from the East Coast.

'Joss Lane,' he said, holding out a hand. Thurman stared at him hard.

'What are you doing creeping about?' Joss asked.

'I could ask the same of you. How'd you get in?'

'Up the wall.'

'Jesus: Spiderman.'

'You?'

'Delightful night-nurse slipped off to the john; I slipped in.'

'You don't seem like the others,' Joss said.

'Could say that. Fucking A-grade whackos with a star: David Korresh would say this place was extreme.'

'Look this is dangerous,' Joss pointed out.

'And I don't know that? I'm not sweating because I've lost my winning ticket for the lottery.'

'Who are you?'

'Freelance journo. I'm doing a piece on Rivers. They have no idea.'

'How long have you been here?'

'Two weeks: I'm almost through orientation, I can't wait to get out of this place but I haven't gotten the right angle yet.'

'You have to be joking. You saw what they did to that guy tonight in the community centre; get him to talk.'

'That's nothing! I'm talking about the real filth, man: the nationals won't pay jack crack for stuff like that. I mean the hard stuff: all these millennium cults are the same, they all got agendas.'

'What do you know about Rivers?'

'He's a conman. He has to be, you never heard him?'

'Only on the film they show you.'

'Jeez, you're lucky, man, it gets worse the longer you stay here. It gets so that you can't think about anything else but his twisted theology. These people are headed for disaster same way as the Heaven's Gate tribe, Jonestown, Aum cult, all those freaks. By definition, he is either right or wrong about Armageddon. If it comes then, hey, he's a big hero, but if it don't there's gonna be fireworks among the folk who believed him.'

'How is he convincing all these people?'

'It's the whole set-up, don't you see it? They live in this highly regulated and disciplined regime where they are totally dominated emotionally and physically. Trick is that they call this an intentional community.'

'What, so they never have to deal with the accusation that they kidnap people?'

'You got it, but it's the same thing all right. Those in here who have committed everything they had in the outside world have nothing else now but their blind following of Rivers: the more isolated they become, the easier it is for the ideas to keep a firm hold.'

'So he has convinced everyone that the millennium means the end?'

'Or the beginning.'

'What do you mean?'

'He's a breakaway sect from mainline Seventh Day Adventist doctrine: he believes that Christ's return will only occur when there have been a sufficient number of Christians purified. He claims to be a messenger from God with the task of cleansing the anointed ones.'

'One hundred and forty-four thousand of them.' Joss recalled his conversation with Trainer in the sauna.

'That's right. He also claims that it is his duty to reveal the secret information contained in the scroll described in chapter five of Revelation: it's supposed to be a description of the events that will occur when Christ returns, and the the world as we know it ends.'

'And presumably you get saved if you hand over your earthly chattels to him.'

'You just about got the measure of it: he's been lining his pockets since day one with all his astronomical bullshit.'

'What's all that about?'

'He claims that several heavenly phenomena will occur simultaneously and that we are already in the cycle that is leading up to the day of judgement.'

'For instance?'

'First was the appearance of the Hale Bop Comet. Its brightest day was recorded as April 6th 1997, one thousand days before the year 2000. A total lunar eclipse followed this all over Africa, Eastern Europe and Asia on September 16th. The next solar eclipse to occur was August 11th 1999 and, according to Rivers's prophecy, the star of Bethlehem, that is the great conjunction of Jupiter and Saturn, will make an appearance in May of the year 2000 and that will be the moment when the parousia or second coming will occur.'

'All that stuff explains why my father got involved, I guess: the only way anyone was going to prove to him that God existed is through the appliance of science,' Joss muttered.

'Who's your old man?' asked Thurman.

'He's called Callum Lane. He's the reason I came here and I intend to get him out.'

'I hate to be the one to break it to you, Joss, but your old man . . .' he paused. 'I don't think he's gonna want to go anywhere.'

'You don't know him.'

'I don't need to.'

'What do you mean? I've seen him for myself, and if I could just get him out of here for a short while I think he'd see things differently,' Joss said angrily. He was about to mention his father's note, but held the information back.

Thurman seemed moved by Joss's vehement defence of his father's position.

'OK, OK, but from where I'm standing it sure as hell looks to me as if your old man has more than spiritual interests at heart here: he's turned Rivers and the chosen few into exceptionally wealthy individuals. Do you really believe that your father isn't profiting as well?'

'That can't be true.' Joss was about to explode.

'It is. I've been deep in this story for the past four months. No room for error, Bucko: your pater swims with the sharks.'

Joss was stunned: he could not fathom, let alone believe, what he was hearing.

'He's just a man who's lost his way.'

Suddenly an alarm sounded downstairs and echoed shrilly through the medical block. Thurman whispered 'Fuck' and bolted through the door. Joss fought back his panic and struggled to think rationally. Whoever it was would expect them to run; Joss cautiously edged out of the room and along the hall heading for the window until the thunder of feet turned him away from his point of entry.

Above his head he saw the sign for the surgical block. Swiftly he made toward it. An operating theatre door gave way as he pushed it forward, but beyond it there was no other means of escape; no windows, no skylight, no chance.

He spun around and was about to push open the door when he heard Trainer's voice.

'Bring him in here.'

Joss had nowhere to go; Trainer would crucify him.

His mind was moving at the speed of light: then he saw it! Above the operating table swung a six-foot bucket surgical light. He climbed on to the table then braced himself and jumped. It had to be perfect: he had to wedge both arms and legs into the bucket's sides at exactly the same time or he would simply plop on to the table. He almost lost it with his tired left leg but just managed to even out the pressure until there he hung, upside down, suspended over the table.

Joss held his breath as the door was kicked open and light illuminated the room. He prayed they would not switch on the operating light as his body obscured the beam. He heard Trainer's voice.

'What do you think you are doing in here?' He heard a whack and a groan.

'Hold him up,' Trainer ordered. Joss heard several more deep blows land and was sickened at the unmistakable noise of crunching bone.

'I haven't done a fucking thing, man.' It was Thurman's recently familiar voice, but this time it was thick with blood. The assault continued with stomach-turning monotony until Thurman had disclosed who he was and who he represented.

'Look what you've done to my fucking teeth, you frigging Nazi,' Thurman complained through a shattered mouth. 'You and your stormtroopers are going to prison.'

Trainer laughed without humour.

'Gag him.'

Joss heard the sound of a scuffle. His fingers and legs were bursting with the strain of suspended stillness and insistent gravity. One of his fingernails had begun to bleed once more and he watched in petrified horror as the blood snaked along the bucket light toward its rim.

'Stick him on there,' Trainer ordered. Joss looked down and there staring up at him was the mangled face of Jim Thurman with a strip of surgical tape fastened across his mouth. Looking down at Thurman, Trainer brandished a flashing scalpel.

'We are not going anywhere, but you are.' And without hesitation he neatly sliced his throat. The last thing Thurman saw was Joss trying not to fall. Struggling not to die, the light in his eyes went out.

'Swab!' Trainer remarked: the others with him laughed.

Joss saw his own trail of blood reach the end of its journey, bleb to a rounded drop and fall. Just at that moment, Trainer turned to his companions.

'Have him disappeared. If anyone asks about him, route the call through me.'

Joss had to hold on. They would surely snuff out his life as simply as they had Thurman's if he weakened. A body bag was produced and the dead journalist was thrust within it.

Joss swore he would put things right, but he had to be alive to do that. The operating theatre was sluiced down, the lights extinguished as easily as the reporter's life; the murderers left.

Finally, Joss dropped to the ground, he was shaking. His stomach churned in revolt from what he had witnessed. He had to get out. First, safely back to the dorm and, second, back on to the mainland where the authorities would have to be informed. He had to act fast, but if he gave any indication to Trainer that he knew what had just occurred he would find himself in a body bag of his own, Callum or no Callum. Firstly though, he needed some items that an ex-junkie knew a hospital could provide.

Jocelyn Lane swore one silent oath of his own that night; one he was determined to keep or die in the attempt. He dropped silently to the floor and began his dark quest.

CHAPTER TWENTY-FIVE

Thurman's pleading eyes pursued Joss through what was left of the night. This was his new reality. Even rogue tabs of acid had failed to conjure demons as vicious as Trainer and his merry helpers. At one time he would have hit the streets and chased down a dealer to fix himself up, but he had responsibilities now; namely, Callum. More than that, Joss reminded himself: Greta was fighting a court case to show the world the grim truth behind the cult. He wanted to help her, but he had no evidence. He threw his mind back to the whispered conversation with the murdered journalist, re-running the spool of his memory. Thurman had mentioned investigating the cult's finances and had been convinced that Callum had made its leaders wealthy. His father's letter made it clear that he wanted out: he might just provide the Millennium Church's Achilles heel. Joss had to work to free his father from the cult's brainwashing techniques, then hunt down the truth. The hazy stranger from the previous evening's dinner had to be ousted and his real father reinstated.

At 6am the morning ritual began again: the same sincere voice, the same trite verbiage. Reluctantly, Joss joined his dorm-mates in their early morning workout, but it would be for the last time, he promised himself. He ensured he was last out of the accommodation block, then swiftly doubled back and was relieved to recover his hidden belongings from the washroom ceiling; he was going to need them. He kissed the playing tile representing the future and placed it with its companions back in his pocket.

Joss stuffed as much breakfast down him as possible before seeking a meeting with Lars.

Joss was well aware that he had to display the same surly uncooperative attitude or Lars would be suspicious. He remembered that his boyhood friend Ben, now a Eurobond trader in Geneva, had once had aspirations for the stage. When going for a difficult role where aggression was a key factor, Ben told Joss how he used to remember all the bad things in his past: he called it 'RADA Rage' and it worked.

Joss concentrated on his mother's death: it did the trick.

'Yes,' Lars said flatly through clear eyes untainted by troubled sleep.

'Came to say goodbye; it's been wonderful.'

Lars considered the news.

'You can't leave until orientation is complete.'

'Fuck that,' he said smiling. 'This place might be fine for Callum but I've got a life to get on with.'

'Your life is here,' Lars snapped.

'What happened to "you are free to leave at any time"?'

'It's the rules.'

'Your rules, not mine. Tried it; hated it; thanks for the mind-expanding experience, Lars. Now I know my father is leaving for the mainland today: I'm going with him.'

Lars's patience was wearing gossamer thin.

'Not today, not . . .'

'Any day?' Joss suggested, his voice dropping to a low threatening whisper, and sounding braver than he felt. 'That's kidnapping isn't it? Bad charge: courts don't like it; kind of interferes with choice. Heavy, heavy prison sentences.'

Lars almost snarled. 'You need correctional help,' he continued. 'I know just the regime.'

'I want to see Trainer, now!'

'I am here,' Trainer said from behind Joss's back.

How does he do that? Joss wondered, always appearing like a bad smell in a crowded lift. He turned around.

'He wants to leave,' Lars explained.

'And I told him . . .'

'That he could,' Trainer concluded reasonably. He turned to face Joss, his expression the very embodiment of sadness and loss.

'I had hoped that we could get to know each other better. You are a remarkable young man, possessed of many talents, talents I had prayed might be put in the service of the Church, but . . .' he gazed off into the distance.

Joss was impressed and, despite all he knew, felt shamed by his selfishness. He struck the emotion away; that was how these places, these mind cults worked. He reminded himself of Trainer's merciless use of the shining scalpel on Thurman's white throat.

'Look, I'm just not ready: there are a lot of things still to resolve in my life.'

'Of course, of course. Nobody stays here against his or her will.'

Joss fought back an ironic smirk.

'But you will come to see your father from time to time: he of course has *no* intention of leaving us.'

'I would like that, Trainer, I really would.' Joss forced himself to sound sincere. He stuck out his hand, which Trainer ignored, gathering Joss into a firm embrace.

'Have your things ready in ten minutes. A boat will take you to the mainland, from there a car will transport you and Callum to Aberdeen for the train south. Where do you intend to go?' he asked releasing Joss from his bear hug.

'London. There are a few old friends I want to look up.'

'Farewell,' Trainer said. Joss moved toward him and hugged him closer, feeling the tense hatred stiffen his entire body.

'Bye,' he whispered.

'I'll be seeing you,' Trainer spat.

Later, Trainer reviewed his decision to allow Joss Lane to leave. The young man was a complicating feature in a complex timetable. After the Reverend's trial was concluded with a joyous acquittal, there would be the triumphal meeting of the chosen in London's Hyde Park. When all that business was concluded, there would be time enough to deal with the obstinate Lane Junior. Trainer had briefed his men to be vigilant and watchful. Callum would be monitored carefully. He flicked the switches hidden underneath his desk which translated to the video screen in front of him. The view leapt around the peaceful Haven; all was well for the moment. He would not allow anything or anybody to shatter their hard-earned tranquillity.

*　　*　　*

They sat on board the 'Scotsman 225' train as it pulled away from the bleakness of Aberdeen station. There were four of them. Joss, his busily distracted father and his two minders sat in the end compartment of the first-class carriage; the train was all but deserted. The boat journey from the island had been a rocking horse swell and Joss was pleased to see that the hired hands looked less than comfortable.

Callum appeared bitterly disappointed to hear Joss was leaving, but brightened immediately when Joss promised that they would be seeing a lot of each other; he didn't stipulate where that would be. The car had sped them over the mountain peaks in silence to the waiting train as his father tapped away at the ever-present laptop computer. The minders watched him carefully whilst he purchased his return ticket to London King's Cross.

The rhythm of the train and its swaying motion through the awesome countryside had an uncomfortable monotonous resonance. Joss kept his bag handy; it was the key to what he had in mind. Half an hour into the journey, Joss offered to buy a round of drinks, which were accepted with surly enthusiasm by the cult members.

On his way to the buffet car between first-class and standard Joss began to set the final train of his plan in motion. He bought a Mercury phone card from the steward and, armed with his credit card, hiked it to its limit by making a series of calls. On his return the minders appeared suspicious.

'Been throwing up myself,' he explained; it was their turn to appear grimly pleased. They took their drinks and sank them swiftly, complaining about the high sugar content, but Joss reassured them by pointing out that it helped to unknot a complaining stomach.

The journey passed and, after leaving Edinburgh Waverley, Joss knew it was time to act. The men were both enjoying an unexpected chance to catch up on the sleep that the Haven's regime denied them; his father was lost in his computer. Joss woke the minders with steaming plastic mugs of coffee, which were once more highly sugared, his father thanking him with a fixed and nervous smile.

Joss held his breath as they distractedly sipped the drinks laced with the drugs he had stolen from the medicine cabinet in the hospital wing the night before. Within half an hour his father and the two minders were deeply asleep. Joss had felt impelled to drug his father as well. He now gathered his father's belongings and took the minders' train tickets, money and every form of identification from their wallets. He bent their credit cards into useless pieces.

A guard approached and Joss proffered the tickets up with a finger to his lips.

'Has my father's wheelchair been arranged?' he whispered. The guard nodded and, despite his intense curiosity as to how this mystery virus struck without warning, wandered silently away. The tannoy system announced that they would be arriving at Newcastle Central station in five minutes.

Joss moved the baggage to the exit and began to coax a deeply comatose Callum to his feet. Whilst he had lost weight he had gained muscle. Joss struggled and the guard re-emerged to aid him.

As they neared the automatic door, the guard whispered, 'Sure you don't need an ambulance?'

'It happens all the time; it's a kind of narcolepsy.'

His helper nodded knowledgeably though he was clearly none the wiser as to what the word meant.

'Aren't the other gentlemen leaving here as well? That's as far as their tickets take them.'

'Change of orders from the company: they're going all the way to London. When they wake up they'll sort it out.'

The train pulled in to the vast Victorian wind tunnel that was Newcastle station. Joss slipped the guard a ten-pound note for his help and manoeuvred Callum into the wheelchair. Three minutes later, as he pushed his father to the taxi rank at the station's entrance, he breathed gratefully as the Scotsman pulled away.

So far so good. He had no idea when the minders would wake up or when the alarm would be sounded, but Joss knew where he had to go: there was only one person who could help him untangle his father's scrambled brain. The flight that he had booked to Paris from Newcastle was scheduled to take off in just under two hours. He had also taken the precaution of booking alternative flights from Manchester at five in the afternoon and could only hope that he had enough time to throw Trainer into utter confusion. His fingers found the tiles as they rattled together in his pocket: the past, the future and love all pushing him onwards to his fate.

CHAPTER TWENTY-SIX

Mason was approaching the end of his examination-in-chief of Dr James Barton, an expert in physiology. He was attempting to establish the first limb of his argument that the entire induction process into the church could have sapped Rose's free will. The doctor was a touch younger than he would have liked, but his good looks and rugby player's frame made up for that. Mason caught the two young women on the jury raising eyebrows at one another when he had taken the oath. Although the two sat at opposite ends of the back row, an allegiance had been formed. Mason made a mental note.

'Now then, doctor, you have examined Rose Moody, have you not?'

'Yes I have,' the doctor replied.

'When was that?'

'I have examined her on three occasions now, but I first saw her in August of last year.' He reached for the notes in front of him. 'Yes, my first report is dated the fifteenth of that month.'

'Thank you, doctor: and the purpose of your examinations was to collate information on the dietary changes experienced by Rose during her time at the Haven?'

'Yes. Essentially, I was looking for the overall effects of prolonged exposure to the type of foods and exercise regime Rose claimed she had undergone.'

'And your conclusion?'

'That any individual, but especially someone of Rose's weight, height and age, would almost certainly have experienced what I can only describe as a breakdown.'

'Not just a physical collapse?'

'No. I would anticipate, given the extremes of lack of adequate vitamin intake and essential nutrients, that not only would the subject suffer physical fatigue, but would rapidly lose the ability, or more importantly the will, to make rational thought possible,' he concluded confidently.

'Thank you, doctor. Would you just wait there, please.'

Thynne rose to his feet quickly, which Mason knew was usually an indication that he wanted to dismiss this witness's evidence as sharply as possible.

'Of course, doctor,' he sneered. 'All of this information and detail you collated came from the Millennium Church by way of disclosure, did it not?'

'I'm sorry?' the doctor replied, breaking his confident smile. 'I'm afraid I don't understand the question: could you repeat it, please.'

Mason looked over his shoulder at Greta, who looked blank: they had no idea what Thynne was leading up to.

'I'll put it another way, then,' Thynne went on, as if offended by this man's ignorance. 'Is this report you have produced based on information upon which we can rely because it was provided for you by the defence?' It was a clever question, which had only one answer.

'No. I have relied solely upon the information as provided by Rose Moody.'

'I see. Exactly as I thought.' He paused, as if framing the question, but of course he already knew exactly what he was going to ask. 'Are we to take it, therefore, that you have not bothered to corroborate anything this young girl has told you?'

'I wouldn't put it like that,' the doctor replied, looking uneasy that his reputation as an expert witness depended entirely on his ability to withstand cross-examination.

'You wouldn't, would you? Well, taking it step by step: you haven't bothered to confirm with those instructing me a single detail of the foods described to you by Rose Moody.'

'No.'

'You haven't bothered to seek permission from those instructing to visit any of the retreats operated by the defendant in this country or in any other country, have you? This report that you have produced is entirely self-serving to the prosecution case and incapable now of corroboration: isn't that the case?'

'It's not that I haven't bothered, it's because I have not been provided with any instructions to do so, or informed that those avenues were open to me.'

'Forgive me, doctor, but are you saying that when the prosecution instructed you in this matter they did not inform you that such facilities were indeed available to you?'

'That's correct,' the doctor declared, seeking now to shift any imputation of incompetence. Mason looked sharply at Charmers the solicitor, sitting in the back row behind Greta. He shrugged his shoulders and mouthed that he had not seen any such authority. Mason jumped up.

'My Lord, the prosecution categorically denies ever having received such an authority from the defendants.'

'I can hand in a copy of the letter, my lord, if necessary: it is dated the 16th January, addressed to Mr Charmers,' said Thynne, thrusting the letter forward with an exasperated look towards the jury. 'Really, my Lord, it is most unsettling to have this sort of pointless interruption.'

'I quite agree,' said Withnail, taking the letter and reading it. 'Mr Mason, your solicitor tells you his office did not receive this letter?'

'That is correct, my Lord.'

'Well, that is highly irregular, because I see this is recorded delivery, signed for on behalf of Mr Charmers's firm. Would you like to see it?'

'Naturally, my Lord. Thank you,' said Mason through clenched teeth. All this was taking place in front of the jury and Withnail seemed in no mood to send them out. He scanned the letter quickly, handing it back to Charmers, but it was pointless: the signature was illegible and could have been anybody's. The solicitor was puce with embarrassment as Geoff Moody glared at them from the gallery.

'I suggest most strongly, Mr Charmers, that a thorough investigation of your organisation would benefit not only your clients but perhaps your bank account, although I anticipate it is an even rarer occurrence that cheques go missing in a solicitor's office,' Withnail joked with the jury and invited Thynne to continue.

The barrister rounded off the demolition by cornering the learned doctor into the cruel admission that this in fact was only his second appearance as an expert witness. It would probably be his last.

Mason pushed on and called Doctor Robyn Odell, who was an expert in injuries occurring during sexual assaults. She stated that in relation to an examination of the vaginal area, it was evident that Rose had been partaking in regular sexual activity. However, this evidence was qualified when she added that there were no areas that showed labial or vaginal wall tearing, normally expected in non-consensual intercourse. Mason managed to question her carefully so that she was able to state that this could be explained by the passage of time between the alleged assault and the examination, and did not rule out the possibility of rape. In putting the case for the defence, Thynne went further in forcing Dr Odell to accept that the existing injuries were equally consistent with regular, promiscuous sex. The expert also accepted that due to the coarsening of the area from regular contact, there was no way of knowing how early Rose Moody's sexual experience had begun. Mason had winced at that. Clearly, Geoff Moody was being set up to take the fall once more.

The next witness for the prosecution, Susan Morris's scant qualifications were met with a derisory snort from Thynne, though Withnail did nothing to rebuke the breach of court etiquette. She briefly detailed her dealings with Rose and outlined how the two of them had formed a bond of trust. The thrust of her evidence was to convince the jury that the trauma Rose suffered was real. But things had changed now that Geoff Moody was a suspect. No one could doubt the girl had been abused; the question was by whom?

Mark Mason wanted more from her. Rose had floundered in her own time in the witness box and he wanted to redress the balance by showing her in a different light.

'How is she now, Miss Morris?'

'A little better, though I doubt she will ever return to her old self.'

She was composed, clipped and professional, her dazzling white blouse and well-cut navy suit completed the picture of competence.

'And you have observed at close quarters her relationship with her father?'

Once more the jury glanced across to where the subjects of the question visibly held hands. Morris smiled lightly.

'Over many months in many different situations.'

She was about to elaborate, then remembered Mason's advice to keep her answers brief and to the point.

'Are they close?' Mason was using simple language, everyday expressions that would mean more to the jury than such technical terms as 'displacement', 'guilt transference' or 'trauma closure'.

'They have a close and loving relationship.'

Mason noticed Thynne was watching the jury's faces with some care, hoping for signs of irony at the description.

'Does that surprise you?'

'Not at all, they were close before Rose's disappearance. Obviously there was a period of readjustment after her release from the Church . . .'

Thynne did not hesitate in objecting.

'My Lord, the word "release" suggests that the complainant was some kind of prisoner. There is no substantial evidence to support that.'

Withnail considered before he pronounced, 'Miss Morris, please refrain from using emotive language in your replies; stick to the facts.'

She seemed unmoved by the rebuke, and held the judge's eyes with her own for a moment too long. Mason quickly interrupted the staring competition.

'What kind of readjustment?'

'There was a lot of anger and resentment toward her father at first, but that is a regular response to a situation of this kind.'

Mason had to tread carefully; this was a vital part of Morris's testimony. He could see that the jury was hanging on her words.

'Please explain, Miss Morris.'

She nodded and mentally prepared her answer before complying.

'Young girls like Rose look up to their fathers and measure other men against them. They believe their fathers can do anything, answer any question, know the secrets of life, and always, always, protect them from harm. When circumstances dictate that is, and was, a fallacy there is often resentment and anger against the father or father figure.'

'You mean that they realise their parents are human like the rest of us?' Mason suggested, in an attempt to keep the language on a common footing.

'Yes, and more. Rose felt dirty and sullied by everything that had happened; she was ashamed that her father knew about the sexual aspects of the case. These emotions turned her against herself and the thing she loves most, her father.'

'Let's be very clear about this, Miss Morris: was Rose angry with her father because he had sexually abused her?'

She appeared puzzled by the question.

'Geoff assault Rose?' she shook her head. 'Frankly I've never heard anything more ludicrous in my life. Whoever raped and abused Rose,' she continued staring unflinchingly at Rivers, 'it was not Geoff Moody. They are both victims. No, you will have to look elsewhere to find the abuser.'

Glancing around, Mason saw to his relief that the jury appeared impressed by the calibre of her opinion and were shifting to get a better look at the defendant's response, but Rivers remained implacable, mute and expressionless.

'Thank you, Miss Morris,' Mason murmured and left her to the tender mercies of Thynne QC. The defence barrister immediately launched an attack on her qualifications, but Morris smiled sweetly and agreed that 'others' might well be better qualified, but they did not have Rose's trust. This found favour with the jury and Thynne became more bombastic and unpleasant in his cross-examination. At every turn she fended off criticism with gentle good humour and graceful compromise, but refused to budge on the central question of whether Geoff Moody might have abused Rose.

'Mr Thynne, you have not seen them for yourself: the love, the trust, the understanding. It is beyond all comprehension that these emotions could survive the level of abuse you are suggesting.'

'But it is possible?' he asked, the lawyer's last desperate question twisting bitterly from his lips, attempting to snare her with her own innate fairness. Morris had worked it out for herself.

'No,' she said, committing personal perjury and forgiving herself immediately. 'It is impossible.'

'So you say, Miss Morris, but of course you are incapable of approaching this girl's account with any degree of objectivity whatsoever, are you not?'

'As her counsellor, naturally I am closely involved, but my professional duty is to remain objective at all times.'

'I can see that, Miss Morris, but what I am suggesting is that if she is as damaged as you would have this court believe, then how can we believe anything she says?'

'I believe her.'

'As you are entitled to, Miss Morris, but the reality of the situation is that Miss Moody has made many claims before without any supporting evidence at all.'

'I was not aware of that until the statement allegedly made by Rose was shown to me.'

'Shall we examine the document?'

'I see no need to revisit that which is manufactured.'

'Indulge me, please, Miss Morris,' Thynne replied condescendingly. 'In it she speaks of the abuse by her father, of her loneliness and despair at being home. She was, in effect, a young girl who was so deprived of love that she would do anything for attention.'

'But not the sort bestowed upon her by the defendant, Mr Thynne.' Morris looked directly at the jury, knowing that her response had hit home.

Thynne continued to wheedle and snap, but the moment was gone and he was aware of it. Eventually he finished with an empty flourish and took his seat.

Mason was pleased; damage had been done to the defendant's cause. It was still not enough, but some of the balance had been restored to the case's equilibrium; but they still needed something more.

Trainer slammed the telephone receiver down with a crash. The shockwave caused a signed photograph of the Reverend to topple to the floor.

'That's where we'll all be if I don't get the Lanes back,' he muttered, retrieving the picture. The British Transport Police had his men in custody; the Lanes had vanished. Callum had access to all the Millennium Church funds and records and had to be found or killed as swiftly as possible; there was no other way. He breathed deeply in order to meditate his way through the situation, then spat, 'Fuck Zen,' and began making phone calls.

He had never really trusted Callum the way the Reverend did. There was something of the 'free ride' in all of Lane senior's dealings, as if he knew a secret, cheaper way of achieving the desired objective.

His first call was to the chief accountant dealing with the internal audit of the Church's fund holdings and expenses. He left instructions for the money man to concentrate on all of Callum Lane's recent dealings with Church wealth and to chase down any unauthorised or unexplained expenditure.

His trawl of Joss Lane's file had detailed the former junkie's appearance before a Dutch court when he was sent to a rehabilitation clinic, but there was no name or address to which Joss had been dispatched. Trainer then made calls to Dutch members of the Church, themselves involved in the justice system, and asked for their help.

Trainer feared the Reverend's response to the disappearance: punishment would be swift. In all likelihood Trainer would lose his high position and the many benefits that brought. No, he concluded, the situation was grave but not terminal.

He began to relax slightly until the telephone rang. A trusted Dutch court official had retrieved Joss Lane's case papers from the court vault. They contained a medical assessment of him by a Doctor Kristina Klammer from the Complott Clinic in the Austrian Alps, and several updates on his detoxification programme. Trainer thanked the Church member, and lied when he promised that the Reverend would hear of his swift work.

So Callum Lane had undertaken to pay for his son's treatment, yet throughout his stay at the Haven he had never once mentioned the existence of his errant son. In Trainer's view, Callum knew no shame, so his masking of his son's predicament must have been for another reason. He spoke once more to the accountant in charge of the audit and narrowed the search down still further.

'Use the search engine and key in the "Complott Clinic". I'll hold.'

Trainer sucked in his cheeks whilst the receiver whirred with the clatter of keyboard-pounding: he had a bad feeling about this. From the other end of the line he heard a whisper.

'Shit!'

'What is it?' Trainer shouted.

'Sending it through now, Mr Trainer,' the accountant replied, and Trainer pulled his computer monitor closer as the modem made the connection. The figures danced up on the screen. Monthly payments had been made for the past year and a half. Each payment was for £40,000 and each payment had been met by the Millennium Church holding fund. Callum Lane had ripped the Church off for almost three-quarters of a million pounds and, whilst his mouth began to dry, Trainer knew that this could be the very tip of the financial iceberg. Realising that the telephone line was still open, he spoke once more.

'Keep searching. Put a block on any further transactions from the accounts that Callum Lane can access.'

There was a pause from the accountant.

'Did you hear what I said?' Trainer barked.

'I did, but I can't do it,' the man replied sheepishly. 'He has all the codes for the next month.'

'Change them, then.'

'If I do, then the system will collapse in chaos. All our money to finance the Hyde Park rally is in place. Our operatives have signed contracts and have obligations that have to be met. As we speak, transfers are occurring.'

'So what the fuck are you saying?'

'There is no need for foul language,' he chided, 'but what I am *fucking* saying, Mr Trainer, is if we close the codes down we may as well cancel the rally, and somehow I cannot imagine the Reverend agreeing to that.'

'Thank you for your assistance,' Trainer whispered. 'It will not be forgotten.' And he sent a mental memo to himself to bring the accountant in for further 'orientation'.

Trainer considered the situation: where would Joss Lane go? He had no friends to speak of, and his father was his only family. Further telephone calls revealed that the Lanes had left the train at Newcastle upon Tyne. Church members then contacted the taxi firm that had taken them to the airport near Ponteland. Trainer keyed into the flight information for the relevant period: there were several destinations available. He checked his security file for a Church member contact, and tracked down a Customs and Excise official, who raided the passenger list.

Paris. The Lanes were in Paris. Now, he pondered, what would take them there? He looked once more at the exorbitant bill, settled unwittingly by the Church, and made a decision. He had no other leads: he would get value for their money and plumb the doctor's mind for ways to catch Joss Lane. He called the clinic and asked to speak to her. There was an apology and an explanation: no, Dr Klammer was not available as she was speaking at a symposium in Paris.

Trainer smiled as he replaced the receiver. The position was not terminal – not for him anyway. Paris would not be 'gay' for the Lanes: he had quite a different kind of experience lined up for them.

Thynne, Callow and Rory Fannon sat in a conference room in the court building. The very Reverend Rivers sat with them, staring over the table-top with his fingers interlocked. His face was reddened by anger, but he fought for control.

'Mr Thynne, sir,' he began, his voice a cold whisper, 'I know the hearts of men and how to reach them. If a man has hate in his soul then I will apply balm to his mental torture. If a man is too timid to take on the Lord's work, then I will steel his very essence until he shines with confidence. What I will not do is fail to understand what I am dealing with.'

'We have done well enough,' Thynne hissed.

'Silence, lawyer,' Rivers boomed. Thynne was about to reply, but the cult leader's cold stare stopped him in his tracks.

'That Morris woman caused us damage; am I right? Tell me I *am* right?'

Callow nodded, Fannon remained aloof, unwilling to engage the overpowering cleric. Rivers shook his head, 'You failed because your pride was hurt and you were bested by an unqualified witness. Now, I am not by nature an unfair man and it is right to say that the evidence of the Moody girl was swept away, particularly by the subtlety of Brother Fannon.'

Fannon shrugged.

Rivers paused, then continued, 'There is no room for error with my work, lawyer. I will not accept second best from a man reputed to be the best. Tell me, Is your heart not in this trial? Have you been listening to the dark one's blandishments?'

'How dare you?' Thynne blustered, unused to an attack from a client.

'I dare because I must. The Lord's work is more important than this trial, but in order for His work to continue I must be *seen* to be innocent.'

'You will be,' Callow murmured.

'Silence,' Rivers thundered. 'This is between the Lord and Mr Thynne. Do you wish to leave this trial, Mr Thynne? Think long and hard before replying. You have a reputation that you desire to expand. This is a keynote trial. It would be a sad and awful day for you and your dependants if you were to lose that hard-earned reputation because of your temper and bad judgement.'

Thynne's colour was high. He was being threatened by a powerful man with almost endless resources and the domineering will to win at all costs.

'No, I wish to remain,' he whispered eventually.

'There, you see?' Rivers said, smiling benignly, 'Your judgement and sanity has returned.' He reached his hand across the table and took Thynne's clammy one in his own.

'Welcome back to the team. Now I know, because we have spoken like true men, that you will not fail me again.' He beamed at the remaining two barristers. 'The Lord does not move in mysterious ways, my friends; you must merely open your eyes and his purpose will shine for you.'

Rory Fannon smiled emptily and whispered, 'Hallelujah.'

CHAPTER TWENTY-SEVEN

A warm ripple of applause swelled from the assembled ranks of psychiatrists, psychologists and addiction counsellors in the Baroque ballroom of the George V hotel in the centre of Paris. Kristina Klammer dipped her head shyly in brief acknowledgement, swept up her full, but unused, notes and retired from the gleaming podium to the row of Louis XIVth chairs set at the rear of the stage. Her plain black Jaeger suit was severe but still could not disguise her attractive figure nor her energy. A simple diamond brooch was her only deference to vanity. At five feet ten, she had the build and the jutting looks of a catwalk model, but her searching mind had taken her down a very different career path. Her black hair was cut short to a shining bob, which accentuated green eyes in a knowing face.

She had been unusually nervous before her address to the symposium and she had caught her voice beginning to wobble at the moment she introduced her topic 'Addiction is Rejection'. It was not one of the conference's key-note speeches, but did mark her journey forward within the international community of addiction experts.

The subject had been Joss Lane. At their last meeting she had promised his name would not be used. But as each stage of his treatment was explained to the assembly she could clearly picture him change from shattered youth to fractured man. This familiarity with her subject gave her the strength to overcome her initial nerves, as she had spoken at length of how a bright and self-reliant young man was transformed into a dull, lethargic, dependent, apathist.

The rejection she referred to was many-fold but in her speech she concentrated on his father's rejection of Joss and his own rejection of the will to live. It was not until she rested back into her seat afterwards that she realised how fond she had become of her former patient. She shook her head; a typical analyst, she could analyse everyone but herself. Besides, she still had work to do with him and had continually scanned the hotel's reception and foyer for his expected presence. This was the endgame and she had been well paid for it, but she couldn't help feeling guilty about the false face she had long worn with him.

The late afternoon approached and dusk began to grip the edges of the full-length windows. Subdued lighting began to replace natural as the Chairman thanked the audience for their attendance, and reminded them of the Gala dinner at 8pm that evening. By then, the ballroom would be cleared for dancing and Kristina had agreed to accompany a Toulouse-based psychiatrist to the event. More applause swept across the room as the speakers were thanked individually for their efforts.

The delegates began to gather their belongings, and stopped to talk in small groups of related interest on the way to the hotel's magnificent cocktail bar. She nodded a few swift 'hello's and 'thank you's on her way to the same destination. As she walked through the immense arch she heard a familiar voice.

'Kinky-shrink, that was some performance. My ears were burning.'

Kristina spun around and there he was, eyes watchful as ever, a half-grin on his familiar face.

'Joss. What are you doing here?'

'No kiss? No hug?' he looked perplexed. 'No, on second thoughts, forget the hug: I've had a lorry load. How about a hello?'

She reached forward and kissing him lightly on both cheeks, she could smell his familiar aftershave. Kristina looked searchingly into his eyes and could gauge that his pupils were properly dilated. She breathed out in relief then felt a twinge of guilt about what would follow.

'No, I haven't fallen from grace, at least not in that way, but I do need your help.'

His eyes flicked around the room as if he were searching for something or watching for something searching for him.

'Are you in trouble, Joss?'

'It's dangerous to be here: can you come with me? Please.'

192

His voice was desperate and pleading: she nodded grimly, knowing this was all part of the charade. Her part in this drama had been written some time before, but Joss was an unwitting player.

'Where are we going?' she asked, turning for the door.

'I broke into your office. I know the Millennium Church paid my bills. Have they contacted you?'

'Not since I arrived in Paris, why?'

'But they've asked about me before?'

'They paid the bills; they were entitled to know how you were progressing.' Or one of them was, she thought.

Joss steered her to the wooden revolving doors at the hotel's portico, which was teeming with delegates and other guests.

'What have you done?' she asked, grasping his arm.

'Trust me, Kris,' he whispered, all the time watchful and tensed. 'I trusted you, remember?'

'Not at first,' she replied honestly.

'We came a long way, though.'

Joss plunged to the deepening gloom outside; it had begun to spit rain.

'What do you want me to do, Joss?' she asked as the top-hatted concierge opened the door to a taxi for them. Joss waved her inside and barked an address on the outskirts of Paris to the driver, who shrugged in a typical Gallic fashion.

Joss planted himself down next to the psychiatrist and scanned the road behind for several seconds without speaking.

'Joss, you are scaring me. What do you want me to do?'

He turned to face her.

'I want you to meet my father.'

The journey passed swiftly whilst Joss brought Kristina up to date with the events of the last few days. As he concluded his account, her widened eyes revealed her apparent horror of what he had done.

'You drugged and kidnapped your own father? For God's sake, Joss, what the hell have you been up to?'

'Saving my father's life,' he replied.

She pretended to be stunned by the carefully orchestrated turn of events.

'Joss, you must be undergoing some delayed delusional fantasy. You have role-played this into reality.'

'It's bizarre but true, all of it.'

She could only shrug.

'You think I'm off my head, don't you?'

She stared out of the window.

'It's quite a shock all this, but I am sure we can get to the bottom of it, as long as we remain calm.'

'I am calm,' he replied.

'That is what concerns me most,' she whispered. 'I have to ensure that your father is not in danger; that is if he is here at all!'

The taxi drew to a halt outside a ragged apartment block; the streets now damp, the streetlights flickering into life. Joss followed her gaze.

'Welcome to Bedlam,' he muttered, furnishing a handful of notes to the scowling, smoking, driver.

Kristina followed him into the tarnished lobby, where a weasel-eyed woman in a housecoat glared at Joss as he pressed the button to open the grey doors of the lift. With a shrug the doors rumbled open and they stepped inside.

'You don't have to come; I just didn't know who else I could turn to. Besides, it was my father who suggested you,' he said, pressing the square plastic button for the fourth floor. They began their silent ascent.

The doors squealed as they spread apart and Joss led the way to apartment 413. She followed him into the gloom of the room. The light was dull and soporific. She smelled the air for the tell-tale stench of drug-use but could not discern any of its distinctive odours. The decor was faded and drab, the furniture equally tired and sagging. To her right was a closed door, blistered with peeling paint.

'Why here?'

'Couldn't think of any place else. I stayed round here when I was Interailing. They won't find us: in this district everybody is a liar.'

'Joss, this is worse than I thought: you are not only delusional, but also paranoid into the bargain.'

He opened the door and moved slowly toward the bed where a large grey-haired man lay strapped on to its width. Kristina could tell by the familiar face that this was indeed Callum Lane.

At their approach he flicked open his eyes and fixed them upon her.

'Joss, what have you done? What have you done?' she whispered as she knelt by the recumbent figure. 'Mr Lane? Are you Mr Lane?' she asked gently, knowing the lie behind her question, whilst placing a light finger on the pulse in his neck.

'My name is Kristina and I am a doctor, here to help you.'

Joss could hear the edge of fear in her voice and with a plunging heart accepted that she believed him to be dangerous. He couldn't really blame her for feeling that way, but he had to convince her of the truth.

'Give me half an hour, that's all; thirty minutes. If you are not convinced by then of the truth, we will call the police together,' he said. She continued to check his father thoroughly.

'Mr Lane, can you talk?'

Callum licked his lips with his tongue. Kristina reached out and grasped a glass of water from the small table beside the bed.

'What have you given him?' she asked, raising his head and allowing him gentle sips of water.

'Barbiturates,' Joss answered. 'I knew what I was doing,' he explained defensively.

'I'm sure you thought you did, but that isn't really the same thing, Joss, is it?'

Her tone was now professional, measured and calm. Then Callum spoke, his voice dry and cracked but with the steadfast conviction of an Old Testament prophet.

'The day is coming: repent now; repent!'

Joss raised his palms as if this should be sufficient corroboration of his story.

'Stoned, Joss, he's probably hallucinating,' she said, anxiously.

'He's been like this since we arrived yesterday: it took me that long to track you down.'

'Renounce the weaknesses of the body, accept the message of the one and only father,' Callum thundered, the volume rising to a zealot's roar.

'This is not my father. He has lucid moments, but not many.' Joss whispered sadly. 'They changed him, traded him in for a younger model with an empty head; can't you see that?'

195

'Joss, I have never met your father, before,' she lied, 'so how can I judge? For all I know he could be suffering from barbiturate poisoning and this is the result.'

'What can I do to convince you that what I told you is true?'

She stood up.

'Let him go.'

'I can't.'

'Why?'

'I will lose him for ever. They will take him back and I will never see him again.'

'The man you saw murdered: the authorities have to be notified,' she reasoned.

'Oh terrific, you're supposed to be my friend and you're treating me like Charlie Manson. What the hell do you think they are going to do?' Joss stood stock-still as he asked the rhetorical question. 'I'll be in a strait-jacket before I've left the apartment.'

'It will be difficult, I accept, but what do you expect me to do?'

'Half an hour, that is all: just talk to him, on your own. You used regression technique with me to get to the key of my addiction, use it on my father.'

'I did that with your permission. I took an oath, the Hippocratic Oath: I have to be true to it.'

'But can't you see he's incapable of commanding his own senses? He wanted me to get him out of the Church, so I did. He must have lucid moments or he couldn't have asked me to.'

'Joss, this is madness.'

'No, Kristina, this is my father.' He bent over and stroked his brow gently. 'Dad, Dad it's me, Joss.'

His father looked toward him, smiled lightly, then hardened his features, as if unable to focus properly.

'Tell me the Oath, tell me the words of the Oath you swore to the Foundation.'

'There are many Oaths, Joss, there is even one I do not yet know, but you are not one of us, you cannot know.'

'Tell me, Dad, tell me. I love you. Tell me for the sake of my mother, your wife.'

His father's eyes began to swim with tears.

'You are tearing him apart, Joss, you cannot do this,' Kristina snapped. Joss felt sickened, but knew he had to continue.

'For her sake, for Jennie's sake, tell me,' he demanded. Callum's face was soaked in sweat, he struggled and pushed against his bonds, his face began to redden. He began to hum a tune, then whisper the words with a cracked voice:

> *Joss and Jill went up the hill*
> *To fetch a pail of water.*
> *Joss fell down and broke his crown.*
> *His Mum came tumbling after.*

Suddenly the bed shook with a convulsion and Kristina clamped hold of Callum's head with both hands.

'Quickly, help me,' she shouted. 'He is trying to swallow his own tongue.'

Joss leapt forward as she turned Callum on to his side and began to slide her fingers into his mouth; it was clenched shut but his eyes were begging for pity.

'Ram your fingers into the space underneath his jaw.'

Joss found the point and did as he was commanded: slowly, reluctantly his father's mouth began to open. She squeezed her fingers in and flipped back his tongue from his throat, then screamed as Callum's teeth bit into her flesh. Joss had no option but to punch his dad on the side of the head; he slumped unconscious onto the bed. Regardless of her own pain, Kristina swiftly inserted a toothbrush from the bathroom into Joss's father's mouth as a restraining bar.

Flopped back onto the floor at the side of the bed, she stared, bewildered, at her lacerated finger. Joss was breathing heavily.

'Still think I'm barking?' he asked between raking gulps of air. She shook her head slowly from side to side. 'Are you going to help?' Joss pushed as he checked the pulse on his father's wrist. Once more she nodded dumbly.

'Do you believe me now?' he continued. Kristina eventually found her voice.

'I've read about that but never seen it before,' she whispered.

'But what does it mean?' Joss asked.

'It means he would rather die than divulge what has happened to him.'

She shook her head once more in disbelief.

'That tune he sang, you recognise it, of course.'

'You've asked me before, Kris,' Joss replied. 'Of course I know it; my mother sang it to me often enough. I just don't know what it means.'

'You have to try harder. It must mean something to your father as well, something vital: it could help us to save him.'

'But can you help him if I can't remember?' Joss pleaded. She looked down on the prostrate man and vainly attempted to rationalise what had just occurred.

'I do not know, Joss, I really do not for the life of me know.'

Joss Lane placed a hand on her shoulder, walked into the bathroom, retrieved a small frayed towel to bind her hand and whispered, 'We have no other option.'

The seed was sown; Kristina was ready to move on to the next phase of the operation.

CHAPTER TWENTY-EIGHT

After the medical evidence, Mark Mason had called other witnesses to deal with the police interviews of PJ Rivers. Though Mason had edited them down, they still consisted of long, turgid pages of denials. Rivers had resolutely refuted any sexual assault on Rose. He could not recollect if he had ever met her, though continually stated he would pray for her tormented soul. Mason watched the eyes of the jury begin to glaze over, then drop with boredom, but the defence had insisted that Rivers's protestations of innocence should be hammered home with dull repetition.

After some minor cross-examination dealing with Rivers's full co-operation with the investigation – including the provision of bodily samples of blood, hair and urine – the prosecution case was at its end. Mason formally closed the matter, then two days of legal argument followed in the absence of the jury, whilst Callow QC pushed for the case to be halted by the judge.

Huge piles of thick law reports climbed in stacks on counsel's benches, like building blocks of the defence's submission that the case should not be allowed to proceed. Photocopies of the decisions of the superior courts bounced backwards and forwards between Callow, Withnail and Mason.

The argument had two limbs; firstly, that the court had no jurisdiction to hear the case and, secondly, that the evidence was so manifestly unbelievable and inconsistent that no jury could properly convict upon it.

Mason had attacked the first argument with some vigour claiming that the English court had jurisdiction because the offences began in England and the mere fact they continued in Scotland did not bar proceedings. This found favour with the judge, who was unhappy that the point had not been raised at the beginning of the trial. It was clear that the judge would find for the prosecution in that dispute.

The second was more problematical. Callow was suggesting, rightly, that whilst the facts were the jury's domain, this was a special case where the jury should not be allowed to decide the guilt of the defendant at all. He argued with vigour, that the entire case for the prosecution was based on the unsubstantiated allegations of a mentally suspect witness and that if the trial were to continue and the jury were to convict, then a potential miscarriage of justice would occur. It was a submission rarely made with such good grounds and Mason knew it. The members of the court waded through a full transcript of Rose's evidence, but it still came down to the stark point that she, and she alone, maintained the abuse had occurred and there was not one iota of corroboration to support her allegations.

Withnail was unsure of himself, barking rebukes at both sides of the dispute and manifesting his unhappiness with the position he had been forced into. The troubled judge had eventually adjourned the case overnight so that he might 'consider in full' the legal disputes. Mason suspected that he would take the problem to one of his more accomplished 'brother' judges for guidance. Eventually, and to the defence team's fury, Withnail allowed the prosecution to continue. Mason was duly relieved, for at least he had got the case beyond 'half-time', and now he would get a chance to cross-examine PJ Rivers himself.

The jury, clearly puzzled by their lengthy expulsion from the proceedings, was given no explanation as they resumed their seats in the box. Mason waited, pen poised for the next act in this curious ballet of justice.

There were raised whispers amongst the three wise men of the defence super-team. Withnail's decision had thrown them momentarily off-balance. Thynne's eyes were riveted on Callow, who shook his head desperately, whilst Fannon seemed half-amused by the fracas.

Mason smiled; it was the first sign of uncertainty. He turned to glance at Rivers who stared straight ahead, apparently oblivious to the lack of firm leadership. The lawyers probably had a table already booked for a celebratory lunch at an expensive restaurant once the trial was over, but today they would dine on Old Bailey sandwiches.

Eventually, Fannon clambered to his feet. Thynne attempted to restrain him with a claw-like hand, which was brushed off in disdain.

'My Lord,' Fannon began, 'ladies and gentlemen of the jury, the defence call the Reverend Rivers to give evidence in his own defence.'

The jury turned as one, as a court dock officer opened the small wooden gate to allow the accused through into the belly of the court. Rivers walked with dignity and strength. His black suit and white shirt were a perfect reflection of the lawyers' own colour co-ordination. A black tie with the cult's trademark single red slash across its widest point was the only unconventional aspect of his attire. Once more Mason was impressed. Each step seemed to resonate with piety and self-belief. Rivers's eyes looked neither up nor down, but appeared fixed on the rightness of where he was and what he was doing.

Once in the witness box, Rivers then surveyed the court, like some prophet in a temple of moneylenders. Mason almost expected him to beg forgiveness for all involved in such indignity. The black-robed usher hovered, seemingly unsure of the next move, though he had sworn in countless witnesses before. Mason was very impressed. Rivers undeniably had presence and power. A King James Bible was offered, but politely refused. Instead Rivers produced a slim volume bound in black leather, which, he explained, contained only the Book of Revelations.

'I shall swear an oath on that which I believe.' His voice, soft and strong, like a bell tolling in the far distance, invited no argument. He held the book aloft in his manicured right hand.

'I swear by all things holy and true, before my Redeemer and in the presence of the unredeemed, that I shall bear true witness before one God in this courtroom today.'

Withnail glanced quickly to Mason for any potential disagreement with the form of the oath sworn. The barrister shrugged non-committally; it didn't matter. If Rose was being truthful, then Rivers was a perjurer, whatever book he chose to lie upon. Fannon took up the examination-in-chief.

'What does that oath mean to you, Reverend?'

Rivers raised one eyebrow slightly at the irreverent tone of the question.

'I would have thought that was obvious,' he replied.

'It is to me, but the members of the jury have not had an opportunity to witness the strength of your beliefs before.'

'An oath is a binding declaration in this life and the next, Mr Fannon. If I were to lie then I would be damned for eternity.' Rivers's face was set in Mount Rushmore stone.

'We need to know about you and your work, Reverend,' Fannon continued. 'You were not always a man of the cloth.'

'I was not, Mr Fannon. I was lost until I was found.' Rivers looked up to the sky and put a hand over his heart.

'Tell us how you were found,' Fannon pressed. Mason could see that the strength and genuine nature of Rivers's beliefs were to be the cornerstone of the defence case. If the jury could be convinced of them then Rose's story would never be believed.

'I was once a bad man enraptured by money and success. I sold things to people who neither wanted them, nor could afford them. The misery I caused was great, may I find forgiveness.'

'You sold health products, is that correct?'

Rivers nodded solemnly. 'Modern day snake oil. Balms and potions with the health content of car-exhaust fumes.'

This had been to form part of Mason's cross-examination. The defence were drawing the sting out of the accused's chequered past by first admitting, then later avoiding the issue.

'Were you successful?'

'Lord, yes,' Rivers said, his voice trailed with misery. 'The devil gave me his blessing and the vain and foolish listened to my words with open ears and empty heads.'

'Why did you stop?' Fannon's lilting voice assumed gravitas for introducing the moment of redemption.

'My saviour intervened. I was punished with great might.'

'How?' The jury was wrapped up tightly in the tale; even the reporters' pens drooped in their hands.

'A heart attack. I was smote with my own weapon. I promised the good people health and did not deliver. The punishment was just and appropriate. I died that night. Three times, my empty heart stopped beating and three times I was brought back to the vale of tears.'

'Were you operated on?' Fannon asked in a whisper.

'A quardruple by-pass. I was in a coma for forty days and nights until I was released from the wilderness of my own greed.'

'Did your experience change you?'

'For ever, Mr Fannon,' Rivers's voice boomed. 'I had been saved. I had been given a chance to redeem myself and others. I was to be the baptist, the birthing father of a new faith; the Millennium Church.'

The jury was fascinated; so was Mason. The man was either an actor of rare distinction or a genuine convert to his own religion and only the jury could decide which.

CHAPTER TWENTY-NINE

Harrison Trainer sat aboard the Church's private jet looking down over the English Channel. The two female cabin staff sat behind him in silence, well aware that to interrupt his personal space and private thought processes was strictly off the in-flight passenger care charter limits. The only sound was the constant hum of the turbines plodding relentlessly on to the French capital.

As they approached Orly airport, Trainer carefully folded a street map of Paris that lay across the drop-leaf table in front of him. He had used a fluorescent marker pen to segment the city into surveillance areas. Already he had marshalled two hundred Parisian Church members, who, armed with photographs of both Joss and Callum Lane, were scouring the hotels, bars and streets, so far without success. That situation couldn't be allowed to continue. Whatever the cost.

The treasury department of the Church had been thrown into chaos when word had leaked out that Callum had been kidnapped. Trainer spent his last few hours at the Haven fielding panic calls from the Church's European business partners, concerned that Callum had failed to show for their scheduled meeting. He had lied his way into buying more time, but crucial financial information was needed from Callum's databank. The fact that he hadn't backed up his computer files before he left the Haven meant not only that he was on the loose holding highly sensitive and utterly irretrievable material, but worse he was accompanied by a son who was shooting from the hip.

Trainer had judiciously avoided alerting the Reverend while the court case was going on, but realised that if he didn't find the Lanes before nightfall he would have to inform Rivers personally of the catastrophe.

Damn that kid, he thought, as the plane taxied toward the terminal where he knew that Dave Tomlin and Alan Moyne would be waiting with a car for him.

Tomlin and Moyne – it always sounded like a slightly seedy firm of solicitors to Trainer – were both medium built, possessed whip-cord reflexes but were essentially anonymous. By the time most people had met them it was too late to react. Their faces were of similar complexion, their hair a similar close-cropped brown, but Tomlin had the dark-rimmed eyes of a sinner and Moyne the clear-eyed gaze of a saint; they had been known in their Army regiment as 'Hell and Heaven'.

On the way into the city centre they recounted to Trainer their efforts so far. They had managed to trace several members of staff at De Gaulle who recalled the handsome young man pushing his distinguished father so lovingly in a wheelchair, but no one could remember how the pair had left the terminal. They had joined other devotees trying out the hotels armed with photographs and bribe money, yet whilst the francs dwindled the trail grew colder still.

Trainer had tried to work out exactly what it was that Joss was doing in Paris; the young man was too clear-thinking to merely flounder from place to place. No, Joss Lane had to have some kind of plan that involved Callum and his doctor. The old man would be unwieldy and unco-operative. Joss would need to enlist some help.

But the tumblers of fate had clicked in his favour with his revelatory call to the Complott. Forty minutes later and he was scanning the conference delegates thronging the foyer of the George V for her face. The organiser had kindly provided a photograph of Dr Klammer, and Tomlin and Moyne were on watch outside with the same visual ammunition.

Trainer's enquiries revealed that, to the annoyance of a certain French quack, Kristina had failed to meet him as arranged for the gala dinner on the previous evening. One bribe later it was clear that she had not collected her belongings from her room. So, Trainer deduced, she would return, or else send for her things: either way it would lead him to the Lanes.

*　　*　　*

Kristina appeared exhausted.

'He is in deep,' she explained to Joss.

Joss sat miserably on the sagging sofa.

'You have to know what you are involved in.'

'Go on,' he invited her.

'The suborning of another's will is idly referred to as brainwashing, but this term is inaccurate: it is more like a vacuuming of the free-will. It robs the victim of the ability to choose. Callum has been swept almost clean.'

'Almost?'

'The fact that he asked you to rescue him shows that the transformation is not complete; but it is very close.'

'What can we do?' Joss asked, a brighter note in his voice now that he believed there was a chance.

'We have to show him that all he believed about the Church was false and wrong; it will not prove easy.'

'How can I help?'

'He keeps mentioning the rhyme that he sang. I don't know why: some fixation. It may be trivial to you, but it is vital to him. You must try to remember. Anything might help.'

Joss was tired; almost too tired to think. Besides, the memories were painful. 'I'll try: that's all I can promise.'

Callum was sleeping. He, too, appeared exhausted.

'I have been forced to use the same techniques that Rivers employs; sleep and food deprivation.'

She moved through to the main room, glanced at the clock and wasn't surprised to see that twenty-four hours had elapsed.

'I will allow him ten minutes more before resuming. I feel every bit like a medieval torturer,' she said wearily. 'I'm supposed to be a supporter of Amnesty International.'

'I don't suppose a lucid argument about the greater good will help?'

Kristina shook her head.

'Means and ends, ends and means: the greater or the lesser good, all arguments by historians with a master's degree in hindsight. I have to deal with the here and now.'

The room hung silent. Joss knew what he had asked of her was against everything she seemed to believe in or held to be right and true.

'I just can't understand how they got him,' Joss eventually muttered. Kristina nodded, her eyes suddenly fixed once more on the job in hand.

'Too many of us believe that it is only the real "losers" who join cults; this is not so. What good are the lonely and the dispossessed to those who seek power? Do you think you can recognise cult members by their clothes and the way they behave?'

Joss shrugged.

'It is often the very brightest who join these organisations,' she continued. 'The Scientologists boast many wealthy and influential people amongst their number, and no one calls them losers. That is the very purpose of proper recruitment Joss; just human nature. If the road-sweeper, however worthy, joins, we tut and shake our heads, but if a famous figure publicly declares their allegiance, we look a little closer, trust a little too much, then, wham!, suddenly you are on the inside looking out.'

'Is that what happened to my dad?'

'He was head-hunted then head-shrunk but they would never have taken him if he had not been so vulnerable.'

'You mean it is my fault?' Joss asked, afraid to hear the answer. She struggled to find a kind way to express the undeniable truth.

'That and the circumstances of your joint loss.'

'Ouch.'

'But I believe that if you can talk to him about the circumstances of your mother's death and what occurred afterwards, it may provide the key.'

'But that almost killed him yesterday.'

'There you are wrong. You asked him to declare the terms of a secret oath he had sworn and used your mother's memory as a weapon to force him to do that; that would not be the point of this exercise.'

'You mean we should try a sort of catharsis, rather than betrayal?' Joss asked.

'Exactly,' Kris replied, 'I am pleased that you have worked it out for yourself.'

'Let's do it then.'

'Steady, Joss, he isn't ready yet. First I must break him further, God forgive me, and then he may be ready. But are you ready, Joss

Lane? Are you able to go to those dark places in the recesses of your mind and remember her death? Are you ready to tell him what the rhyme means?'

Joss shook his head sadly and shrugged. He didn't want to return to that time in his life; it was worse, much worse than what had followed.

Kris flicked her attention once more to the tarnished clock on the mantle.

'I have work to do; be ready.'

Joss was alone once more and exhausted. The tick of the clock soothed him into an oblivious sleep.

Inside the bedroom, Callum Lane opened one eye slightly and fixed it on her steadily.

'Is he ready?'

'Let him sleep for a while; he will be more disoriented.'

'He has to tell us this time,' Callum said in a low whisper.

'I couldn't get it out of him at the clinic,' she replied and looked down to her bandaged hand. 'You didn't have to bite me so hard.'

'Had to keep in character. Besides, these are desperate times.'

'He is your own son,' she whispered through clenched teeth. 'It might destroy him.'

Callum Lane smiled.

'If I don't find what I need it will destroy me; I have no choice.'

Joss woke with a start when Kris shouted out: 'Come through, your father needs to talk to you in private; it's about your mother.'

He had slept for seven hours whilst Kristina Klammer had worked on his father.

This is too quick

You're not ready

Kristina appeared in the doorway.

'I don't know how it came about – the sleep, the fatigue, any number of things – but he has already said how much he loves you,

Joss. This is your moment, seize it, it may never come again.' Her words seemed flat and emotionless, almost rehearsed.

Joss walked through the grim portal knowing he was about to revisit the worst time of his life, and waiting there would be his parents, his friends and, most of all, Greta.

By force of habit and desperation he fingered the well-thumbed. 'Go' counters still nestling in his pocket. 'Love' was Greta and his mother, 'the past' was his mother's death, and the 'future' would be decided now.

CHAPTER THIRTY

June 1996: Surrey, England.

Joss cleared the surface, his head dripping with the swimming pool's heavily chlorinated water. Sunlight threw dancing prisms across the shimmering surface to the tiled side where Greta's long, brown legs kicked lazily. Tom, Barney and Ben sculled like basking sharks in the warmed shallows, their own sun-French-kissed bodies like slippery seals.

'Show off,' Greta shouted, after his two lengths underwater were successfully completed. Joss tried not to gasp for breath: that would not be cool, and cool was the only way to be. Greta watched him, her fine mouth turned up in amusement.

'You are allowed to breathe, you know: you are, after all, vaguely human, or so my limited experience of biology tells me.'

She was two years into a three-year Law degree and Joss adored her. It wasn't hard; they all did. Greta, at twenty-three, was more mature than the four of them could ever be, even cumulatively. She had walked straight from the pages of Harper's and Queen, pausing only to read the Times Law Reports *and turn her slim body into heavier muscle by her love of dangerous sports and 'In Extremis' in particular. Her long blonde hair, coloured by her mother's Norwegian birth, was wet and lightly bleached.*

Liam Gallagher belted out 'Wonderwall' from the ghetto blaster by the edge of the pool, and his heartfelt lyrics spelt out precisely what Greta meant to Joss. Ben, Tom and Barney swam idly across to them. They had all met through their love of sport but there was a common glue that bonded them all together; the love of cranking the thing up one further notch. They had just returned from two weeks' climbing and snowboarding in the French Alps. There had been some hairy moments, one in particular, when Joss had been forced to clamber down a dangerously narrow crevice to rescue a maniacally giggling Tom, who was convulsed by the situation. He was training to fly Harriers with the Fleet Air Arm and would soon earn his wings.

Ben was the more studious of the three, a specialist climber who would work out a route with meticulous detail then ignore it on the basis that if he could 'suss the sucker out' it was therefore too easy to bother with. When he wasn't hanging by his fingertips he was training for a life in international banking. He was highly rated by Callum, Joss's father.

Barney was the funniest of the bunch, dry to the point of parchment; he could reduce a room full of people to helpless laughter with one word or cause a fight with a single glance. His chosen method of attempted suicide was cave- and deep-sea-diving. It was as if he hid himself in a silent world to shut himself up.

Barney approached them first. 'Lungs like an alligator; looks to match.'

'Drown, cherub,' Joss laughed, pushing Barney's blonde, tousled hair under the water.

'You'd have to keep him under for a decade,' Ben said. 'Perhaps we could lease him to some Pacific pearl divers; it's the only way he'll ever turn a profit.' The fledgling banker was strong in him.

'They'd have to lock up their dolphins,' Tom added, with his warm smile, as Barney arose grinning his trademark gap-toothed grin. Greta smiled indulgently.

'What time is everyone arriving?'

'For the watery-'rave?' Joss quipped. His mother and father were away on business in the capital and not expected back until late the next day. 'In an hour or so,' he continued, placing his arms over the lip of the pool and folding them over each other.

'They all want to catch the last rays, before they "surf the rave". The Spine is coming fully armed for the occasion,' Joss concluded flippantly, referring to Spineless Eric, their friendly purveyor of recreational drugs. Greta climbed to her long legs and dove elegantly into the crisp water without creating a splash.

'Not too happy about our chemical friend?' Ben asked.

'You know Greta,' Joss said. 'Highs are all right, in her view, as long as they are natural ones.'

'Can't get more natural than the great weed in the sky,' Tom muttered.

'It's not the garden produce she minds, it's the pharmaceuticals,' Joss explained pointlessly. They knew her views. Greta made them plain enough and now she was furiously lapping the pool to rid herself of the frustration.

'Got a point though,' Barney said, for once his cute face serious. 'When I'm diving in a cave and I find the route out; now that's a high.'

'No, that's luck,' Joss snapped.

'Steady, Lois,' Barney warned, knowing full well that Joss hated Superman's girlfriend's name. Joss eyes his friend warily.

'If I broke your nose, now that would stop you looking cute. Who knows, you could even be brutally handsome.'

'Don't be pissy with us, just because Greta is hacked off with you,' Tom warned.

'Lose the edge, Joss,' Ben suggested. 'It suits you like a pair of bell-bottoms.'

Joss risked a reluctant smile and turned to Barney Calladine.

'You wouldn't suit rugged good looks; you'd have to have your hair straightened.'

Barney shrugged. 'Could always wet my nose and stick it in a light socket.'

But Joss knew he had struck a low blow to one of his closest friends and Barney was covering up with a limp suggestion.

'Pimms?' Tom suggested. 'We shouldn't eat on an empty stomach.'

'Only if it's mixed with dry ginger and fresh mint,' Ben said, climbing out of the pool.

'And vodka,' Barney added. The others looked at him quizzically. 'Invented it yesterday,' he explained. 'Call it "Pimestroika": guaranteed to bring your personal Kremlin to its knees.'

'To the revolution,' Joss shouted.

'Storm the Winter Palace,' Tom bellowed.

'Just mix the drink, comrade,' Ben said, smiling indulgently at

213

*his mates. Greta left the pool without a word or a backward glance
and Joss saw the sun dive behind a cloud.*

Back in the apartment Callum watched Joss talk through heavy-
lidded eyes, red-rimmed by deprivation, but also wary and angry.

'You murdered your body with that filthy stuff; the Church will
teach you the true way.'

But Joss noticed that the thunder and the crash of his earlier
pronouncements were now mercifully absent. Callum waited for
a reply. Joss was minded to respond with some inappropriate and
smug metaphor, but this was not the time for jokes: he doubted if
it ever would be again.

'Dad, the Church is guilty of many things: particularly murder.'

Callum shook his head and pulled the flowered counterpane
closer around his chest. It was touching; like a child fearing the
night and everything that dreams could bring.

'Most people arrived on time,' Joss continued as he rubbed a spot
on his thigh, where a childhood break brought him early arthritic
pain; Callum watched his activity.

'I took you to hospital myself,' he muttered. 'Carried you to the
car, felt terrible, built the tree-house you fell from.'

'No,' Joss argued gently, 'you *bought* the tree-house I fell from.
I would have loved it more if you had made it yourself.'

'I wasn't a good father,' Callum whispered.

'I wasn't a good son,' Joss replied, 'but I didn't expect my mother
to come back so late to the house.'

*Things were getting out of hand. Spineless Eric had supplied the
gear, as per contract, and the floodlights illuminated the pool.
At any one time there were between 75 to 100 ravers in and
around the premises moving animatedly to the Ibiza sound. The
boys had a couple of joints as they planned their next expedition;
base jumping in the Tyrol. Greta had chilled out slightly and Joss,
who had just dropped an E, waited for the jaw clamp and the
munchies to grip him simultaneously. Things became decidedly
weird after that.*

*The expected 'loving up' was displaced by multi-coloured hal-
lucinations of hideous intensity; he'd been given some form of
acid. The last thing he could remember, before being windswept
by the chemicals, was seeing his mother. He hoped it was merely
an illusion, part of the chemical effect. But there she was, calm and
charming as ever. He saw her shrug her shoulders at the advantage
he had taken of her absence as she took a drink offered too, too
quickly by a grinning Spineless Eric; then he had blacked out.*

*When he woke, the police and ambulancemen were there, fran-
tically attempting to revive her, but it was pointless. At some later
stage when the spiked drink ravaged her brain, it seemed that she
had wandered to the deserted pool and quietly drowned. The ravers
could not be seen for dust, and Spineless Eric, true to his name,
had established an alibi for the crucial time. At the inquest, in the
absence of 'reliable evidence', the Coroner asked the jury to return
a verdict of misadventure; his father had not spoken to Joss from
that day until their meeting in the Haven.*

'I loved her,' Joss stuttered, his eyes ablaze with the wrongness of
it all. 'The way she was, the way she did things, her kindness, the
whole package.'

'She wasn't a package,' Callum shouted. 'She was my wife.'

'And my mother,' Joss whispered. 'Why do you think I tried to
destroy myself? Do you really believe that one single nano-second
has passed when I haven't hated myself for what happened to
her? Do you think I haven't wished it were me at the bottom of
the pool?'

'I wanted it to be you as well,' Callum said wearily. 'In some
ways I still do, but where are we now? We only have each other
Joss, or do we?'

'I think we could start to get to know each other. I think I would
like to try, but the ball is in your court. Do you really want to go
back to that place, with those people?'

'Yes and no. They gave me comfort when I was grieving for
you both and affection when the world had turned cold. How can
I betray them?'

'They took away the you in you. How could you know it at

the time? Everything was hopeless. I can't blame you, but do you blame me?'

'Yes and no; it's too early.'

His father was staring into the middle distance, but at least he was dealing with the suggestion as a possibility.

'There's something I can't get out of my mind, Joss. It's like it's on a continuous loop in my memory: an echo of better days. I know if you explain it to me then we can start again.'

'The nursery rhyme my mother used to sing to me as a child?'

His father nodded. 'She loved the innocence of that rhyme.'

'I don't think we have time for this, Dad: they will be looking for us and I think we are in danger.'

'I want to know.' Callum's voice was demanding and strong.

'I can't tell you what I don't know.'

His father's eyes flashed in anger.

'Well try harder. You remember her singing it?'

Joss nodded.

'Where did she sing it? Was there a special room or place?'

'I can't remember; I don't want to remember. Please be quiet.'

'Just who is in charge here?'

'Kristina, and me. You haven't been well.'

'On the contrary, I've never been in better shape,' Callum said gloomily. 'I was kidnapped by my own son, tied to a bed, and some shrink has exhausted me beyond endurance.'

'She did the same to me,' Joss replied. His father looked blank, then spoke.

'I keep getting these messages from the back of my head, these urges to call the Church, to confess and betray you; I feel the fear.'

'Can you fight them?'

'If I couldn't, I wouldn't have told you about them.'

Joss considered the reply.

'You could be lying.'

'Yes, yes I could: you'll just have to trust me.'

'Should I?'

'Only you can know the answer, Joss.'

'You need to get some sleep now,' Joss replied, tucking his father into bed. He watched as exhaustion overtook Callum, and

216

then gazed around the tatty bedroom. Spying his father's laptop at the foot of the groaning, shabby sofa, he guiltily picked it up and switched it on. He needed to know more about the Church and Callum's involvement with them. Thurman, the dead journalist, had been adamant that his father 'swam with the sharks'. Joss wanted to know just how deep he had swum. Thurman could have been wrong, but then again . . .

There was a user code to begin the programme and Joss remembered his father always used to use the letters 'MV' for 'merchant venturer'. He typed them in and was relieved to see that his father was a creature of habit. This password, though, was only sufficient to operate the overall system, and not particular software. Each and every time Joss attempted to read a specific document he was denied access. At home, to his father's annoyance, he would use the computer in the study to surf the net and play noisy, violent games. His father had therefore regularly changed the codes and Joss had regularly cracked them. It was a trick Ben the banker had shown him, which involved hacking directly into the C drive memory. People believe that once information is wiped from a computer's memory, then it is lost for good, little do they realise that programmers always place back doors into protected programmes for a quick entry. Joss entered the system and, using Ben's method, he was eventually able to find the burglary point of the software; this gave him access.

Joss was no financial wizard, and the spreadsheets and pie charts he now examined might as well have been in a foreign language. They all related to the finances of the Millennium Church. Joss took copies of all the files he could find and stored them on floppy disks. Whilst his understanding of the content of the files was suspect, one thing was absolutely clear: whatever came into the Church's accounts was routed through Zurich. If Joss was to keep Rivers away from Callum, he would need a lever, something to bargain with. He might also be able to help Greta with some insider-dealing knowledge of the Church.

If everything that Thurman had told him was true, then maybe he could help sink this ship after all.

At that moment Kristina returned after a walk to clear her head and anxiously accosted Joss. 'And?'

217

'You worked a miracle,' Joss said, stooping down to kiss her on the cheek.

'I broke a sacred oath,' she spat. 'This should see me struck off.'

'I doubt it,' Joss said, uncomfortably.

'But I myself must live with the truth, I must come to terms somehow with what I've done.'

'Thanks,' Joss said, but any thanks seemed insufficient and paltry by comparison.

'Did you find out anything about the rhyme, Joss?'

'Jesus,' he spat, 'what is it about an old song that has everyone so exercised?'

She shrugged.

'It's just that Callum . . .'

'You talk as if you know him,' he said suspiciously.

Her face flushed.

'Only as a recent patient,' she stammered unconvincingly.

Joss watched her warily. It felt like there was something going on here that he was not privy to: some sort of secret agenda. Or was Kristina right? Was he just being paranoid?

'I am going to return to the hotel for my things; there is also one very angry doctor to placate.'

'Don't do that,' Joss ordered. 'Send for them; Callum's still unstable, and I think we could all be in big trouble.'

'Possibly, but I have done all I can for him, the rest is between the two of you.'

'He might relapse.'

'I doubt it. He is troubled, yes, but the malignity has been lanced. However, he needs his mind to be kept as busy as possible. He also needs nursing.'

'Are you volunteering?'

She shook her head. 'The Lane family are not my only patients. But I have a suggestion: Elsa from the clinic; she adores you. I can have her flown over to tend to your father.'

Joss smiled, it would be an ideal solution to the problem.

'Terrific.'

Half an hour later the arrangements had been made and Elsa had bubbled with joy at the prospect of the job in hand. Kristina kissed Joss goodbye at the lift door.

'Be careful,' he warned.

'I have nothing to fear,' she replied.

'Indulge me.'

'As you please,' she sniffed, haughtier than she had intended. 'Call me later and let me know how he is. Meanwhile, I have some shopping and relaxation to attend to. I'll be fine.'

Joss demanded her hotel room number, then watched Kristina depart. He felt an unaccountable fear for her.

Kristina Klammer entered her hotel room, exhausted by the pretence and play-acting; and all for nothing. Joss still refused to give up the secret of the rhyme. It had been eighteen long months ago that Callum Lane had briefed her on his requirements during a secret visit to the clinic. He needed his son to remember something that he had forgotten, he said. Callum was never specific about what exactly that something was, but its discovery consumed Joss's father who plagued her for a result. All the time Joss had been at the clinic, she had worked slavishly to solve the problem. But the wolves were closing in on Callum's door and, before she had been able to complete her task, she had been ordered to pronounce Joss cured and free to leave. Her one act of decency had been to allow the letter from his ex-girlfriend through the normal censoring procedure.

All this charade had been Callum's idea. She had been briefed to construct a scenario that would subject him to the ultimate pressure. A tour de force of guilt to break his son to the point where he would remember what the words of the poem meant. But they had failed. Kristina would play no further part in the enterprise.

Her hand reached for the light switch, but the room lit up before she could touch it. She was about to scream when a hand clamped over her mouth. Another man, small and stocky, dressed in black, stood before her, smiling grimly.

'Doctor Klammer, I presume,' he drawled in an American accent.

She nodded, too terrified to speak.

'I know you won't want to breach client confidentiality,' he continued. 'But I'm afraid one of your patients is causing me and my colleagues more than a little concern.'

219

He walked up to her and punched her hard and full in the stomach. She tried to double up with the pain, but the person behind her continued his firm grip.

'Now let's have a little chat about the deeply dysfunctional Lane family.'

Three hours later, as his father slept and Joss idly watched the small black and white television in the apartment, Kristina's picture flashed up on a news item.

'Morte': the word struck him like a Juggernaut. Joss's French was reasonable enough to know what it meant. Morte. Dead. The news camera panned up to the height of her hotel room window then plummeted down to the floor below, where the area was cordoned off by police tape. He heard the word 'fenêtre' and surmised that Kristina had fallen through the window.

His mouth had gone Sahara-dry and his pulse was speeding like an Ibizan raver. He winced as his own face appeared on the screen and his name was mentioned under the word 'suspect'. Kristina Klammer – his Kris, his friend and his healer – was dead. And Joss was certain he knew who had killed her. Joss reached for the remaining barbiturates he had liberated from the Haven. Once, he would have swallowed them down as quickly as possible and waited for cowardly sleep, but this was different: he wanted to be fully alert, he wanted revenge. Suddenly, there was nothing he wouldn't do to bring these mind-bending murderers to their knees.

Callum couldn't be trusted fully yet, and as his father slept Joss tied him to the bed once more. Then he filled a syringe with the crushed drugs and injected them into his unconscious captive. Callum's eyes crashed open.

'What are you doing?' he demanded, as he pushed and surged against his bonds.

'Kristina's dead: it can only be Trainer, he's thrown her out of a window,' Joss replied breathlessly.

'She will have told him where we are,' Callum slurred: the drug was starting to take effect. 'You must let me go,' he whispered.

'I'll keep you safe, Dad, don't worry.'

'You do *not* understand what is really happening here: release me!'

Joss was too busy thinking ahead: he had to secure his father, then meet Elsa, the nurse who would care for him at the airport.

'She'll never have told them, Dad. I won't be more than an hour.'

Callum's eyes were beginning to glaze. He beckoned to his son as he whispered something, and Joss dropped an ear down to listen.

'You stupid little prick: you have killed us both.'

Joss shook his head. It was the drugs talking; it had to be. He left on his mission.

CHAPTER THIRTY-ONE

Joss stepped over another prostrate self-staining drunk as he made his way through the white-tiled, cavernous corridors of the Metro. He boarded the northbound train heading for Charles de Gaulle international airport. At last, as he settled into his seat and buried his face in the pointless pages of a hastily chosen magazine, he felt anonymous enough to think, unhindered by the constant panic-bolts he'd been suffering ever since he'd left his father in the apartment. Now Callum had another 30 millilitres of phenobarbitone cocktail inside him, he'd sleep through an earthquake.

Problem One sorted. All he had to do now was get to the airport and pick up Elsa, who was arriving on the 21.40 flight from Berne, but first he needed wheels. Car rental from the airport was a no go: he figured Trainer's men or the police would be on the lookout at all major departure points in the city.

Suddenly his logic was pierced by another emotional meteor: Kristina. Jesus Christ, what had they done to her? She had been so much part of his memorable past that he had never contemplated a real future without her. He squeezed his eyes shut and tried to force her kind, thoughtful face out of his mind.

All sense of normality had now disappeared. There was only this new and bizarre world, and how much longer he was to remain in it didn't hang totally on his own wayward sense of self-preservation for once. Trainer and his cronies were murderers – that much was brutally obvious – but the truth that stared him starkly in the face was the fact that if they could kill a gentle woman like Kristina, they were certainly going to lose no sleep over him. Whatever he knew, or they thought he knew, he was making them very nervous.

The train snaked under the city until he sprang off in a quick-step on the outskirts of Paris, two stops before the airport. He walked for a little while, grateful for the slightly misty evening air, before rounding on to a faintly seedy commercial stretch on the Rue le Bobigny.

First call was an all-night *bureau d'échange* where he scored some Swiss Francs and German Marks in small denominations. Next, he located the nearest car hire place, and within the hour he was mobile in a throaty little Renault.

The car park at the airport was the usual frantic squeeze, but eventually he zipped into a bay close to the lifts. He spotted a telephone kiosk to the right of the stairs and firstly checked with the airport information desk on Elsa's flight from Switzerland. Then he telephoned Greta Larson; she had to know what was happening. This was all tied in to the cult, and they might just be able to help each other. Besides, he didn't want her to believe that he was a suspect in Kristina's death. God only knew what she thought him capable of; but he had to try to get his side of the story across. Her answerphone met him with a brief message, and he spoke:

'Greta, I know you don't want to hear from me right now, but this is more important than a casual shag with a stranger. You will hear bad things about me; they aren't true. But you were right about the Millennium Church. I'm on their trail now and I'll be in touch. If I come across anything, anything at all, I'll find you. That's all. Take care.' Joss stared at the mouthpiece for a second, then tried to collect his thoughts. He couldn't be sure whether Kristina had told her killers anything before she died, so the less time he spent in the terminal building the better.

At least Elsa's plane was on time, giving him more than an hour to wait. He moved back to the car and switched on the radio, hoping for more news of Kristina's murder, but there was only one more brief reference to it on the half-hourly news-slot.

The glove compartment contained a complimentary map of Europe and a skeleton street-plan of Paris, which he used to plan his exit on to *le périphérique* and out of the city from the apartment. He sat and took in some deep breaths, trying to relax the tightening in his muscles. He had to think and act clearly.

With fifteen minutes to go, he held the 3½in floppy disks he had used to copy the files from Callum's computer. He had been gripping them tightly, almost willing them to tell him what to do, then he placed them back into the safety of the back pocket in his jeans. There was nothing else for it: he had to go to Zurich. Instinctively, he realised that the only way out of this ruthless game was by knockout, and the place to start had to be the money trail and Ben the Banker.

First, he had to get Elsa away from the terminal without drawing attention to himself, and just in case there were any obstacles he removed the piston barrel from the crooklock and secreted it up the sleeve of his Gore-tex jacket. He moved swiftly across the car park. It felt good to be active at last, as he reached the lift.

Keep calm.

But don't lose the edge!

As he reached the long glass corridor to the arrivals terminal his whole body was pulsating with apprehension, but how he loved that rush. There was a set of pale double doors ahead of him, partially obscured by a family of six excited youngsters seriously hassling their mother, who was clearly desperate for the return of her husband. A lot of squeaky voices making 'Pa-pa, Pa-pa' sounds drifted into his ears as he got closer. A sign above the doors twenty metres away said it all: *'Ceux qui laissent leurs véhicules le faisent à leurs risques et périls'*.

Joss gave a small, ironic smile as his foot knocked a child's doll and sent it skittering along the floor ahead.

'Excusez-moi, madame,' he said in his worst French accent to the struggling woman who was still trying in vain to shepherd her brood along to the door. She turned toward him.

'Oui, monsieur,' she snapped, while attempting to break up a squabble among the children.

'You dropped this,' he said, offering the figure, which turned out to be an Action Man soldier.

'Ah, merci, merci,' she said gratefully before returning her attention back to the children, leaving Joss holding the snarling little warmonger. *'Henri, tu a laissé tomber ton Bruno.'*

One of the kids, about five years old with Buddy Holly-style eyegear and spiky black hair, wandered up to him and tugged at his hand.

'Merci, monsieur,' he said with a grin cheekier than Bilko.

'You're most welcome,' Joss replied, as the mother looked on anxiously. 'Come on, hurry up or you'll miss Papa's plane.' The woman smiled warmly as he gave a nod of encouragement for her to carry on while he walked along with Henri.

The door to the terminal was just ahead now. The worst that could happen was that Trainer himself would be waiting for him on the other side, scrutinising every face that passed through, with his insect eyes taking everything in. Christ! – Joss gripped the little hand tightly – what was he doing? He could be leading this precious little child into a murder zone.

He swept the paranoia aside as he breezed through the door, keeping his head down. If anyone was waiting for him there then he was going to die. He tried to rationalise the situation. No one would dare produce a gun in such a public place, he was sure of that; but he was also sure that if the moment was right a sniper wouldn't hesitate.

He walked with the family to the ropes trammelling the arrivees' exit. He was lucky, the place was packed, so he edged his way to the back alone of the crowd and took shelter against the far wall.

He checked the electronic information board chattering away above the crowds. Where was it? The plane, the damn plane.

Athens, Budapest, London, Los Angeles . . . *Come on, where are you?* Bombay, Berlin, then he caught it: Swiss Air SW4532 Berne.

'Disembarking now. Disembarking now,' the sign flashed.

People were beginning to wander out of the customs hall: some weary travellers, some returning relatives, but no middle-aged nurse . . . yet.

Come on, Elsa, the coast's clear. let's get out of here. Now. Before there's no time left. For any of us.

The beating got louder in his chest, as one after another the passengers trooped out and greeted loved ones: excited hugs all round, but still no Elsa. He tightened his grip on the metal tube, flat and secure in his palm. If Trainer was around then he would whip it out in one swift and brutal motion. Jesus, what was he saying to himself?

Keep calm, Joss.

Nice and easy.

The inner voice that Kristina had taught him to heed came to his aid and protection. He scanned the landscape once more; and the crowds of people. He loosened his grip on his weapon and wiped his palms against his trousers. He could feel the dampness permeating through the fabric. Every muscle was coiled tight, tense and ready.

Then he saw one of them. Late thirties; blond crew cut, chisel chin with a black overcoat; forty metres to the left, moving down the opposite staircase; alert expression; scanning the faces, not the ticker board.

Paranoia, panic or plan?

Better choose right.

He chose to plan. Turning away from the stairs, Joss headed toward a taxi driver who was standing near the ropes clutching a white board with an unpronounceable name written on it. Joss pulled out a 100-franc note from his jacket pocket, still keeping his back to the stairs. He couldn't bear to look round, even if he dared. He thrust the money into the hand of the startled man and signed in the air for a pen. The man obliged, puzzled but intrigued.

Joss took the board and wrote on the other side:

Elsa. E. Block East car park, 6th level, bay 12.

He took the board in both hands and demonstrated to the driver, flipping the card from one side to the other in his fingers.

'Ah, message.' The man shrugged and put the money in his pocket. 'No problem.'

Joss thanked him, pulled his collar high around his neck and headed for the main exit. As he approached with the crowds he lost sight of Chisel-face. Not that good then, Trainer, are you? he thought. He thought too soon.

At the doors ahead he saw his man again, talking to another man of heavier build and dark hair who didn't fall into the cultural visitor category. Joss was sufficiently above average height that he could see over the heads of the people in front of him. He was sure there were only two of them. No sign of Trainer himself: at least, not at this exit point.

Desperately, he searched around for alternatives. Seconds later, he sidled off to the left of the main stream of pedestrian traffic and walked with the opposite flow, heading for the upper level and viewing gallery. He nipped under the stairs leading up there and spotted a door marked '*réservé au personnel de l'aéroport*'.

He heard something that didn't register with him at first – just another voice in the crowd greeting a relative. It was just a little louder than the rest. His attention was still rooted firmly on the escape door. If the taxi driver hadn't repeated himself so loudly, he would have ignored it.

'I tell you, madam, it was given to me only moments ago. Look, there he is, I tell you, there he is.'

Then it registered. Joss turned his head. It was too late: although Chisel-face hadn't seen what the commotion was, he certainly spotted Joss and immediately reached for his inside pocket. Joss couldn't take the chance: he could only hope that Elsa had finally believed the taxi driver, kept her mouth shut and would head for the car park.

Meanwhile, he had to shake off these two goons. Check that, he thought: there might be more than just a shake involved. He slid through the door, took the left option and turned down a small staircase leading into a cafeteria obviously catering for transient airline staff. No time to think, only execute. So he didn't stop for the shouts of protest from the group of stewardesses when he barged into their table, spilling everything in sight. As chairs screeched and glasses went crashing to the floor in his wake, a few screams from frightened young girls pierced the chaos. What the hell, he wasn't in the mood for making dates anyway.

He crossed the cafeteria just before Chisel-face burst into the room with a determined focus in his eyes. Joss belted through the glass doors and emerged into another large lounge overlooking the tarmac runways outside. The huge silver undercarriage of a 747 was lit up and standing closest to the floor-to-ceiling windows.

He sprinted the length of the room, which contained only a few people relaxing and watching the ground crews in black and yellow boiler suits going about their industrious business. They hovered around the majestic jumbo, gigantic against the night sky like little parasite fish darting around whales in the ocean. He knew that the security staff would have been alerted by now, and he had to find an exit. He frantically scanned the signs ahead of him.

Which way, which way?

228

The lights outside bounced up and down as he ran.

Plan, Joss.

Bingo.

He checked the blue diagram above, depicting a set of suitcases and an arrow to the right. Then he spotted a long corridor at right angles, fifty metres away. Just then, as he was rushing towards it, he heard shouts behind him and a loud yelp as Chisel-face went hurtling to the floor with an enthusiastic pilot locked on to his ankles.

Joss took his chance and crashed through the emergency exit signs directly to his right, setting off an internal alarm. He found himself on a galleried walkway encircling the observation areas of the huge concrete hangars. He guessed the walkways were used for authorised guided tours, so they must lead somewhere. Fortunately, the personnel working on aircraft below him couldn't hear the clatter of his shoes as he sped across the mesh metal walkway.

They also couldn't hear the first spit of the gun in Chisel-face's hand. The bullet whistled within inches of Joss's left ankle, sparking off the flooring with a welder's flash. He kept running, straining from side to side, doing his best to minimise the target. The only thing he could think of was why Chisel-face hadn't gone for the head shot. Jesus, he was even beginning to think like these guys. Then, through the gaps below him, about a five-metre drop, he spied a moving conveyor belt.

No time to think: just execute.

He jumped on it, hoping that the rubber flaps at the end would give way to a soft landing down a chute to the baggage handlers emptying the luggage from the 747.

He was wrong.

Sirens. He could hear sirens. He shook his head, realising he had been rendered unconscious by the fall and felt a bump to the back of his skull. Sirens; Christ, for a moment he had forgotten about the security services: they would be tearing the place upside-down searching for the cause of this disorder. He could only hope that Elsa had got to the car before the airport was closed off. They would suspect anything from terrorists to drug-smugglers judging by the trail of destruction left behind in his wake.

Straight ahead of him was a fenced-off maintenance-vehicles' compound, which offered good cover to enable him to get to the rear end of the car park. From there, he could easily scale the outside face of the multi-storey by the substantial guttering.

He pushed ahead and scuttled around the perimeter until he found a spot furthest away from the terminal buildings. Traffic was moving inside the compound and a few forlorn-looking portacabins to his right contained groups of shiftworkers. No one noticed him swiftly tumble over the fence and snake under a petrol tanker.

Just then, he heard a siren wailing into earshot and getting stronger with each second. Not one, but two cars bleating a discordant scream as they closed in. He could just about see the gate to the compound manned by a single security guard.

The police cars sprayed groundwater in great arcs as they slid to rest next to the entrance. Joss strained to hear the frantic exchange between the drivers, but the semantics didn't matter: he knew all too well whom they were looking for. They received another communication and sped off. Another car, this time an unmarked Citroën, replaced it. A flash of blond hair emerging from the rear seat of the vehicle was more than enough to tell him that Chisel-face and his companions had more influence on the situation than he did. Did the Millennium Church's influence extend as far as the French authorities?

He couldn't waste any time pondering those particular conundrums, and he certainly wasn't prepared to see whether he could barter his way out of the situation. He had to move and move quickly. He watched as other men spilled out of the cars and began filing into the compound about a hundred metres away from him.

Plan and execute.

He planned.

The sky was pale and moonless, but over the tops of the huts and the far end of the compound Joss could see the dim glow of the yellow phosphorous autoroute leading away and beyond to the stronger tint of Paris neon.

He moved.

Slowly at first but then, as his confidence grew, with more speed he clung to the ground, creeping his way along the row of metal underbellies. Axles and low-slung trailers impeded his progress, but before long he had covered the distance to the far end of the compound and emerged just behind the first in a series of ten or more wooden storage sheds.

Suddenly, he was sure he could hear the faintest rustle of footsteps just around the corner. He darted for cover in the gap between the first and second sheds.

One set, at least; more probably, two. They had crept around the perimeter on the other side and were edging their way between the fence and the sheds. There it was again. Joss stood motionless, holding his breath as the sound moved closer to him from the darkness. Then a flash of torchlight.

A spasm of fear shot through him like an electric shock following through with a panic bolt.

Should he run?

No: be calm until the panic passes.

Then execute.

Silence.

Slowly and carefully, he moved to the end of the shed and listened again. A movement behind him caused him to turn sharply. He cowered down behind an oildrum. Then he caught them – sound and vision together: a shadow on the steps of the third shed along. A second figure joined the first, shoes creaking. There was nothing for a moment, then they muttered something and moved away to the steps of the next shed along, ducking under the windows as they went.

The car park was no more than sixty metres away: with the fence close by, he could get to the first floor without any difficulty at all.

One of the men searched the shed while the other stayed outside watching, waiting, with the steely blue moonlit glint of a gun in his hand. They knew he was there, somewhere. They must want him real bad. They were sensible and efficient and in the next five minutes they would find him.

Plan and execute.

It was like a paralysis.

Silent and still.

Move when the time is right.

231

His instinct told him: silent and still. The men searched another hut quickly, then another. They came up to the shed against which he was lying. Same pattern: one went inside while the other stood watch. Only two metres away now: another second and it would be too late.

The inertia broke in a snap as Joss threw himself at the figure with his full weight. The man went crashing to the ground with barely time to scream as Joss whipped the tube across his temple.

'Tomlin, you all right?'

An English voice, rough and very ready. Joss pushed himself flat against the shed wall and waited for the other man to appear. He almost felt like he should apologise for his anger as he struck the man a single, vicious blow to the back of his neck.

Before his victim hit the ground, Joss was already legging it for the fence, and in one tremendous effort he leapt on to the mesh, gripping the top, and scrambled over the gap on to the first level of the car park. Crouching down, he checked around: no security. They must still be searching inside the airport, he thought. Now for Elsa.

The stairwell looked clear and he headed for it without a sound. Five flights later he sprang out of the doors and saw her standing by the car.

Thank God.

He sprinted over to her and smiled affectionately.

'Thanks for coming. Sorry I couldn't be there to greet you: I had to take a leak.'

'Looks like you didn't make it,' Elsa replied, indicating his clothes which were still covered in the grease and oil from his earlier crawl.

'Yeah, I kinda got lost. Come on, I'll fill you in on the way.'

'The way where?'

'It's a long story. Get in.'

'Where's Doctor Klammer?' she asked, lifting up her small suitcase.

'Throw it in the back, Elsa: just get moving.'

'Joss, what's going on?'

'I only wish I knew, honestly. She's dead, Elsa. Kristina's dead.'

232

'What? But I only spoke to her . . .'

'I know, I know, I was there. Come on, there's no time.'

'Joss, please, I feel . . . how can this be true?'

'Believe me, I wish to God it wasn't, Elsa, but if we don't get out of here now I'm afraid we could be knocking on the Pearly Gates with her.'

'Oh, Joss.' She dropped the suitcase to the floor, where she stood rooted to the spot, shock spreading across her face like a cyclone.

Shit, he thought, *I could have handled this one a little better*. At least he'd had a few hours to become accustomed to the new reality. He moved around to her side of the car and gently placed his arm around her shoulders, drawing her close to him. She swallowed hard until she could hold it back no longer. Surprisingly, what came out wasn't the wailing sobs he'd expected, but a stream of expletives mouthed angrily into his shoulder. He felt a warm ray of hope as he knew at least his father would be safe with this remarkable woman.

CHAPTER THIRTY-TWO

The buzz of late-night diners' conversation hummed around the restaurant in smart Soho. Mark Mason sipped a brandy awaiting the return of Rory Fannon. He had been surprised by Fannon's invitation to dinner. Whilst there was nothing to stop counsel dining together during a case, the combative nature of this dispute had engendered a 'gloves off' mentality.

The day had concluded with Rivers's detailed account of the growth of the Millennium Church throughout the world. By Mason's estimation he would be in the box for another couple of days at least.

Fannon had stopped by a table that had a senior solicitor from a successful law firm at its head and back-slapped his way into another important, criminal brief. The defence QC then returned to his place opposite Mason.

'Always take care of business,' Fannon muttered as a silver bucket containing a bottle of vintage champagne was placed before the solicitor and his party. They nodded their appreciation to Fannon, who raised his glass in recognition.

'Bit obvious, isn't it?' Mason said.

'Difficult to miss then, old son,' Fannon replied, with a satisfied smile.

'I don't mean to appear ungracious, Rory, but what's this all about? I've sat through a very fine dinner and we've bullshitted our way through great tales of the Bailey, but . . .'

'Why did I ask you in the first place?' Fannon concluded for him. 'Don't know really. Thynne and Callow are dry to the point of arid, just needed a bit of human contact, I suppose.'

'Come on, you're an old stager: you must want something from me.'

Fannon looked deep into the thick, viscous liquid of his own brandy balloon.

'How do you think our boy's doing, Mark?'

'Something troubling you?' Mason asked.

'My clerk persuaded me to accept the case, you know: wasn't so keen myself.'

'Like you said in the robing room on day one: "school fees to pay".'

'I did, didn't I?' Fannon shrugged. 'I'll start believing my own blarney next.'

'He wasn't going to give evidence, was he: not until you forced the issue?'

The Reverend is none too happy with me,' Fannon replied with a smirk. 'There was a smidgen of confusion at the time. I thought Callow was going to crap himself when Withnail allowed the case to continue.'

'Why did you call him? He said everything he needed to in his police interviews. Rose was given a thorough going-over in cross and you've got a hundred alibi witnesses for the times of the assaults.'

Fannon's eyes seemed to cloud over.

'Didn't seem fair that's all.'

But Mason suspected there was more to it than that.

'I mean, the girl's a mess for some reason. I think the father's obsessive but I doubt he's an abuser.'

'I hope the jury share that view,' Mason whispered.

'I have a daughter the same age, you know,' Fannon continued. 'I'm blessed that nothing like that has ever happened to her: don't know what I'd do if it ever did, but the man scares me.' His voice trailed off.

'No one told you that you have to like your client. I mean, how many murderers have you swapped phone numbers with?' Mason said reasonably.

'I said I feared him, not disliked him. The power of the man's will is incredible.'

'That's why the cult members follow him,' Mason suggested. Fannon shook his head.

'I shouldn't talk about the case, but we all do it. I've seen paedophiles, rapists, buggerers and sadists, self-mutilators and child-killers, but Rivers . . . No, he takes the biscuit barrel. It's not the torment in a criminal's soul, it's the lack of any real soul at all that scares the shit out of me.'

'A barrister with a conscience; is that an oxymoron?'

'You're living proof that it's not,' Fannon replied. 'The only moron is me for taking this case.'

Mason took a belt from his drink and swallowed hard.

'I've had my own regrets,' he confided.

'Don't beat yourself up about it,' Fannon chided.

'Seems we are both in the business of self-flagellation tonight.'

Fannon paused for a moment, glanced around the room suspiciously, then leaned forward.

'Your man Rivers there,' he began, 'very organised, controlled, but I've seen him in conference, asked him a few difficult questions.'

'Rory, don't, you're breaching client privilege.'

'Only if I give you content, and I'm not completely suicidal,' the Irish lawyer said. 'But if you get him riled, the jury might just see a different Right fucking Reverend Rivers.'

He stood to leave.

'I'll pay the bill on the way out. Goodnight, Mark.'

'Thanks, Rory,' Mason said.

'What for? Indifferent food in an over-priced canteen?'

'For being candid.'

'Me? I said nothing you didn't know already. We all have our weak points: find his.' And with that, Fannon left.

Later, as he turned off the bedroom light, Mark Mason chewed over Fannon's bitter words. There had to be a chink in Rivers's holy armour, a weakness in the metal that would allow an arrow of insight to penetrate fatally: he could only pray that he could direct his aim truly.

CHAPTER THIRTY-THREE

Joss had driven Elsa back to the shabby apartment, her rich expletives turning to sorrow. She had immediately checked his father's vital signs and promised to care for him as best she could. Joss left for Kristina's hotel, knowing how dangerous it would be now that his photograph had appeared on television; but he needed more information. Joss was certain that the two men he had attacked at the airport were part of Trainer's team. That meant that Kristina had told them of Elsa's arrival, he could only hope that she had not told them the location of the flat where his father was. The area around the hotel was cordoned off and thronged with police; it was much too fraught with danger to approach further. He decided to return to his father and Elsa before leaving for Zurich.

He parked the throaty hire car around the corner and made for the apartment block. As he approached, Joss heard a disturbance from the shabby foyer and, ducking into the shadows, he saw Chisel-face emerge his head bandaged, carrying a prostrate Callum Lane, feet first. His colleague followed behind with the rest of his slumped father in his arms. Trainer carried up the rear, glancing from side to side as if he could sense Joss's presence. They threw Callum into the boot of a waiting car, closed it and sped off. Joss was too stunned to react.

Elsa! He ran inside, ignored the lift and raced up the stairs to the fourth floor. The door was open and he feared the worst. Barging in, Joss found her on the sofa, bleeding from a head wound but still breathing. He sat her up. 'Elsa, Elsa, wake up, please wake up.' After a short time, and to his relief, her eyes blinked open. She stared around the room, attempting to remember where she was and what had occurred.

'Bastards,' she spat. 'I could not do anything, Joss,' she added, raising her hands to her bloodied head.

'It's my fault. I should have known,' Joss muttered.

'The little one, the American, he left a message, something like: the police are with them; it would be pointless to complain. Come in, or your father dies.'

Joss cleaned up her wounds whilst he considered his options. Whilst he was on the run Callum would stay alive. The moment he capitulated would be their last. He could only free his father if he had something to bargain with. Joss felt the reassuring presence of the floppy disks in his jeans pocket and knew what he must do.

It took him less time than he expected getting to the outskirts of the city via the *périphérique*. Although the traffic was solid it moved swiftly enough, and he began to relax a little in the darkness of the car.

He crossed the Seine and headed for the tollbooth leading on to the N15 E7 Paris-to-Dijon autoroute.

It was a good 250 kilometres to Dijon and he pressed the little car hard down the concrete highway, while trying to figure out what the hell was really going down with these freaks. It stood to reason that they felt very uncomfortable about his reappearance, but what was so important that they would kill seemingly anyone who had access to his father? A renewed sense of fear and gratitude pulsed through him when he thought of the risk that Elsa had taken. Joss had put her up in a plush hotel, where she could rest for a couple of days and lick her wounds.

It didn't surprise him at all that people like Rivers would be only too happy to have his father working for him. Callum Lane was one of the world's great tax-avoidance experts. He knew all the dodges and the swerves. He more than knew them, he devoured them: every tax haven, every Trust, any currency. He had loved such wheeling and dealing ever since Joss could remember. He had tried so hard to turn his son into a chip off the old block. It never worked: by the time Joss had reached 14 years of age, he was finding every excuse in the world to get away from home and into the open; away from Callum with his charts, his pink newspaper and his lifelong fight with the Inland Revenue.

When not at boarding school in Oxfordshire, itself a more athletic than academic public school, he organised his own vacations. Summer camps, adventure weekends, even a milk round during one holiday, which his father thought admirably capitalist and his mother declared dangerous. Callum never realised that these part-time jobs rescued Joss from the breakfast ritual of the *Financial Times*, but his mother did. Lost in the past, he pushed on to Dijon, then Strasbourg, his crossing point at Delle Porrentrux in the west of Switzerland, towards his ultimate destination of Zurich.

Trainer held Callum Lane's cheek in one hand and slapped the other with hard stinging smacks.

'Wakey, wakey, brother Callum; it's confession time.'

Joss's father slid open his eyes slyly.

'Thank God,' he sighed, 'you found me.'

The room was dark and bare. He recognised Tomlin and Moyne, who were stripped down to T-shirts and looked ready for action.

'Why have you tied me up?' he asked innocently.

Trainer smiled and pulled up a chair opposite.

'This is the bit of the movie where the bad guys get to have their fun, Callum.' He nodded to Tomlin, who produced a rivet gun and experimentally fired one into the floorboard. It spat, and the wood shattered with the impact of the metal.

'I thought something ironic was in order: a modern-day crucifixion, perhaps.'

Callum Lane began to shake.

'You saw how it was,' he stammered. 'He had me tied up, and drugged up to the eyeballs; I was kidnapped.'

Trainer shook his head, then nodded to Tomlin. Callum's mouth was clamped by Moyne as Tomlin slowly removed Callum's shoes and aimed the gun at his smallest toe.

'I am the resurrection and the light,' Trainer whispered as the rivet tore into his foot. Callum shuddered, and attempted to scream his pain away, but the grip on his mouth refused his need.

'Confession is good for the soul,' Trainer said.

'And for the sole of the foot,' Tomlin grunted his appreciation of the comment. The hand was removed from Callum's mouth.

'Why are you doing this to me?' Callum pleaded, his face twisted with agony. 'Tell me, how have I wronged you, brother?'

Trainer nodded once more.

'Wait,' Callum shouted. Trainer hesitated.

'Brother? But one even greater than the Reverend was betrayed with a kiss, how have you betrayed us?'

Callum swallowed hard before speaking.

'It was through love. The boy needed help; I helped him. Doesn't the Reverend teach us that we must sacrifice in order to achieve true understanding?'

Trainer smiled warmly.

'You have interpreted this for your own ends and have not made any sacrifice, but stolen from your brothers and sisters.'

'Then I must be punished, but let the Reverend decide what my punishment will be.'

Trainer considered his response.

'I feel that our leader has other matters to attend to. I am his trusted disciple and must take it upon myself to mete out punishment.'

He nodded once more, and another projectile surged into Callum's foot, accompanied by his scream. This time his burning pain was allowed freedom of expression. Trainer leaned his chin on his hand.

'You will run out of toes eventually; then we must consider other items of your anatomy.' He glanced down to Callum's groin, which was soaking wet. 'We have spoken to the Klammer woman, or shall we call her the flying doctor? Your conversion to our way of thinking is a sham: admit this or lose another digit.'

This time there was no hesitation.

'Yes, fuck you, you poisonous dwarf. I used the funds to pay for his treatment.'

Trainer nodded. 'This is better, though personally a little insulting.'

He leaned forward and ground his heel on Callum Lane's tortured foot. This time he squealed.

'Forgive me, brother,' Trainer said. 'I shall pray to be forgiven for my spite. You clearly have no real affection for the boy: why did you do it? And this time look inside your soul for the truth.'

'His mother stole some documents from me before her death,'

Callum said, breathing harshly, his forehead dripping with sweat.
'She left a clue in her will only Joss can understand. If he ever
finds those documents it will destroy us all.'

Trainer closed his eyes in deep contemplation.

'Let me try to understand fully,' he began. 'I gather that the
marital home was not a happy one before your wife's untimely
death and she made provision for her own safety?'

Callum nodded.

'Yet she died, and the documentary time-bomb still ticks?'

Joss's father nodded once more.

'And this would involve some of the past dealings you have had
with the Church?'

'Bell, book and candle,' Callum spat.

'Indeed the very artefacts used by the Roman Catholic Church
for an exorcism.'

'I can bring him in,' Callum said. 'You can't do it without me.'

'Perhaps. Where has he gone?' Trainer demanded.

'I have no idea, but I would tell you if I knew.'

Trainer looked upon his captive with complete disgust.

'Yes, I believe you would. Does the boy have any idea of what
you were up to?'

Lane senior shook his head: 'He couldn't have; there's no
way.'

'So he will trade,' Trainer pronounced.

'He's bright enough to seek leverage,' Callum offered.

'And how could he find that, I wonder.'

'Did you bring my laptop computer?'

Trainer glanced across to the far side of the dingy room. Moyne
retrieved the item in question. Callum informed them of the required
codes and they searched the memory for recent access. Trainer
glanced through the files.

'Your son obtained the details of our money route,' he concluded.

'You still need me to bring him in?' Callum enquired anxiously.

Trainer nodded. 'Your life expectancy lasts until we have your
son, and not one second longer. Do not expect your death to be
quick or merciful.' He turned to his men and whispered, 'Zurich.'

*   *   *

243

Joss reached Switzerland, feeling relieved, at 2am. The last time he'd crossed the Limmat he was Interailing as a student. Nothing much had changed. Zurich was still the same as any other city from the outside in. Heavy industrial complexes in the satellite towns flashed by as he headed along, and it wasn't until he reached the Limmatstrasse that he began to recall the buildings of the old town around the Hauptbahnhof station on the west bank of the river. He circled the Platz promenade and turned on to Bahnhofquai carefully, observing the very precise road manners of the Swiss drivers, who show great deference to the trams whizzing around the city streets.

Joss manoeuvred the car across the Rudolph Brun Bridge and travelled east along the Muhlegasse trying to spot a hostel. The light was gradually breaking as he found a place along the Zahringerstrasse called Hotel Martahaus, where a group of backpackers were making their way down the steps.

Joss parked the car and took his haversack from the boot. He covered the short walk quickly, feeling the cold after the raging heater in the Renault. A young man sat, reading a magazine, behind a heavily varnished reception desk. This was fine, thought Joss.

'Hi. Do you have any space?' he said in English as he approached.

'Sixty-six francs for a single, thirty-two if you don't mind sharing in the dorm.' The man replied easily in Joss's language.

'Single, please,' said Joss.

'Lounge is down the hall. Breakfast from six.'

'Thanks, I'll bear that in mind, but I'm kind of tired. I think I'll get my head down first.'

'Travelling far?' asked the man, nodding at Joss's rucksack.

'No, just come up from Italy,' Joss lied easily. 'Heading back down there in a couple of days: just came up to find someone.'

'Ah, I understand. A woman, no?' The man's eyes widened considerably with that look of shared interest. They were after all in the middle of the red-light district. 'I can recommend a good establishment: clean, no fuss, you know what I mean.'

'I do, but no thanks: maybe later.' The last thing Joss needed now was a prostitute.

He paid with two fifty-franc notes and promised the man the

balance later that day when he'd had a chance to change some money. This lying lark was getting too easy, he thought, as he climbed the staircase decorated with unconvincing prints by the great waterside artists of the city.

The room was basic, but at least it had a shower and a clean set of towels. He threw himself onto the bed and turned on his back, staring at the ceiling. As he did so, the thin plasterboard wall shook ominously. The fan heater in the corner of the room was down to its final breaths: as he flicked the switch next to his bedside cabinet it stirred into action with a thud, and the burnt oaky smell of a filament in trouble began circling the room. For a while, he did nothing but lie still, before finally drifting off into a dreamless sleep.

The Niederdorfstrasse district woke early: at five he was disturbed by the clinking of beer crates stocking up the bars and clubs of the old town. A few minutes later and the water pipes in the hotel began to creak into full rattle as the early travellers and guesthouse staff took their showers.

Joss lay for a while, listening to a conversation outside his window between two maids. The tension of the previous night's activity seemed strangely distant now. He felt numb to the touch of ordinary people and their lives. At around 7 am the house was in full swing, with jocular chatter going on among the guests tramping past his room along the corridor to the staircase. Joss realised then that the dreamless snatches of respite were over, so he got up and showered slowly. Before long, his thoughts turned to food, forced on him by biting stomach cramps ably assisted by his tiredness. He pulled on a black polo-neck sweater and jeans and left in search of breakfast. He slipped past the young man at the desk without further conversation and found himself on the street. He turned left and headed for the Sellargrabben, where he knew there were a number of twenty-four-hour eateries that catered for transport workers. Eventually, he found a suitable one and ordered the basic all-day trough from the breakfast buffet for ten francs. He lingered over his food, enjoying the banter of the workers chuntering on around him, and thought about what to do next.

It was obvious.

In the café there was a public telephone, so he purchased two tax cards from the rounded proprietor for forty francs and rang

information. It wasn't long before he was armed with Ben's number
at Crédit Suisse in Geneva. As he waited for the call to be answered,
he thought how fortunate it was that one of his best friends had
turned out to love the money market just as much as his father
once had. The receptionist at the Geneva bank answered the phone
in perfectly pronounced English.

'Good morning, Crédit Suisse First Boston International Trading.
How can I help you?'

'Good morning. Could I possibly speak to Ben Nilan?'

'One moment please.' The line hummed a ditto before the
connection was made.

'Ben Nilan.'

'"Winter, spring, summer or fall",' Joss whispered into the
mouthpiece, repeating the first chorus line of James Taylor's
classic. There was silence.

'Who's that?' demanded the voice.

'"All you got to do is call and I'll be there, yes I will: you got
a . . ."'

'Friend,' Ben finished then went on angrily, 'OK, quit fooling
around. Who is this?'

'It's Joss.'

Silence.

'Ben, are you still there?'

'Of course I am, you dipstick. Where the hell have you been?'

'No time, Ben, I need your help, old pal.'

'Whoa, hold on a sec, Lone Ranger, you can't expect just to catch
the master of the universe in a helpful mood before he's had his
first meeting of the day. If I remember, the last time I gave you
a helping hand I didn't hear from you again for how long? Go on,
remind me. Oh yes, I know: it's until now.'

'Sorry, Ben, things have been kind of complex.'

'Is that the word for it these days? No matter, I expect you'll tell
me when you're ready. What's the brush?'

'I need information.'

'If I have it you can have it: apart from the colour of my
girlfriend's underwear,' he quipped.

'Was a time when we even shared that.'

'Long time ago.'

'OK. I guessed you would be pissed off at me but, honestly, there is a good reason.'

'I'll bet, knowing you, Joss, there always will be. I'm just never sure if it's the right one.'

'Look, I need to get behind some numbered accounts in Zurich.'

'Ha, ha.'

'What's the matter?'

'See you some time after the next millennium, cowboy: no can do.'

'Come on, Ben, I'm desperate.'

'That may be, but you're talking major-league criminal activity here. I can't afford the drop in salary to prison wages.'

'Was a time when you didn't care.'

'Was a time when I didn't have a mortgage and a kid to look after, Joss. Wake up to adulthood.'

'Jesus!'

'That's what I said when Christian popped out.'

'Cool name.'

'Hot babe: best thing I ever did, hitching a ride with her.'

'What, better than the base jumping in Venezuela?'

'Different kind of thrill. Besides, I've put on a few pounds since then: I'd probably bounce off the floor.'

'I'd always be there to stop you,' said Joss, leaving between them the shared memory of when he really had prevented Ben from falling six thousand feet to a certain death. And he knew it.

'Where are you?' Ben asked after a short silence.

'Zurich.'

'Stay put: I'll be there mid-afternoon. Meet me in the cybercafé at number 5 Rossengasse, next to the Hotel St Georges, at four. This better be good, Joss.'

'Trust me, Ben.'

'I always did.'

CHAPTER THIRTY-FOUR

The first part of Rivers's marathon performance in the witness box was drawing to a close. After witnessing the zeal of his religious beliefs on the first day of evidence, the jury's interest had subsequently waned. Fannon, barely masking his disdain, had paid lip-service to the catalogue of charitable works financed and administered by the Millennium Church.

The message was clear and unequivocal: the Church does great deeds, Rivers is head of the Church, therefore he is good. It was a deductive syllogism of stark logic. There were times when even the accused's passion seemed to slip, but a note from Thynne soon steered the subject matter to pertinence.

Fannon had then painstakingly questioned Rivers about his whereabouts in relation to each and every allegation of abuse, and Rivers gave chapter and verse from his diary of 'good works', as he called them. There were always other members of the Church who would in due course swear their own oath and provide alibis for their leader.

Rivers had no recollection of Rose Moody, he said. He claimed he might have met her once, but then there were so many young people in such need of his guidance and counsel. Rose and Geoff had sat transfixed in the public gallery as Rivers spoke, the girl appearing thinner and more frail with every denial, her father ruddy-faced with outrage. Mark Mason tapped his pen thoughtfully, as Fannon made a last check with Thynne and Callow that all matters had been dealt with, then fixed Rivers with a level gaze.

'And have you told the truth, Reverend Rivers?'

The accused appeared annoyed by the question, obviously under the impression that his words were unchallengeable.

'The oath I swore is binding,' he spat, but some members of

249

the jury looked between Fannon and his client with undisguised interest. Clearly there was discord in the defence camp.

'Please remain at the stand, I am sure my learned friend has some further questions for you.'

Fannon glanced across to Mason and winked. Rivers saw him and narrowed his eyes. Mason wondered how long Rory would remain on the team. He climbed slowly to his feet.

'A snake oil salesman?' he began.

Rivers looked puzzled.

'I don't understand,' he muttered.

'You began your evidence by describing your past life, before you founded the Church: you described yourself with those exact words.'

'I see, and now you are going to suggest that I have not changed, I suppose.' Rivers was affronted, then calmed himself. 'But, Mr Mason, I am sorry, you are just doing your job. Please ask any questions you see fit.'

'Why, thank you: it is nice to have your permission,' Mason responded acidly. 'But your permission is vital to the Church, is it not?'

'I don't follow,' Rivers said.

'You run a tight ship; your word is law; you are "the baptist", the "birthing father" of the Millennium Church?'

'I give what guidance I can.'

'It is a Church of rigorous discipline, is it not?' Mason continued.

Rivers nodded. 'Many are weak; they must be guided by the strong.'

'And the strongest of all is you?' Mason asked, eyeing the jury who all seemed rapt by the exchange.

'I was chosen, therefore power and dominion were granted to me by the all-powerful.'

'A new soul, another convert, must be a cause of great celebration to the Church?'

'Indeed, heaven rejoices,' Rivers clasped his hands together. Mason noted that a couple of the jury shook their heads suspiciously; the English despised public fervour about everything but football.

'You must keep a register of the saved?'

'There are so many,' Rivers replied.

'Precisely the reason that a careful record must be kept of them all. Their names, ages, sex, origin and progress.'

'I have many who work for me,' he said reasonably, but Mason was aware of the irritation in his voice.

'You mean who work for God,' Mason corrected him, with the tone of a teacher, chastising a pupil's gauche reply.

'That was what I meant to say,' Rivers whispered.

'We all heard what you said, and I suggest that is precisely what this case is all about; your own private church for your own dark needs.'

Rivers firmed his mouth into a thin line.

'The Church is open to all. I have no needs other than salvation: besides, it is well known that I am celibate.'

'It's the first Rose Moody's heard about it,' Mason muttered across to the jury. Thynne was on his feet immediately, but Withnail stayed him with a meaty hand.

'Put your case. I will not tolerate gamesmanship and biased comment in my court.'

Unless it's you that's doing it, Mason thought.

'But before your, how shall I describe it? Epiphany?'

Rivers nodded. 'For once your description is accurate.'

'You had some difficulty with celibacy?' Mason watched for any discoloration of the defendant's face, but he had been well prepared.

'I was lost, a sinner. I fell to temptation: little wonder that I was punished so.'

'You had many affairs?' Mason pressed.

'Many indeed; I slaked my lust to my bitter shame.'

'It took much time and many affairs before your shame became apparent,' Mason commented. Thynne was climbing to his feet, but Rivers raised one finger towards him.

'I will not be silenced by mere rules of law.' He turned towards the jury. 'I have nothing to hide but much to be ashamed of. There were many women . . .'

'Young women, weren't they?' Mason continued, determined not to give the moral high-ground to the experienced preacher.

'Their ages were irrelevant,' he blustered.

251

Mason controlled his breathing, he had absolutely no evidence to back up his allegations: he was working on a hunch born from instinct and the fact that sexual preferences rarely changed for the better.

'But you liked them young didn't you? Fresh and virginal; like Rose!'

'I have never met the girl,' Rivers shouted, then began his own deep breathing exercises in an attempt to control his temper. Rory was right: there was a button to press.

'Why did you have the girls' hymens examined before they were allowed into the Church?'

Rivers's mouth was gaping slightly.

'You see, Reverend,' Mason said, forcing as much disdain into Rivers's clerical title as he could, 'Rose told us of her examination at the Haven and that part of her evidence was never challenged by your barristers in cross-examination. Now are you telling this court that it was not on your orders that young girls were examined in this way?'

Rivers was attempting to gather his composure.

'It is only when we know how far they have fallen that we can save them.'

'So you accept that she is telling the truth about that?'

'It sounds much worse than it is, but we need to know about them.'

Mason leaned over counsel's bench, his hands flat upon the surface.

'Is she telling the truth?'

'Yes,' he whispered.

'Louder.'

'Yes,' Rivers shouted.

'But what will a ruptured hymen tell you about any young girl? It could happen in any number of ways not involving intercourse, could it not?'

'We needed to know, that's all.'

The jury appeared stern and judgemental.

'Then why not just ask them? After all, they were with you because they chose to be: you were their father, their leader. They would not lie to you; or didn't you believe them?'

Rivers was breathing shallowly.

'It was necessary.'

'But God knew, or has he stopped talking to you? That's if he ever spoke to you at all.'

Rivers's finger was pointing straight at Mason.

'The Lord knows me and my work. You are the mouthpiece of doubt; a devil's advocate.'

Thynne was on his feet once more, whilst Mason smiled and Withnail commanded order be restored. Mason was rebuked, but the jury, no the jury had peeked inside the vat of boiling self-justification and didn't seem to like the smell.

The rest of Rivers's cross-examination was adjourned until the next day.

Fannon slipped a note across the bench.

Found the button; pressed it. Aren't you glad I didn't challenge Rose about her examination? P.S. I don't think my services will be required for much longer. R.F.

For the first time since the case began Mark Mason believed that they were in with a chance. Rivers watched him and scowled.

CHAPTER THIRTY-FIVE

The cybercafé was predictably high-tech. Stainless steel benches and brightly polished metal tiles on the floor gave a rhythmic echo as people scurried around the busy interior. Rows of expensive-looking hardware in matching matt-black consoles sat twitching and blinking, beckoning their flightless navigators to faraway places on the global net. Overhead, the exposed foil-covered airducted-heating system snaked through the metal joistwork giving the entire place the feel of a testosterone-driven spaceship.

Joss managed, he thought, to blend into the mixture of customers well enough and purchased for a few francs the use of a terminal at the very rear of the establishment facing the front door, who he noticed a gleaming silver telephone, and took the opportunity to call Greta Larson's chambers' numbers, but was informed that she had left for court. Sighing, he made a mental note to call her later, after the court rose for the day.

He nursed a piping hot coffee while staring into the computer screen in front of him without the remotest idea as to how to operate the new systems. Years spent travelling a different superhighway on chemical overdrive had left him relatively ignorant of the recent techno-revolution.

His embarrassment must have shown as the teenage girl at the next terminal looked over at him pitifully then shouted for the attention of people at the main desk, being too engrossed herself to offer assistance.

The group at the desk contained three silver-Lycra-clad young women, all wearing identical black wigs each cut into a severe geometric bob. Standing next to them, holding a mobile telephone, was a curious-looking creature whom Joss had noticed earlier mincing around in a rather affected manner.

He hoped his helpless expression would attract the attention of at least one of the girls. He was wrong. They looked over at him but none set off in his direction. The creature, however, was moving towards him with a predatory gaze.

He turned out to be the café's proprietor, a young man with a shock of fluorescent green and orange striped hair shaved at the sides. His faintly ridiculous pig-like features were accentuated by the two gold sleepers protruding from his flared nostrils.

'Virgin spaceman?' he enquired in English having correctly guessed Joss's nationality. Was it that obvious?

'Without a helmet, I'm afraid,' Joss replied quickly.

'It is no big deal.'

'Not to you, maybe.'

'Seriously, my friend, you can be driving this baby in nanoseconds, I guarantee it.' He licked his lips just a little too suggestively for Joss's liking.

'I think you're overestimating my road skills.'

'So negative.'

'So realistic.'

'Rene Hildbrand.' The young man smiled, holding out his hand.

'David Reed.' Joss accepted with a geekish grin, now comfortably changing his personality with each stranger he met. The proprietor grabbed one of the dainty, ergonomically designed stools and wheeled it over next to Joss at the terminal. He rolled back the sleeves of his black polo-neck to the elbows and cracked his fingers in the manner of a concert pianist, but Joss couldn't erase the vision of a slightly tacky, albeit modern, vaudeville act.

'OK, David Reed, let's surf,' he said grandly in his best pantomime English accent.

'Take it away, time traveller,' Joss quipped trusting that he was responding in the appropriate spirit.

'This screen allows you access to the net: first you need to log on with your own user identification. It's all linked here in the café anyway, so you do not have to worry about the technical details: just choose a handle for yourself, so if you contact a chat site other users will know who they're talking to. Understand?'

'Sure, you mean I need a snappy title.'

'You got it.'

'OK, what about Dreamer?'

'Why Dreamer?'

'Why not?'

'OK, Dreamer it is. Simply type in your handle in the first dialogue box here and then the computer will finish your log-on procedure, indicating that you are based here at the Zurich Cybercafé.'

'Neat,' Joss said in genuine fascination. The screen bleeped its way rapidly through a series of pages set against a background of asteroids flashing towards them. The technology had changed immensely since its fledgling days.

'It certainly is,' agreed Rene with more than a decent degree of self-satisfaction. 'Now we are in cyberspace where would you like to go?'

'I don't know: anywhere, I guess. Just show me something interesting.'

'I know just the website for a lonely traveller like you.' Rene smiled while his fingers danced over the keys. Within seconds the screen sprang into millions of tiny gaily coloured segments. Joss should have guessed but he didn't.

The brightly coloured banner headline at the top of the Internet page advertised a gay and lesbian chat site. Rene glanced sideways at Joss searching for a reaction. Joss's eyes widened.

'Hey, no offence, but I'm not lonely for that sort of company.'

'A little defensive, I would say.'

'Not really, it's just not my casino.'

'You'll never pick up the prize if you don't enter the lottery.'

Joss smiled at the café owner's tenacity and was just trying to formulate an appropriate response when thankfully he spotted Ben in a blue shirt and yellow necktie bustling to the rescue like the cavalry through the glass doors from the street outside.

He turned to Rene. 'Thanks for the flying lessons, Rene, but I am expecting company and it's just arrived.' He nodded towards Ben who was casing the faces in the joint.

Rene glanced over his shoulder and huffily grunted, 'Mmm, looks like you already lost.' He jumped up and marched past Ben back to the desk, cutting across his path with all the aplomb of a snooty Siamese cat.

'What did I say?' Ben said as he approached.

'I guess he just doesn't think you're trendy enough for his tardis,' Joss laughed. 'I mean, look at you: Jesus, man, what happened to you? Baby banker complete with pinstripe romper.'

'Like it?' said Ben, holding his arms out and brushing off a piece of imaginary lint from the front of his elegant chalkstripe suit.

'Like it? I love it: it's going to be like hanging out with Gordon Gecko.'

'Cut the crap, Joss.'

'They already cut it and you're wearing it, big boy,' Joss countered, their natural rivalry surfacing immediately despite the intervening years.

'You mad that I hit the jackpot, is that it?' Ben smirked as the two men embraced warmly. Their friendship still zipped together tighter than the ropes between them on a freezing mountainside all that time ago.

They stood sizing each other for a moment or two, each flashing silently through the past before Ben picked up the pace.

'So that's why you dragged me all the frigging way from my comfortable office, my very attractive secretary, my very, very beautiful wife and my one and only handsome heir is it?'

'Is what?'

'Is that why you called, dork, because you freaked and I didn't?'

'Oh, sorry, big boy, I got distracted for a sec: thought I was hearing the sounds of a smartarse warbler.'

'No, siree: just the sweet, sweet tune of success.'

'You gone an' done real well for yourself, boss, I can see that,' Joss slurred in mocking mid-West American drawl.

'Yup, I sure have, and I ain't gonna have no jailbird come a wreckin' my party.' They paused; the banter could only take them so far. Joss frowned.

'Seriously, Ben, you've obviously cracked the system: I would like nothing better than to tempt you back to the edge but I know you'll be a great dad.'

'I'm pleased you said that, Joss: you see I've become kind of attached to the freedom of movement principle. And I think what you were talking about on the telephone is diametrically opposed to achieving that lifestyle.'

258

'I'm not asking you to do anything I wouldn't do myself, Ben: I'm in deep with this thing and I need your expertise.'

'First time I've ever heard you beg for help, but it's the same answer, Joss: there are just too many risks involved in what you're proposing.'

'First time I've heard you shy off a risk, Ben.'

'Maybe, but things have changed while you've been lying on your back plotting a fucking bank job: I've been nurturing a different set of values.'

'You think I'm planning to rob a bank?'

'What else?'

'I don't want to steal anybody's money, Ben: what do you take me for?'

'I dunno any more, Joss: give me a break here you will you?' Ben looked at Joss, pleadingly. 'You have to remember that in the last two years all I've heard about you is that you turned into some sort of dumb spaced-out messenger boy for drug lords. That's hardly the sort of friend you can take home for dinner these days now is it?'

'All right, I catch your drift, but honestly, Ben, you have to listen to me.'

'No, you have to listen to me. I'm going to help you.'

'Great.'

'Before you start doing cartwheels, I said I'm going to help and that means getting you back on the tracks. Now there's an opening in our trading room for a trainee broker in samurai bonds on the Japanese domestic market. I reckon you can blag your way through an interview and I'll give you the reference: what do you say?'

'I say *you* haven't got a clue.'

'The money may not be brilliant to kick off but it'll keep body and soul together and maybe build a pontoon with your old man.'

'My old man's strung out, Ben, that's what all this is about.'

'Come again?'

'To put you straight, I haven't been lying on my back thinking about ripping off a bank in some cockroach-infested cell.'

'Shame.'

'Funny guy. Dad swung a deal for me after the Amsterdam fiasco.'

'So where you been?'

'Chilling.'

'Are you clean?'

'As the day I was born. I got banished to a rehab unit in the Alps.'

'OK, I'll go for that, but your old man: what's the score with him?'

'He's flipped big style.'

'Not Callum Lane? Jesus, he's one of my fucking heroes, man.'

'I recommend a new pin-up, then: he's lost it.'

'What happened?'

'Only went and got himself involved with some lunatics calling themselves the Millennium Church. You heard of them?'

'Some sort of religious cult. Yeah, I heard of them. So what's he doing there: sorting out their finances?'

'You could say that.'

'What do you mean, Joss?'

'I don't know for sure how they got to him, but he's no employee: he's a regular God-squad lieutenant.'

'Jesus, I can't understand it. What did he do with his tax-scamming company?'

'Collapsed.'

'I hate to tell you this, Joss: he may be my number one striker in a fantasy finance team but his reputation for fast dealing goes a long way. Are you sure he isn't working a scam himself?'

'Look, you just don't get it, do you. I broke him free from these religious weirdoes, then some goons from the scripture-grippers grabbed him, back in Paris. He's coming out of his trance in front of a hostile crowd. I've seen them in action and they don't mess about.'

'Is he in danger?'

'We're all in danger now.'

'Whoa, what do you mean?'

'They kill people, Ben.'

'Kind of rubs against the Bible, Joss: you sure you're not hallucinating?'

'Give me a break, for Christ's sake, Ben: they almost got me in Paris. I watched them virtually decapitate a fucking journalist, they've offed my therapist and they aren't going to stop there.'

'Steady on, Joss.' Ben gazed warily around the café, and dropped his voice. 'I'm sorry, this is very freaky. What are you trying to find out?'

'I know my father is important to them, but I get the feeling it's something much bigger than his money we're talking about.'

'Like what?'

'I don't know, but I've got these account numbers and I need to see what's going on. If I can get hold of any evidence of malpractice by the Church I can bring them down. It's the only way I can get my father out of this shit.'

'This is way out of your league, Joss: leave it alone.'

'I can't.'

'Why not? Your old man's one of them, isn't he? Just walk away from it.'

'It's not just me involved now.'

'Hold fire a moment: what are you telling me here?'

'The leader of the Church is on trial in London and Greta is helping to ride the white horse of the prosecution.'

'Jesus, how come?'

'Long story, but one of the cult's former members claims that this Reverend Rivers guy is a child abductor and rapist. The reality is that the trial isn't going her way. She needs us to help, Ben. I can't let her down again.'

'There goes that "us" thing again.'

'OK, I can see why you wouldn't want to get involved here, Ben, on account of just me and Greta: but what about all the other victims of this guy? I mean, I saw their parents outside the court: surely they deserve some sort of justice?'

Ben grimaced at him and shook his head. 'You always were a persuasive bastard. I could do it, but it's not going to be easy.'

'I never thought it would be, but you're the only person I know who would have a clue where to start.'

'Give me the numbers.'

Joss passed Ben the floppy disks containing the material from his father's laptop.

'How do we get in, then?' Joss asked.

'Only two ways.'

'Shoot.'

261

'I don't suppose you've got about £100,000 handy?'

'Correct.'

'So that's the first way out of the picture. Pity.'

'What, you mean bribe someone?'

'Money talks in Zurich, Joss.'

'It figures.'

'No pun intended, right.'

'Forget it: I don't have the money. What's the other option?'

'Hack in through the domestic banking network.'

'Now you're talking, whizzkid.'

'There's no guarantee that the account will be accessible. It's bound to be protected by a security blanket, but we can try.'

'What do we need?'

'A stolen credit card for Crédit Suisse: preferably a cloned one.'

'A what?'

'Just what I say: a cloned card with the digital information taken from a real credit card. That way they are harder to trace.'

'I haven't got a clue where you're coming from, Ben, but it sounds as if you know what you're talking about.'

'Something every good trader should know: we have to find out sometimes whether our clients can afford to trade.'

'So?'

'We occasionally check their numbered accounts to see whether they're good for the money. It's strictly a Desperate Dan measure, though, and obviously is not authorised through our head office, but they know it goes on.'

'What if you get caught?'

'You're on your own.'

'Whatever you do in your spare time, bud, you know what I mean.'

'That sort of thing.'

'So the worst that can happen is you lose your job, right?'

'Not exactly, but that would be bad enough. We're talking about being struck off, criminal proceedings, the full works.'

'I know I'm asking a lot, Ben, you don't have to keep reminding me; but I know you can do it. It's like the irresistible force meeting the immovable object.'

'OK, so move me.'

'How hard do I have to push you? Sounds as if you've been there already.'

'All right, against my better judgement I'll do it, but don't get too excited my friend: first we have to have the card.'

'No problem.'

'How? You don't know anyone in Zurich: we'll have to go back to Geneva.'

'No time, Ben.'

'So what have you got in mind?'

'Wherever there's drugs, there's stolen credit cards, Ben: that's one thing I did learn.'

CHAPTER THIRTY-SIX

In spite of his extreme tiredness, Mark did not sleep well at all. His wife was complaining that he was spending far too much time at work and consequently less time than he should with his family. The case was everything at the moment: it had to be, at least until the next case came up. The inevitable argument had followed: the one that always started with him saying he worked so that she didn't have to, and ended with her saying it was his choice to have children in the first place. It was a nowhere argument: the kind that they'd been having all too frequently recently.

He dozed, and woke with a start every time the tube jolted to a stop. Somewhere up above him beyond the stuffy little carriage a whole world existed but it didn't seem real to him. His world was whizzing around in his brain trying to find the heat of the moment. He had annoyed Rivers yesterday, but he knew it wouldn't last. Sooner or later Rivers would grasp the reality of the situation. Mark didn't have the big nail yet, the one needed to drive home the case. He had been right from the very start: this was all about credibility, and if he could cast even the slightest doubt in the jury's minds, then they might just be in with a chance.

Of course the jury were suspicious of this man's motives: after all, he was from anyone's point of view no ordinary person; a holy man who had obviously amassed great personal wealth, although he appeared ambivalent toward it. In this, coupled with his ability to consume the space of any room with his physical presence, he presented a threat to the very ordinariness of everyone around him.

It was, however, inconceivable to think that during the course of this trial the jury had not interested themselves even briefly in the salacious tabloid tales surrounding the case. More and more would-be litigants against the Millennium Church were selling their stories to hungry reporters. The articles were carefully pieced together so as not to contravene any contempt laws, but subliminally at least the jury must have caught a whiff that they were there to judge the Millennium Church itself, in all its glory.

The sky loomed heavy with angry clouds as Mason walked the short distance from Temple tube station to chambers. As he walked, the question kept recurring in his brain: just how were they going to shatter Rivers's credibility with hard evidence? He knew that if they didn't succeed in this, then the defence would butcher an uncorroborated prosecution case in the jury's eyes when it came to the closing speeches. He breezed into chambers to find a welcome legal aid cheque, and a cup of hot mocha from the deli which helped to chase away the pressure for a few moments.

His clerk slapped a newspaper on the desk and commented, 'You seem to have a bit of gift for this prosecution business, Mr Mason,' pointing to the headline on page three. Mark picked it up to find a detailed report of his cross-examination of Rivers, punctuated with ample poetic licence. He smiled wryly at the clerk who was on a percentage and never liked the chambers' policy of criminal defence work only. The more the merrier was the only policy he understood.

Greta appeared at the door reading a case report.

'What do you think, Greta?' Mason asked.

'What about?' she replied distractedly.

'About Rivers's performance yesterday. Where have you been, my dear, the whole world is talking about it,' he said, in finest thespian delivery.

'I don't know. You had him rattled, but surely he must work out the game plan eventually.'

'What do you mean?' said Mark watching her perch gracefully on the window seat. He knew exactly what she meant, for he'd thought precisely the same thing only minutes ago. He just wanted to hear her say it.

'If he realises the only reason you're goading him is because you have no ammo apart from Rose, then . . .'

'Then what, Greta?' pressed Mark, feeling immodestly pleased that it was he who had taught her to look beyond the evidence and feel for the pulse of a case, even though the case in question seemed a hopeless prospect.

'Then he calms down and cruises home with a smile on his face.'

'You're absolutely right. See what you have here?' he said turning to the clerk.

'What's that, Mr Mason?'

'You have got yourself a genuine class act,' he replied, gesturing to Greta. 'She knows how to read the rhythm of a brief: a gift not to be overlooked, may I remind you.'

'I know that, Mr Mason, our Miss Larson is becoming very popular with the punters.'

'Did you hear that, Greta?' Mark smiled. 'What confidence our learned clerk has in your future: I only wish that mine were so rosy. No pun intended of course.' He winked at Greta who smiled back coyly. She was always grateful for a good word in the clerk's ear from someone senior. As he looked at her framed in the window he had a different kind of thought. An 'if only things were different' type of thought.

'We'd better get to court,' Greta said briskly, diffusing the sudden tension between them.

'I'll get a cab ordered: it's raining now,' said the clerk heading for the door. 'Oh, by the way, there was a message for you, Miss Larson, from that bloke again.'

'Which bloke?' she asked, a little anxiously.

'Joss Lane. I couldn't make head nor tail of it. It's in the clerks room: shall I send it up?'

'It's all right,' she hesitated. 'I'll grab it on the way out.'

'OK, the cab will be waiting by the time you come down.'

'Thanks.' She moved to follow him out of the room.

'Love life improving, Greta?' Mark asked but immediately wished he hadn't.

'I thought we'd been through this one: you're the patient, remember?' she snapped at him.

'Sorry,' he said humbly as she walked out without looking back.

*   *   *

267

It was thirty minutes later after a silent cab journey when finally she looked him in the eye just as they were walking into court.

'I'm sorry I snapped at you before, I was kind of wound up.'

'You don't say,' he smiled.

'It was that message: this guy is driving me crazy,' she said pausing at the door.

'Lucky guy.'

'I just hope his luck hasn't run out, Mark.'

'What do you mean?'

'Forget it. Anyway the Moodys are the ones who need some luck.'

'It's not luck we need, it's evidence; and you don't have to say you're sorry, Greta. I know it's none of my business what you do in your private life.'

'You lying bastard,' she said playfully, 'you told me I was your business last week.'

'You knew what I mean.'

'I know. Don't worry about it.'

'Answer me one thing: is this the guy you were telling me about; the one whose father is the numbers man?'

'The self and same. I think he's mixing things up a bit.'

They walked into court and took up their positions. The public gallery and press box were crammed again.

Rivers appeared composed once more. He sat in the witness box awaiting the arrival of the judge, reading nonchalantly from his own clerical text. Along the advocates' row, Thynne and Callow sat in silence, their junior barristers mirroring the static tableaux; Fannon was missing, presumed dead in the criminal water. Mason shuffled across.

'Morning, gentlemen: Rory missed his train?'

Thynne glanced up over silver half-rim glasses. 'Surplus to requirements, Mason. Our client believed his heart wasn't really quite in it.'

Mason smiled thinly. He was sorry that a decent man had been sacked from a job he was so adept at, but he wasn't surprised. Rory had been brought on board to charm the jury with his closing speech, and now Thynne would coldly shoulder the responsibility.

'Will you be much longer with him?' Thynne weedled. 'Some of us do have a practice to maintain.'

'Not too much longer,' Mason lied, in the expected chicanery of the courtroom. 'Just one or two minor matters to clear up.'

Thynne nodded knowingly, a master of disinformation facing a worthy rival.

'I think you'll find him a little different today,' he whispered, whilst Callow sniffed disparagingly.

'Nasty cold,' Mason commented, as he returned to the prosecutor's side of the bench.

The jury trooped in, several of them stealing sharp glances at Rivers, who bowed gracefully.

Don't overdo it, old son, Mark thought, as the court was commanded to attention.

A long day passed in clinical cross-examination. Rivers had been well briefed on the folly of his previous day's performance and today he maintained a low-level charm and good manners at all times. Mason examined, in minutiae, the numerous alibis the defence would be presenting. He was not doing this to rile Rivers at this stage, but to provide a firm platform for establishing the inconsistency of the future witnesses' accounts.

By lunchtime the jury were wilting; by the close of the day the bloom of their interest was almost dead. But it had to be done this way, if Mason was to prove beyond a shadow of a doubt that Rivers was lying. Just before the court rose for the day, Mason threw in one incongruous question.

'Do you know Joss Lane?'

Rivers had been thrown off his confident course and hesitated for a moment too long. His cheek twitched before he denied ever having heard the name before, but Mason knew he was on to something. As he left court, he took Greta to one side and steered her into a corner.

'Did you see the look on his face, Greta?'

'I saw it all right, but how did you know he'd react like that?'

'I didn't: it was a guess based on what you told me last week. I think you'd better start explaining to me what's going on, don't you?'

'I really don't know myself, Mark.'

'Come off it, Greta, what's there to be afraid of? Are you hiding anything from me?'

'It's not like that at all.'

'Then what is it like?' he said sternly.

'I may be kind of responsible.'

'Tell me, for God's sake,' he pleaded.

'It's Joss Lane: I think he may be in danger because of me.'

'What kind of danger are we talking about here?'

'I don't know: he's not your regular kind of guy. I'm not sure if I can rely on a single word he says.'

'But what did you mean before when you said he was mixing things up a bit?' Mark pressed.

'He thinks he may be on to something that could help us.'

'Track him down, Greta. I don't care what you do; I want anything that he can lay his hands on. Rivers is lying, I am going to be the one who nails him to the cross. Your man spells trouble to him; you could tell by the look in Rivers's eyes when I mentioned his name back in court. Something is stirring in their camp and I want to know exactly what that something is.'

CHAPTER THIRTY-SEVEN

The distinguishing feature of Zurich's drugs problem is that, more than anywhere else in the world, the junkies stand out. It was legend amongst visiting young travellers that the place to avoid was the area at the back of the National Museum, where backpackers were easy pickings for the colony of heroin addicts who roamed the streets. Eventually, the authorities abandoned a free sterilised needle policy back in 1991 when crime in the city peaked and the place had became known as needle park. Joss, being a traveller with a habit, had been forced into the zone.

Now, as he walked into the Platz promenade he bumped into the first of a row of haggard-looking bodies strung out along the wall, covered in a variety of rags and cardboard. Makeshift rooms delineated by barriers of shopping trolleys angled away to his right, naturally leading his eyes to a circular group gathered around a burning oil drum. That was where he had to go.

Among all tribes of users there was always one who, despite the fact that he realised their lives were shitty enough already, had to rule the roost. He was the one who organised the scores, getting a better volume for dealing in bulk from the pushers. He was the one who sold the collective morning haul of stolen goods from nights spent burgling and days spent shoplifting. The others went along with it just because they couldn't be bothered to do anything about it.

If you couldn't bear to go and walk the streets alone then you had to live with the dictatorship or kill it. It was one of the purest capitalist societies going because the dealer's dealer up the ladder didn't care who was buying the smack, just how often he paid for it. So what if one of the toe-rags revolted and slit the throat of his leader? Promote him.

271

It was that man that Joss needed to talk to.

As he approached the fire he could see a large man wearing a dirty white sweatshirt who would have been in the prime of his life, were it not for the tell-tale sunken-eyed look of an addict beyond redemption. He was chopping wood, watched by a group of washouts. He was still a big man: couldn't have been on H for too long, guessed Joss; judging by his weight, he probably didn't have too much of a problem overthrowing the previous king.

A single star splintered from the edge of the blade as the big man brought the axe down. With controlled power his blow split the log with a single clean sweep. The two half-logs, their newly exposed interiors bright glistening yellow wood, quivered, toppled and fell. The junkies' leader reached for another log, all the while never taking his eyes off Joss, who had found no difficulty squeezing into the circle. The noise of the axe splitting wood and the dry tumble of cleft logs disturbed the peaceful sounds of gentle crackling from the fire. Joss kept his eyes down.

Eventually, a freak to Joss's right began a slow chant. He was far away in some distant dreamland of his own. But the leader did nothing to quell the uneasy atmosphere. He lifted the next log easily with one hand and carefully positioned it on the chopping block. His expression revealed only a blank concern for what he was doing here and now.

A waif-like young girl, no more than seventeen years old, Joss guessed, with dirty brown matted hair and a weasel face stepped forward from the gathering to put a hand on his shoulder.

The man stopped moving. Like a forest creature abruptly sensing a predator he remained statue-still, wary and yet somehow lifeless.

'You are wanted, Stephan,' said the weasel.

As though he were a machine activated to obey a command, he lowered the axe to the ground. The girl took it from him and placed it upright against the chopping block. Stephan hesitated.

A smackhead's hesitation, Joss noted.

He gave Joss the sort of thousand-metre stare that made him look like he had forgotten for a moment which dimension he was operating in. Suddenly he seemed worried. Nervous.

A junkie's nervousness.

The man's gaze was fixed on the untidy pile of logs he'd chopped but not stacked. Without taking his eyes off the logs, he spoke directly to Joss.

'What do you want?'

To Joss's amazement, he spoke in perfectly good English with barely a trace of an accent.

'Help.'

'We all need help, mister: what have you got?'

'I got some cash.'

'That means a lot more round here.'

'I thought it might,' said Joss, chancing his arm that the guy was in good humour.

'You said you need help.'

'That's right: I need a credit card.'

'Go to a bank.'

'What do you think this is about? Do I look like the sort who can just walk in and say "give me a gold Amex".'

'You don't look so bad to me,' the Weasel chipped in, then she turned her eyes sharply away when Joss tried to smile at her. He knew he shouldn't.

'You want my bitch as well, stranger? You can have her for nothing.' Stephan suddenly swung his arm back and swiped his hand across the girl's face without warning. She went spinning to the floor and lay whimpering as a trail of blood trickled down her nose. 'Slut,' Stephan spat at her. 'You were saying, stranger?'

'I was saying I need a credit card, a cloned one. I thought you may be able to point me in the right direction, but I guess I was wrong. You're just an arsehole.'

'What did you say?' Stephan asked, his eyes wide with the rush.

'In case you didn't understand, fuckwit, I called you an arsehole.'

The big man's hands immediately reached for the handle of the axe but Joss was too quick. Moving with maniacal speed, he dived for Stephan's legs and sent the group scattering in fear. He crunched his fist into the junkie's groin and simultaneously swept his legs away at the knees, felling him with a heavy thud to his chin. The big man screamed out in pain and the axe dropped out of reach.

Joss seized the advantage and hurriedly turned the heaving frame over, then delivered a full blow to the face. A satisfying crack of nasal bone sounded louder than the fire spits. Joss was about to smash another fist into Stephan's face when his hand was grabbed from behind.

'I think you've proved your point, stranger,' said Weasel. 'Now leave him alone.'

'He's a piece of shit.'

'But he's the only piece of shit I've got; now stop.'

Joss let his hand drop and let go of Stephan's sweatshirt; he was out cold anyway. He turned to the Weasel.

'Do you know where I can get what I need?'

'Come with me,' she said while stooping down to wipe the blood from the side of Stephan's head. She gently laid him back on the floor and placed her thin cotton windcheater under him. As she rose wearing just a vest, Joss could see the smooth scar tissue across her wrists and the old scabs of needle sites in the crooks of her arms. Joss shuddered at the memory of his own addiction.

They didn't speak as they walked the short distance to a café amongst a row of shops opposite the train station. A large Mercedes was parked outside with a squarely-built goon leaning against the bonnet. He eyed Weasel with disdain and then suspiciously gave Joss the once-over. Weasel muttered something that Joss didn't catch and the man nodded dismissively. They walked through the door.

Once inside, Joss knew exactly whom the Mercedes belonged to. He was the only customer apart from the obligatory vixen clamped next to him like a human limpet. In the corner booth, a middle-aged man with close-cropped black hair, wearing a shiny blue mohair suit was counting money.

Drug money.

He was in the right place.

As he approached, Joss could see the piles of currency on the table neatly divided. A half-smoked joint was burning in the ashtray and a steaming hot espresso sat to the man's left. On his right was the Latino fox: a girl with impossibly long eyelashes and very large breasts. She had one hand under the table, the other round her companion's shoulder, and her lips were stuck fast to his pock-marked face.

No one said a word.

Weasel ushered him forward.

The gun came out from under the table as soon as Joss sat down. He quickly raised his arms.

Stupid, stupid boy,

What the hell are you doing here?

You've just kicked the daylights out of one of this guy's street dealers and he's got a gun in your face.

For once his inner voice had been sleeping.

'I wasn't expecting company, Eva,' the man said to Weasel.

'I'm sorry, Jacques,' she spluttered. 'This guy here he says he needs a card and Stephan's had a bit of an accident.' Joss secretly thanked her for concealing the details of Stephan's misfortune.

'What kind of card?'

'Cloned. Maximum twenty-four-hour exposure before theft report possible,' Joss said repeating Ben's instructions.

'Bank?'

'Crédit Suisse.'

'Five hundred dollars.'

'I only have four hundred.'

'Goodbye then.'

'OK, OK, five hundred dollars.' He didn't have time to haggle over the price but still resented the fact that he had to pay this lowlife.

'You're a fast learner. Leave the money on the table, walk out the door and return here in fifteen minutes.'

It was as easy as falling off a log, Joss thought as he rose from the booth.

Joss placed the cash on the table and carefully edged his way out of the café. He lingered around at the corner for a couple of seconds before spotting a sign for fax service at the train station opposite. He sprinted across the road and walked into the shop. He sent the fax to Greta's chambers.

Dear Greta. The chase is afoot; pray God we are not too late. Made contact with an old friend; should have some

news tomorrow. Looks like very dirty laundry and Callum
is now with sheet-stainers.

Love Joss.

The message was oblique enough to be misleading to a nosy
stranger. He could only hope that Greta could read the subtext
and would trust him.

Trainer was flanked by Tomlin and Moyne in a plush hotel
suite near to the Church's principal bank. Callum Lane limped
around, complaining about his foot until Tomlin silenced him
by approximating the spit of the rivet gun with his own mouth.
Trainer had plumbed the depths of Lane senior's own expertise
with the murkier side of finance and had then sought a meeting
with a senior bank official, who had fawningly denied that there
could be a breach of security.

Trainer was less sure: Joss Lane had come a long way in a
very short time, not through luck but through perseverance. The
pastel-shaded, five-star accommodation offered every luxury, but
Trainer felt uncomfortable. He had allowed this situation to develop
out of control and would be held to account if it progressed any
further. He had arranged a dedicated line to the bank that would
inform them of any transactions that had been been previously
arranged. For now, they would wait until Joss made his next move,
and when he did they would be ready to move on him with the might
of the Lord and a sack full of weapons.

CHAPTER THIRTY-EIGHT

'Voltaire once said that if you see a Swiss banker jump out of a window, follow him for there is surely money to be made,' Ben opined as he wired the wafer-thin modem into the comport at the side of his laptop.

'Looks like he was right,' responded Joss as he gazed around the hotel room in which they stood. The windows were large and domineering with intricate plasterwork giving a magisterial theme to the place. The curtains were made from luxurious heavy velvet in swirling shapes of emerald and deep gold. The thick pile carpet was a contrasting ruby-rich claret with manicured rugs strategically placed around the floor. A huge four-poster bed dominated the centre and intricate marquetry furniture made a separate sitting area.

Joss took his shoes off in respect.

'How are we doing?'

'Getting there: I just have to clock into the internal billing system of the hotel and that gives us access to the external data lines which they use to charge customers' accounts when they are checking in and out.'

'What do we do then?'

'We piggyback a ride on the modem signal, find out the right connection to Crédit Suisse central operating system, and from there we have to hunt down the account. It could take some time.'

'Which . . .'

'We haven't got. Yeah, I hear you, Joss, but we're talking about a search of 630 domestic banks and over 200 foreign banks.'

'What difference does that make?'

'We don't know which bank the account is held in.'

'So why did we need a Crédit Suisse card in particular?'

'Nothing special.'

'I'll bet.'

'OK, so I thought I'd take a little peek at one of my punters: he's been getting a bit shaky lately and I think he's trading too big.'

'See: I told you that you would enjoy this.'

'Ask me again when I find out I'm in big shit if he's over-exposed. I've lengthened his credit line.'

They waited a short while for a transaction to go through from the reception downstairs. It didn't take long before Ben had trained his own modem to link with the central computer at Crédit Suisse. A central information screen appeared for access to personal accounts and Ben swept in the details from the credit card that Joss had picked up. Downstairs at reception the clerk dealing with the bill was completely unaware of the real reason why the first swipe of the card he was holding hadn't been successful.

'These machines are so temperamental,' he'd said to the customer while he gave it a second run through. It chattered out the printed receipt oblivious to the fact that Ben's phantom card was still in the system.

'I knew it,' shouted Ben. 'That two-faced little shyster Hertz.'

'What have you got?' asked Joss.

'He's only carrying two million in his fucking deposit trading account.'

'This your client we're talking about?'

'I'm going to cut him off at the neck. If I don't let him make a few winning bets that means one more person to share the pot with.'

'Come on, Ben, let's move on: remember what we're really here to do.'

'OK, I'm going to move back to the options page and look for associated banks because I've never come across this sequential numbering before.'

'What's that?'

'It's the way the account numbers are grouped: I think it's a foreign bank and pretty obscure. Probably very private.'

'Is it here in Zurich?'

'Definitely.'

'How can you tell?'

'Look at the first group of numbers.'

'Eight, eight, eight, seven, six, seven.'

'That's right: they indicate that the bank is registered in the Canton of Zurich and is licensed to take all sorts of deposits, cash, credit, bullion and the like.'

'What about the rest?'

'Like I say, we just have to enter the numbers and hope for the best on a trial and error basis.'

'This could take forever.'

'Have patience, Joss I think the computer will prompt because it's unique.'

'What? It's not going to show us the way, is it?'

'Kind of. You see, trading is going on all the time between different computers without the need for human intervention.'

'Get out of here!'

'I'm serious. Look, when a large unit trust or insurance company buys into the stock markets of the world, they do so usually on strict guidelines. For instance, they will only buy shares at a given price. No amount of persuasion by brokers will work. So they eliminate the problem anyway and simply programme their accounts to buy and sell at predetermined markers and the computers basket trade with one another. This account looks like a very specialist trading account to me. I think the numbering system is the give-away.'

'Go to it.'

'OK, we start with the Saudi banks. Pass me the phone book.'

Three hours later, Joss decided to collect his things from the hostel and drive back over to Ben's hotel. He left Ben working through the system of jumping from bank to bank via the Crédit Suisse central computer using the fake card to fabricate transactions between its account and the target bank account numbers that Callum's laptop had supplied.

As he drove back over the Munsterbruke and parked up at the side of the Hotel Glockenhof, he was hopeful that Ben would by now have accessed the account details, but something else suddenly crossed his vision. A man he'd seen before, he was sure of it, was walking into the lobby of the hotel. He stopped for a moment, catching his breath.

He was seeing things, surely.

Flashback, Joss. Get rid.

He walked a little unsteadily up the stairs to the hotel. It was an expensive lobby: just like the guestrooms, furnished tastefully but without much individuality. Functional.

Keep functional, Joss.

Survey the area.

The regulation deep red carpet looked about as classy as the heavily made-up girls behind the reception desk. He checked the exit routes. He checked the punters. There were quite a number of people coming and going, most of them middle-aged and most of them British or American.

Joss spotted him again, or at least he thought he did, before he disappeared from view. Joss stopped abruptly beside a pillar. He lost track of how long he stood there motionless. The man had gone into the gents off to the left, but was he the only one?

Was it him at all?

Joss was sure it was one of Trainer's men from Orly airport: not Chisel-face, the other one. He looked at his watch more frequently to see just how much time this paranoia trip was wasting.

Then he clocked a face he knew for sure. He recognised Trainer immediately, stepping out of a car outside the glass fronted lobby. He whipped his back to the windows. He could pick out Trainer's footsteps within a few feet of him, striding towards the reception desk. Joss was sweating with fear.

He couldn't make out what Trainer was saying to the receptionist but he couldn't be here by coincidence.

Jesus Christ, he had to get to Ben.

Eventually, Trainer re-emerged and gave a discreet nod to the other man Joss had correctly identified as one of his cronies. They walked directly towards him, turning only at the last minute to sit at a table no more than a metre away from his pillar.

Joss breathed deep and quietly and got ready to make a swift exit the other way, through the front doors.

He thought he'd done it.

Evasive action.

But then he heard a sharp intake of breath just as he was about to set off and his heart stopped.

Nothing happened.

Trainer got up with the slightest creak of leather from the chair.

Joss turned in time to see him walk over to the other side of the lobby and turn his back on the reception desk, buying a newspaper at the gift counter near the far window.

There were only three other people in the lobby; an elderly couple just on their way out, and Chisel-face's mate, whose head was covered in tight black curls, standing at the reception desk filling in a form. The receptionist handed him a key. The man walked over to the lift and Joss saw him press the button for the sixth floor.

Trainer glanced at the lift indicator, saw where it stopped and stepped into the next lift. Joss watched the lift indicator too. It had stopped on the sixth floor.

Ben's on the sixth floor.

Joss did what he had originally intended to do and walked out the way he'd come in then sprinted round to the back alley. He had to get to Ben's room before Trainer and his cronies reached it.

He had to know how many people were chasing him.

He took the fire escape. It didn't take long to get to the sixth floor. He found what he should have anticipated: the fire door only opened from the inside and there was no way to get in. He jumped down to the fifth floor; no luck there either. He went up again past the sixth and could see Trainer and the man with the tight curls entering a room just two doors along from Ben's.

On the seventh floor someone had been careless with the firedoor, which remained slightly ajar.

Joss inserted his fingers easily into the crack and pulled the bar. He was in the corridor.

It was thickly carpeted and mercifully empty. He tiptoed along until he got to the lift, pushed the down button and held his breath in case someone unfortunate popped out.

Suddenly he saw Trainer. He was in the corridor, just coming out of the room Joss had seen him enter earlier. He'd heard the lift doors opening and turned to lock the door behind him. Joss slipped out of the lift and round the corner into the stairwell. When he stepped back, Trainer had gone. He quickly made his way to Ben's room and slipped the key in the lock. Relief streamed from every pore as he saw Ben's familiar back crouched over the laptop.

'We've got to move Ben, now.'

'What, like now?'

'Like yesterday, Ben: move it. Unplug it,' he ordered, motioning to the plug in the wall.

'I already have.'

'What do you mean?'

'I have in my hand a piece of paper . . .'

'You did it,' Joss exclaimed.

'I certainly did.'

A knock. Then another. A pause, then a bullet came whistling through the door.

Trainer.

Chisel-face

'The window,' Joss whispered.

Ben nodded. 'Ledge is big enough: we can run round to the fire escape.'

As the door handle began to turn, Joss and Ben were seventy feet above the streets of Zurich. They clattered down the fire escape without looking back. Joss could hear their pursuers shouting as bullets ricocheted off the ironwork around them. They hit the bottom running, Joss leading the way, sprinting down the side alley towards the car. They jumped in; then, with fumbling fingers, Joss inserted the key, gunned the engine, and snarled away from the scene. He could see Chisel-face and Curly-mop in the rear-view mirror. Both were gesticulating wildly; Joss gave them the finger. He and Ben were driving away from Zurich with an armful of dynamite. Only trouble was, they had yet to realise just how powerful it was.

Trainer leaned into Callum Lane's face until their foreheads were touching and, barely breathing, whispered, 'Don't tell me about computer viruses, tell me what happened.'

They were in a private room in the Kholl Bank as they and the bank's employees furiously attempted to discover exactly what Joss and his friend had done.

'It's not as simple as that; the virus is eating everything in sight,' Callum replied, dropping his eyes and moving away from the confrontation.

'Give me a fucking educated guess, then, Brother Lane!' Trainer bellowed. Tomlin and Moyne sat sheepishly in the corner of the stark, over-lit room.

Callum shrugged. 'Before the virus ate the records I started at the end of the transfer. They will know about the supply to the Venice operation.'

Trainer kicked the table over on to its side.

'And,' Callum continued, 'there is money missing.'

Trainer halted in his tracks, as if frozen.

'How much?' he asked, his voice wavering with anticipation.

'Too much.'

'How fucking much?' he asked, flatly.

'Enough to buy my life back?'

Trainer shook his head. 'There isn't that much money in the world.' He paused for thought, then turned to Tomlin and Moyne. 'Mobilise all our people. The thieves are driving: block every route between here and Venice. They have to be taken alive, but that doesn't mean they can't be hurt badly in the process.'

CHAPTER THIRTY-NINE

Joss concentrated on maintaining an even speed, afraid to push on the incline and strain the small engine. He willed the car higher up the mountain road. His eyes fastened on the pitted track ahead, searching for any potential hazards after the heavy falls of snow in the Alps. They were heading for Venice via the mountain route.

'So tell me again, why Venice?' Joss asked.

'Let me explain my sheer, audacious genius and how the virus works, then all will be revealed,' Ben replied, still higher than a satellite through adrenaline. Joss shrugged. 'Three hundred lines of simple DOS programming, that's how.'

'In plain English, please,' Joss implored.

'Someone had created a programme that is a mutant of an ancient virus designed to tackle pirate operators of kids' computer games in the Far East back in the seventies.'

'Someone at the bank you mean?'

'Or someone who set up the account computer system at Kholl Bank.'

'So what have they done, exactly?'

'They've adapted that old virus and built it into their own system to destroy the historical data when security is breached by unauthorised access.'

'So, come on, what have we got then?'

'The account is, as I suspected, a trading account.'

'How can you tell?'

'Because it balances back to nil at the end of each trading day.'

'So what's that mean?'

'Some big sums of money are passing through it each day and going somewhere else.'

'How do you know that for sure?' Joss asked, continuing to stare at the road ahead through the encroaching gloom.

'Look, no one operates that kind of account for anything other than gambling on arbitrage deals or hiding money they don't want people to know about. Either way, you couldn't get clearance from the bank to trade unless it was getting big commission.'

Joss could see that Ben's agile mind was racing through the financial spaghetti junction.

'Can you tell where the money is going?' he asked. Ben narrowed his eyes.

'It looks to me as if it's heading for the Channel Islands, probably Jersey, and from there, I've no doubt, shipped somewhere else. It's a classic laundering operation, and it has your dad's fingerprints all over it.'

Joss ignored the comment. It was not the time to apportion blame; he had to save his father's life. He pushed on.

'What will happen now that the virus has attacked the account: is there no record left?'

'I doubt it. They want to keep this very secret.'

'What kind of money are we talking about?'

'Hundreds of millions: more money than you could ever imagine kind of money. It could be that what we are seeing on this trading account is not in fact the Church's money. I mean, cash donations of five million are not even made to the Vatican let alone some whacko outfit, are they?'

'So it's possible they're fronting for someone?'

'Or a lot of people. Could be they are skimming money off someone else.'

'Ripping off the hands that feed them.'

'Something like that.'

'So setting the virus off is going to cause some mayhem anyhow?' Joss asked, becoming more interested as Ben explained the extent of the cult's problems.

'It will effectively render the account worthless. No one can tell from here where the money's gone, apart from us: to everyone else it is floating around on the financial net, but . . .' he paused and shook his head, 'right now it's sitting in my employers' suspense account in Geneva with my reference on it.'

286

'Jesus Christ, I'm sorry, Ben.'

'Hey, what's a few million between friends? I can say it's an inheritance when the regulators ask me in for coffee and biscuits.' He paused again as the magnitude of his action struck home, then seemed to jump one point further. 'Hey, wait a minute, Joss: if this account is what I think it is, then the money involved is the sort that nobody wants.'

'What do you mean?'

'Look, don't you see? If it is a laundering operation then whoever it ends up with is going have to explain it away to the authorities.'

'So I don't get it.'

'So it stands to reason that while it's missing they ain't going to be making a song and dance about it, are they?'

'Can you tell the source of the cash?'

'I chased down thousands of sources; from private donations to big business, from pennies to millions of pounds. But that's not what matters: it's where it goes next that's important, and that's why we're going to Venice.'

Joss shook his head, which was swimming in a sea of money and corruption. His foot was tired from its hovering position on the accelerator.

'Ben, can you give me that message again for the benefit of the hard of thinking?'

'Donations to the Church are supposed to be for religious and charitable purposes. Why, then, is the main recipient Ruga Fondamenta glass company in Venice? The sums involved would buy a lot of stained glass; millions of church windows, in fact.'

Joss glanced sideways at his friend.

'Why the hell would a glass company be getting that kind of money?'

Ben smiled grimly.

'It was earmarked through a buffer company for the victims of the Sicilian earthquake, for medicine.'

'Bastards,' Joss spat.

'It's working capital for something else, Joss; something very big.'

Joss dropped the engine down a gear as the incline increased.

287

'We still haven't got enough to go back to Greta with.'

Ben shook his head.

'We've got evidence that they are ripping off their converts.'

'Still not enough. I need something to nail Rivers and the Church right down. It's not just about Callum; it's about all the victims,' Joss said softly.

'What about the money?' Ben asked.

'Leave it in your account in Geneva. Let's call it a compensation fund for the people whose lives the Church has destroyed, but one thing's for sure: it isn't going back. It's about time they paid a few debts.'

All at once there was a flash of light moving up and down dead ahead. As Joss slowed, he could see two or three men standing in the way; one of them was signalling him down. Jesus Christ, just as he thought they had got out of Zurich without a sniff of Trainer.

What next?

He told Ben to duck down out of sight and try to roll out of the car as Joss was slowing down on the blind side of the men in front.

They would be searching for two men.

Think Joss.

Think fast.

A series of rocky outcrops trailing round the bend would provide cover for Ben to get on the rear side of them. Ben quietly opened the door just as Joss stuck the full beam into the faces of the roadblock, and gently rolled into the soft snow.

Joss pushed the car on the extra twenty metres. He didn't recognise any of the men. As he slowed to a halt and slid the window down, one of them came forward.

Suddenly, there was a deafening report and the approaching man collapsed to his knees. A scream followed from another of the men as a second shot thunder-clapped, and then another. Joss stared uncomprehendingly as the two men fell sideways. Then the car door opened and his passenger crashed back into the seat holding what for the whole world looked like a pistol.

'Jesus Christ, Ben what the hell?'

'Go on, just drive, drive, man.' Ben was clutching his head, which was bleeding heavily.

Joss's mechanism for response had deserted him.

'Come on, Joss: they were there to kill us.'

'But the gun?'

'I got it off the one I rolled on top of.'

Joss slammed his foot on the accelerator and they lurched ahead, the car's wheels fighting for grip on the snowy surface. He turned again to speak to Ben but the words wouldn't come out. Ben was sitting forward, one hand on the dash peering out. The car slipped to the left violently.

Joss was concentrating so hard that at first he didn't see the flickering lights behind them. They were below him now as they edged up the mountain side but clearly visible.

Twin lights close together and now Joss could hear the sounds of a roaring four-wheel-drive engine. The road had suddenly become steeper and the car hesitated on another corner before recapturing its precarious momentum. They barely managed to avoid a sloping wall of brown ice with rock outcrops as they swept round the hairpin.

'Careful, Joss.'

'You're telling me to be careful. Jesus, Ben, did you kill that guy?' Joss screamed.

'Aimed for his knees. Careful, Joss,' his friend repeated forcefully.

Joss followed his gaze ahead and suddenly saw the reason for his anxiety. A deep black trench was cut into the side of the road ahead. It could have been a drainage trench: it appeared from the plastic pipes lying around the roadside that the works were recent.

There were two flat planks like railway sleepers in waiting for them, but Joss didn't fancy their chances in the slightest.

He felt a pain in his gut as the two beams from the four-wheeler behind them dazzled in his rear-view mirror.

'Cross it,' shouted Ben.

'What, that?'

'Yes, you idiot, that: cross it quick.'

Joss inched the car forward, praying that he had lined up right.

'Drive,' screamed Ben as the back window shattered around them. It was impossible to see down. There was a sensation of swaying, above an inky void. The engine of the pursuing vehicle was deafening.

They went for it.

The car purred over the chasm and lurched off the other side.

'Wait,' shouted Ben as he jumped out of the car and hurled one of the planks, like a caber, into the valley below. He scrambled alongside the plucky Renault as Joss depressed the accelerator as far as it would go. Ben clung onto the frame and managed to haul himself into the seat.

They saw the lights of the jeep disappear over the edge and then seconds later heard the explosion below.

They bumped along the top road for another kilometre in absolute silence. Suddenly, the car slumped sideways and the wing crashed into the side wall of the cliff. They ground to a halt with the front wheel caught in a culvert. Joss tried to reverse out and as he looked behind he saw the searchlight from the helicopter above them.

Suddenly the car broke free with a tremendous jolt backwards, just taking them out of the stream of bullets that hammered down on them from the sky. The light wavered and Joss was able to get a grip with the back wheels on a trench of gravel catapulting them forward again: a straight stretch going downhill into the town of Uetilberg. Ben opened the window and pumped off two rounds of the pistol behind them more in hope than anything else.

They were no more than three kilometres from the town when, without warning, Joss felt a sickening thud and heard a scream from Ben. The car had slammed into the retaining wall at the bottom of the road. The impact had caused the dash to cave in and was trapping Ben hard against the gear column. Joss had a couple of glass fragments stuck in his face but otherwise was mobile.

He jumped out of the car, snatching his battered rucksack from the back seat, as the helicopter circled above the crash scene looking for a place to land. In the distance he could hear the sound of a police siren approaching. Joss tucked himself neatly behind a boulder and was maniacally relieved when the helicopter pilot gave up as the police car arrived. Joss made for the drainage ditch alongside the road and started for the town.

He felt bad about Ben but at least he would be safe. At the very worst he'd have a couple of broken ribs and would need a few stitches to the head. Joss had removed the financial records from the dashboard so the police could do nothing other than hold

Ben for questioning until they figured out whether being shot at is a criminal offence.

He emerged from the ditch cold and wet and headed for the bus station and the first ride out of town.

The bus said Milan.

Yes Milan. That'll do: Milan airport to Venice.

There's nowhere else to go, Joss.

So Milan it was.

CHAPTER FORTY

J oss had landed at the hectic Treviso airport outside Venice in the choking heat of mid-afternoon, on the flight from Milan. The typical Venetian lethargy towards customs and authority had buoyed his confidence when disembarking, and the number 6 bus would take him the 30 minute journey to the centre of Venice.

He had bought his ticket from the *tabacchi* stand directly outside the dusty terminal, along with two plump *tramezzini* to encourage his flat appetite, but felt nothing but trepidation toward his task. All he had to go on was a link between the Ruga Fondamenta glass company and the Millennium Church, and the fact that he knew that the company was to be found on the Island of Murano, the very centre of the glass-blowing industry.

It had been some time since he had visited Venice but he expected the vastly over-priced Piazza San Marco to have retained all of its beautiful arrogance and its surly ability to separate the unwary from their Lire. The Piazza kept the city solvent its gondolas and wavering tenors an expensive adjunct to the tourist industry; but this time Joss was here on business; serious business.

He spread out the map, purchased at the *tabacchi* shop, on his knee as the bus continued its journey towards the city's epicentre. Venice consists of 118 islands tied by some 400 bridges over the ever-encroaching water. Six sestieri, or districts, contribute their own distinct identities to the whole, three either side of the Canal Grande.

It was the water that made him think of Barney Calladine; lunatic cave diver and old friend. Whilst waiting at Milan airport, he had traced his former 'In Extremis' partner. Barney's mother had told him about the Club Med diving school, where apparently Barney was having a fine old time condescending to the men and charming their girlfriends, whilst charging outrageous sums to show them how to breathe through an aqualung in the dangerous waters of the hotel swimming pool.

Barney had been dragged from a barbecue and toga party to the poolside bar telephone.

'Barney Calladine, the boy from Atlantis, how may I help you?'

At first his bouncy joy was swept away when Joss quietly whispered his name, but within seconds it returned.

'You never wrote, so I broke off the engagement. Men!' he humphed. Joss had laughed appreciatively, then attempted to enlist his help. Barney was all laughs up front, but like many jokers his jocularity masked a deeply serious worldview. Joss explained some, but not all, of his predicament, then concluded:

'I know you're on to a good thing, Barney, and I have no right to ask.'

'Good thing, you say? Hardly: the Med is so full of crap it's like cave diving, and the women, well the women are fantastic. Hang on, I think I've just talked myself into staying.'

'I understand,' Joss had replied.

'Then you understand nothing, Joss. Give me the name of a hotel where I can reach you.'

Joss rummaged in the attic of his memory for the name of a *pensione* he had stayed at on his last trip.

'Can you bring all the equipment with you?'

'I run the school. If it needs repairing it gets repaired. I reckon it will take me about half a day.'

'Barney?'

'Oh no, he's going to thank me in that gooey, mushy sincere voice of his. Look, you are cutting in to my recreation time, Lane, and there is a particularly louche hairdresser from Watford waiting to see me do a handstand in my toga: tomorrow.'

Joss glanced at the other passengers on the bus but they were on the whole fairly unremarkable. He could smell the city's approach before he could see it. The bus's ineffective air-conditioning system saw to that.

As a child, Joss had been allowed by his mother to stay up late one night to watch the Nick Roeg movie *Don't Look Now*. The scene where the dwarf in the bright red plastic mac had savagely dispatched a heavy-eyed Donald Sutherland still gave him nightmares. That remained his over-riding image of the city of Venice; beauty, corruption and unexpected death. He shook away the recollection.

A tanned female backpacker glanced across at him and smiled. Joss almost returned the gesture then remembered Monica and the honey trap in London and scowled at her instead.

The bus negotiated the remaining part of the journey with staccato progress, the Venetian traffic as loud and heavy as the fetid air. It pulled into the terminal in the Pizzale Roma with a shuddering kick, and Joss joined the others to disembark. The girl who had smiled at him earlier hefted a weighty Bergen backpack on to her broad shoulders and complained to her lank-haired friend that the place smelled.

'It's a bus depot, of course it smells,' Joss muttered as he slid past.

It was quicker to walk in Venice. The entire city centre and its major attractions could be navigated in an hour. The sun was just a low fiery ball on the point of its daily extinction by the earth's rotation as Joss sauntered along the canalside, marvelling at the vision that had built the city and the neglect that was allowing it to slide back to its watery origins.

He had covered this route before. He and Greta, playful, hand in hand, laughing at the warbling gondoliers and their wheezing accordions. He and Greta, eyes wide when the bill for two coffees and grappa exceeded the cost of a night in the West End, then smiling as if they were experienced in these mundane ways of the world and leaving a hefty tip for a slyly smirking waiter. He and Greta, making love in a cheap hotel in the afternoon, richer than he would ever be again but too dumb to be aware of it.

The *pensione* in Cannaregio was as he remembered it; the 'Al Gobbo'. He and Greta had called it the 'Hotel Spit' when he had selected it for them out of the *Rough Guide,* but for a one-star it was more genteel than most of its lowly counterparts on the adjacent Lista di Spagna, and their room had overlooked a small but attractive garden. When he and Greta lay in the sweet afterglow of sex the mimosas had gladly offered up their scent to counteract the water's stench.

Within ten minutes the owner had welcomed him sleepily but was unable to provide the same room, and in a way Joss was relieved. A reluctant tap splashed cool water into the aged but rigorously scrubbed bath and Joss took half an hour to wash away the residue of his journey. He tried to clear his mind of all things except the task that lay ahead, but Greta's sweet face swept continually into view; smiling, laughing, determined and then finally, at his mother's inquest, unforgiving and harsh. He splashed himself with soothing hot water in a vain attempt to scour away the deep chill of regret and loss.

Daylight was losing its grip on the watery landscape as Joss, now changed into loose chinos, tan boat-shoes and a white linen shirt, made his way to a bar on the Calle Priulli. It was lively and loud, a stop-off point for young men in suits – ties loosened and calf leather cases gathered around expensively clad feet – to have a cold beer and an animated discussion. A jukebox, almost muted by the competing chatter of the patrons, hummed Van Morrison's 'Brown-eyed Girl.' Joss ordered a glass of Prosecco Rose from the busy waiter and was forced into a bottle by the mere raising of the man's thick eyebrows. Joss shrugged: what the hell. Barney would arrive in the morning, then the work could begin.

Just then he spied the phone box outside, and when it was finally vacated by the heavily petting couple within, he strode over to make it his own. He had the number memorised and dialled it effortlessly.

Her breathless voice whispered, 'Greta Larson.' He paused.

'It's me,' he said, waiting forlornly for her voice to give some intimation of potential forgiveness.

'Thank God,' she said, pure business. 'Where are you?'

'In Venice.'

'Joss, Rose Moody went to pieces and Rivers looked very surprised when he was asked about you in court; what have you got?'

The speed and fervour of her information and demand almost robbed him of breath.

'I've got some financial stuff on the Church from Zurich: they are ripping all their members off; it's completely crooked. That led me here. They've got Callum . . . I have to get right to the rock bottom of this; they won't hesitate to kill him.'

'I don't know what to say,' Greta whispered sadly, 'but Mark and I need all the help we can get.'

'You two almost sound like a couple,' he said bitterly. She ignored his unfair comment.

'Fax me what you have, I'll get it to Mark: he'll know what to do with it.'

He hurriedly noted her home fax machine's number.

'Are you in danger?' she asked and Joss's heart soared over Beecher's Brook.

'I can handle it,' he replied nonchalantly. Greta sighed with frustration at his Schwarzennegger reply. 'I mean I'll be careful: don't worry.'

'I always worry about you.'

'Do you mean that?'

'This isn't the time, Joss,' she said, her voice brisk and business-like.

'If you get anything, anything at all, send it. Rivers is getting away with murder.'

'He already has,' Joss replied bleakly.

'What?'

'Just a turn of phrase,' he said, not wishing to burden her further. She had enough to cope with; they all did. It was enough that she still cared; at least there was hope.

'I'll be seeing you, Greta.'

'Make sure of it.' Silence consumed them both until he heard the buzz of a dead line at the other end.

Later, when he had faxed the documentation through, he lay down on the bed in his room and swore to himself to do everything in his power and strength to help Greta and redeem himself in her eyes.

No more than three kilometres away, Joss's father looked over to the dazzling lights of Venice from the Island of Murano. Trainer had been mainly silent after news of Joss's dramatic escape in the mountains had reached then: four dead, two wounded and a young banker in protective custody. The window he gazed through was heavily barred and the room was a stale holding cell for Callum Lane. It was eight feet by eight, with crumbling plasterwork from the encroaching waters of the nearby canal. A key turned in the lock and Trainer walked in, bearing a tray of olives and peasant, sour-dough bread. He placed it on the rough table.

'Have to keep you alive till we get the money back,' he explained.

'Is that your conclusion or the Reverend's?' Callum asked. Trainer smiled beatifically.

'He will come, that boy of yours. Strange,' Trainer mused, sitting on the single hard-plank chair and scooping a glistening black olive into his mouth with a satisfied smack. 'He is courageous and intelligent. The apple must have fallen a long way from the tree: or does he take after his mother?'

Callum shrugged without reply.

'We will wait,' Trainer continued. 'He will come; he needs answers. He thinks he will find them here, but all he will find is torture until he gives us the £50 million back, then death. I think I'll make you confess everything first; just to break his soul before I take his life.'

Trainer stood and walked towards the door.

'*Bon appetit,*' he breathed as he closed, then locked the door behind him.

Callum Lane stared through the bars of his cell, and waited for Joss to come.

CHAPTER FORTY-ONE

Mark Mason had a problem. He had the fax from Greta, which appeared to provide proof of suspicious movements of Church funds, but this presented two problems in itself. Firstly, in all likelihood Joss Lane had come by this information dishonestly and, secondly, these were privileged banking documents. He consoled himself with one thought; that he could not have disclosed the bank documents at the proper time because he did not know of their existence. How to call them in as evidence, however, was an entirely different matter.

He mused over the problem as he waited to recommence his cross-examination.

The courtroom had taken on the usual quiet lethargy of a long-running case. Just another day at the office, the assembled workers slumped in resigned desperation, drugged by the dreary sameness of it all. Mason thought their attitude might well change when he began his unexpected, financial, assault; this was not a time for subtlety.

'Mr Rivers,' he began, 'please look at these documents.' An usher took them languidly to the witness.

'What documents?' Callow QC said loudly, leafing through the yellow flagged box files before him. Mason pressed on.

'They relate to monies taken from the Millennium Church.'

'What is this, my Lord?' Callow blustered. 'The defence have no record of any financial documents forming part of the prosecution case.' He swivelled around to confirm the same with his flustered junior barrister.

'They have only just become available to us: I now formally serve them as additional evidence,' Mason said with a confident flourish. He had to strike now, in front of the jury.

'Just how much dishonest money are you making from your followers?'

The jury almost jumped to attention, as he had planned.

Withnail's face was purple: he looked on the verge of a volcanic, cranial explosion.

'You are in contempt of this court, Mason,' he threatened through clenched teeth. 'One more word in the presence of the jury will see you in the cells. Take the jury to their room. Now!'

Rivers was shaken. Thynne and Callow stared angrily in Mason's direction. Withnail looked ready to beat him to death with his own Archbold. The press scribbled the evening's banner headline and Mark Mason knew his future was on the line.

After the jury were led away, Thynne had only one comment to make: 'The jury must be discharged.' His voice was heavy with anticipated triumph, but Withnail was reluctant to accept the prospect of a re-trial and he would not escape his duty by declaring bias.

'In all my years, Mr Mason, I have never witnessed a more flagrant disregard of the rules of court procedure. You will, of course, be reported to your head of chambers, for what good that will do; but more importantly you will be reported to the Bar Council: this could see you disbarred.'

'As your Lordship pleases,' Mason replied quietly, 'but as far as this trial is concerned, I propose that your Lordship rebukes me in front of the jury, after which I shall of course apologise. Then your Lordship will find it appropriate to tell the jury to disregard the topic altogether.'

Thynne was on his feet immediately. 'That is tosh; utter nonsense. They must be discharged; the prejudice to my client is immense. Do it now!' As soon as the last phrase left his lips, Thynne blanched, but Withnail had stomached quite enough from arrogant lawyers for one day. Mason spoke quickly to drive home the impact of his opponent's language.

'My learned friend is saying that if your Lordship instructs the jury to ignore the topic, they in turn will ignore you.'

Withnail fixed him with a savage gaze.

'I know precisely what his words meant. I was a barrister for many years, you know. Your games have all been played before.'

'What does your Lordship intend?' Mason pushed, but he could see that the judge had no intention of sitting through the entire case again.

'Let the jury return and the case recommence,' he murmured. 'But let it be known, Mr Mason, any further sharp practice on your part *will* see the jury discharged and you yourself in the dock.'

Outwardly Mason was nodding humbly; inwardly he glowed, knowing that the jury could not possibly ignore the allegation he'd just made, and Rivers was one step closer to his own prison stripes.

CHAPTER FORTY-TWO

arney Calladine's hair was long, golden and curly, tied back with a batik ribbon. His walnut-brown cherubic face, with its famous single dimple, still grinned knowingly at the vast amusement life provided. Baggy surfer's shorts accentuated his small frame but an 'Einstein was an Alien' cut-off T-shirt drew immediate attention to his compact strength; he hugged Joss.

'You look like the guy who did a runner from the Turkish prison in *Midnight Express*.'

'This is my *Trainspotting* look,' Joss answered. They stood in the walled garden of the *pensione* in the late morning sunshine.

'I wrote,' Barney explained defensively.

'I know; well, at least, I know now.'

'Solitary confinement?' Barney enquired, slumping down on a wrought-iron bench and crossing his legs.

'Something like that.' Joss joined him on the seat.

'You always were one of the Lost Boys.'

Joss looked at him and Barney was smiling. 'Still, you seem to have found yourself now. What's the gig?'

'Have you got the equipment?'

'Locked in the owner's office. Top of the range: two riverbank reeds and a hand-knitted balaclava each.'

'Just the job,' Joss replied with his own stern smile. Barney could always be relied upon to come up with the most reliable gear available. 'Any problem about taking time off?'

Barney shrugged and narrowed his eyes towards the low, milky, sun.

'I quit. Well they don't know yet, but it was time to move on.'

'Barney!' Joss exclaimed, genuinely moved by his friend's sacrifice

'Don't sweat it. Anyway, I've been treading water ever since . . . you know.'

Joss nodded slowly. 'Any news from the others?' he asked, attempting to avoid the subject of his mother's death.

'Not for a while. Ben's in . . .'

'I've seen Ben,' Joss interrupted. Barney swivelled his head slightly and raised his eyebrows challengingly.

'So we're all in this?'

'It's not what I wanted,' Joss muttered.

'Very little is,' Barney retorted. 'Well, Tom is back holding the torch of liberty high in Germany and buzzing the flaxen milkmaids in his Harrier, and Greta . . .'

'Yes,' Joss pressed.

'I heard she got married. Sorry.' Barney dropped his eyes to the flowering mimosas.

'Married?' It was as if Joss had been stunned with a cattle prod. Why hadn't she mentioned it when he had seen her in London? Then he checked himself; the last time he had seen Greta face to face he'd had a naked woman in his hotel room and it was hardly the time for a trip down memory lane.

'Well why not? Your boyfriend is a junkie who was all but charged with his mother's death by the coroner: not a lot to wait for, is it?'

Joss stood up and began to pace back and forward, his hands deep in his pockets, brow furrowed, and for the first time in months he felt the call of the dragon. His wrists ached along with his fluctuating heart, his stomach was in freefall miles below him in the garden. There was always the hope until now. When everything was at its bleakest in the clinic, when even the methadone failed to reconnect him to himself, he welded the craving to his need for Greta: Greta had been his champion and now she was married to someone else.

'I don't know the details,' Barney murmured. 'I know it was quick.'

'Whirlwind; terrific. But she never said a word to me.'

Barney stood and walked toward his friend, reached up and placed his arms on Joss's shoulders.

'You'd gone, Joss – just pissed off without a word, a missing person – she was frantic. Then the days rolled on, weeks, months, not one freaking word from the great Joss Lane. She's no Miss Haversham.'

'Stuff the Dickens,' Joss spat.

'A very honest writer if a little wordy in places,' Barney mused. 'But you have to put her out of your mind for now. Don't we have stuff to do?'

Joss could not drive the unwanted information from his mind. Suddenly, he felt a stinging blow to his face. His anger flared. Barney was smiling.

'Do you remember that time?' Joss struggled to find the connection. 'Lost on Helvellen: Barney Calladine panics and loses it when the freezing fog turns to snow, Joss Lane cracks him in the face, leads him higher to the snowline then digs them both in. Next morning with a bruised face and an injured ego they are rescued.' Barney smiled grimly. 'But you never told the others.'

Joss shrugged. 'You would have done the same for me.'

'Doubtful then, but give me the chance now.'

There was silence for a moment as they both recollected the shared life-threatening experience.

'Now,' Barney continued, 'give me the entire back-story, then we'll visit this place, what is it called?'

'Murano,' Joss replied.

'Well, what can happen to a couple of likely lads in the middle of such a civilised city?'

Joss felt a light seismic tremor course from his lower vertebrae up to the peak of his spine, where it gripped the back of his neck: despite this, he began his tale.

The number 52 *vaporetto* chugged across the lagoon from the Fondamente Nuove stop toward San Michele and Murano. The waterways, the aquatic equivalent of a British motorway, were thronged with waterborne traffic.

It was low tide and Joss could make out the *bricole* route-markers that guided the unwary away from the hidden mud flats where hire boats had once been seen regularly stranded on what the locals called *laguna morta*; dead water. The novelty of rescue had given way to a marked reluctance to allow enthusiastic tourists to beach themselves in hire boats, but after an hour and the exchange of a hefty deposit they had secured a skiff for a return visit.

Barney threw pieces of bread to the gulls that screeched and flapped around the boat. He had remained silent ever since the extent of the problem had been explained. Joss had given him every possible opportunity to renege on their agreement, but Barney's resolve was die-cast and Joss now watched him mentally marking out their route by visual reference to the flat landscape.

After stopping briefly in San Michele, they breached the choppy water to Murano, the island of the glassblowers. Other passengers were making their way there too, heading to the Museum of Glass where objects of awe-inspiring beauty and awful kitsch fought for space in the highly polished display cabinets. Joss and Barney scouted around the perimeter of the island for a landing place. They found a suitable point at the southeast of the island. A small, murky canal led to the back of the Ruga Fondamente Company.

All the island's foundries were open to the public, including the Ruga. A stunning Venetian girl with faultless English showed them around the proudly-presented display room. However it was not the exhibits on display that interested Joss and Barney, but what lay hidden behind the façade; any clues or evidence that might find the continuation of the trail back to PJ Rivers and the Millennium Church.

After half an hour, Joss tipped the guide generously: she thanked him and asked where they were staying and whether she could assist further. Barney smirked, Joss blushed and the guide laughed at his Englishness.

Soon they were lumbering back over the water, the tide fully on the turn, and once more they were silent: there was nothing further to discuss for the moment, there was only work to be done.

At the rear of the Ruga, Harrison Trainer, flanked by Alan Moyne and Dave Tomlin, questioned the girl thoroughly. Trainer remembered her as a former inhabitant of the Haven, some two years before. He was pleased with her initiative in attempting to trace Joss's accommodation and make further contact that evening, but had learned long before that it was pointless to chase the enemy

306

when the enemy was hell-bent on chasing you. He dismissed her with the promise that Reverend Rivers himself would hear of her fine work then winked at his brothers-in-arms.

'Almost time, lads,' Moyne grunted, whilst Tomlin returned the wink. Things were going to turn out just fine after all.

CHAPTER FORTY-THREE

Joss watched in awed fascination as Barney carboloaded three plates of linguini and an entire ciabbata bread. The air outside the tiny restaurant was feisty with hot wind from the lagoon and Joss was quietly irritable.

'You must have hollow legs.'

Barney shrugged.

'Must have a hollow brain to be going along with all this.'

The rebuke was well deserved; this wasn't Barney's battle. Joss passed him another bread stick; Barney took it and munched thoughtfully.

'If these weirdos are as heavy as you say, what's to stop them making us disappear the way that journo did?'

Joss snapped his own crisp stick into small pieces.

'Fifty million quid, and the collective brains and ingenuity of the Lane–Calladine organisation.'

Barney pushed back his plate.

'Now that last part scares me,' he said, smiling uncertainly. They had spent the late afternoon loading up the hired boat with the diving equipment. A hefty bribe to the owner improved the prospects of it still being there on their return.

'Let's go over it again,' Barney demanded. It was his way. Time and time again, until the continuous repetition of the details of the plan became as natural a progression as breathing in then exhaling. Joss took out the map on which Barney had marked their navigational route through the treacherous mud flats, hugging the side of the island until the secluded tie-off point, and then the swim through the murky waters of the canal to the back of the Ruga Fondamente foundry.

'What about when we get inside?'

'Play it by ear,' Joss replied. 'After all, it worked for Beethoven and he was deaf.'

Barney nodded and added, 'But not dumb.'

'Neither are we,' Joss shot back.

'Neither are they,' Barney muttered. Joss had no response. His friend was right. Rivers had not built his empire on luck alone: the man and his lieutenants were thinkers not talkers, doers not dalliers: Kristina Klammer's death and the murder of Thurman were the clearest evidence of that.

'We get the evidence to cripple them,' Joss pronounced.

'Accepted,' Barney said, as he waved his arm to the waiter to bring them the bill, 'But we may only find a tacky but expensive glass ashtray.'

'I hope so, Barney, I really do.'

Barney watched his friend's face carefully, searching for clues as to how frightened he really should be and, though the breeze was a warm *sirocco*, he shuddered.

Joss sculled whilst Barney whispered directional orders down the eleven feet of the boat. They travelled without light, unwilling to signal their approach to the islanders, and on one occasion were all but capsized by a ferry's wash. Joss had held onto the side and the aqualungs as the craft rocked crazily: he almost lost an oar, but a lunge from the nimble Barney soon had it docked back.

The moon was unobscured and hurled its beam down on them; it seemed to Joss like a prison searchlight at a midnight escape. He continued to dip the oars gently into the cold water, his dry suit, worn over his clothes, superheating with the continued effort.

It took well over an hour to reach the dark contours of the island of Murano. They sat in silence once Barney had tied them up to a well-rooted silver birch tree, and Joss breathed deeply until his respiration rate was even once more.

Barney quietly ran through the many necessary checks on the tanks, facemasks, hoses and spear guns. He expertly secured their guide rope onto the anchor chain of the boat by tying a complicated knot that Joss knew would unravel at the correct moment with a tiny pull in the right direction. Barney was a marvel in these situations.

Joss reminded himself there had never been a similar situation before, but that did nothing to detract from the economical way in which Calladine performed. It was as if he were purpose-built for times such as this.

They each secured the other's tanks, snapping on clips and belts for security. Barney swung his legs over the craft's side whilst Joss leant the other way to counterbalance the shift in weight. Once this was achieved, Barney held the boat steady as Joss mirrored his activity. Barney waited for him to swim around to the side nearest the land then secured the two together with a further rope; Barney would lead and Joss, his aquatic Siamese twin, would follow.

They fixed their mouthpieces and Joss gave his friend the thumb-up, Barney gave him the finger and Joss smiled. He watched as his buddy-diver took one last look to orientate himself, checked the direction against the Braille compass he used for cave diving, and ducked under the water.

At first the water was clear and visibility was reasonable, but this had been expected. It was at the point where the canal mouth met the main body of water that the silt began to spin, thicken, then blind. On their earlier trip Barney had paced out the distance between their diving point and the back of the foundry. He had cut their guide rope to the same length, so that when they could go no further, they knew they had arrived. Joss felt as though he was choking. He wasn't – the sweet-sickening air from the tanks guarded against that – but it was the raging blindness that sucked up his fear. Myriad, tiny shoals of canal dirt crowded his vision wherever he turned his head.

How could Barney do this stuff? How could he swim utterly without sight, down claustrophobic caves no bigger than the cir-cumference of his waist? Joss had accompanied him once, down some well-travelled caves in Cheshire:

'Kid's stuff,' Barney had said as they prepared to dive. Joss had lasted twenty minutes before the wide walls began to crowd in and rob him of his senses. Barney had never commented on the occurrence, but there had been a look of deep concern on his face after their swift return to daylight and open space.

Joss kicked slowly and evenly and decided that, if he could not see, he might as well close his eyes. This helped: not much, but

311

the swirling effect of the watery debris on his optic nerve was now negated. Barney had estimated the canal's depth at roughly fifteen feet. Joss had asked him about the possibility of air bubbles rising to the surface and giving their position away, but his friend had merely remarked, that it would be midnight or later by the time they reached the island, and that if anyone was looking for air bubbles then they would be in 'deep shit' anyway. Joss had to agree with his friend's stark evaluation.

It seemed like an eternity but it could not have been longer than ten minutes of slow, patient swimming before Joss felt the backward tug of the guide rope at his waist. He stopped swimming. Almost immediately, Barney's momentum was halted by Joss's static condition. Joss felt a hand on his shoulder give him a gentle squeeze, then felt a movement in the water followed by a tug on his line; Barney was moving to the canalside and rising as he did. Joss allowed himself to drift, but in accordance with their earlier agreement held his breath until they broke the surface with a gentle splash. Barney's facemask was the only visible sign of their presence and skimmed the surface by just millimetres; Joss followed his example.

The back of the foundry was black and looming, its bulky outline towering over the still water by the canalside. A small, brightly-painted craft bobbed on the surface, moored by a thick hemp rope to a squat, metal mushroom. Barney led them forward. Once they had breached the distance, he began to unbuckle his tank: Joss followed suit. They laid the tanks down in the belly of the boat, careful to lift them gently from the telltale water. Then Barney tied their guide rope onto its submerged anchor chain and swam away to an adjacent set of steps, carved out of the canalside centuries before. Gingerly he climbed, crouching as he did, until his head breached the line of vision. He began to move away into the shadows: Joss followed his friend into the gloom.

Once they were safely away from their landing point, Barney wordlessly passed command of the mission over to Joss. There were three major outbuildings, ugly and constructed for function rather than form. From the earlier guided tour, Joss knew that the two vast flanking buildings were glassblowing sheds, heated to melting point by ceaselessly burning fires. The central building was the main storage area: he had decided to concentrate his search there.

Joss's main weapon was the element of surprise: who would expect a midnight assault on a glass factory by two divers? It was madness and could never be anticipated. Their spear guns were still strapped to their backs, and though the spears were in place it was too dangerous to have the firing mechanism cocked whilst swimming. He watched Barney put that right.

They padded quietly across to the doorway. It was locked, as he had anticipated, but a heavy pair of bolt-croppers soon dispensed with the padlock and they were inside. Joss removed a small but extremely powerful torch with a pencil-thin beam from his belt. Before them, vast racks of glassware sparkled the beam's reflection back at them. Ornaments of every description crowded the high wooden pallets in cramped rows. This was the legitimate merchandise; Joss wanted to know what the illegitimate produce could be. He had put his brain and imagination on the rack in a filed attempt to reason the thing out, but so far without success.

They continued their search, but each aisle merely led to another, then another, a maze of translucent crystal. It was Barney who spotted the crates, marked 'freight' then 'Berlin' at the loading bay. As this was the only merchandise that was not on open display, Joss jemmied open the top of the first one. The kapok filling spilled out as he delved within its interior.

Then he felt them: tiny vials, not of glass as he had expected, but of flexible plastic. There were hundreds of them, all filled with a clear liquid. Joss ripped the top off the first and smelled it: nothing. He was about to taste the liquid to identify it when Barney grabbed it from him.

'Are you absolutely fucking insane, Lane?' Barney whispered through gritted teeth. 'Let me,' he demanded. Joss saw him take a tiny sip, which he proceeded to spit onto the floor.

'Tastes like liquid Ecstasy,' he said, and it was at that point that all the lights inside the huge, glittering storeroom exploded into life.

Barney crouched low and brought the spear gun around to bear on the main thrust of the light, an overhead beam of ferocious intensity. Joss slid down behind the crate and raised his hand over his eye to shade it from the dazzle whilst he scanned furiously around the huge room for a reference point to their danger.

'Good to see you, Joss,' Trainer's voice boomed through an overhead address system. He almost replied, but that would fix his position and it was not yet clear if Trainer knew exactly where he was. He reached into the crate and removed a handful of the plastic vials, which he stuffed inside a waterproof pocket.

'You are outnumbered, out-gunned and out of luck,' Trainer said, and Joss could almost hear him smiling.

'When did you last see your father?' Trainer mocked in reference to the famous painting. 'He really needs to speak to you.' Then, heart-breakingly, Callum spoke.

'Joss, son, it's Dad. You have to give yourself up or they will kill us all.'

Joss was torn, but knew that surrender meant certain death: at least this way they had a chance. Trainer needed to know where the money was and that couldn't be discovered if Joss was dead. He glanced at Barney and indicated that they should begin to crawl back the way they had entered; his friend nodded and began to wriggle away.

'You have caused us some problems,' Trainer said, 'but that is over now. Come out and we will talk: do it, or I will shoot your father limb by limb.'

So that was it, Joss thought, no deal to cut: Trainer was not even attempting to trick him by mentioning the possibility of a stand-off. He heard the sound of a single gun-shot, which was followed by his father's tortured scream. Joss was torn by the dilemma.

Think, Joss.

They can't bargain if he is dead.

They can't kill him, can they?

Trainer hadn't ordered them to keep still and that could only mean that they were not in Trainer's line of vision.

Barney had stopped by an open space between the towering pallets. Joss knew what his friend was thinking: the open ground would give Trainer a clear view and a free shot. Then Barney spun onto his back and raised the spear gun to take aim at the most powerful light source. He counted down to three, mouthing the words. As Barney fired the barbed projectile, Joss heaved all his weight into the nearest mountain of glass.

The spear shattered the glaring light with an explosive pop, but that was as silence compared with the shattering stutter of machine-pistol fire that greeted its dimming.

'Fire at their legs,' Trainer screamed over the cacophony. Joss saw the wooden pallet he had jolted rock on its heel then its toes before beginning the monumental freefall into the next, then that into its neighbour in a crystal domino run. Shards of glass erupted all around them as bullets tore into the surrounding area. Shrapnelled wood spun madly about their heads as together they rose and ran towards the exit.

Joss had his own spear gun in front of him as they slammed the door open. A spitting patter of gunfire danced around his fleeing feet. At the steel door, Joss paused momentarily to jam a bolt through the flapping clasp as Barney made straight for the water.

Trainer believed he had anticipated everything: everything, that was, except an underwater raid at the rear of the premises. His men had been stationed outside the front at two crossfire points; he himself had been monitoring the display area when he had heard the movement within. Against his own orders he had broken radio silence to order his men back to the capture zone. Now Lane had jammed the door and precious seconds elapsed whilst they retraced their route through the shattered interior and around the back.

On their arrival at the water's edge they used powerful searchlights to throw the area into shadowy relief. The two raiders had been wearing diving suits, and the three of them now watched for tell-tale bubbles. Trainer swept the foot of the canal-side where a gaudily coloured boat rocked gently with recent momentum and there, percolating through the murk, were the rising breaths of the two. Tomlin squatted low, bringing his machine-pistol to bear on the watery traceline, but Trainer gripped his shoulder.

'No. They'll have to come up when the air runs out.'

But after ten long minutes there was still no movement.

'Come on, come on, Lane, come up,' Trainer whispered. His men were watching the area intently. Then the bubbles halted abruptly.

'This is it,' he said through gritted teeth. 'Get them out of the water and back in the foundry.'

A further two minutes elapsed and Trainer began to feel the chill wind of suspicion.

'Get in the water,' he ordered Tomlin.

'They've got spear-guns: you get in the water,' Tomlin replied, unwilling to even the fight by submerging himself in his quarry's chosen battleground. He glanced at Moyne, who averted his gaze back to the water and said, 'They must be dead by now.'

'Spray the top of the water, scare them up,' Trainer ordered. They churned the water with rapid fire. Trainer waited for the gasping bodies to rise and was disappointed once more. He could only guess at this stage that they had tied themselves down to the jetty. It was over. He had to recover the corpses and dispose of the evidence. He dropped himself into the water knowing the stolen money was gone for good and he was finished.

Three hundred yards away, Joss and Barney broke the surface for air. They had only one tank between them. Barney had secured the other to the anchor chain and fixed the oxygen on slow release, whilst they swam back up the guide rope, pausing every thirty seconds to share the mouthpiece of the oxygen cylinder. Joss was on the point of panicking every time his body craved the life-giving oxygen, although his faith in his friend to bring them through kept the demons of doubt at bay; but only just. Barney's face was contorted with pain as he slid silently into the belly of the boat. Joss jettisoned the almost-depleted tank and clambered in next to him.

'You OK?' he whispered. Barney nodded his head down to his foot where two toes had been shot off.

'Jesus, Barney . . .'

'Shut up; I'm the talkative one. Bind it, looks worse than it is, quickly. That trick won't keep them back for long. Once the tank runs out they'll know.'

Joss got to work, almost sick at the sight of his brave friend's blood, but sicker at the thought of the lifelong disfigurement his friend had suffered, and his part in causing it.

'Get us out of here, Joss, they weren't just shooting to end my ballet career.'

Joss picked up the oars and rowed as swiftly and as silently as his exhausted body would allow. When Barney started groaning it seemed to amplify in Joss's ears to a scream. He took one of the plastic ampoules from his pocket, ripped off its top, not daring to allow any of the once-sweet juice to touch his own dry lips and tipped it into his wounded friend's mouth.

'Sweet dreams, Barney,' he muttered and began to row again. In the distance the screech of a police launch's siren cleft the night air and grew in intensity as they approached. Joss began to pull away from their course.

Trainer grudgingly acknowledged that Joss Lane had bested him again. His reluctant trawl of the water offered up the heavily punctured air-tank but no corpses. He had a choice: he could either speed after them in a boat, risking the attention of witnesses and a fatal brush with authority, or he could remove the evidence of the crates of ampoules destined for Berlin. He chose the latter course. Lane would be bound to inform the police of his suspicions, albeit anonymously, and they were bound to investigate the Ruga. In a curious way Lane's escape from death had saved his own life; at least for the moment. The ever-resourceful Joss would continue his search and Trainer had more than an inkling of where his travels would take him next, and next time there would be no mistakes.

The jetty had been deserted on their arrival back at the mooring point. Joss had no choice. Barney was delirious with pain and highly loved-up with the liquid drug. He needed hospital attention for his foot, which was seeping blood through the makeshift bandage. This was an obvious gunshot wound and any Venetian doctor would be legally bound to report the matter to the police. Joss could not take chances with the investigation and they could not admit to the raid on the foundry.

'Barney, can you hear me, mate?'

As he shook him, his friend began to stir lightly.

'I love the sound of breaking glass,' Barney sang tunelessly, through cracked lips.

'I'm getting you to a hospital. They'll look after you: I can't. I'll get word to you.'

'Word up,' Barney muttered, his brain furiously making musical connections to Joss's dialogue.

'Keep singing, mate,' Joss said quietly and made his way to a phone box. There he made three swift calls; one to the police, informing them of a large drugs haul in the Ruga's premises, one to the emergency services detailing the whereabouts of his wounded friend and another to Greta asking her to dig around for information on the Berlin company that the drugs were to be freighted to. He swiftly returned to Barney Calladine, who seemed slightly more alert.

'I've got to go now, Barney. Say nothing: the British Consul will be involved; you'll be safe.'

But as the words tumbled out they sounded hollow and uncertain. Barney appeared puzzled, then blinked open his eyes briefly.

'Joss, when you get home, check out Spineless Eric,' he muttered, referring to their one-time dealer.

'What are you talking about?'

'Just a whisper I heard.'

But then Barney's eyes had glazed over once more. Joss, stunned and tired, confused and dazzled by the entire turn of events, kissed his friend gently as he whispered, 'I will make it up to you, I promise,' and slid through the shadows; he was on his way to Berlin.

CHAPTER FORTY-FOUR

Joss looked down through the wispy morning clouds hanging over Berlin like paint-starved brush strokes. He could see the jagged scar etching its way across the urban landscape, parts of the wall now indistinguishable from the air by virtue of the large scale re-developments going on all over the city as it struggled to accommodate yet another chapter in its illustrious history.

He had managed to secure a flight out of Marco Polo airport in Venice by taking a standby on a long haul from Bahrain, which had stopped to refuel on its way to pick up at Berlin and Amsterdam. Given that the flight had originated from the Middle East, they landed at Schonefeld airport on the eastern side of the city. Joss was the only passenger to get off and the airport was virtually deserted. He needed to speak to Greta. Someone else had to know what was happening, and he needed to know how the case against Rivers was progressing. It was early enough to catch her at home. Joss used some loose change and called her number, waiting apprehensively as the connection was made.

'Greta Larson.' Her voice was thick and breathy with sleep and he desperately wanted to hold her close and pretend this was all a bad dream.

'It's Joss.' Immediately she brightened.

'Where are you, Lane? What is going on?'

'Barney's been shot,' he said and heard her gasp. 'He's going to be OK; at least I think so.'

'What the hell are you up to?'

Joss sighed: why were problems always of his own making in her eyes?

'We found the cult's drug operation in Venice. They will have cleared it out by now, but it's financed by the church. I saw it.'

319

'Are you hurt?'

'I was lucky,' he replied. 'They've still got Callum, but I think he's safe for now.'

'Explain?' she asked, and Joss could almost hear her mentally filing away the information for potential use in the trial.

'I've liberated some of their working capital.'

'Have you stolen it?' she snapped.

'I don't intend to keep it,' he bit back. 'It's leverage.' But Greta's silence showed that she was unconvinced.

'The drugs were bound for Berlin.'

'And that's where you are now?'

'Correct,' he replied. 'I need you to call Niall Robertson, my dad's solicitor: you can trust him,' Joss continued as the telephone display warned him that his time and money were running out.

'No! You trust him, Joss,' she snapped.

The final warning beeps interrupted his flow.

'How's the trial going? Are you nailing the bastard to the wall?'

But Joss never heard her reply as the phone went dead. He replaced the receiver, then walked to the airport café and ordered coffee. The bill of lading he had taken from one of the boxes at the Ruga Fondementa was still in his pocket. He picked it out and examined it for the umpteenth time.

The shipment was headed for the KK import/export agency in Potsdammer Platz. Joss planned to pay a visit to the KK agency eventually, but first he needed to hole up and contact Tom Redkin; the final member of 'In Extremis.' He finished his coffee and sauntered over to the news-stand where he bought a VIBB atlas and an early edition of the London *Times* to read on the journey into the city centre. He unfolded the atlas on a table next to the entrance to the bus terminal and checked the listings for the U- and S-Bahn systems. He worked out that he could take the number 171 bus to Flughafen where a connection with the S-Bahn overground train would take him to zoo station.

He got to the train station without difficulty but soon realised that the massive expansion of the network to accommodate the increased capacity of the city since reunification was making for big delays. No matter; he settled into a bucket seat on the platform and watched the pedestrian traffic as Berlin came awake. It was just after 9am.

On arriving at the Zoologischer Garten, recognised for years as the centre of western Berlin, he walked out of the elaborate concourse with its huge, high, glass roof. It didn't take long to walk down to the Kaiser Wilhelm memorial church with its crumbling tower reminding everyone of the city's former glory. Soon he found himself in the middle of the Kurfurstendamm with its smart shops and slick bars, and decided to find digs in a small side street. Once safely installed in his room at the hotel Alpenland he tried to contact Tom at RAF Gatow in the north-west of the city.

His old friend couldn't be contacted so he left a message and drifted off into a kind of sleep with his head still spinning.

Time to plan, Joss.

Dream and plan.

The telephone woke him two hours later its shrill pitch biting into his trance.

'Yeah,' he answered. Dry throat. Tight and sticky with exhaustion.

'Mr Joss Delaney, you have a call,' stated the receptionist.

'Thanks, put it through.'

'Jesus Christ, Joss what do you think you're doing?' It was Tom sounding distinctly unimpressed.

'Nice to hear from you as well, compadre,' Joss croaked, raising himself up and propping a pillow behind his aching neck.

'You've got a nerve.'

'So did you once. Get off my back, Tom; I'm in trouble and I need your help.'

'You don't say. Two fucking years, Joss. We all had to go through it: you realise that, don't you.'

'Do you honestly believe that I could ever forget, Tom: she was my mother, don't you remember that?'

'Listen up. There is an Interpol search for you, Joss: they say you may be involved with the killing of your shrink.'

'What do you think? Do you believe them?'

'I don't know what to think, Joss. I tried to contact Ben only to find out from his wife that he's in police custody with some

321

heavy-hitting bank on his case. Then I get a call from Barney's mother saying he's in hospital with a bullet in his leg.'

'Foot.'

'What?'

'It was Barney's foot, not his leg.'

'Oh that's brilliant, Joss. I'm so sorry: you see, I get kind of loose with my language when it comes down to my friends getting shot.'

'I know it must seem out of control.'

'That's an understatement. Jesus Christ, if the brass find out that I'm in contact with you I'll get court martialled.'

'Has anyone questioned you about any of this?'

'Only Interpol.'

'I didn't kill her, Tom.'

'I hope not. What the hell is going on, Joss?'

'You wouldn't believe it.'

'Try me.'

Joss spent the next half-hour explaining to Tom all the events of the last week and how it was that he came to be in Berlin.

'Look, you have to give yourself up: it's the only way. I can get someone from the consulate to be there with you right away. I'll even come over myself.'

'I can't, Tom: I have to get some concrete evidence that this organisation is corrupt down to the core, and then I've got to bargain for Callum's life. Don't you see that?'

'But how? All you have is your word and right now that's not worth a great deal, is it?'

'Maybe not, but if I can get to this import/export company I am one step closer.'

'What do you want from me?'

'I need a safe passage out of Berlin and back to London.'

'Not asking for much then?'

'Come on, Tom, I know you can get me out. If I try to fly into any commercial airport in the UK I'm bound to get stopped.'

'Are you suggesting that I get you in on Royal Air Force transport?'

'Exactly. Barney told me that you were flying all sorts of

stuff including those Hercules transporter planes: surely there's enough room.'

'Don't be stupid, Joss. If you get caught then I'm in deep shit.'

'If I get caught, I promise I won't implicate you.'

'You seem to have lost your powers of reasoning: they already suspect that you will try to contact me; that's why I'm using a friend's phone.'

'You know I wouldn't ask if there was any other way.'

'Do I?'

'Come off it, Tom. I need you.'

'What are your plans now?'

'I'm going to go down to this place in the Potsdammer Platz and ask some questions.'

'Are you sure you're up to this, Joss?'

'I don't know, but I have to try: you know how it is, Tom.'

'Look, I'll get you out but you will have to meet me at the north end of Tegel airport at 3.00am tomorrow: there's a scheduled flight into RAF Brize Norton.'

'Thanks, Tom: I'll never forget this.'

'I won't let you. Good luck.'

Joss couldn't blame Tom for his hostility, but at the end of the day he knew Tom would come through for him. One by one he had asked his friends for help and one by one they had given generously and paid the price. He could only hope that Tom's name wouldn't appear on the list of casualties marked 'The friends of Joss Lane'.

CHAPTER FORTY-FIVE

I t was very dark and Joss was being ultra cautious. He managed
to find the KK building on the north side of the new piazza
in Potsdammer Platz. Street lighting did not cover most of the
site while it was still being installed, and for that he was grateful.
The building, all steel and glass, reminded him of the film set of
Blade Runner. He walked the perimeter, checking the positions of
the various security sheds, but their inhabitants didn't seem that
interested in anything other than the small television sets, which
seemed obligatory in each hut.

He could make out the warehousing section, the largest building
in the sector, and just to the left of the main gates he saw a wagon
bearing an Italian registration mark.

You're in the right place, Joss.
That means it's dangerous.
You could die here.

The wagon driver was waiting patiently at the gates while a
dishevelled security guard in a shabby blue uniform was finishing
a telephone call in the hut. Eventually, he walked to the driver's
side and within seconds the load was waved through into the body
of the warehouse.

Joss looked around wildly. There didn't seem to be a way in other
than past the same guard. Just then the unfinished road to the right
suddenly lit with the headlamps of a lone vehicle speeding west.
The driver glanced over in his direction but didn't see Joss as he
ducked behind a container.

He crouched down, clutching the disposable camera he'd bought
earlier that day in his coat pocket.

Think, Joss.
Think and plan.

He didn't have time.

A footstep to his left. Then another, followed by two more. He saw them before they saw him, but one thing was clear: it was definitely him they were looking for:

How did they know where he was? He was sure he hadn't been followed. He curled even tighter behind the container, waiting for the men to round the corner, then they would be upon him. The first man walked into Joss's clenched fist. Hard and fast straight between his lip and the tip of his nose. The crack was sickening.

But he didn't go down and now there were two of them. The second man came hurtling round the bend, his eyes bright with feral hunger. The razor blade in his hand tripped a rhythm as he played it, expertly twirling it around his fingers.

'Cut him,' the first said through the blood and shattered bone. The man's pupils were wide as he closed in, beginning to circle Joss who had his back to the wall.

A lunge, and Joss felt the blade slice the air by his cheek. He dodged to the right and the man was off balance. Joss could take him now easily but he slid off down to the end of the warehouse and into the rear storage area.

Only the razor man followed; the other had clearly gone for assistance. Joss edged behind a tray of wooden pallets waiting for his pursuer.

Come on.

Execute, Joss.

He heard the steps shuffling by.

Do it now, Joss.

He lurched to his left while the razor man moved in with the grace of an acrobat. The razor arched down, shining under the floodlights of the goods yard, cutting for his face. Joss ducked under his attacker's arm, slamming his wrist down on his shoulder. The weapon clattered to the floor. He dropped down into a crouch and allowed the assailant's momentum to carry him over his shoulder. He cocked his leg behind the razor man's ankle kicking it forward while he thrust his body upward.

It was ugly but it worked.

Joss left the man lying face down, spitting blood, as he sprinted across the goods yard hearing three, maybe four, voices.

Confused voices.

They had lost track of him. But it was no good being at ground level: he had to climb.

Have to take those photographs, Joss.

They're evidence.

Greta needs evidence.

It had been far too long since he'd scaled anything higher than the wall at the Haven, but now he had no option: every entrance to the warehouse was blocked and the drugs must be inside.

Silence fell. He could hear his own ragged breathing and feel his heart thundering like a tympanum. They were looking in the wrong place.

Don't look a gift horse in the mouth.

Beside his feet was a reel of thick rope used for strapping loads to the wagons. He quickly unwound it from the bobbin and hurried over to the sheer face of the warehouse. He checked it at somewhere near 150 feet of closely-pointed, granite ashlar block. About twenty feet above him he could see a winch mechanism protruding out of the wall and he hurled the rope over it. He swiftly knotted a makeshift harness, which immediately cut brutally into his thighs.

Fortunately, the surface of the wall was pitted and provided him with a decent grip as he slowly began his ascent, knowing that when he reached the winch he could move over to the metal guttering taking him all the way to the roof.

He was there in seconds, one final surge taking him onto the winch. He gathered the rope and wound it around his body as he clambered up the drainpipe and onto the roof space.

The glass atrium above the warehouse floor gave him a full view of the unloading below. All he had to do now was get into the damn place. He needed to be closer to get the shots.

He was in luck.

The skylight didn't even have a clasp lock on it. He carefully lowered himself into the corridor at the eastern side of the building. He was in control now. No second thoughts; only the desire to execute.

No one in sight: they must all be outside searching the yard by now. He reached a door at the end of the passage and flung it open. A stairwell leading down.

Looking good, Joss.

He ran down the steps, his momentum carrying him into every turn of the stairs, bouncing off the walls like a human pinball.

Right turn.

Faster, Joss, faster.

Left turn.

Finally, he reached the warehouse floor. A thick steel door was all that separated him from the unloading process.

A shout. From above. The stairs: they were coming down the stairs.

Move, Joss.

Move now.

He burst through the door and into the bright, blinding, fluorescent strip lights of the warehouse floor. The wagon was directly in front of him, about five or six men unloading crates; the same crates he had seen at the Ruga Fondementa.

Behind him, an engine roared into life: he span round to see the fork-lift heading straight for him.

Cornered. Like a rat. A rat in Trainer's trap. Trainer's face peered out at him through the mesh windscreen. Gone was the controlled expression with which Joss was familiar, his features were now snarled into focused fury. The crate loaders fled in all directions leaving Joss pinned down with two metal spikes racing toward him.

No game plan, Joss.

No time.

Only instinct.

Only In Extremis.

He leapt onto the right-hand prong just as it crashed into the steel door behind him. The door buckled under the impact and shunted Trainer headfirst into the mesh. Joss heard the gunfire open up behind the door but it would do them no good; the door was jammed in tight.

A second later Trainer sparked into life and tried frantically to shift the gear stick into reverse. Joss clambered over the engine block desperately fighting for breath. He dropped to the other side, just as Trainer extracted the machine with a violent shudder, and he started to sprint along the long aisle to his left. The engine revved louder as Trainer pursued him with blood streaming down his face in dark rivulets. The mesh windscreen was flapping against the side of the cab as it careered along, forcing Joss ever closer to the end of the rows of shelving.

It can't be.

Only way is up, Joss.

The only way is up.

His inner voice screamed loudly in his head, competing with the reverberating pounding of his heart as Trainer closed in on him. Spotting an empty gap in the shelving just above head-height, Joss prepared himself for the jump. Three metres away a layer of wooden pallets gave him the necessary springboard and Joss exploded into the jump, summoning every sinewy muscle in his body. He sailed onto the second shelf and crashed into a row of boxes while Trainer went slamming into the breeze block wall at the end of the row.

No time Joss.

Finish it.

Before it finishes you.

He sprang down onto the roof of the cab through the cloud of dust thrown up by the impact and scrambled to open the cab door. Trainer was slumped across the huge steering wheel with the shift stick embedded in his chest wall. Joss pulled him off with more care than he deserved and looked into his lifeless eyes. Trainer stared back at him, just the trace of a thin smile etching itself across his lips. He opened his mouth slightly and Joss could see the thick blood filling his throat.

Leave him, Joss.

Leave him now.

Leave him for dead.

He didn't.

Instead he reached over Trainer's crumpled legs for the handgun lying at his feet. It was one instinct too many because he didn't witness Harrison Trainer's last act on the planet, but he felt its effects.

The hypodermic syringe forced itself into the vein behind Joss's right leg as he screamed in agony. He grasped for the pistol and flung his full weight into Trainer's temple. Now he didn't have to leave him for dead.

329

Trainer died with a smile on his lips that no God would allow into heaven.

Joss fell back onto the warehouse floor clutching at the syringe embedded in his leg. He could feel the first acid-rush burning up his leg searching for his heart. He had to move and move quickly. He had been injected with heroin but how much of it he didn't know.

He crept along the gangway and out of a small door at the rear. It was only a short stagger to the perimeter fencing but the drug was already beginning to take hold.

Stay awake, Joss.

You have to.

In the car park of the building opposite he could see a small van, pounding techno music escaping from its darkened interior along with the smoke of two cigarettes. He approached from the rear and opened the passenger side door. The girl stared in horror as he thrust the pistol into her mouth and edged into the car. Her boyfriend held up his hands as Joss closed the door and gestured for him to start the engine.

'Drive,' he said slowly, making a great effort to ensure the words came out properly. 'Drive to Tegal airport and you won't be harmed.'

The young man nodded and placed his shaking hands onto the steering wheel. Joss noticed the clock on the dash: it was 2.15 am. He had to remain conscious at all costs. He focused on the tiles, forever present on his person. Yes, Love was Greta and his mother; yes, the past was his acceptance of Jennie Lane's death; and in all likelihood the future was his imminent death.

Later that same morning, Mark and Greta were sitting in the conference room with just the table-top between them. Mark realised there was something wrong with her.

'Is it Joss?' he asked.

'Yes,' she replied, keeping her eyes fixed on him.

'What's happened?'

'I don't want to involve you, Mark: he's in big trouble.'

'So is this case, Greta. I'll take the risk.'

'You don't have to keep reminding me'.

'I'm sorry, but come on, Greta.'

'I think he's got something on Rivers's drugs operation and he's traced it down to Berlin.'

'Great, so what's the problem: let's get him here.'

'It's not that easy; it's how he's come about the evidence that worries me.'

'We don't have a case without something concrete, and you know it.'

Mason sighed deeply and toyed with the starched bands around his wing collar. Greta had her fingers laced together; they were all anxious.

'You don't know what he's like,' she explained.

'Then tell me,' Mason requested, leaning back and crossing his long legs at the ankles.

'He's brave to the point of foolhardy. Impetuous and stubborn: yes, he's bloody stubborn all right, but he's also focused. He won't let up till it's over.'

'That's the trouble; it could all be over, if I don't call him as a prosecution witness.'

'Can't you buy him more time?' Greta asked.

'If I go any slower the jury will have died of natural causes,' Mason replied. He had painstakingly questioned the countless alibi witnesses from the cult into terminal detail. Their shiny, glowing faces wrapped in innocence were buying Rivers a 'get out of jail free' card. Whilst discrepancies had cropped up during the course of their cross-examinations, they were insufficient to cause the jury any further disquiet.

'The jury needs to know what Joss knows: hear him speak at first hand about his experiences at the Haven and subsequently.'

'Will you be allowed to call him, Mark? We've closed the case.'

Mason considered: he'd thought of little else since witnessing Rivers's response to Joss Lane's name.

'There is a way. Because the evidence has arisen *ex-improviso* I can call him with the judge's leave. We have to argue that the evidence has only become apparent during the course of the trial.

Greta nodded. 'So we need him.'

331

'And fast,' Mason emphasised. 'But he was sure about the drugs?'

'Positive: thinks it's some kind of Ecstasy.'

Mason considered.

'Greta, you have to get him back for me; for Rose.'

Greta frowned with the burden of her responsibility.

'It's all about justice, Greta: whatever Joss has done can't be as bad as Rivers's crimes, can it?' he asked.

'You're absolutely right, Mark, I know.'

'But we can't mess it up this time. Rose would never get through a retrial if I just go blasting in on hearsay: I need facts, something tangible the jury can use to tip themselves over the edge to a conviction.'

They sat looking at each other during the long pause that followed, ignorant of the fact that Joss Lane was presently the only human occupant of a diplomatic mailbag heading back to London in the back of an RAF transporter plane.

CHAPTER FORTY-SIX

Greta watched him carefully, unsure of what she now felt for the boy she had once loved. He had changed, almost beyond recognition, as if a battle-weary older brother, grizzled with fatigue, had taken his place. She could only begin to imagine what he had been through, but his body was barely living testimony of the truth.

The court had risen for the weekend, so Greta could devote the entire day to Joss.

This was the second day of his withdrawal from the 90 per cent pure heroin that had been jabbed into his battered body: it had almost been too much for his system to withstand. Since Tom had brought him to her home in an RAF ambulance, she had watched over him as he groaned in delight, then shivered, gibbered and screamed at the demons of addiction. He had been stabilised for twelve hours now, but refused to make any sense.

Tom had filled her in on what he knew of the story; the rest she could piece together from Joss's previous phone calls. Since then she held a vigil over his life.

The room was cleared of any materials that he might injure himself with: all that remained was a bed, padded at the sides with additional duvets and pillows, and a chair for her to sit and watch and think.

Joss Lane: her Joss once, then Junkie Joss, cured Joss and now reluctant addict Joss once more. She had ached for him for a long time until the familiarity of drudging duty dulled the edges of her loss and made it an acceptable numbness: not so much the aching of a phantom limb; more the remembering how to use a damaged limb once more. There had been men: not too many, but enough to convince her that it would be a lengthy search before she would rediscover herself through unflinching devotion.

He flailed around and groaned. She smelt his stench, then immediately and uncomplainingly changed the bedclothes and bathed him for the seventh time that day. This was the reality of drugs: not the brief, orgasmic delight of the hit, but the subsequent vomit, urine and body toxins that sweated and leaked from every human orifice like a fractured human dam.

Having set the washing machine rumbling away once more with its soiled load, she returned to the room: he was awake, eyes flashing around to attempt orientation.

'You must be thirsty.'

His face contorted in alarm.

'I must be hallucinating.' Joss's voice was thick and cracked, like a twisted husk. 'I'll see my mother next,' he muttered, as tears ran slowly down his stubbled cheeks.

'This is real, Joss. It's really me. Tom brought you.'

'Yeah, of course: then you'll turn into a flesh-eating zombie.'

'I am flesh,' said Greta softly, then took his hand and placed it gently on her cheek. He tried to pull it away, but the last days had burgled his body of any residual strength, and as he felt her pale, warm skin he turned his face to her.

'Greta,' he whispered.

'Sleep, Joss. That stuff nearly snuffed you out.'

'How long have I been here?'

Greta whispered the story of his departure from Berlin and his arrival at her home, whilst Joss, eyes welded to her face, stayed silent. He seemed about to speak on several occasions, then, mouth gaping, shrugged away his proposed question.

'Say it, Lane: whatever it is can't be that bad.'

Joss looked at her intently. He had waited, prayed and promised anything and everything for this moment, yet now it was here he was stricken with fear and silence. Now, close and intimate for the first time in years he could see her as she really was. She had grown older, yet more beautiful in the way that those blessed with cheekbones like pale, angular bruises do. Her flowing hair was now cropped short and shaved up the nape of her long neck, and her grey eyes gazed at him, wise and knowing.

'Where is your husband?'

What had been intended as a friendly enquiry came out as a stumbling accusation.

'I don't have a . . . wait a second. You've been talking to Barney Calladine?'

Joss nodded, though cramps began to contort his guts. Greta smiled. It was a beautiful smile. Then she laughed.

'Some joke,' he complained.

'Some misunderstanding. Look, that was an immigration thing for a political refugee from the free representation unit. He was about to be deported and wouldn't have survived five minutes back in Africa, so . . .'

'You married him. Have to get myself deported.'

Greta dropped her gaze down to her lap.

'Didn't work. Immigration have seen it all before.' She stood up slowly. 'Two months later I was a widow. Anyway, what the hell has that got to do with you, Lane?'

Her face was now hard and harsh as it had been at the inquest.

'Where were you? Hiding? Moping? Burying yourself in smack and self-pity? What about the rest of us? How were we meant to cope?'

'I know,' he muttered.

'You know nothing, or you would not have run away.'

'Greta, I've stopped running. I decided to live instead. You kept me alive, at least the thought of you did.'

There was a pause as she looked away towards the shuttered window, then swung her eyes once more to him.

'You know, it's not just the dead you are responsible for: the living are owed something too.'

The cramps could be ignored no further and her fury rendered him miserable and pained. He contorted on the bed, aware that his bowel control had turned to jelly.

'I'm sorry . . .'

'Joss, it's all right, really.' Her voice was now considerate. Her eyes closed in shame and exhaustion, but he warmed his misery with one thought: she did not have anyone else in her life; there was still hope.

*   *   *

335

PJ Rivers stood before his congregation in the gymnasium of the Haven. He held his arms wide to them as they, in turn, took the sacrament of the communal heartbeat. The commune had swelled to over five hundred spirits, each brought by another spirit into the fold of the Millennium Church. He watched in delighted awe, and marvelled at the level of their commitment to the movement and to him, their venerated and beloved leader. Soon the chosen would band together for the greatest day of the Millennium Church's history. He had promised them Armageddon and if it failed to occur it could only be through their own unworthiness.

He bid them open their trusting eyes, and as one they obeyed.

'We have suffered a terrible loss,' he began, the 's' trailing in a slither behind the sentence. 'One who was once amongst us is now gone.'

All faces were riven with anticipated despair.

'A true spirit, a valiant servant of the cause now ripped from his family by those who would destroy us all.'

A low moan began to gather in the audience. He raised one hand to silence them.

'But his death does not weaken us; it makes us stronger.'

His pronouncement was met with the nodding of hundreds of heads.

'Many of you knew Harrison Trainer and knew him to be the best of us. His spirit is a shining example to all. Whilst you go about your tasks today, fix his face . . .' Rivers waved to his right, where a six-foot portrait of Trainer was produced and placed centre-stage, '. . . in your mind's eye. If the task is too great, remember it was never too great for Coach Harrison, then strive and succeed. Now go and honour him. You too might be chosen.'

Rivers watched them file away, heads bowed in reverence to his valediction, until the gymnasium was deserted. Then Tomlin and Moyne entered from the back of the staging area with Callum Lane. Rivers fixed him with a baleful glare.

'It went well,' Callum began. 'The notion of the dead as a totem for the living is as ancient as man himself,' he said with fawning delight.

'I have been fully briefed on your fall from grace, Brother Lane,'

Rivers whispered. 'Even Judas Scariot had the eventual decency to take his own life.' Callum dropped his head in mock shame.

'It's the boy that concerns me,' Rivers continued. 'Our little loose end.'

'No more than that, PJ; never more than that,' Callum said, dropping reverently to his knees.

'But better than you could ever be,' Rivers hissed, 'yet he has stolen from the temple and must be punished. He must be humiliated and publicly shamed in order to be cleansed. Afterwards we will speak with the boy.'

Callum Lane nodded his agreement.

'He has yet to learn of your treachery,' Rivers continued, his voice rising to Old Testament vibrato. 'So your day of atonement will be delayed, but not avoided. All adventures must come to an end.'

Rivers placed a gentle hand on Joss's father's neck, then turned to Tomlin and Moyne.

'Hurt him,' he ordered, then smiled and made his way out from the hall to the airstrip and the waiting jury.

CHAPTER FORTY-SEVEN

I t was as if his body, once cleansed by the clinic, had remembered the chore of detoxification. Joss had grown in strength and anxiety in equal proportions. Greta watched over him with the over-keen eye of the amateur, aware of the risks to his survival.

Joss stirred from another drenched dream, hair super-glued to his aching forehead. During his lucid moments he had enquired of her what had happened to the other members of In Extremis; the news wasn't good. He flicked open his eyes, alarmed at her grim demeanour.

'That bad?'

Greta shrugged her shoulders. 'Could be worse.' She really didn't want to go into this yet, whilst Joss was recovering swiftly, he was still snowflake-fragile.

'Need to know, Greta: tell me.'

'Ben's been suspended from the bank and is under investigation for computer fraud.'

'It's the Church who should be investigated for fraud,' he fired back.

'Maybe so, but the authorities are holding his passport. Barney is still in Venice under police guard at the hospital. They think he's some kind of terrorist.'

'Shit. What about Uncle Niall and the consulate?'

'I spoke to the vice-consul. Niall never contacted him.'

'But you said you spoke to him; he promised. Jesus, something must have happened to him.'

Greta's face clouded. She bit her lip and said nothing.

'But things seem to happen to people around me, don't they,

Greta?' His voice was flat and toneless. Greta could only nod in agreement. 'Tell me about Tom.'

'In the glasshouse. You can't just use the Royal Air Force's equipment like your dad's car, and expect to get away with it, but he knew that: he told me not to worry.'

Joss's face was a mask of misery.

'In my arrogance and ignorance, I have destroyed them. Again.'

'This isn't the time, Joss,' Greta chided gently, but he knew her too well: if she'd disagreed with his guilty conclusion she would have spoken out. But Joss's mind was already pushing on.

'Greta, my dad!' Joss glanced away to the afternoon's fading light where it dropped by the window in a fading pool.

'Use your logic, Joss. You have a classic Mexican stand-off: you have the money; they have your father. They will contact you once you surface; you have to be prepared for it.'

It was almost too much. He began to rub his hands through his damp hair in a fury of friction.

'Focus, Lane, focus,' Greta shouted. 'I'm not going to lose you again.' She slapped his face hard, with a stinging crack. 'This may well be exactly what they want; have you considered that?'

The immediate pain hurt but helped. But her words; her words echoed his own when kidnapping his father and deciding against police involvement.

'Who is going to believe an ex-junkie?' he asked miserably.

Greta placed her hands on his cheeks and leaned close, until her nose almost touched his, and her fiercely intelligent eyes bore into his.

'I do, and the jury should, too.'

He felt like he should kiss her, and as if she had read his thoughts, she turned and placed her moist lips on his rough cheek, then moved away. Joss hugged his trembling body with his arms.

'When am I scheduled to give evidence?' he asked.

'Tomorrow,' Greta answered. Joss nodded gravely.

'I need to see Niall first and find out why he hasn't helped Barney.'

Greta shook her head.

340

'You're not up to it.'

'They all came through for me and I'm tired of letting people down.'

It was a little after eight that same evening when Greta and Joss left her apartment. Storm clouds loomed swollen over the London skyline as they entered the black cab in Islington. Joss would hear no arguments to the contrary once he had spoken to the British Consulate in Venice; they had never heard of Niall Robertson, let alone spoken to him. When the realisation hit him it was as if the very gangplank of his recent history had been burned before his smarting eyes. Once more, it was only Greta's sheer strength that stopped him tumbling down.

Joss had always scoffed at the conspiracy theorists who claimed that the world was being run by this alien or that subterranean-dwelling super-community. He had laughed himself insensible at the wacky abductees and crystal-lovers; the witches, white black and dish-water grey; false Christs and anti-Christs; dead-sea scrollers, holy white-knuckle rollers and dope-head solstice lovers. They were no more than disenfranchised from the mainstream, verbally incontinent with unprovable truths; but this was different. The Millennium Church was made up of a palpable mass of money, power and relentless direction. It lived and breathed in the relative open-air, preying on the natural human fear of death: this was different, and he knew it.

Like casting the runes, he had to discern some hidden intent to all that had befallen him. He had to find some meaning behind the dark sequence of events. Perhaps his father's best friend could help him to decipher the code.

Greta had ordered the cab driver to head for Uncle Niall's flat in Canary Wharf. Joss was chilly, though the black cab's heater pumped out recycled London air in a facsimile of natural heat. Greta stared mournfully out of the misted window where light drizzle ran like crocodile tears down the glass.

'It's hard to be sure of anything any more,' he whispered.

'Be sure of the boys,' she replied, 'and me.'

'I keep thinking; they would have all been happy if I hadn't come knocking at their doors,' Joss said, watching a fat raindrop glide down the car window.

'This is not the time for "if onlys",' she replied. 'Let's keep a grip on the here and now.'

But recent events had banished any real hope he might have had that anything could ever be straightforward again.

Forty minutes later and twenty pounds poorer, they emerged and were soon dampened down with the ever-increasing rain. Inside the chrome and glass edifice, as the uniformed concierge took their details and briefly telephoned the information through to the recipient, Joss peered at the man and wondered whether he was part of it as well. He tutted away his ludicrous suspicion with a now rare smile.

'What is it?' Greta asked.

'Simple case of Lane paranoia; nothing unusual.'

The concierge nodded to the mouthpiece then replaced it abruptly.

'You can go up, it's on the . . .'

'I know where it is,' Joss said quickly and moved toward the plush speed-lift. The carpet was thick pile with a Regency stripe; he felt his loafers sink into it. The mirrored ceiling and walls reflected their features into infinity and Joss could see how wasted he looked.

A ping at the fourteenth floor sprang the lift doors open and there stood Niall Robertson to greet them. The little man's face was flushed as they shook hands. He knew Greta from before, but not well; they'd been introduced at the odd drinks party at the Lane home. Now he kissed her hand gallantly.

'My but it's good to see you, laddo, though I have seen you looking a little fitter than the dishrag you are now. Come in, come in,' he said, gesturing towards the open door of his luxurious rooms. Once they were seated inside, drinks offered and refused, Joss cast an eye around the interior; it was professionally designed and beautifully presented. Fine art deco predominated with an undercurrent of modern that was sympathetic and yet at the same time strangely incongruous.

'Now bring me up to date with everything that's happened, lad, leave nothing to chance; something you think irrelevant might well be important to an old hack like me.' He winked at Greta, who barely managed to smile in response.

'Why didn't you help Barney Calladine as you promised?'

Niall's face coloured higher.

'Don't trust me now, is that it, Joss? Have your adventures drained you of all natural human reliance?'

Joss caught the heavy edge in his voice and glanced quickly to Greta who watched the display through narrowed eyes.

'Of course I trust you, Uncle Niall, it's just that things have been completely out of whack recently and a little information wouldn't go amiss, that's all.'

'Trust, Joss, trust. Me and your old man, that's how it worked, horses for courses, him on the flat with his speed, me over the fences with my stamina; never let us down.'

'I'm not my father,' Joss replied quickly; too quickly.

'More's the pity, lad, more's the pity.'

'I don't deserve that, Uncle Niall.'

Robertson fixed him with a withering stare.

'You call me Uncle, yet you treat me with the contempt of a stranger; it's a sad day, Joss.'

'He's been through a lot,' Greta said, protectively.

'Young lady, when this young man needed you, you deserted him. Let's not allow any feelings of guilt to get in the way of sound common sense, shall we?'

'You goat,' she spat. 'You sanctimonious . . .'

'Greta, leave it,' Joss instructed, though his own expression was less than conciliatory.

'Like I said, Niall,' he continued.

'So I'm not your Uncle any more,' he barked. 'That's the way it is, is it? Well, I never thought I would live to see it, your mother . . .'

'Shut up about my mother,' Joss warned. Niall lifted his hands and crossed himself.

'Why didn't you help Barney Calladine?' Joss continued, his languid voice betraying none of his agitation.

'The boy was in too deep.'

'Too deep into what?'

'I spoke to the consul and the vice-consul about his plight, poor lad; crippled as well.'

At the mention of the vice-consul, Joss could almost feel Greta's hot intake of breath but, though his stomach plummeted down to the basement of the building, he kept his face straightened and his mind focused.

'But you did try?'

'Any friend of yours,' Niall replied, standing to replenish his glass.

'Well that's OK then. Look, I'm sorry.' Joss felt his face burn with what appeared like embarrassment but was in fact rage.

'Let me tell you all about it.' Joss paused, smiled sheepishly, then said, 'Uncle Niall.'

Joss almost puked when the solicitor nodded sagely and said, 'I said some harsh things, lad, and for that I am deeply ashamed. Now, tell me the truth, the whole truth and nothing but the truth.'

And for the next hour Joss Lane did precisely the opposite.

CHAPTER FORTY-EIGHT

J oss Lane glared at Rivers. Open and naked, the loathing swept across the barristers, solicitors and press box, then nailed the jury down with anticipation. Mason watched him carefully; Joss had to be handled with great care. A witness, boiling with hatred, was potentially worse than no witness at all. He could rob the prosecution's evidence of any integrity and bad-mouth the rightness of the cause.

Joss stared; just stared. Unmoving, unblinking, fixed and ready. Mason could see that his breathing was sombre and steady. He was so pumped up it appeared he was calm. He checked through the detailed statement that Joss had dictated to Charmers; it read like the purest pulp fiction. It had been served on the defence in the proper way. Then, a lengthy legal debate had followed in the absence of the jury. Withnail had surprised him. It appeared he had taken a healthy dislike to Rivers and he swept away Thynne and Callow's objections to the late calling of the evidence.

They now awaited the judge and the air was dense. Greta sat behind him, next to Charmers, her hands knotted together with anxiety. Rose and Geoff Moody huddled arm against arm, waiting for their champion to tell the truth. Mason had never felt such tension; it grabbed his throat and his stomach in a fleshy vice.

The judge strode on. His robes appeared to fit him better, as if the coming storm had lent him an air of much-needed majesty. Joss affirmed. The Bible was dismissed kindly; his only god was what was right; mere lip service to convention was unacceptable. The oath he swore bound him in his heart; he was there to tell the truth.

Mason stood and bowed gravely to Withnail. He didn't know why, but he felt as if they were all on the verge of something

345

unforgettable, like the judges at Nuremberg naming crimes against humanity. Withnail spoke.

'Mr Mason. I have read the evidence that this witness intends to give. That forces upon me a duty under the law.'

He studied Joss for a moment in silence.

'Mr Lane?' Joss nodded sternly. 'In English law you have a privilege. That right ensures that you cannot be compelled to answer any question that may incriminate you in any crime; unless you choose to answer. Do you understand?'

'Perfectly, my lord,' Joss replied, his voice steady. 'I am here to tell the truth, the whole truth and nothing but the truth. It sounds like a cliché but it means something to me.'

Mason glanced toward Thynne who appeared at ease with the proceedings, and felt a chill in his legal bones.

'Now, Mr Lane, let us begin at the beginning . . .'

For four long hours Joss recounted the events from his arrival in London two weeks earlier to his return. Withnail, for once, took a detailed note of all his evidence. The jury listened intently to his animated description of all that had occurred. From time to time, Mason stole a glance at Thynne who seemed preternaturally calm in the face of the evidential vortex; once more he felt an anticipatory shudder. The luncheon adjournment was delayed so that Joss might give his testimony in one large bite.

They visited the Highlands, Paris, Zurich, Venice and Berlin and sweated the heroin out of their own bodies in sympathy with Joss. Eventually, the trail of danger and discovery brought them, and Joss, back to the present.

The defence had made no objections to any of his evidence. Mason had trod carefully, fully aware of the judicial, suspended sentence dangling over his own future. Even portions of Joss's account that had no thread of admissability were ignored.

'And is that the truth of all that occurred?' Mason concluded.

Joss risked a grim smile.

'That's how it happened.'

Mason sat. Now, Thynne stood up and dropped his half-rims to majesterial level on the bridge of his nose.

'Things do rather seem to happen to you, don't they, Mr Lane?' he began.

Joss shrugged.

'Is that a question?' he replied.

Thynne smiled wanly.

'Perhaps not,' he conceded. 'When did you last have heroin in your body?'

'I've told you, when and how.'

'Ah yes, the dogged Mr Trainer; thank you for reminding us all. But your involvement with "smack" has not always been so involuntary, has it?'

Joss returned Thynne's gaze flatly. 'No. I was a junkie.'

'Surely more than that?'

'I don't follow,' Joss replied.

'Your dependence on drugs was such that you underwent eighteen months of detoxification and therapy at an expensive rehabilitation clinic?'

'You know that,' Joss snapped.

'And that treatment was paid for by the Millennium Church?'

'So I discovered,' Joss looked angry.

'They didn't want you to know that did they, Mr Lane? They never asked for thanks? Never presented you with a bill? Their kindness saved your life!'

'My doctor saved my life; they paid for it.'

'Your doctor? Ah yes, Miss Klammer. She diagnosed you as delusional and psychotic?'

'Something like that,' Joss replied.

'Delusional: now that means you were prone to believing things that were not true?'

Joss sucked in his cheeks.

'I was once; not any longer.'

'And all you have told us is, to the best of your belief, real?'

Thynne looked at the jury who appeared perplexed by the direction of the questioning.

'I know it's the truth.'

'You stand there, you affirmed, and you really believe all that you have told us truly occurred?'

'It did. Look, I was there; I know!'

'Very well. Let's leave the matter of your subjective reality to one side for one moment. You went into rehabilitation rather than prison? You were caught smuggling drugs; class A drugs; smack; Charlie; shit; horse; the dragon?'

Joss began to colour. 'Look, I was pretty low.'

'Surely, one cannot get lower than a drug dealer?'

'Not till I met the Millennium Church; those people are true scum.'

'And you, a junkie, a dealer, kidnapper of your own father, man of violence, fugitive, think yourself superior to a recognised religion?'

'I've seen what I have seen. I make no excuses for myself.'

'Your dependence on hard drugs began after a certain tragic event in your life, did it not?'

'You shit,' Joss whispered through bared teeth.

'Control yourself, Lane,' the judge demanded.

'Your mother's untimely death at a party you organised?' Thynne continued. 'She was given a drink spiked with LSD, was she not?'

'Yes,' Joss replied, biting his lower lip.

'You hold yourself responsible for her death, don't you?'

'For God's sake, have you no compassion?' Joss shouted.

'Answer the question,' Thynne demanded.

'I do, every day, in every way.'

'That is touching,' Thynne commented dryly. 'You abandoned your father and your friends, even the woman you loved after that?'

'I am not proud of what I did.' Joss looked across to Greta who nodded her encouragement.

'Quite a rosy resumé,' Thynne said. 'But I keep coming back to the curious nature of your reality.'

'I accept it is curious, but it is real,' Joss stated firmly.

Thynne turned to his junior barrister and nodded. In turn the lawyer nodded to a solicitor at the court door.

'As real as this?' Thynne asked, his voice laced with sarcasm. Joss and the court all turned, some of the jury craning their necks to see along the angle.

Callum Lane limped through the door. Joss was stunned. He had expected many things, but not this.

'Dad,' he shouted. 'Are you all right? Have they hurt you?'

Callum ignored him, walked towards Rivers and shook his hand firmly, whilst saying, 'I'm so sorry, Reverend, he isn't well; he is sick, very, very sick.'

Withnail was too stunned by the turn of events to react, but Thynne recognised the advantage and grasped it firmly. 'Mr Lane, you haven't changed, have you? You are delusional and paranoid and your evidence is worthless.'

Joss could only open and close his mouth like a landed fish, drowning in the alien oxygen as Thynne continued his assault on the shredded vestiges of the prosecution case.

'My Lord, in due course Mr Callum Lane will give evidence against his own son that he was drugged, kidnapped, then held prisoner against his will.'

Joss shook his head. 'Dad, Dad, tell them the fucking truth.'

Callum Lane shook his head sadly. 'I'm sorry son, but I'm going to.'

Mark Mason rubbed his face with his hands; it was over, lost and destroyed. The jury, forced by dint of hard work and Rose Moody's courage to an open mind, had slammed it shut again on the case of the Crown versus Rivers.

CHAPTER FORTY-NINE

J oss's hangover was crushing. Greta had taken him to a
wine bar in Fleet Street where the two of them had drunk
themselves through misery, into false courage, then back into
the despair of reality, before being asked to leave at around 7pm.

They had been refused entry at several restaurants before Greta
charmed, then bribed, a cab driver to pour them out at her Islington
address. They had then devolved down to the gibbering conversation
of the hopelessly pissed and he awoke to find himself naked in
her bed. Greta had taken the couch and, when he woke her, was
sympathetic.

'They were ready for you; that's all.'

Today they would await the jury's verdict. Mason was robust
and confident in his closing address to them, stressing the shattered
nature of Rose Moody. He accepted, as they all must, that she
had been abused; the question was by whom. Joss was deeply
impressed by the power of his oration. Without referring to any
notes, he flicked with speed and accuracy through the welter of
evidence that the jury had heard over the past two weeks. Rose
and Geoff seemed nervous, yet hopeful; Greta spoke little. But there
was a flatness of reaction on the faces of the jury. Mason closed
by allowing his last words to permeate into the jury's collective
conscience:

'Protect her and you will protect others. Without your courage
the abuse will grow and grow until we are all sullied by its
terrible effects.' But Callum Lane's evidence had severely dented
the prosecution case.

Then Thynne addressed them. His normal terrorist reign of
sarcasm was replaced with a fervent speech on the subject of the
sad ruin of Rose Moody by her own father, the kindness shown to

the girl by the Church and the statement made by her, that was in his words:

'The terrible, shameful, truth.' He led them on a morally guided tour of the Millennium Church's good works and then turned to the 'deeply delusional Joss Lane'. He pointed a long, bony finger in Joss's direction, declaiming:

'Wherever there are great men doing great works, the infidel and the insane will invent rumour in an attempt to steer the right-minded away from the light of truth. Even his own father has told you of his fixated madness.'

Joss gritted his teeth, but the jury seemed to be nodding their heads in agreement.

Finally, Withnail summed up the case to them. For once he stressed the prosecution's 'very heavy burden to prove the case, so that you are sure'. He then reminded them at length of the fallibility of Rose Moody and her father's angry outburst. Eventually, he instructed the jury to elect one of their number as foreman and asked them to retire to consider their verdict in the matter.

Outside the court, Joss attempted to speak to Rose, but a glare from her father told him all he needed to know. He felt wretched and well beneath contempt. Mark Mason spoke to him.

'These things happen: they shouldn't; but they do.'

'What will they decide?' Joss asked.

'Juries are curious animals,' the lawyer answered. 'Sometimes they come back, look the defendant straight in the eye and smile; then they convict. Another time they will look everywhere but the accused and appear nervous and unhappy; they acquit. One just does not know.'

But something in Mason's words told Joss differently.

'He's going to walk, isn't he? The bastard is going to walk!'

Mason shrugged. 'Whilst they are out anything can happen. I remember an eco-warrior case, a couple of years ago. On the face of it, Jenny Fox looked guilty as Hindley, but the jury eventually disagreed.'

'This isn't that type of case though, is it, Mr Mason?' Joss pressed, and Mason stared into his eyes.

'It was never going to be an easy case; that's probably why I took it. Don't feel too bad: it was potentially over before you gave your evidence.'

'I didn't help, though did I?'

'No, I'm rather afraid you didn't,' Mason replied, and wandered away.

Later, in the canteen, as the jury's deliberations passed their third hour, Joss and Greta sat silently over cups of tepid tea. The detritus of the legal system bickered, smoked and bragged around them in the plastic seats.

'I still have to find my father,' he muttered, his shoulders hunched and chin down. 'The bastards have him somewhere; but I'll find him.'

'Are you sure he wants to be found?' Greta replied. Joss was about to give a terse response, then slumped once more into silence. An announcement broke the moment.

'The jury are returning in the case of the Crown versus Rivers. Will all interested parties please reconvene immediately.'

Joss looked to Greta who smiled thinly, but her fine face was consumed with worry. He placed a cold hand on hers and they made their way into the belly of the court. From his vantage point, Joss could see the backs of all the barristers' wigs, tails hanging down to raven-black gowns. The judge sat in quiet contemplation awaiting the jury's return. The press were hungry: whatever the outcome it was going to be hot copy.

He strained his neck, attempting to catch a glimpse of Rivers, but could only make out a brief glimpse of hair. Rose and Geoff had been allowed to sit with Charmers behind Mark Mason.

There was a solemn knock and the jury processed in. They looked down at their feet; was that good or bad? They seemed nervous; did that help or hinder? They fidgeted; did that mean guilty or not guilty? Joss's mind was a swirl of questions that would soon be answered. He knew one thing, though; that all their lives would be altered irrevocably in the next few seconds.

'Would your foreman please stand,' the court clerk said sombrely. A tall man in a casual sweater, wearing thick-rimmed spectacles, clambered to his feet.

'Answer my next question yes or no; has the jury reached a verdict on which you are all agreed?'

'We have, my Lord,' the foreman replied with a nervous stammer.

'And on the first count of rape, do you find the defendant guilty or not guilty?'

There seemed to be a pause, a hesitation that stretched interminably, and Joss's eyes zoomed in on the foreman's thin mouth, watching for the choice of consonant that would alter all their worlds.

'Not guilty, my lord.'

There was uproar. The Rivers supporters in the public gallery broke out into applause, but were silenced with one hand by their leader. Joss shook his head dumbly as the identical response was given to each and every count on the indictment. Greta touched his arm, but he shook her off.

After Rivers was acquitted, Withnail spoke.

'They are proper verdicts, if I may say so, members of the jury. The costs of the defence will be met by the prosecution. Reverend Rivers, you have been found not guilty in the eyes of the law: you are free to go.'

All the public gallery stood as one. Joss's devastation knew no boundaries, but just then a movement caught his eye. Geoff Moody began to run across the back of the court and Joss could see the glint of a knife in his hands.

'I'll give you justice, you bastard,' he screamed, and began to lunge towards the man in the dock. Before he could reach him, however, a police officer tripped him from behind and he fell in a desolate heap at Rivers's feet.

As other officials pounced and took away Moody's knife, Joss watched Rivers's face. Flat and smug, he placed a hand on his attacker's head and blessed him. Joss now knew there was no God. He took the tiles that had been his mentors and his guide and dropped them, then crushed them underfoot; the past, the future, love; all gone. But he had to atone.

CHAPTER FIFTY

The expression on Rose Moody's face had finished him. After the acquittal, Joss and Greta passed Rivers's press conference on the pavement outside the Old Bailey. The parents of the 'missing 32' waved their banners forlornly, but the message was clear; Rivers was unstoppable. Or was he? Joss still had the money from the Swiss accounts and the Church had his father.

Later, at Greta's home, he lifted the telephone receiver and called the number of the Church's headquarters. After three interdictions he was transferred to a final number. It was answered within three rings and PJ Rivers and Joss Lane spoke as serious men do.

Joss had been busy, all the time weighing up then down the alternatives and methods at his disposal. Rivers had understandably been open to the suggestion of a meeting on neutral territory and Joss booked a conference room at the Wembley Hilton. Joss knew that on the eve of the Hyde Park rally Rivers was loathe to take the risk of Joss running to the tabloid press with more 'wild allegations': besides, he wanted his money back. Callum would have been proud, and if his plan worked he would get his father back soon.

Greta was stationed in a room adjacent to the conference facility with the video and audio equipment purchased from an industrial intelligence shop near Sloane Square. The microphone was concealed in the flower arrangement, so obvious a place that it would never be considered, and the tiny camera in a clock. Joss spoke into his own microphone, concealed about his person, and was rewarded with an acknowledgement of its working status from Greta.

The room was sparse and pastel: hues of dusty pink cloaked the walls; the velour seating and silk flowers were also pink.

A call from the concierge's desk informed him of Rivers's arrival and very soon a knock at the door heralded the cult leader's presence.

'Come,' Joss said, his voice sounding more deep and confident than he actually felt. Rivers let the door swing open, and as it did his reptilian eyes swept the room. Satisfied, he nodded to his left and right, where Chisel-face and Curly-top appeared.

'Gentlemen, how are you?' Joss said with a sneer. They both bristled in response. 'Wait outside,' Rivers commanded and closed the door behind him. Joss sat relaxed, legs crossed, one palm flat on the ash desk.

'Will the lovely lady barrister be joining us?' Rivers asked.

'Too busy picking up the pieces of Rose Moody's life,' Joss replied, smiling savagely.

Rivers nodded once. 'Still I'm sure she isn't too far away,' and he seemed almost to gaze through the wall, then smiled.

'You have learned from your adventures Joss: I have had the opportunity of reading and hearing a great deal about you over the past few weeks. Less impetuous, more measured. Your recent difficulties have aided your development.'

'Not yours, though,' Joss snapped back.

'Tell me your concerns, Joss,' Rivers continued, his face solemn, like a priest on television. He walked around the room and took a chair opposite Joss.

'I want my father back, and all charges dropped against my friends and Geoff Moody.'

'And what will I have in return?'

'I know where the money is; you don't. If you did, you wouldn't be talking to me now.'

'A handy piece of deduction, though not necessarily true.'

'But how sure are you?' Joss countered.

'As sure as I am that you are recording this conversation by some means; as sure as I am that this juvenile trap could be avoided by an innocent child.'

Joss felt his face whiten.

'Joss, my dear Jocelyn, the position I hold was not one given to me on a plate; I did not win it in a charity raffle. I know the hearts of men, their motives and desires, their methods and their madness. It is through this knowledge, and only this, that I have flourished. Like your father, I have trained myself to think as my own opponent would, and react accordingly.'

'Where is my father?'

'The sainted Callum is closer, much closer than you think: that is why we can speak candidly and your record of our meeting is rendered worthless.'

Joss was puzzled, but if candour was expected he would not disappoint.

'But why? Why all this? Those young people? Those lives?'

Rivers pondered the multi-question.

'Why anything? Why this room? Why you? Why me? Why Callum? It just is, the way things are and will be. Because.'

'That's it, is it? your unified theory of the Universe? Because you can and no one stops you? Terrific, I'm a convert: forgive me, Reverend Rivers, for I have sinned.'

For once the cult leader's sanguine attitude was rattled.

'I did not come here to raise your consciousness, Joss.'

'It doesn't need it,' Joss barked. 'But I need to know I'm right about you.'

'You cannot judge me,' the cult leader hissed.

'Someone has to,' Joss responded. His eyes found Rivers's and latched onto them.

'Not in this world,' Rivers gently whispered. Joss shook his head.

'You really believe your own shit. There I was, wrong again, pegging you down as just another con man in a caftan, out to squeeze the money from the fools, when you actually fucking think it's all for real.'

'You can have no appreciation of how real it is,' Rivers thundered, his voice shaking with conviction.

'What, as real as Jim Thurman? As real as the thirty-two missing kids? As real as Rose Moody's virginity?'

'No!' Rivers whispered, 'as real as this.' He stood abruptly. Joss tensed, ready for some kind of attack. Instead, Rivers walked angrily towards the door and wrenched it open. There in the frame stood Callum Lane once more.

'Dad . . . what? . . .'

His father walked through into the room, a fixed smile on his face.

Joss stood up. 'If you've hurt him . . .'

'Why would I hurt the finest servant the Church has ever had?' Rivers's voice was full of spiteful pride.

'Dad, what the hell is going on?' Joss asked, walking toward him. Callum walked around to the side of the table where Rivers had sat earlier and took a seat.

'Sit, Joss,' he commanded. Joss slumped down into his chair, barely able to understand the dynamic about-turn of events.

'You see,' Rivers began, 'you can record what you will and tell all, but you cannot destroy me: if you do so, you will destroy your own father, and that, dear Joss, is not an option you will take.'

Joss realised his mouth was hanging open, and clamped it shut.

Rivers produced an envelope from his pocket and threw it onto the table. 'Take a look. A certain young lady recently confided in me that she had been filmed in a certain compromising way. These are stills from one of many such works of art.'

Furiously, Joss tore the envelope open and wrenched the colour photographs from it. To his horror, he saw Callum, naked, his face contorted with lust, and underneath, naked and frightened, Rose Moody.

'I have been tried and acquitted, Joss: your father does not have that benefit under the law.' Rivers said, taking a seat and smiling benignly. He paused and pursed his lips.

'You fucked her, like she said, you sick shit,' Joss exploded.

'It was God's will. I follow the path of his choosing. I do not expect mere mortals to understand. That is why the jury believed me; they will not believe Callum.'

'He didn't know what he was doing; he would never have gone along with it,' Joss stammered. 'He was under your influence; you made him.' Rivers shook his head benignly,

'Who knows what a man will and will not do when he has the opportunity. There is nothing like young flesh to warm an old man's bones. Who wouldn't sell their very soul for just one more thrust of pure sex? Why not feel young and strong again?'

Joss was speechless.

'This is why you cannot harm me, because you will ruin your own father into the bargain.'

Joss now understood why Rivers had been so arrogant and free with his words. Once more, the cult leader had bested him. How could he save his father now without handing the money over?

'So you win,' he whispered.

'One gets used to it,' Rivers answered smugly. Joss stared into his father's eyes and felt a tear begin to fill his own, bound and gagged by the debt he owed his mother.

'Dad . . .'

'Join us, Joss,' his father replied.

'What happened to you?'

'I found the way, the only true path.'

'But he has abused his own followers, and taken innocent lives just to satisfy your lust.'

'Those who are not worthy must render to those who are.'

'For fuck's sake, Dad, what . . .'

'Any further talk is futile,' Rivers said. 'Come, Callum, there is work to be done.'

His father rose sedately and, barely nodding to his son, began to leave.

'I shall await your decision with interest, Joss,' Rivers said. 'You have until after the rally tomorrow. Give me the money back or I will hand your father over to the authorities. After robbing him of your mother, isn't it the least you can do?'

'One thing, Rivers,' Joss said miserably. 'What was the oath that he took?'

Rivers smirked before replying.

'An oath as old as the Dead Sea scrolls: he swore to offer up his first-born son as a sacrifice.' And with that they left Joss to his helpless misery.

CHAPTER FIFTY-ONE

And one conversation changed everything, immutably and forever.

After Rivers and Callum's departure, a grim-faced Greta had brought in the video equipment they had hired and placed the footage of the meeting on the table. She reached to the clock where the tiny camera was hidden and switched it off. She had no words. Joss stared blankly into space. They made their way back to her apartment in bleak silence whilst inappropriate sunshine filled the shabby streets of London.

Once home, Joss's silence had turned to rage, sparked by the television coverage of the forthcoming Hyde Park rally. Pundits and commentators described the phenomenon in fascinated awe. Cameras showed the complex arrangements at the meeting's epicentre. Vast marquees, refreshment stalls and merchandising sporting the now-famous Millennium Church logo dotted the periphery whilst a gigantic video screen and banks of matte black speakers dominated the purpose-built stage.

Greta nodded her agreement as he raged, fuelled by betrayal and impotence, into the late evening. And one conversation changed everything, immutably and forever. He came at 10pm and apologised for the lateness of the hour. He held an embossed business card which introduced him as Kenneth Hamer, 'solicitor' and 'commissioner for oaths' Joss would have laughed at the last part if the situation were not so grim. Hamer was tall and robust, smartly dressed in light pinstripe and carried a gentleness about him unusual in a lawyer.

'I have been looking for you for some time young man' he said in a rolling west-country burr.

Joss shook his head, 'Want to tell me what this is about?' he asked. Greta scrutinised his card and recognised the firm as worthy and reliable.

Hamer looked toward the couch.

'Sorry,' Joss apologised, 'please, sit.' The solicitor smiled forgivingly and sat. 'I am sorry for your troubles. I read about them in the newspaper, but as I said I have been searching for you for a long time; you see I was your mother's solicitor.'

Joss looked dumbly at Greta, then back to Hamer.

'I thought Niall Robertson dealt with all the family business.'

Hamer shook his head.

'I'm afraid your mother lost confidence in his – how should I put it? his impartiality. But it does me no service to denigrate another professional man in his absence. In any event, I drew up your mother's original will and her last codicil on the day of her death.'

'She didn't leave a will,' Joss argued, his forehead creasing with consternation, then the legal penny dropped. 'At least that is what Niall Robertson told me.'

Hamer raised his eyebrows but did not comment on Joss's words.

'Lying little shit,' Greta whispered.

'She did,' Hamer continued, and he reached down and unclipped his seasoned brown leather briefcase, 'as I have it here.' He produced the document with a gentle flourish.

'Let me explain a little background,' he continued with a wistful smile. 'Up to the day of your mother's untimely death, your father had been the main beneficiary to the estate. That changed when she came to the city to see me. Jennie was agitated, I remember it well. She was to meet your father for dinner, and if my recollection is correct,' he mused and Joss didn't doubt the accuracy of his memory for a second, 'It was the day of your graduation and she wished to tell you of her intentions.'

Joss shook his head, 'I'm not getting this, Mr Hamer.'

'You will, I'm afraid,' the lawyer replied. 'The codicil, that is a later amendment to a will, was duly entered and witnessed by myself and my partner,' he said waving the paper tantalisingly close to Joss's face. 'It made you the only beneficiary. You are a wealthy young man.'

'But I was told that my father inherited the estate,' Joss said,

'No doubt by Mr Robertson. Clearly, Jennie had good reason to change her legal representation. Your father attempted to have the will contested. He and Mr Robertson claimed that you could not benefit from your own crime in relation to your mother's death, as is the law, but as you had not been charged with a criminal offence their action foundered. If you had not reappeared, then after seven years you would have been pronounced legally dead and your father would have taken the inheritance.'

'My dad would never have done that, I know he wouldn't.'

Hamer smiled sympathetically.

'I can only tell you what I know, Mr Lane, but before you read the terms of the will, there is, I'm afraid more heartache for you.'

Greta moved toward Joss and squeezed his arm.

'Spit it out Mr Hamer, my day can only get better,' Joss said, reassured by the comfort of Greta's contact.

Hamer nodded wisely, 'When I spoke to your mother on that terrible day, she also instructed me to begin divorce proceedings against your father.'

Joss dropped his head into his hands,

'I was wrong,' he muttered, 'it can get worse.'

'What were the grounds?' Greta asked.

The solicitor frowned, 'We did not speak about the reasons then, only her intention. She arranged an appointment with our family partner. As I said earlier, Mr Lane, I am sorry for your troubles.'

The solicitor handed the document to him, Joss refused it.

'No you tell me Mr Hamer,' he pleaded. The lawyer raised his bushy eyebrows.

'Very well,' he began. 'The estate is large and has accrued interest and is now valued at three quarters of a million pounds.'

'I don't care about the money,' Joss said. 'Was there any message?'

'Of a kind,' Hamer continued, 'though it is rather oblique.'

'What is it?' Joss demanded.

Hamer dropped his eyes to the bottom of the will where the codicil was attached, he read:

' "My dearest love, Joss, you must find the truth,"

'Then it continues,

> *"Joss and Jill went up the hill*
> *To fetch a pail of water.*
> *Joss fell down and broke his crown.*
> *His Mum came tumbling after."*

Joss's world began to explode in his head. For months Klammer had plagued him with continued requests about the song. The instructions could only have come from his father as he had access to the terms of the will. Then in Paris they had continued their joint endeavour to find out what it meant to him.

'Does it mean anything to you?' Greta asked, 'It has to have some sort of significance. Something she didn't want your father to get his hands on, perhaps?'

'I can't deal with all of this,' he sighed, slumping back and rubbing his face with his hands.

'You have to, Joss,' Greta demanded, pulling his hands down. 'Think, think.'

Joss cast his mind back to Jennie, his mother. He conjured up her sweet face, smiling close into his own when he was a boy. He could feel her breath on his cheek and her arms about his tiny waist, lifting him and swirling him around like a toddler carousel. In the past his recollections had always been clouded by the avenging spectre of Callum in the background, but now the knowledge of his mother's intention to end their marriage had swept the spectre away. He saw her running and smiling, looking to the sky in the park when the heavens opened and a deluge swept them wet with warm rain. He began to hum the song, in a small voice that was an echo of the small boy who grew into Joss; it made Greta's eyes fill, *'Joss and Jill went up the hill, to fetch a pail of water.'*

Joss could see her now in Regent's Park, strong and protective, pulling him by the hand, towards a huge fallen tree, hidden behind some thick bushes. It was hollow and dry there, where she cuddled him close and they sang the storm away.

He could feel the tears course down his face, his voice broke into racked sobs.

'I know where it is. Her own father had discovered it when he was a boy. I've been blocking the memory for years.' He turned to the solicitor, who was looking away, embarrassed by the distress he had caused.

'Thank you, Mr Hamer.'

The decent man nodded, 'You need to be together, Mr Lane. Please contact me when you are ready.'

Greta escorted him to the door whilst Joss continued to weep. When she returned, Joss was reaching for his jacket, his features hardened into granite. 'It's late, but not too late,' he said. Greta looked to him for an explanation. Joss's eyes were set, focused on an invisible object with an expression of complete hatred.

'Tell me what you're going to do,' she pressed, urgently.

'We never really know anybody do we? I mean not right down to the bone, the deep places.'

'I don't understand Joss; what are you planning?'

'I have to make it up to her. I wasn't there when she needed me.'

'You're not making any sense,' Greta whispered.

'It all makes perfect sense to me,' he replied.

Greta was afraid. She had seen that look of unshakeable determination before and it was always before he risked his life in some daring escapade.

'You have to let me in.'

'Better if you don't know, Greta,' he looked deep into her eyes. 'I am so sorry I got you into all this; you don't deserve it. You're too precious to risk. I'm going to walk out of your life and this time I won't be coming back.'

Greta snapped.

'This isn't fucking *High Noon*. You're not Gary Cooper and I'm not Grace Kelly. You think you're just going to walk down the main street at midday with your six-shooter? Well think again, Sheriff.'

Joss smiled and walked towards the video they had shot in the hotel conference room, picked it up and slid it in his jacket pocket. Greta began to rush around the flat, furiously changing into day wear and didn't hear the click of the door as he left. Greta shouted his name but there was no reply. She sprinted down the corridor but by the time she hit the three o'clock streets he had gone.

'You bastard, Lane,' she swore. 'You're not running away from me again.'

Joss took a taxi to Regent's Park. En route he stopped at an all-night service station and bought a powerful torch and a nine-inch screwdriver. Clambering over the Victorian railings in the black night, he attempted to get his bearings. Wondering if he could trust his recovered memory, he walked gingerly around until he spotted a bandstand he remembered close by. Joss kept a wary eye on the nearby road, aware that police patrols sometimes scoured the park for itinerants, drunks and junkies. But tonight he seemed to have the vast space to himself. The earlier rain had given way to an unbelievable freshness in the air and his heightened emotions seemed able to smell the carbon cycle in motion. She was going to divorce Callum. He shook his head as he walked, cracking sticks with his feet and shining the torch beam in front. He hadn't really been around much for the previous three years before her death. Always away, travelling, studying, but mainly partying, whilst she was miserable. What was it she needed to tell him that was so vital that she did not want Callum to have access to it? Joss could not begin to guess. He hoped that in the intervening months the tree had not been tampered with. The thicket of hedge was as his mind's eye remembered it, only more so. The years had broadened and densed the morass of leaves and branches. Cautiously, he forced a path through its uncooperative interior with the aid of the torch and the screwdriver. He was snagged and cut several times, but he kept going until he reached a tiny clearing. There, supine, lay the great, hollow, log. Joss scrambled toward it.

Think Joss

Where would she hide something?

It was at least forty feet in length. The bark was split and mildewed. He shone the beam inside and heard the scuttle of some small night creature; a vole or mouse, as its dark home was invaded by his light. After ten minutes of checking the decaying mulch on the log's floor, he swept his beam up to the top of the woody cylinder; still nothing. Joss retreated once more to think. His mother was intelligent enough to realise that they would not be the only park visitors to have discovered the fallen giant. She would have hidden her last gift to him somewhere it wouldn't be stumbled upon. Joss trained the beam onto the tree's exterior and attempted to put himself in his mother's place.

Suddenly he noticed a thick knot of dead, black, fungus, as large as a tenpin bowling ball underneath one of the oak's branches. Grimacing he plunged his screwdriver inside it and dug around. It released a deep, pungent odour and he was about to give up when he heard a metallic scrape. Tearing away the remnants of the growth, his fingers touched upon a small, metal box. He brought it up into the light of his torch and his heart welled when he recognised it as his own. It was his special tin he'd kept as a boy. A secret tin for special things; the words 'Joss' and 'Keep Out' were written on the lid in an infantile scrawl. Joss took the box and climbed inside the hollow once more, curled his feet up to his chest, and gently prised it open. Inside there was a letter wrapped in a plastic protection folder, and a small key. He removed the message from its covering and could see that on it was written,

'To my darling boy, Joss'

Blinking away his tears, Joss used the screwdriver to open the envelope and began to read,

'My dear Joss,
    You remembered! I knew you would. This place always held a special memory for me. The two of us, so close, so warm; together. Sadly this also means that I am gone, but it is the living who carry the burden of remembering, not the dead. I always loved you, Joss, remember that. He did too at least until he changed. Callum wasn't always so harsh with you as he became. That was my fault. You need to know the truth. I fell in love with another man, a mountain climber. It doesn't matter how we met, but we did. I was going to leave your father, then I became pregnant with you. The mountaineer died in a fall; he was your real father. It was kept a secret until you were older. Callum wanted other

367

children and we tried and tried until a visit to a fertility clinic proved my downfall. Callum was infertile and I had to tell him the truth. After that he changed.'

Joss was stricken with a numb understanding; his father was distant towards him because he wasn't his father at all. He read on.

'He kept a string of women but I had no right to complain. I was happy as long as I had you. Your father's business went from strength to strength. He and Niall were unstoppable. It was as if they had a magical monetary touch that turned base metal into gold, but I discovered the truth. Their business is based on lies and falsehoods. All they have done has been achieved by corruption and bribery. I know because I have seen the evidence. The key you have is for a safety deposit box held by Ken Hamer, my solicitor. In it you will find all the details of the wrongs they have done. Their principal partner in all this is an American called Rivers. They are in it up to their necks. I could not live with the knowledge any longer and have tonight, the night of your graduation, told him I intend to divorce him and expose them all. I am very afraid, Joss. Perhaps I went too far, but I know the man you call father will not allow me to ruin him. Soon I will see you my son, at the graduation party. I can only pray that you never have to read this letter. As you have, please let me ask for forgiveness. We ran though the rain, hand in hand, and I loved you then and love you now.'

Joss could control himself no longer and his body convulsed with wracking sobs. Hugging his knees towards him, he cried and cried until he could cry no more. Afterwards, he knew what he must do.

The morning broke bright and razor clear. The weather report from the Met Office promised PJ Rivers unbroken sunshine for his finest day; but that was as it should be, he told himself. Final preparations were in place and Rivers had bathed away his feverish anticipation, then eaten a full, but secret, fried breakfast.

Callum Lane was in the adjoining room with a young and tender female believer, enjoying one of the many fruits the Church provided. Rivers had enjoyed the dismissal of Joss Lane the day before, seeing the dismay on his face. The young buck was finished and, once all financial matters had been put to rights, he would be dealt with accordingly.

A telephone call informed him that the cortege was waiting outside the hotel's entrance, as were the world's press, as were 100,000 fervent disciples. Rivers wore a single-breasted bespoke suit, petrol blue, with a brilliant white shirt and sober sky-blue tie with parting-of-the-Red-Sea slash; so appropriate, he told himself, checking one last time in the chevalier mirror and striding purposefully out to his security guards.

'Such a perfect day,' he announced brightly; it had begun.

Joss was high in the scaffolding. A cloudless sky met him at eye level as he surveyed the scene below. Before him, the stage held prominence, simple in its starkness yet startling in its intent. At its centre was the ancient wooden podium, synonymous with a Millennium Church meeting. It looked as though it had been ripped out of a Gothic cathedral, and stood eight feet high with a twisting snake of worn steps to its interior. A burnished brass rail gripped its scarred top and glowed warmly in the sun's rays.

Behind the podium towered the gigantic video screen that would beam Rivers into millions of homes. Beneath it ran a banner, crimson on snow white, with italic script, that read:

'COME CROSS THE RIVER OF FAITH WITH ME!'

and below that a sketch of a child's outstretched hand, chubby and inviting. Simple; yet stunning. By peeping over the tarpaulin parapet that hid him from view, Joss could see that even by eleven in the morning the crowds had begun to gather, all wearing their 'Rivers Run Deep' sweatshirts, baseball jackets, caps and tracksuits.

He had found the climb, at 4am, relatively simple, and just as the dawn sneaked over the park's lush interior he had ducked from view and reflected. After leaving Regent's Park he had flagged down a black cab and asked to be taken to his mother's solicitor's office. He borrowed a pen and scribbled a note to Ken Hamer, enclosing his mother's letter and the key. The solicitor was a decent man and would ensure the evidence found its way to the right hands. Joss shook his head; he was still struggling to come to terms with the truth. His mother had been given a spiked drink at his graduation party, and there was only one person present who would have arranged for her to get it. Joss would make his move soon, when the great PJ Rivers arrived and presented himself to his loving followers.

Greta walked with the others to the rally. She had spent long, fruitless hours searching for Joss in Regents Park. When the dawn broke, she surmised that Joss would be heading towards his father and Rivers in Hyde Park. Police barriers funnelled the faithful toward the beating heart of the meeting and she could feel the intensity of their joint belief. The excitement and anticipation amassed almost palpably in the air. Reporters aided by camera crews invited sound-bites of adoration from the masses and Greta could discern a dozen different languages in the babble.

She scanned the crowd, watching anxiously for a glimpse of him. She thought, wrongly, on three occasions that she had caught a fleeting glimpse. But it was just wishful thinking. Greta was, in fact, no more than a kilometre away from Joss, but it might as well have been a continent.

The stretch limousine nosed gently through the crowd, its interior hidden by smoked glass. Within, sat Rivers, Callum Lane, Tomlin and Moyne.

'You have come a long way,' Callum said with a fawning smile.

'Yes, yes,' Rivers accepted. 'Come, cross the river with me,' he added in a deep, sonorous voice. The other two laughed and he smirked. 'But they,' he indicated the slowly moving crowd, 'made it so easy. Take an idea – the simpler the better – wrap it up prettily, add a tincture of mortality, mix carefully, then shażam; the faithful drop to their knees.'

'You are too modest,' Callum said. 'You have been wholly dedicated to the cause.'

'Destiny is not dedication,' Rivers whispered. 'This was meant to be; preordained.'

Callum sucked his cheeks in slightly. 'Whatever you say.'

'But your help has been invaluable.'

'It was my pleasure,' Callum said, meaning every word.

'After we bring the faithful to their knees you will atone,' Rivers said quietly.

Joss was twelve feet away from the technicians' booth to his left, but still hidden from view. He could see the technicians though the windows, lazily twisting dials and making last-minute adjustments to their equipment. Joss nervously fingered the hunting knife in a sheath secured to his belt which he had bought from a derelict. He prayed he wouldn't have to use it, but he knew he would if he had to. He half-remembered a quote from his school days, attributed to Edmund Burke, that 'evil would win out if enough good men did nothing'. Joss would do whatever it took.

He still found his mother's last message hard to cope with but it harked back to something Barney had said after the raid on the Ruga Fondamente when Barney was stoned on the liquid E: 'Speak to Spineless Eric.' Joss's mind had been racing overtime, and he now believed he had completed the picture. His father, he almost choked on the description, must have got the gear off Eric and given it to his mother.

A roar from the crowd averted his attention to the arrival of a dazzling white limousine that swept sedately through their welcoming arms and around to the rear of the stage. Soon the performance would begin.

Hawk-eyed security men, hand-picked and able, watched the crowd suspiciously and formed a human wall of rippling muscle as Rivers leapt gracefully from the car's interior. The roar became deafening thunder as the stirring sound of Beethoven's *Pastoral Symphony* began to seep from the banks of speakers.

371

Then Joss saw him, impossibly youthful, spilling vigour as he bestrode the stage. The crowd cheered, waved and clapped.

'Jesus!' Joss whispered. 'This isn't a religion; it's rock and roll.' And then he began his assault.

All attention was focused on the stage except Greta's. She was still desperately searching the crowd for a sight of Joss, and then suddenly, she saw him crawling along a gantry to the technical control booth facing the stage.

Joss could see two of them, both with their backs turned as he wrenched open the door and dived inside, the knife gleaming in front of him wickedly.

'Christ,' one of the technicians shouted. The other whispered, 'We've got trouble,' into a radio headpiece, before Joss ripped it from him and smashed it under his foot.

'Co-operate,' Joss hissed; they both nodded. 'Now, what is to be shown on the video screen?'

'The usual,' one of them said. 'The Rivers video. It's expected.'

Joss remembered the programme in question from the viewing room in the Haven.

'When?'

'When the applause dies down and he formally welcomes them all.'

Joss reached into his jacket pocket and produced his own video.

'Not today,' he said icily. 'Do it.'

Greta was fighting her way through the phalanx of the crowd, cursing and shouting to be allowed passage. To her left, three men with radio headpieces bulldozered through toward the raised booth, parting the people like a loose zip. The noise began to die down and Greta turned her head to see Rivers raise his hands to silence them. Obediently, they did as they were asked. She couldn't move.

'Joss,' she screamed in the silence and Rivers's face swivelled towards her, then the booth. He acknowledged the security guards' progress then continued.

'Come,' he shouted from the pulpit, 'cross the river with me,' as a row of hands, beginning at the stage's front, reached out to clasp their neighbours' in a show of solidarity. Greta was trapped in a cage of flesh.

Joss had his finger on the play button, ready to depress it with a single push. Rivers had gambled and lost. He had fallen through arrogance and pride. His error was to believe that Joss's love of his family would prevent him from destroying Callum, but his mother's letter had changed all that.

'Well fuck you, father,' he muttered as Rivers concluded his welcome and looked toward Joss in the booth. He could see fear in Rivers's eyes and Joss was glad. He pressed the button and before the vasts crowd the video recording of the previous day's confrontation sprang up in images one hundred feet across.

'You fucked her, like she said, you sick shit,' his own voice boomed.

'It was God's will. I follow the path of his choosing. I do not expect mere mortals to understand. That is why the jury believed me; they will not believe Callum.'

The tape ran on, the crowd silent and desperate.

'Who knows what a man will and will not do when he has his opportunity. There is nothing like young flesh to warm an old man's bones.'

A murmur of betrayal and disgust began to well from the crowd's throats.

'Who wouldn't sell their very soul just for one more thrust of pure sex? Why not feel young and strong again?'

Because it is wrong, Joss thought, as the crowd began to mutter and push toward the stage. Greta watched the minders scramble up the ladder to the booth, the lead one producing a pistol.

'That is why you cannot harm me, because you will ruin your own father into the bargain.' Rivers's image continued on the video screen whilst the real one raised his hands to silence the crowd. At first his authority caused the sea of bodies to ebb, then the crush from behind propelled them onwards again.

'People, my people, let me speak,' he demanded, and once more the crowd stilled momentarily; then they were thrusting toward him again. Rivers's security men were pushing futilely against the awful crush of bodies. Other followers, still loyal, fought to force open a channel of escape for the Reverend and pockets of vicious fighting broke out. Fists and heads, teeth and fingernails scoured and tore as the monster of belief attacked itself.

'No,' Rivers thundered in vain against the encroaching mass. 'It was not meant to be this way. This is not my destiny.'

He began to sidle away from the approaching crowd.

Joss watched, frozen by the terrible spectacle. This wasn't what he wanted but he was powerless to put the brakes on the awesome juggernaught he had set in motion.

Time to go Joss, His inner voice warned. *You don't need me anymore. Goodbye.*

The security guards and many followers were attempting to climb the scaffolding to get to the communication booth. Joss felt it begin to rock with the vast weight of the climbers. He glanced down to Rivers, who was now cowering inside the pulpit above the melee, pointing and gesticulating at the crowd. He was eight feet above them, giving his last ever sermon.

The scaffolding shook again and Joss heard the fixing bolts start to sheer. The tower began to wobble and Joss could hear the screams of the terrified climbers as they began to realise their fate. A security attendant burst through the door to the booth and aimed his weapon at Joss, but Joss didn't see him; he was too busy watching Rivers being plucked from his pulpit by his lapsed followers. Joss's face split with joy that at last he had done something worthwhile.

The first bullet smashed his arm, the second sliced through his leg, a third through his ribcage. Joss lay on the floor, still smiling, and whilst the blood poured from his wounds he whispered one word: 'Mother.' The scaffolding could take no more and began to crumple and separate. The booth began to tip and Joss felt that he was flying through the clean air of the Austrian Alps once again as he and the huge edifice crashed down, like the Walls of Jericho, onto the final resting place of Rivers and Callum Lane.

As his final breath left Joss's lips, he shouted out one word: 'Greta.'

EPILOGUE

Greta carried the simple bunch of daffodils past the church gate to the well-tended graveyard. So much had happened since the fateful day of the Hyde Park rally. Rivers had been crushed to death by the combined weight of the furious believers and the tumbling scaffolding. Religious leaders wept at the tragedy but asked whether, in the light of the subsequent revelations about the cult, it was not the 'Wrath of God'. Callum Lane and 87 other followers had also lost their lives in the desperate, angry crush and the falling steel. She herself had been lucky. As the throng pushed toward the stage she had sidled towards the corner, away from the concentration of the crowd until the collapse. Eventually, she had clambered through to where Joss lay, clawing at the bodies and the debris and seen his terrible wounds.

Now she walked towards the grave. The world's newspapers had carried the story and its aftermath for many long weeks. Jennie Lane's solicitor had called a news conference and exposed the truth. The world now knew Rivers for what he was; a rapist and charlatan. The story had grown and grown as each piece was fitted together by the press. Joss Lane and his friends were hailed as heroes. Barney now walked with a stick but was sought after in the diving community as someone who had 'been there'. Ben had been offered a new job with an international computer giant who wanted to protect its clients from people just like him; and Tom's defence of a fallen comrade was lauded by the Air Force.

Joss had left instructions in a letter to Geoff Moody containing details of the money he had recovered from the Church. It was all to be the subject of a massive public enquiry to be headed Mr Justice Mason QC. Rose Moody's story was now, at last, believed.

Greta knelt before the grave, a soft wind blowing her hair as she gently laid the floral offering on the cold earth. The death was avoidable, she knew that; everyone did. Greta felt a tear slide down her face. Just then she heard a noise behind her, and turned quickly, thinking for a moment she had heard his voice. But it was Ben, Barney and Tom.

'Thanks for coming. Joss and his mother would have appreciated it.'

They all looked down on the grave.

'I don't suppose we ever really knew him,' Greta whispered.

'We loved him though,' Ben said, his voice wavering.

'Sometimes that has to be enough,' Tom muttered, blinking back tears.

Barney began to speak, then shook his head, unable to provide adequate words. Greta gave him a hug, then hugged each of then in turn.

'Just think how many lives he saved by what he did,' Barney eventually said.

'Grandstanding to the end, you mean?' Ben said with a wry smile. It was an inappropriate comment; exactly what Joss himself might have said.

Tom's shy grin pushed through the rain clouds of their shared misery. 'Typical Joss Lane: does the deed, then leaves us all to clean up after the party.'

'Fucking loveable show-off, you mean; Butch and Sundance rolled into one,' Barney said, wiping the tears from his cherubic face.

They smiled at each other, content in the knowledge that they had been privileged to share some time with a remarkable human being.

Greta hugged them all again as if by pressing his closest friends she could be one step closer to Joss in his final resting place. For the missing 32 and their families there might now be a kind of peace; but never peace of mind.

And Joss Lane – motherless son, ex-junkie and extreme sportsman – would be grinning; for the special people, he had loved and trusted, disappointed and saved, who would be starting the rest of their lives here and now.